NOTHING RHYMES WITH SILVER

1

DAVID LEE

NOTHING RHYMES WITH SILVER

1

Matador
9 De Montfort Mews
Leicester LE1 7FW, UK
Tel: (+44) 116 255 9311 / 9312
Email: books@troubador.co.uk
Web: www.troubador.co.uk/matador

ISBN 10: 1-905886-04-7
ISBN 13: 978-1-905996-04-3

Cover illustration: Ian Legge

Typeset in 11pt Stempel Garamond by Troubador Publishing Ltd, Leicester, UK
Printed in the UK by The Cromwell Press Ltd, Trowbridge, Wilts, UK

Matador is an imprint of Troubador Publishing Ltd

Dedicated to all who drink too much, smoke too much and never go to bed before dawn

8 Bar Introduction

HEAVYWEIGHT CHAMPION of the world, Joe Louis was supposed to have said, just before his title fight with Billy Conn, who was much lighter and faster than Louis, "Billy can run around the ring, but he can't hide." Came the fight and Conn ran for twelve rounds. But came the unlucky thirteenth, and mighty Joe finally caught up with him: one left hook later, Billy Conn became Billy Gone! The guy had no chance.

I reckon my chances are even less than Billy's, because I'm running and hiding too, not from a left hook, but from a nine millimetre shell in the back of the head! Logic tell me there has to be a contract out on me. I mean, nobody does what I did to the head of a New York City Mafia family without getting "visited" sooner or later. I am just sitting around here in Havana Cuba waiting for the bell to come up for my thirteenth round.

So, I guess by the time you get around to reading this, I'll probably be dead. And, who cares? I know I don't any more. Frankly, life out here has become nothing but a weightless, meaningless, limbo. Every day I do the same damned thing: I come here to the 'Bar Cuba Libre' and sit at the same rickety, cigarette-scarred table, just outside the bar itself, where it is shady all day because four years ago a hurricane twisted the outside shade in such a way that the sun never visits this side of the bar, and I drink And I think. And I drink and think, and think and drink until mercifully, I can't think anymore...

...Somewhere down the street to my right, a radio is beating out a rumba. I can't quite hear the tune, but I can catch the beat. To my left is a school. Like everything else here, it is broken down and unrepaired. Maybe this is why I love Cuba, and especially Havana, so much. We are both irreparably fucked up.

Yesterday afternoon, one of the school kids, instead of going straight home to Mamma like a good little boy ought to do, crossed over the road to where I was sitting and said to me (in Spanish of course), "Hey Senor, how is it that you never talk to anyone but just sit there drinking?" He was about twelve years old, a thin, poorly-dressed kid with large dark oval eyes that stared straight through me.

"Fuck off," I said (in Spanish, of course).

Did this kid expect me to explain, in Spanish yet, why I'm doing what I'm doing? Or why it is that I need a bottle of rum with a dozen beer chasers every day, just so that I can go over, without the pain becoming too unbearable, exactly the same memories I went over yesterday and the day before that and back to when I first came here over thirty years ago?

And while we are on the subject of "why": why is it that as you get older everything becomes harder? These days, walking, eating, peeing are all hard for me. I've even reached the stage where my arteries are harder than my cock. Even remembering, becomes harder with every passing, lousy day.

Maybe that is why I wrote down all these memories, some still crystal fresh in my mind, others tattered and frayed by the processes of age, time, and I guess, too much of that good Cuban rum...

...Memories. Passing but persistent scenarios of high times and low times; of opportunities grabbed and chances that silently slipped away like a snake in the night. But memories are all I have left. And that is what this book is about. Should you have the staying power or maybe, the obstinate determination to read the whole damn thing, this I guarantee: you will learn of a great, maddeningly impossible love. You will also get the inside dope on what drives a previously nice, sweet guy to callous, crude, murder.

Naturally, all the conversations will not be verbatim. After all, some of the incidents took place as long as sixty years ago. And who can remember the kind of words you used when you were a kid? So if the dialogue sometimes seems a little too grown-up for a kid, just live with it. But everything you read will be the clean, untarnished truth. God knows, I've gone over it enough times to ensure that.

Anyway, now that it is written down, it'll save me the bother, not to mention the pain, of having to rethink it. All I will need to do is open my Book of Life, and there it will be.

Who knows? With a bit of luck, drinking might become a pleasure again instead of the painkilling drug it is right now.

Chapter 1

DO YOU BELIEVE in the Fates? I do. I reckon that up there somewhere, there is a vast company of Fates, rather like a major firm of accountants. When you are born, a dossier is created in your name which is then handed over to the suitable department. From there it is passed on to your own personal operator who almost invariably turns out to be some grey-suited grey-faced, humourless shit-head of a bureaucratic Fate. Of course, sometimes you get lucky and fluke yourself a nice Fate—some good guy who fixes for you to win the football-pools or a grand lottery or something. Or even for you to get the girl. Not just any girl, but THE girl.

But that's an aberration. Normally, the nice, good, fun-loving Fates are reserved to control the affairs of the rich, handsome and privileged, whereas the Fates that handle the fortunes of most black people must come from a special Motherfucker's department. Maybe they mistook me for being black.

And there also must be apprentice Fates. After all, it has to be an ever-growing business. Probably these tyro Fates are wheeled in to handle people's destinies in times of deep emergency, like wars. Once there is a war raging, the official experienced Fates are so damned busy deciding on the millions of people who are going to live and die, that they are forced to hand over some of their less important dossiers to young and often mischievous Sprites, which is what must have happened in my case I'm damned sure. Came the 1939-45 war and the Fates, realising that this was liable to be their busiest-ever time, took handfuls of files down off the shelves to share out, among their junior acolytes, saying to them something like, "Here, go away and play with these, and leave us alone. We're gonna be helluva busy for the next few years."

In retrospect, I can see that the trainee Fate who got me was not only a mean bastard, but he also must have possessed a warped sense of humour. When he opened my file and read, 'Jake Silver, 213 Brixton Road, London SW9,' he must have thought, "What kind of a crazy name is that? Silver? Is he going to be a pirate or something? I must give this pretentious son of a bitch the full works." And he sure as hell did!

But before this shitty Sprite started working his voodoo hoodoo on me, in other words, between the years when I was born in August 1929 and the beginning of World War Two, life was in the main, sweet, loving fun. So it seems reasonable to assume that the Fate who got the original job of covering those first ten years of my life, was a decent and probably unassuming Mister Nice-guy Fate. He saw to it that I was agile and healthy, barring the usual kid's diseases, like measles and all that jazz, and that I had a smart enquiring mind which enabled me to read before I was four years of age. I also inherited my father's natural musical ability, although I think my genes, rather than any Fate, were responsible for that.

My father, Isaac, but known to all as Ike, was a little over six feet tall with a slim athletic build, and, I am reliably informed by all who knew him, good-looking. He was a photographer by trade, but, had he the choice, I'm goddamned sure he would have been a piano player. In fact, at the time he tied the knot with my mother, back in December 1926, Ike was actually working as a pianist in a silent movie house.

I can just see him sitting there in the semi-dark, cigarette-hazed cinema, peering up at the grainy grey film, dreaming up music to fit the flickering action on the screen: banging out the tremolos when Pauline was in peril, or maybe knocking out some ragtime to accompany the antics of Harry Langdon or Buster Keaton. Or maybe even creating some quasi-Arab love music for sex-idol Rudolph Valentino to seduce not only the heroine by, but half the women in the audience as well!

By the time I came along, the silent movie era had given way to talkies. So my old man had to find another way to bring in the moolah. That was when and why he became a photographer. He managed to persuade a local department store to let him set up a studio on their ground floor. I still have a snapshot of him standing in front of his little studio, cigarette as ever, stuck in the corner of his mouth (he was a 60-a-day man). Behind him, the studio front bears the legend, 'Come and be snapped. 10 snapshots for a shilling'.

It must have been a pretty successful venture, because within a short time he had studios in two other department stores. And what with his getting a few photographic gigs at weddings, bar mitzvahs and Masonic merry-makings, etc., we were doing a lot better, bread-wise than most, although my pop never lost his love for the piano. Every night, when he came home after closing down his studios, he'd go through the same routine: pour himself a large Black Label scotch, take it over to our Broadwood upright piano, put his drink on top of it, set an ashtray down on the last four notes of the treble end of the keyboard, light a Gold Flake cigarette, and proceed to unravel the cares and tensions of the day through the music of Jerome Kern, George Gershwin, Richard Rogers, Fats Waller and others.

My mother, Eve, was at the time of her marriage, a dark-haired, petite and very pretty little thing, possessed of a lively sense of humour, and, according to my aunt Sarah, who was her older sister, constantly pursued by the local studs.

After she and my old man wed, they lived first in the East End of London, in Brick Lane to be precise, because she wanted to be near her mother. But the suffocating living-in-each-others'-pockets style of life so typical of Jewish ghettos everywhere, did not appeal to my smart man-about-town Dad. So, about six months after I came along, my mother gave up her job making fur hats at her Uncle's sweat-shop, and we moved to what was then the quiet leafy suburb of Brixton. (I understand it has now become London's Harlem in every way but the jazz.)

We occupied the lower two floors and basement of a big old house at 213 Brixton Road. We also had exclusive use of the large back garden. It had a huge sprawling oak tree dominating the middle of it, which when I was a bit older, was great for climbing and hiding in. We also had a raspberry bush, planted by my father but given over to me to water and tend generally. Best of all was the potting shed. By the time I was four, this shed had become my personal castle or cowboy shack in which I would plot the destruction of my enemies, be they evil knights whom I would dispatch in a sword fight, or Red Indians who I would shoot down just as callously and casually as white Americans once did in reality. Of course there was no TV in those days, so my fantasy games were not adulterated or completely fucked up like so many kids' games are nowadays.

By the time I was seven years old, I had two great and equal loves; cricket and jazz. (I was also in love with Joan Blondell, but that was a completely different kind of love.) The former came about as a result of my father becoming a member of Surrey County Cricket Club, which meant that I could sit in the members' pavilion with him and watch great cricketers from every county; bowlers like Harold Larwood or Hedley Verity, and batsmen such as Hutton or Compton and kvell as they cracked whatever was bowled up to them, all over the ground and sometimes out of it. No sooner had we got home, it would be a rush for my half-size cricket bat. I actually felt, as my Dad bowled underarm to me with a tennis ball, that I was all of those great batsmen rolled into one, and then some.

As to how jazz music came into my life at such an early age and in such an unlikely place as what was then, quiet middle-class Brixton must have been due to that Mr Nice-Guy Fate who still had charge of my welfare.

Uncle Harry, who was married to my mother's elder sister Sarah, was rich. So, when they took possession of their new super-duper RGD radiogram (with an eight-record changer, yet), they gave us their old cast-off gramophone. I can remember it as clearly as I should be able to remember yesterday, but no longer can these days. It was dark mahogany, oblong in shape, with the turntable at the top that was got at by lifting a spring-loaded lid, so that once you released the catch it would ride up all by itself, which was wildly fascinating to me at the time. The lower half of the cabinet was for storing records.

I recall clearly how excited I was as I watched the two delivery men carry it in and plug it into the light socket. We did not yet have wall plugs in our 'music room'. We called it that, I guess, because it contained the piano, some sheet music, and a photograph of Louis Armstrong autographed 'To my man Ike', with the great man's signature underneath.

As soon as the two installers had left, I delved into the record cabinet and found two records left inside, either by mistake or some miraculous accident. One was of Bing Crosby crooning out a tune called, 'Moonburn'. But as good as Bing sang and as beautifully as Joe Sullivan played the piano, it was the other disc which had such a profound effect on me. It was "St. Louis Blues" sung by the Queen of the Blues, Bessie Smith, which from the first time I heard it, filled me with so much joy, that listening to it made the hair on the back of my neck prickle and cold chills scutter down my spine.

I played that "St Louis Blues" track so many times that my parents grew to hate, even more than Bessie did, seeing (or hearing), that evening sun go down. Finally, they confiscated it, but not before I had memorised every note (not to mention every surface click). Typically, the more I could not hear it, the more I needed to. I became fixated by it. I searched the entire house to try and discover where they had hidden my Bessie, but without success. In desperation I went to the piano and taught myself to play it, chords and all. Best of all, I found it quite easy to do. So I started to teach myself some other tunes I liked, and by the time my eighth birthday came around, I could fumble through about a dozen numbers like, "Stardust," or 'The Man I Love', with all the correct, albeit basic, harmonies.

But then, in the late Spring of 1938, something new came into my life shattering all the quiet contentment I had hitherto enjoyed: Naziism.

My first recollection of it was my mother telling me that in future my father would be accompanying me to and from school because there were Fascists roaming the streets, beating up Jewish schoolchildren. When I asked her why they were doing it she said, "Why? God only knows why. Because they don't like Jewish children I suppose. But anyway don't ask silly questions," and wagging a warning finger to stress the point, she said, "Now listen to what I'm telling you. Never leave school without waiting for your father. Understand?" I nodded, although in truth it made no sense to me. I could not comprehend that anyone would hate me simply for being Jewish. It all became only too clear a couple of weeks later.

I was explaining to my very closest pal, Jimmy Abel, why I could not go back to his house with him for tea, because I was not allowed to leave the school without my father collecting me. Jimmy was, short, thin, pale and always seem to have a thin trickle of colourless snot drooling onto his upper lip, which every so often, he would wipe away with his sleeve. He was also a broad cockney.

"Why 'as 'e gotta do that? Cancha fin' yer own way 'ome then?

"Don't be daft," I replied. "It's to stop them Fascists from getting me."

"Wot, are you a Jewboy of sumfink?" His face was a mask of horrified snotty, stupefaction.

"Yeah."

He recoiled, like he'd been stung by a wasp.

"My Dad says I'm not allowed to play wiv any of you dirty Jewboys."

Quite naturally we fought and were parted only by the fortuitous arrival of my father. But from then on, Jimmy Abel, previously my best friend, now became my bitterest enemy. He ganged up with three other kids who would use up their school breaks and ruin mine, by following me everywhere I went, shouting in unison, "G'back to where ya cum from, dirty little Jewboy."

The humiliation of those taunts would usually become too much for me and I would turn on my tormentors and the inevitable punch-ups would ensue. But being neither a Bruce Lee nor a Mohammed Ali, this one-against-four fracas usually ended with my getting a nasty beating before the teacher on playground duty moved in to break it up. It was becoming increasingly usual to be picked up by my father, with me sporting a black eye or split lip or torn clothing and very often all three. When he would ask me to account for my condition, for some reason I could not tell him the full story.

"Some kids called me a dirty Jewboy, and I beat them up. That's all."

"Are you sure you are OK? He would ask.

"Yeah I'm fine," I would say, even though the bruises from the punches and the kicks hurt like hell.

And so began a period of my life overladen with depression and trepidation—and pain.

I found myself evermore shunned and outcast at school. Even those kids who were probably not in the least bit anti-Jewish, now gave me a wide berth, I suppose either because they preferred the safe camaraderie of running with the crowd or because they did not want to risk the kind of beatings I was getting, simply for being seen talking to a 'Jewboy'.

Most painful of all, I was cut out of the games I used to so look forward to during the morning and afternoon breaks. I can still remember the deep hurt I felt from these exclusions. I tried complaining to Mr Baker, the teacher on playground duty that I had not been allowed to join in the playground cricket game because Jimmy Abel who captained one of the teams shouted, "We don't want no Jewboys playin' wiv us." Naturally, all the other kids sided with him against me.

"Well, in that case, stand over there and watch," he answered unconcernedly.

Each day the misery seemed to get worse. No sooner did I open my eyes in the morning than the realisation of what lay ahead would come at me in a rush to smother me in inescapable misery. Every morning, after we arrived at school and I had airily bade my father goodbye as if I didn't have a worry in the world (whether this act really fooled him I never found out), I would walk through the large, black-painted iron school gates, steeling myself against whatever horrors the day might hold for me.

Of course, if I'd had the wisdom and humility to tell my father the truth about my school life, or allowed my mother to see even half the bruises that had turned my back and ribs into a study in black and blue, I would have been taken away from that school pronto, and the misery would have ended. But I just could not, nor would not do so, because it would have meant that I had lost the battle, and I had a streak of obstinate defiance within me that would not allow me to admit defeat. Even sillier, I had no understanding of what I was fighting about.

Things finally came to a head when Ian Sproakes, a founder member of Jimmy Abel's gang and one of my most hated tormentors, put his hand up to ask the teacher if he could be 'excused'. As he walked out of the room it suddenly occurred to me that by going to the lavatory on his own, I could finally confront him without his gang.

The moment the teacher turned his back to write something on the blackboard, I sneaked out of the classroom. I went down the hall to the door marked 'Boys Toilet'. As I was coming in, he was just turning from the urinal, still in the process of buttoning his fly. I wasted neither time nor words. I just socked him as hard as I could knocking him onto his backside. I must have caused a bad gash on the inside of his upper lip, because blood was pouring blood down his chin and on to his sweater.

He scrambled to his feet and ran screaming and bleeding out of the lavatory, helped on his way by another punch on his ear which I landed as he ran past me down the hall to the Headmaster's office, to which I was summoned shortly after.

When Mr Roseberry, the Headmaster, demanded an explanation from me for "This quite dastardly deed," I blurted out my story of Jew hatred and was about to show him my bruises as proof of the ordeal I had suffered at the hands,(and feet), of Ian Sproakes and the rest of his gang, but he cut me off.

"ENOUGH," he yelled, holding his hand up in an accidental (or Freudian), Fascist salute.

"What rubbish is this?" he spat out the words through lips tightened in rage. He was a tall bony fellow with a long pale bony face. He looked a lot like the skull painted on pirates' flags.

He pointed a long, bony, forefinger at me. "I don't like lies and I have no time for liars, Silver. I haven't the foggiest idea how a boy of your age dreamed up all this nonsense about Jew-baiting and such. But don't think you can fool me, young fella-me-lad."

I tried to interrupt him but before I could even frame the first syllable, he yelled, "SHUT UP WHEN I AM SPEAKING." Then, after a terrible silence, he went on, "It is quite clear to me that you carry some evil hate within you Master Silver, and young Sproakes just happened to be there to bear the brunt of your vicious temper. He got up out of his chair and made his way round to where a tear-stained Ian Sproakes was nursing his now badly puffed-up and bloody mouth with a grubby blood-stained handkerchief.

"Now off you go Sproakes," he said in a soft sympathetic voice. "Go back to your class and tell your teacher that you have to see the nurse." He patted him gently on his head. "She'll make it all better, I'm quite sure. Now off you go." Sproakes stood up and turned to leave, but not before glaring at me, baleful hatred in his eyes.

Then Mr Roseberry made his way over to the tall corner cupboard. I watched him unlock it with a key selected from a large key chain that he had extracted from his jacket pocket. Reaching into the now opened cupboard, he brought out a long thickish cane. After a couple of terrifying test swishes, he turned to face me, holding the cane in his right hand, gently tapping his left palm with it. Then, in a menacingly quiet voice, he said: "People of your ilk must learn that you are guests in our country. If you insist on living here, then you must learn to drop the evil ways of your people and live as we do. The kind of violence that killed our Lord Jesus Christ might have seemed alright to you people out in the Middle East, but it does not go here, Master Silver."

While he spoke, he slowly walked around me tapping the cane against his left palm and never taking his flat, cold, grey eyes off me for a second.

"As you people seem to think that you are so superior that you can use violence on any person you disagree with, even including the Son of God, I am going to teach you a lesson in humility that you will not forget in a hurry."

Then, in a harder-edged voice, "Now drop your pants, keep your feet where they are, and bend over and hold on to the desk."

I was determined not to cry, but as I unbuckled the belt around my grey short trousers and felt them slide down my legs and settle round my ankles, I could not prevent hot tears from rolling down my face. I reached over to grab the edge of the large dark brown desk, but as I was not allowed to move my feet even though I was standing over three feet away, I was forced to 'fall' forward and grab the desk edge as I fell, throwing all my weight onto my hands and arms. It was like being half-way through a press-up.

I felt his deathly-cold fingers reach into the waist of my underpants and pull them down to my knees. Then he pulled the tail of my shirt up over my head. As he did so, he addressed my bare arse: "Now, Silver, I am going to give you six of the best for telling lies, and another six of the best for your terrible assault on young Ian Sproakes."

I thought about making one last final appeal, but what with the tears now streaming down my face and the aching in my upper arms from the semi press-up position I had been forced to adopt, I thought it best to say nothing and get it over with.

After the twelfth thwack, Mr Roseberry, now breathing heavily from the exertion of beating me, said as he sat back down on the big chair behind his desk, "Right, Silver, you can pull your trousers up now and after you have done so, stand there and do not move." I was desperate to rub my aching and stinging backside and upper thighs, as well as wipe my tear-filled eyes but was too afraid to do so. I just did as instructed while he very slowly wrote a letter. I can still clearly recall the biting, stinging pain I felt as I watched his pen moving very slowly and scratchily across the paper. Then presumably to elongate my suffering, he folded it very carefully and deliberately into the envelope he had slowly and carefully extracted from a drawer in the desk, and addressed in his florid hand-writing. After painstakingly licking and re-licking the envelope flap and sticking it down, he handed me the letter, saying as he did so, "Go and get your things and go straight home and give this letter to your parents. Now, get out of my sight."

Once out of the headmaster's office I tried to rub my aching, stinging backside, but it was too sore for anything but the gentlest patting. So having wiped the tears from my face, I slowly walked home, each step stinging like hell.

As I let myself in through our kitchen door, I found my mother busily cleaning the stove. It only took one glance at my face for her to say, "So what's wrong?"

"Nothing much," I said trying to sound normal and casual. "I got the cane and was sent home. Here is a letter from Mr. Roseberry."

"I knew you'd been fighting," she said accusingly; as she tore open the envelope. "Now maybe, I'll find out what it was all about." After she had finished reading the letter, she glared angrily at me saying "I can't believe that a son of mine would act in this terrible fashion. Now I am going to read you what Mr Roseberry has written and then I will want an explanation from you my lad. Now sit down while I read it."

But my arse and the backs of my thighs were hurting like hell so I just stood there as she read it out to me.

"Dear Mr and Mrs Silver," she read, "I am sorry to have to tell you that your son Jacob has been behaving in such a violent manner as to lead me to conclude that he has no place in this school. It seems that all he wishes to do is fight and bully other pupils. I understand from the teachers on playground duty that they have had to break up fights on an almost daily basis and that your son is always at the centre of them. I was forced to cane him today after a particularly brutal and unprovoked attack on another boy in his class. This disruption of school discipline is no good for the school and not acceptable to me.

I must say that I would have expected that people of your persuasion would be far more careful in ensuring that their children are made aware of the privilege they enjoy from the education they receive in this country from a Christian Hall of learning.

Your faithful servant, R.S.G. Roseberry"

Well now, will you kindly tell me what this is all about?" she said, as she folded the letter back into its envelope.

Somehow I got the idea that my mother was siding with my enemies, and that was just too much for me to take. I started to cry, at the same time blubbing and sobbing out the entire story. At last I got the sympathy I was looking for. She came over to me as I sobbed out my tale of woe and hugged me tightly muttering things like, "Oh my God." Or, "My poor baby," and other typically maternal noises.

Then she hugged me too tight.

"Ouch," I said as I slid out of her arms.

"What's wrong?" she asked, her voice full of concern. I noticed that she was crying too.

"You were pressing on one of my bruises, that's all."

"Let me see them," she said as she started undoing my shirt buttons. Once out of my shirt, she turned me slowly round saying in a shocked whisper, "Oh my God," as she saw for the first time the bruises and welts on my upper torso. I noticed that she was pressing one fisted hand into her cheek, an action she reserved exclusively for when she was in shock.

"So why didn't you tell your teacher what was happening to you?" she asked quietly, after she had very gently fingered each bruise and welt.

"I did," I mumbled as I put my shirt back on.

"Well if your teachers knew, why didn't they put a stop to it?"

"They did—sometimes" I mumbled. Then after a pause she said in a voice full of sympathy:

"You must have been in terrible pain. Why didn't you tell me what was going on?"

"I didn't want to" I replied. "And anyway, my bottom hurts much more than these old bruises."

"Let me see."

But I was already at the age where exposing my arse to my mother was an embarrassment.

"No, it's OK Mum, it'll soon be better." I tried to sound cheerful and optimistic. It didn't work.

"Let me see," she said using the tone of voice which I knew from experience meant there was no room for further argument.

Slowly and very gingerly, I let down my trousers. "And the underpants" she said. I took them off, at the same time trying to hide the pain I was feeling as the elastic top of my underpants slid over Mr Roseberry's heavy handiwork.

Then I turned around to show her. Not having had the opportunity to look at my backside in a mirror, I had no idea what the damage looked like. My mother knelt down behind me. As she gently examined me, she said in a quiet but deadly serious voice: "This was done by Mr Roseberry this morning?"

"Yes." I said.

She stood up, turned me round and after kissing me gently on my tear-stained cheek, said, "Now I want you to go and lie on your bed. I'm going to phone your father, and then I'll phone the doctor."

About an hour must have passed, before my father finally got home. His arrival was greeted by a loud telling-off from my mother. "Leave the boy alone, let him learn to fight his own battles," she yelled, as he stepped though the front door, clearly echoing something my father must have said previously. I could hear them getting nearer and my mother's non-stop voice getting louder, As my bedroom opened she was shouting angrily "And to think I listened to you,. I must have been mad."

He came into the room, my mother following closely behind. No sooner did she see me lying very wisely on my belly, than she started to cry. She quickly moved around and in front of my father to dramatically pull down my underpants, saying at the same time through her sobbing,

"Now see what they did to our son."

"Hello Jake," my father said in his usual voice, ignoring my mother's tear-filled histrionics, "What's all this about you being attacked by a gang of Jew-hating little swines?"

I repeated the whole sorry tale for my father, whilst he examined the bruises on my back and then moved his fingers down my damaged backside which he touched gently, but painfully nevertheless. Then taking me by the shoulders, he gently turned me over, saying as he did so, "Now let's get a look at the front of you." Whilst he gently examined my bruised and beaten body, I noticed that his face was deathly pale. He sat down on the bed next to me and took out his fountain pen, telling my mother at the same time to get him something to write on.

After I had finished my saga, he said "Well you taught one of them a damn good lesson. That was very good and I'm very proud of you."

As my Old Man rarely handed out compliments to me, it made me feel good, and proud. It also destroyed any doubts I might have had about whacking Ian Sproakes.

Then he said quietly and matter-of-factly, "Now I need you to give me the names of the boys involved, and the names of the teachers on playground duty who let this happen to you. He wrote each name down on the writing pad that my mother had by now provided for him. When that was done, he asked in a strangely steely voice:

"Now how many times did you say the Headmaster hit you with the cane, son?"

"He gave me twelve of the best, Dad. And he made me take my trousers and underpants down."

My father said nothing for a while. Then he asked if I knew where any of the boys lived. I only knew one of them and that was the address of my ex-best friend Jimmy Abel. My father made a careful note of it also.

"Now you just lie there and wait for the doctor. I'm sure he'll have something to take the pain away." Then he and my mother, who had been standing with hands interlaced across her chest, and tears still rolling down her face, went out of the room together.

It was three of four days before I could get around without suffering too much pain, even with the medicine and the ointment the doctor had prescribed. I remember my father jokingly referring to me at that time as "the pain in the arse." But once the pain had gone and my parents had assured me that I was not going back to that school, the horror of it soon dissipated.. And that basically was the finish of my boyhood run-in with the Jew-hating Moseley Black shirts (named after Sir Oswald Moseley, the leader of Britain's Nazi party).

It was to be another seven years before I found out the corollary of that little chapter in my young life. Uncle Harry told me that the very next day my father found out the address of the Headmaster, went to his house and gave him such a merciless beating that he had to spend a week in hospital. Uncle Harry also told me with pride, how he had provided my father with a watertight alibi, proving beyond any doubt to the police (to whom Mr Roseberry had complained), that he was definitely somewhere else at the time of the Headmaster's comeuppance. As to the teachers on playground duty and the fathers of the boys who had ganged up on me, my father, aided by some rather hefty members of the Greenshirts (which was an anti-Nazi, anti-Moseley group, largely financed by my uncle Harry), visited each of them in turn, leaving them in no doubt that victimising little Jewish children was a very ill-advised and dangerous policy, which could often end up with bones being broken, the bones in question being theirs.

But whatever I had done to annoy my hitherto friendly Fate, by the early part of 1939, he must have decided that all was forgiven, because, after a couple of weeks to recuperate, I was enrolled in a new school.

My parents, having decided that the only way to ensure that nothing like what had happened ever occurred again, enrolled me in a Jewish school, 'The South London School for Jews', or the SLSJ, as it was known. It turned to be by far the happiest of all my school years. Not only was it peaceful and pleasant; it also contained an amazingly high percentage of talented kids.

There were four fourteen year old boys who sang in close harmony and imitated musical instruments, like the Mills Brothers were doing so successfully at the time. We also had a thirteen year old boy, Joey Segal, and an absolutely sensational-looking girl named Mandy Mosselman who were, or seemed to me at the time, to be as brilliant a tap-dancing duo as Fred Astaire and Ginger Rogers, whose dance routines they slavishly copied. I instantly fell head over heels in love with Mandy, but it was the non-affair of the season. After all, what thirteen year old girl – and a sensationally beautiful one at that—needs the attention of a ten year old kid? Then there was Adrian Goldberg, one year older than me, who did what were to us, hilarious impressions of Charlie Chaplin, Gracie Fields, Greta Garbo, James Cagney and many others, including our teachers.

Once I let it be known that I could play the piano, I was allowed into this wildly enthusiastic show-biz coterie. Everybody knows that Judy Garland and Mickey Rooney did it over and over again in the movies, but in real life, we did it first! We wrote, designed, and performed our own show for Parents' Day, complete with hand-painted scenery and specially designed costumes. We were even clever enough to write our own satirical parodies about the things that went on in school and even about the teachers, all the lyrics being set to popular tunes of the day.

I was the 'band'. I had to accompany two singing acts, play suitable music as background for Adrian Goldberg's impression act as well as playing and joining in the singing of our satirical songs. I also played (after my father showed me how), 'Fascinating Rhythm' and the treacherously difficult 'I Won't Dance' for Joey and Mandy's tap dancing act. I also did my own solo turn, playing what at the time, I thought was a red-hot version of 'Night and Day'.

I clearly remember how proud my parents were of me, and how complimentary my father was about my playing when they took me home after the show.

I was as ecstatically happy at this school as I had been morosely miserable at the previous one. It was to me what a school should be—and the diametric opposite of my previous one. Here at the SLSJ, the teachers (not all of whom were Jewish), were supportive and helpful and the sense of school camaraderie warm and strong.

But education be damned; the reasons I loved this school were my "show-biz" buddies and most of all, being close to the love of my ten-year old life, Mandy Mosselmann.

Thinking back on it. I suppose my parents must have been thrilled at seeing how enthusiastic I had become about my new school. I knew they were relieved by the SLJS arranging for me, and the three other Jewish kids from my area of town, to have a daily escort to and from school by four eighteen-year old boys from the Jewish Maccabi boxing squad. But in retrospect, I guess they must have realised that it was not the SLSJ's educational standards that fired my enthusiasm. I had already told them that Mandy's favourite tune was 'All This and Heaven too'. And the very fact that I would play this tune twenty times a night after coming home from school must have left them in no doubt as to the main reason for my desire to get to school everyday.

Then, on a warm, sunny, early September day, World War Two began.

And it was on this day that my Mr Good-Guy Fate got replaced by a spite-filled, shite-filled, motherfucker of a sprite who quickly saw to it that the tempo of my young life was changed from up-beat allegro to down-beat lousando.

Chapter 2

I CLEARLY REMEMBER my father coming home on his first leave. The day after the war began, he and a couple of his pals volunteered to join the Army, but they put my father in to the navy instead. They seemed interested in his photographic skills, and he was posted to Portsmouth for what they called 'Special Training'.

I recall my feelings of pride on seeing my dad, now a smartly-dressed Petty Officer. But I also remember feeling that he was strangely different to the way he was before he enlisted. He seemed quieter and more introspective now. He was also given to suddenly coming over to me and giving me hugs and even kisses, something he would never have done previously, and which caused me to feel uncomfortable and embarrassed. In truth, although I hate to admit it, the normalcy of my life didn't return until he had completed his leave and returned to his naval unit.

When the daily madness of the blitz struck London, suddenly there were far less kids in my class, or in the school generally. Many of them were sent by their parents to obscure places in the country to escape Goering's Luftwaffe. Adrian Goldberg the impressionist, and I were the only members of our show-biz gang who had not left London to live with their out-of-town, or even American friends and relatives. I was of course especially desolate when my beautiful Mandy Mosselman went off to live out the war in Dublin.

I didn't know it then, but I realise now, that by the beginning of 1941 my new fucked-up Fate must have felt confident enough to start flexing his muscles, so to speak. I was still going to school as usual, but on my own now, my other two mates had been evacuated to Devon and my four bodyguards conscripted into the army. In any case, the war had cleared all the Fascists off the streets. On this particular day in the middle of January, I went to school to find that the entire street, one side of which had been almost entirely occupied by my school, was now a roped-off, rubble-filled disaster area. Even though I was staring at the smashed bricks and twisted metal, the shards of glass and the jagged ends of wooden beams that only a few hours earlier had been my school, I somehow could not get it into my head that my beloved SLSJ was no more. I went up to a policeman who was standing there, arms folded, and asked him what I should do.

"If I were you, I'd go 'ome lad. Count yourself lucky." Pointing with his thumb over his shoulder at the still-smoking wreckage, he said, "If you was to ask me, I would guess that 'itler 'as given you a few days off school, lucky blighter." So I went home.

When I told my mother what had happened she reacted like an archetypical Jewish mother, which surprised me somewhat because it was not the way she usually behaved.

"My God," she cried, her fisted hand pressing into her cheek, "If those swine had dropped their bombs this morning instead of last night, my beautiful son would be dead right now."

There and then she decided that rather than risk my life in some other school, I would have my schooling at home. To facilitate this, she hired a tutor. He turned out to be an oldish man with a wooden leg, who had at some time or other, taught at the prestigious St Paul's school. I was lectured by my mother very seriously about how lucky I was to have such an important person to supervise my education.

"But why can't I just go to another school?" Staying at home all day, and without any school friends was not my idea of an education.

"Because," she said, "We must be together at all times until the war is over. That way if one of us is killed, we both get killed."

Due to this piece of lop-sided logic, I was stuck in the house except when I accompanied her on totally boring shopping expeditions. It was a terrible come-down after the fun and excitement that I had been having at school. With all my friends now out of town or living too far away to visit me, all I had to relieve the otherwise gloomy boredom of life was listening to the radio, or playing my half dozen jazz records over and over again. Or playing the piano. The piano won, hands down. I concentrated far more on my piano playing than I did on my academic studies, although, if I remember correctly, I did manage to get through them pretty well.

One morning, Mr Gibbons, my tutor, heard me playing as he was entering the house. At the end of my lesson he confided in me how much he loved 'Night and Day' and other Cole Porter tunes. So, whenever my mother went shopping, which she now often did whilst I was having my lessons (the 'we must never be apart' schtick having been amended over the weeks to mean that she could go out without me but I was never allowed out without her), I would spend the last ten minutes of the lesson time playing the two or three Cole Porter tunes I knew, for Mr Gibbons.

His reaction was strange in the extreme.

No sooner had I started to play, than he would get up from his chair to lurch up and down the far side of the room, his false leg scraping the floor, his hands clenched together in front of his chest. Sometimes he would suddenly shout out in a voice seemingly wrenched from the very depths of his being, "Aah Paris (he pronounced it 'Perris'), Paris, where has it all gone to?." Or, especially when I went into my childish attempt at a rhapsodic rendition of' I've Got You Under My Skin', he would say quietly but in a voice choked with pain, "Perris, Perris, we were so heppy in Perris" Now, as I think back on it, I realise that those tunes must have stirred up some deep and terrible memories for this man. If I had been older, I would have had great sympathy for poor old peg-legged Mr Gibbons. As it was, after I had got over the initial shock of it, all it caused me was amusement. It also gave me an exaggerated opinion of my playing ability, insofar as it could create such a profound effect in a grown man.

Sitting here at the 'Bar Cuba Libra', a million miles away from that life, as I remember his sad bitter voice, I relate it to my own dismal disaster of a life, and I feel much closer to him now, than I ever did then when I was in the same room with him.

But to get back to my story (and with two thirds of a bottle of good Cuban rum inside me, there ain't no place else for me to go), what I did not know at that time was that my new shit-face Fate was ready to out-Fuehrer the Fuehrer himself!

Because on December 12 1942, he launched his own private and murderous blitzkrieg against the person of little Jake Silver.

Chapter 3

ODDLY ENOUGH, the day began brilliantly. My mother and I had just finished our breakfast of that wartime powdered dreck on toast, when we heard the key opening the front door. My father had been granted a last minute 48 hour leave prior to his posting overseas. He suddenly seemed taller and broader to me. He was clearly very fit. Even the way he walked across the kitchen to hug me displayed his new athleticism.

He had brought with him as a present for me, the American pressing of the Benny Goodman Trio playing 'Someday Sweetheart' (which, if you do not know it, contains some piano playing by Teddy Wilson of quite astonishing virtuosity and invention). Naturally, I rushed to the gramophone to play it, while my father and mother, arms around each other, followed me into the music room. To my surprise, and for some reason, my intense embarrassment, they danced around the room to the music. When the record ended and before I could turn it over to listen to the other side, my father said, "Jake, let me hear how you are getting on with the piano." I can still remember how nervous I felt as I sat down to play. Apart from the fact that my father was a much better pianist than I was, his absence had somehow brought an element of estrangement into what had been an extremely close relationship. And if that weren't enough, he had changed in some intangible fashion. The larky, love-of-life, full-of-fun man was gone. Now, even when he was smiling, there was seriousness at the back of his eyes. He was also much quieter now. So, playing to him was quite stressful for me.

I remembered I played 'Over the Rainbow' and then a show-off piece called 'Midnight in Mayfair'. In the middle of the second piece he came over to stand by the piano to watch and listen. When I was finished I turned to look at him. I noticed immediately that his eyes had lost that 'I've-been-told-by-the-doctor-I-only-have-three-months-to-live' look. Suddenly he was like the Ike Silver of old. All at once he had become my Dad again. He looked across at my mother, saying as he ruffled my thick thatch of almost black hair, "Y'know, I think we have the makings of a real piano player here." She said, "If he would give as much time to his schoolwork as he gives to playing the piano, we'd have the makings of an Einstein instead."

Later on in the morning after the inevitable cup of mid-morning tea, my father, presumably because he wanted to be alone with my mother for obvious reasons (although, quite naturally, it did not cross my mind at the time), gave me a pound note and told me I could go out and spend it on anything I liked. When I said that I was not allowed out of the house without my mother, Ike just laughed and said that Hitler was only bombing at night and that, as long as I was home by three o'clock in the afternoon, there was plenty of time for us to die together. To my great relief, my mother agreed, with the proviso that if I got hungry I was to come home, rather than eat "The muck they serve in cafes these days."

For the first time in months, I was going out on my own with a whole pound note burning away in my pocket. I was like a genie let out of a bottle. I ran the two miles to Acre Lane where there was a big record shop. I bought two records, a Fats Waller piano solo and another by the Artie Shaw big band. Then still having a few hours of freedom, and over ten shillings left, I took a bus ride to my old school, but found the entire street boarded up. So, I took a stroll down the nearby Walworth Road to look in the shop windows. I came to one selling curtains and bales of cloth, and there, standing outside, was Joey Segal, my tip-top tap-dancing pal from school. It was so good to see him. It was like being back at school again. Actually, it was even better than that. It had been a great day for me all round. I had seen my father, I had been allowed out on my own after three months of being stuck in the house with my mother, and I was also the possessor of two great new jazz records, apart from the Benny Goodman disc that my father had brought for me, and still had plenty of money left over.

Joey told me he was home for a few days, to escape the bomb-free but dreary life in Darlington, County Durham. We spent a great couple of hours together, which I had to break up to meet my three o'clock dead-line.

I was in the middle of explaining to him, prior to leaving, how to get to my house, so that he could come and listen to my jazz records and such, when, surprise, surprise, the air-raid warning sounded. Even though I had no personal fear about being on my own during the approaching air-raid, I was a bit worried about how my mother would react.

We immediately went into Joey's parents shop, where it had been my intention to phone home, but, even before the triad glissandi of the air-raid warning had finished its threat-filled wail, the anti-aircraft guns started banging away. Immediately, I was pressed into action by Joey's father, who made me pull down the window blinds whilst Joey locked and bolted the shop door. Meanwhile his mother was busily lighting candles and pushing them into little candle-holders which she had brought out from under the serving counter. Whilst all this frantic activity was going on, Mr Segal was carefully removing the money from the large brass-bound cash register and dumping it into a brown paper bag, saying as he did so, "Ve don' get looted a second time."

By now some bombs were falling and aeroplane engines could be clearly heard. We were hurriedly given a candle each and told to hurry down to the shop's basement, which turned out to be a small room without any window or, as far as I could see, any means of obtaining even a whiff of fresh air. And it smelled like it!

The long nightly occupancies of this airless little room (because the Luftwaffe was bombing London all night and every night), had polluted the air with an even mix of sweat, bad breath and chopped liver.

The basement itself contained one prison-sized cot, placed so that the door banged into it if you opened it too wide. Against the opposite wall were two old and very tatty armchairs. There was a tiny, round, brown coloured table set in the middle of the cellar, upon which was a half-eaten loaf of dark rye bread. On the floor next to the table were the covered-over bowls, which I subsequently discovered contained the various spreads with which they filled their nightly sandwiches. Against the wall on the right of the door was a single wooden-frame chair with a cane back and sagging cane seat. Mrs Segal pointed to it. "You sit there Jake dear," she said as she made her way to the armchair nearest the food table. She was a large-boned woman, with thick wiry grey-streaked black hair, cut and shaped into what was known in those days as a 'victory roll'. Like her son, she had large pitch-black eyes with thick, black eyebrows arched over them. Unlike her son, who had a thin straight mouth, she had full fleshy lips which curved downwards at the corners, giving her what I thought at the time was a sad expression. Now, in retrospect, I realise it was a sensuous mouth. She also had very white teeth made to look even whiter by the thick redness of her lips. She spoke in a deep husky voice, devoid of any foreign accent. Joey, who was sitting in the armchair next to her, had clearly inherited the physical characteristics of her side of the family rather than his father's. As a result he was approaching six feet in height, with broad shoulders and slim hips which, together with his thick black curly hair and flashing white teeth made him exactly into what a tap dancer should look like.

Mr Segal,(I never found out his first name because his son called him Dad, and his wife always addressed him as 'dear'), was short and stubby with a bulbous body shaped like a rugby football. He had a large round face and what hair he had left on his balding head, was black and shiny. His facial features seemed to me to be too small for his face. It was as if a smaller face had somehow been implanted over, the original one. As a result, his eyes seemed too close together and his aquiline nose and small mouth were like two little children lost in a large park. He lay on the rickety rattling bed, handkerchief in one hand with which he was forever mopping his perspiring face.

Mrs Segal, meantime (I did find out her name, it was Greta), was calmly slicing the rye bread for the sandwiches; Joey was just staring into space. I sat on my rickety chair looking at each one in turn, and wondering if conversation was in order.

Mr Segal seemed so intent on listening to the racket that was going on outside that it seemed a shame to break into his concentration. He lay there rigid, listening to the air raid with an intensity normally reserved for listening to Igor Stravinsky or Art Tatum or somebody.

The truth was he was shit scared. Like most Londoners, I was not at all frightened of Hitler's bombers. Having endured at least one raid every day or night for over a year now, we looked upon them more as a nuisance than anything else, rather as Africans do with their mosquitoes, or the Australians their flies; an annoying intrusion but a fact of life and there is not much you can do about it. There were of course those who didn't see it that way, Mister Segal being one of them and my Mother being another, which is why I was very worried as to how she must be feeling over my absence. I felt sure that after this I would never be allowed out on my own again until the war was over.

But Mr Segal's terror was entirely new to me. I could not help noticing how he reacted to every bang. When a bomb was near and the entire cellar shook from the vibration, his tubby little body would arch from the bed and with sweat pouring from every pore he would cry out, "Oyoyoyoy, I tink ve all die." Even when the bombing started to get more distant, he would react to the smallest thud, his body tensing as he said to nobody in particular, "Oy, denks to God, I tink they go avay."

So we sat there listening to the thick earthy crunch of bombs, some of which would cause the earth to shake so badly that the chair you were sitting on would actually move a few inches, and dust and fragments of wall and ceiling would bespeckle your hair and clothes giving you the appearance of someone with a terrible case of dandruff.

After about an hour, the gunfire, the bombs, and the roar of aeroplane engines had decrescendoed to a rapidly approaching silence. In the meantime, I had given myself nausea from eating the over-thick chicken schmaltz with which Greta Segal had daubed the rye bread, prior to adding the strips of chicken to the sandwiches.

Finally, when he was sure the air raid was past, Mr Segal now raised himself to a sitting position and smiling broadly said to me, "You see Jakie ve live to fight anudder day."

Then came the upward glissando, signalling the All Clear. I jumped to my feet as soon as it began.

"I must go right away, I'm afraid. My mum and dad will be very worried about me."

"Of course, Jake dear," said Mrs Segal, as she also stood up.

"Thank you very much for the food," I said politely, even though it was lying like a heavy brick in my gut.

After arranging with Joey what time he would visit me on the coming Saturday, I asked Mr Segal if I might use the phone to call my parents and tell them that I was okay.

"Ve don't hev a telephone Jackie." (I hated being called 'Jakie' but I guess I was too well brought up to correct a grown-up). "You hurry home, mine boy," he said patting me on the head, "Joey vill pop out to the shop next door and use their phone. Don't vorry, your mudder and fadder will know in a coupla minutes."

"My phone number's Reliance one seven three one," I shouted as I ran up the stairs followed by Joey clutching the shop's front door-key. As I ran out of the opened door down the street to the bus stop, I heard Joey's voice yelling at me, "I'll phone you Saturday morning." Still running and without turning round, I waved my hand in recognition. That was the last time I was ever to see him.

The bus was packed when it finally showed up. As I was pushing my way inside, I heard the conductor yelling in his hoarse cockney voice, "This bus finishes at the Oval. We aint goin' dahn the Brixton Road."

I managed to wangle myself past half a dozen jammed-together standing passengers, until I got halfway up the bus, where I stayed, wedged between a short, fat lady, who smelled as if she hadn't had a bath for a year, and an old thin man, in an old, black overcoat, that smelled strongly of dog-shit, which mixed none too kindly with the strong smell of gin coming off his breath. I could hear the ting-ting of the conductors ticketing machine as he made his way up the bus. Then I heard him shout an answer to a question put to him by a passenger I could neither see nor hear: “Nah, we cahn’ go dahn Brixton Road. I fink there’s a bomb or summink dahn there.”

I had by now become completely inured to bombs exploding nearby, but this was the first time one had actually struck the street in which I lived, and I was quite excited about it. As the old bus bumped and rumbled along I was wondering which part of my road had been struck, when the conductor’s hoarse shout shattered my idling thoughts. “Okay. Everybody orf. ’Ere’s as far as we’re goin’. Everybody orf.”

We all shuffled off the bus. I was tickled pink at the thought of telling my mother how I had got all the way home without having to pay any bus fare. It was after five o’clock in the afternoon and pitch dark, because in wartime London, all streetlights were forbidden. In retrospect, I’m buggered if I know why this was considered necessary because the Luftwaffe seemed to find its way around just as well with them on or off.

In those long-ago days, all road vehicles had to have masks over their headlights to stop them being visible to the German bombers. So as I made my way down Brixton Road, in the eerie, black, moonless, air-frosted night, it was hard to tell one vehicle from another. Of course you could always tell if it was a fire engine rushing your way because of its distinctive clanging bell. If you heard a high-pitched repeated ting-a-linging bell, you knew it was either police car or an ambulance. As I briskly made my way home down Brixton Road on that late afternoon, I was sure that I had never heard so many clanging or ting-a-linging vehicles in my life, as they sped past me in both directions, all of which was very exciting to twelve year-old me.

I was now becoming aware an ever stronger smell of burning hanging in the frozen air. Another hundred yards or so further on and swirling smoke was starting to become visible in the dim headlights of the passing emergency vehicles. A large figure suddenly materialised into my view. As I got closer I saw that it was a policeman wearing a white-painted steel hat, instead of the usual tall blue helmet. His right palm was held up towards me.

“Sorry son, you can’t go any further I’m afraid.” His voice was deep and husky, probably made more so by the acrid, swirling smoke. The smell of burning was very strong now.

"But I live down here. My parents will be waiting for me," I said.

"You say that you live in Brixton Road?" He came up close and loomed over me. I could see now that he was an oldish man, tall and beefy, with a large heavy-jowled face, blackened with soot stains around his lips and eyes. He was staring at me intently. I stared right back.

"Yes, I live at number two hundred and thirteen. My mum and dad will be worried about me."

The policeman said nothing for a full half minute. He just looked down at me expressionlessly. Then he said in a warm and friendly voice,

"I think you'd better come with me son," and he put his arm around my shoulder just like my father often did, and led me down to the next intersection, which was not more than a couple of hundred yards from my house.

I can still remember gabbing on to the burly copper as we walked, about how I'd promised to be home earlier, and how the air-raid had made me late, and how my parents would be so worried. The copper said nothing. He just let me chatter away until we got to the crossroads, where there was a black Wolsey police car parked, with two policemen sitting in the front seats.

The driver let down his window as he saw us approaching.

"Wait here son," they copper said, leaving me on the opposite side of the road, while he crossed over to speak with the driver. This gave me the opportunity to look through the gloom to see what was actually going on further down the road. I could not see very far because of the blackness of the night combined with the drifting smoke, but I could make out a couple of fire-engines parked diagonally in the middle of the road. There was also a dull orange glow tinting the grey, swirling, frost-laden mist.

"Come over 'ere, son," my policeman shouted over to me. His head was close to the driver's, his crooked right elbow resting on the open car window, whilst he was waving me over with his left.

As I came towards him, he said to me, his voice casual and fatherly. "These chaps'll look after you now. They'll see you're alright, don't you worry. Then as he pulled himself upright, he turned a smiling face to me and said, "I've got to get back on duty now, me lad." I watched him as he started walking back in the direction from which we had come. Suddenly he stopped, turned and shouted, "Good luck son." And he let the choking, smoky blackness swallow him up.

The passenger-policeman reached over and opened the rear door behind the driver. At the same time the driver turned an expressionless face to me and said in a toneless tired voice, "Get in the back son."

"Where are we going?" I asked as I was clambering into the back seat.

"Down to the station," the passenger policeman said in a voice as flat and toneless as the driver's.

"Is that where my parents are? Because they'll be very worried about me by now."

It was quite a time before either of them said anything. Then the driver said "We've had to clear this whole area. We've got all the residents down at the station."

"I live at two hundred and thirteen Brixton Road. Do you know if my house got damaged?"

There was an even longer pause before the driver said,

"Look son, I've got to concentrate on driving. Do you mind saving your questions until we get to the station? The duty sergeant will be able to tell you everything then."

After that we drove on in silence. I got out my two new jazz records to look at the labels, but it was too dark to see them. So I spent the rest of the journey looking out at the black night and thinking how I was going to tell my mother and father about poor Mr Segal shivering and shaking just because of a few bombs. Then I moved on to thinking about what Joey and I would do when he visited me on Saturday.

Suddenly the car swung hard to the left, through large gate-posts which should have had iron gates attached, but which had been removed, like everyone else's, to be melted down to make armaments.

As we parked next to two other police cars, the passenger policeman reached over me to open my door. "Okay, out we get" he said as tonelessly as before.

I got out and with the two coppers on either side of me, we walked across the small courtyard, up four stone steps, through heavy, double swing doors, down a narrow corridor, past a noisy room filled with policemen smoking, and drinking from large mugs, or playing cards and darts, and then on through two large grubby, paint-chipped swing doors, into a big room with long wooden benches running round three sides of it. The fourth side was taken up with a long table, behind which was a short tubby police sergeant, in a black woollen sweater with his sergeant's stripes sewn onto the sleeves.

On either side of him were two middle-aged ladies. One looked like a bag of unwanted bones with a bun at the nape of her scrawny neck and pince-nez gripping her long, bony nose not more than an inch from its pointed tip.. I was immediately reminded of Margaret Hamilton, who played the witch in 'The Wizard of Oz'. The other lady was another matter entirely. She was smartly dressed in a dark green polo-neck sweater and a flowery patterned scarf carefully knotted at one side, the way fighter pilots wore them. Her shoulder-length auburn hair seemed to me to be fashionably styled rather like those typical true-blue Brrrritish heroines of the war movies. Both women had uneven stacks of files in bulging file-covers of different colours in front of them, in which they seemed to be constantly searching for specific information to pass over to the police sergeant who would copy them into a huge thick ledger he had open in front of him.

We had got to within about six feet of the table when one of my two accompanying policemen suddenly gripping my shoulder firmly, said, "Okay, stop here." They left me standing whilst they went over to the big table and, bending right over, held a whispered conversation with the desk sergeant, who listened to what they were saying without looking up from his ledger even for a second.

Having nothing to do whilst this was going on, I looked around me. There were about twenty people scattered around the long wooden benches. Apart from two old men, one of whom had a large bandage around his head and who was either unconscious or asleep, all the rest were women. They were all either sobbing quietly or just staring sightlessly in front of them, swollen-eyed from having cried in the recent past, their sodden handerkerchiefs pressed against their half-open mouths in a stunned silence.

The atmosphere of shock and depression that pervaded the room suddenly got to me. All at once I felt myself enshrouded in a thick, grey, pall of loneliness, alienating me from everything and everybody. I was suddenly desperate to feel the warmth and safety of my mother and father's presence. I was not the kind of kid who cried a lot, but the quiet sobbing misery around me, together with the eerie unreality of what had been happening to me ever since I got off the bus, caused tears to suddenly blur my vision.

I had no sooner finished wiping my eyes with my overcoat sleeve, than I saw the desk sergeant say something which caused both my police escorts to turn and look at me for a short second. The aristocratic, war-movie heroine type looked up from her work at the same time as did the Wicked Witch of the North.

For a moment time seemed to stop. It was like a still life of blank staring faces. Then, just as suddenly, life began from where it had left off as once again and they went back to their talking and file-searching. The sergeant now slowly put down his pen, stretched his heavy frame across to the telephone that was only just within his reach, dialled three numbers and talked very briefly and very, very quietly into the mouthpiece.

As he put the phone back on its rest, he said something to the policemen, who then turned round and came towards me.

"I want to see my mum and dad," I shouted at them in as brave a voice as I could muster through my panic.

"Alright, alright," the car driver said holding up his hand to indicate that I should be quiet.

"We've got to go back on duty now son. That lady there," he pointed to the quasi-film star:

"She'll look after you from now on."

"But where is my mum and d—"

"All the best, son," he said over my pleading and over his shoulder as he and his partner crossed the room and disappeared through the large double doors.

The lady immediately got up from behind the desk and came over to me. She was tall, slim and elegant. She smiled fondly at me as she approached.

"Your name is Jake?" she asked.

"Yes"

"What a nice name. My name is Penny." She held out her hand to me. "How do you do."

As I returned her handshake, I said, "My parents were expecting me at half past three. That is over two hours ago. They'll be jolly worried about me."

Her smile never faded for a moment, as she replied,

"Of course. Follow me Jake."

As I think back on it now, I realise that she would have made a helluva airline stewardess: or a Queen maybe. Airline stewardesses, Queens and members of the aristocracy must get special training to smile regardless of the circumstances.

"Your Majesty, may I present Hubert Schmuckface. He is dying from leprosy and cancer. He is going to die within six weeks in mortal agony."

"Oh how interesting," she would reply with a frozen, soldered-on smile, oblivious and uncaring of poor old Hubert's problems. This is because royalty, the aristocracy and airline stewardesses have this one thing in common; they just don't give a shit. They just keep smiling and fuck the lot of us.

Of course I was not aware of it then. So I just trailed along behind her as she strolled in stately fashion through the double doors, past the recreation room, along to the end of the drab cream and green painted hall, up a flight of stairs, down another cream and green hallway, up another flight of stairs, along a short hallway and into a small room at the end.

We went straight in without her knocking first, so I guessed she must have known that there would be no-one in it. The room was bare save for a small, table standing naked in the middle of it, a single wooden chair behind it and two more on the side nearest us as we entered.
Apart from that there was nothing else in the room bar a single electric light with a small green shade dangling on a foot long piece of flex from the ceiling adding a depressing yellow hue to the dull, empty walls.

"Would you like me to get you a nice hot sweet cup of tea, Jake?" The smile never left her face.

"Yes, that would be nice," I said, pretending to act normally in this frighteningly alien atmosphere.

"Well, you just sit down over there on the far side of the table and I'll be back in a jiffy."

She was just about to close the door behind her when the ever-smiling head popped back inside and added, "And I'll bring you a nice piece of cake as well." And then, like the Cheshire cat, the smile disappeared and her with it. I sat down in the chair she had selected for me. There were no magazines to peruse, and due to the blackout regulations, I couldn't even look out of the window.

So I just sat with my two records on my lap thinking about where my mother and father could possibly be. Surely the police knew where they were. If they didn't, then why had they brought me here to the police station? Maybe they'd been injured in the air-raid. If that was so, why hadn't the police already told me? Or maybe my parents were actually helping those people who'd been injured in the raid. In that case, I reckoned, the police would not know their exact whereabouts and so they would keep me here until the emergency was over, and they came to collect me. 'That's it', I decided. 'Christ, they might even get a medal for bravery under fire!' I was quite excited by that thought.

Just as I was into the best bit of my fantasy, where the three of us are about to be presented to the King to receive our medals, the door was thrust open and a bull of a man barged into the room. He was short, thick-set and with a neck so thick, his over-tight shirt collar bit into it. He had an aura of boundless energy. Where normal people walked, he bustled. Even taking the seat opposite me was done with an animal-like ferocity.

He was dressed in a typically British, Saville Row type double-breasted blue pin-stripe suit with unpadded shoulders, narrow sleeves, and so over-tight around the waist that his arse stuck out. He also had a typically British white shirt with a starched narrow white collar. It looks just fine if you have a short thick neck like this man had. But if you are thin with a long thin neck these British-cut shirts look terrible. If you don't believe me, check out any old movie featuring Michael Dennison.

Behind Energy Man came two others. The first was tall, fair-haired, and with pale watery eyes and parchment pale complexion. The second was short thin and wearing a pair of round metal-framed glasses that made his eyes look bulging and larger than they actually were. He was dressed in a terribly ill-fitting shit-brown coloured sports jacket, so badly creased as to make you think that it doubled as a pyjama top. His grey flannel trousers were so overlarge and baggy, that if he had an identical twin brother, both of them could have occupied them at the same time and no-one would have known. You may wonder why a kid of twelve would be so observant of how people dress. The reason was, that my Father was a sharp dresser, and he had lectured me many times about the importance of colour-coding one's shirt and socks with the suit you are wearing, and stuff like that. As a result, up to about ten years ago, I was always very clothes-conscious Nowadays I am only booze conscious—and sometimes unconscious!

I also noticed that this shabby individual carried with him what appeared to be a doctor's bag.

Energy Man thrust his right hand across the table for me to shake.

"Hello. My name is Roger Huntingdon – er, Commander Roger Huntingdon actually. And these two are my associates," he said, waving his left hand roughly in their direction whilst never taking his eyes off me. They gave me a head-nod acknowledgement as he did so.

"And you, I understand, are Master Jake Silver. Am I correct?"

He spoke with the kind of impeccable, clipped, military-British accent that put one in mind of our 'gellent cheps' who were so brilliantly and bravely winning the war for us in the propaganda movies of the time. We were still shaking hands as I nodded and said, "Yes sir, my name is Jake Silver."

"Good, good," he said as he sat down in the chair opposite me. He snapped his fingers towards where his pale-faced assistant was standing, who, seemingly able to read his mind, passed to him a clipboard he had been carrying, although I had not noticed it until then.

The Commander studied it for a while. Then he said, without looking up,

"We don't seem to have any details of your next-of-kin." He lifted his gaze from the clipboard to stare at me once more with his ice-blue eyes. "Surely, you must have a married older sister or brother, or even an Aunt or Uncle or something?"

"I am an only child, I am afraid sir," I replied, returning his gaze. "But I do have an Aunt Sarah and Uncle Harry," I added.

"Good, good," he said. Then, as he reached into his inside pocket for his fountain pen he said, in an off-hand sort of way: "I don't suppose you remember their address, do you?"

"No," I said. "But I do remember their telephone number"

"Good, good" he said again, and wrote it down as I gave it to him. Then, while still seemingly studying the piece of paper on his clipboard, he asked "And do you like your Aunt Sarah and your Uncle Harry?"

It stopped me in my tracks for a minute because it was something I had never given any thought to previously. They were just people we would visit from time to time. Apart from their typically grown-up questions about how I was getting on at school etc., we never ever really talked. They would talk with Mum and Dad, whilst I would hang around with their son Ivan, who was older than me by about six years.

I liked Ivan a lot. Apart from the fact that he always treated me like someone of his own age, there were two other over-riding reasons why I liked him. The first was that he loved jazz as much as I did. And the second was that his Father being very rich indulged him with sufficient cash to buy any jazz record he fancied. He also thought that I was a red hot jazz pianist, which didn't hurt either.

So, I assured the Commander that I liked my relatives a lot. "Good, good," he said yet again, but this time absent mindedly as he stared at me in the kind of shrewd, knowing way that people do when they are trying to size you up.

Then quite suddenly, he leapt out of his chair to pace panther-fashion around the room, fingers interlinked behind his back, chin thrust forward. Just as suddenly he started to speak:

"Jake my lad, this is a pretty beastly war. Lots of good British people have already died, and lots more will I am afraid. But we should never forget that to die in defence of one's country is a great honour—maybe the greatest honour of all...

When I think back on it now, I can't believe I fell for such utter nonsense.. But I did, maybe because it was a real life Commander talking to me like I was a grown-up. Or maybe it was because I had seen too many British war movies.

"...and those that they leave behind can bask in the glory of their dearly departed..."

Thankfully, the Commander's cornball cliches were cut short by the noise of the door being opened. It was Penny, carefully backing into the room bearing a tray of tea and cakes.

"Ah, refreshments," said the Commander. "Thank you so much Lady Penelope." ('So', I thought, 'she really is an aristocrat'. That seemed to me to be even better than being the heroine of a war movie.)

"Here, let me help you set it down on the table.," the Commander said as he relieved her of the tray. Having landed it successfully on the table he stood back to allow the Lady to pour the tea, place a wedge of cake into each saucer, and hand them to each of us, saying our names as she did so. As soon as it was done, the Commander bustled to the door and, holding it open, said to Lady Penelope, "Thank you so much." He said it in such a way that she was left in no doubt that he wanted her out of the room and pronto.

"Oh. Well I'll be awf then," she said brightly, looking at each of us in turn, the aristocratic smile still successfully glued into place, the aristocratic horse-teeth flashily white.

Almost before she was out of the room, the Commander turned to Paleface and said quietly, but in the same voice of unchallengeable authority, "And I wonder if you wouldn't mind running along as well Tommy old chap."

He nodded and left, leaving the room to the Commander, Mister Baggy Pants and myself.

Immediately, the Commander banged his tea and cake down on the table and in an almost ferocious way, grabbed a chair, swung it round and sat astride it, so that he was facing me, arms folded and resting on top of the seat-back. He stared at me intently, watching me eat my cake and sip my tea.

"Jake," he said quietly: "Can I trust you to keep a secret?"

I have never felt quite so important as I felt at that moment. Here was a real, live, Commander, about to trust me with a top secret. At felt like Jack Hawkins, Richard Todd and Kenneth More, all rolled into one!

As I put my cup and saucer down on the table, I said in as grown -up voice as I could muster:

"Oh yes. Absolutely."

Then, just to prove how security conscious I was, I pointed to Baggy Pants, who was leaning against the door, directly behind the Commander, his little leather bag at his feet:

"What about him?" I asked the Commander. "Can he listen too?"

He looked round at him for a second and then back to me saying "Oh him? He's alright. He's a doctor."

I could not quite see the logic of his reply, but as it seemed okay to him, it was okay by me.

"Lean forward Jake my boy, I don't want to speak too loudly."

I leaned forward as far as the table would allow.

"Do you know where Tower Pier is"? His voice had taken on a quiet, conspiratorial tone.

"No, I'm sorry" I said..

"Well, it's a mooring point in the Thames, between Tower Bridge and London Bridge."

"Oh, right," I said, searching for something serious and war movie-like to say.

"There is a battle cruiser moored there right now, at the express command of His Majesty. It is there because having returned after an arduous but highly successful tour of duty in the Atlantic, His Majesty wanted to go aboard and meet the officers and men, in order to congratulate them on a job well done."

He suddenly lifted himself out of his chair again and, with hands locked behind his back, went back to his animal-like prowling around the small room, continuing to speak as he did so.

"It had been arranged for His Majesty to go aboard at twelve-thirty precisely, for drinks in the wardroom with the officers. Then, a spot of lunch, after which there was to be a small investiture followed by a low-level fly-past by a squadron of Seafires from Fleet Air-arm. Thereafter, the King had a meeting planned with Winston Churchill for five o'clock precisely." He suddenly broke off his exciting narrative, to come back to the table, grab his tea-cup and empty it at a draught before going on:

"Somehow or other, Jerry had got wind of the whole thing and decided to mount a sneak raid, the object being to sink the cruiser at its moorings and kill His Majesty at the same time."

"Hell," I said, now totally caught up in this real 'Boy's Own' kind of drama.

"Worse still," he said, resuming his pacing. "Because of the low-level fly-past, we had to take down the balloon-barrage in the area, thus allowing Jerry to come in at a really low altitude without too many problems."

He allowed a dramatic pause, to let the deep seriousness of the situation to sink in.

"Hell," I said again, sensing that it had been left to me to fill in the

Commander's dramatic pause, but not knowing quite how to do it. Thankfully, the Commander went back to his 'Boy's Own'story..

"They dispatched six Heinkels to do the job. They came across the Channel at almost sea-level, streaking across Southern England, below the level at which our electronic spotter equipment can operate."

"Christ," I said. I was now genuinely absorbed. After all, this kind of stuff is food and drink to an imaginative twelve year-old boy.

"Then, we had an incredibly lucky break," the Commander said, still pacing the room, his eyes staring fixedly at the floor in front of him.

"The King, whilst on board, received a message from the Prime Minister saying that due to an unforeseen emergency, he humbly requested that his meeting with His Majesty be put forward by one half an hour, to four-thirty. This called for the re-scheduling of the fly-past by the Seafires from three-thirty to three o'clock, which happened to be the exact time that the Germans had planned to bomb the cruiser. By the time we knew what was going on, Jerry was only ten minutes flying time away from their target"

Again, he left a silence to allow me time to get the picture clearly into my head. He needn't have bothered. My heart was actually racing with excitement. This was far better than any of the war-movies I had seen. I remember how I was already mentally rehearsing the way I was going pass on this thriller to my parents.

"The Heinkels were already in the process of climbing to five hundred feet in order to make their bombing runs before we could even get our air-raid sirens into action. We also alerted the leader of the flypast squadron, who turned the entire formation, and flew directly at Jerry. Well sir, when those Nazi pilots saw fifteen Seafires bearing down on them, they did the usual Hun thing. They turned and fled back to where they had come from, but with our boys right up their backsides. Then, damn them, in order to get more speed into their getaway, they just unloaded all their bombs, without any regard for the civilian population beneath them."

"That's typical of them Nazis," I interjected, realising at the same time, that this is what had been going on over our heads, while I was sitting in Mister and Mrs. Segal's cellar munching my way through those over-schmaltzed, lead-weight, chicken sandwiches.

"Well," the Commander continued in true Kenneth More style, "Our boys shot down four of the swine and badly damaged a fifth."

"Jolly good. Marvellous," I shouted with excitement. If I remember rightly, I even clapped my hands at the same time.

Now the Commander stopped his pacing as suddenly as he had started it. He strode back to the chair facing me on the opposite side of the table, turned it around, sat down and took a cigarette from a silver cigarette-case he had retrieved from his inside pocket. It is etched permanently into my memory, exactly how he carefully tapped one end on the table before lighting it with his gold lighter. I watched him as he inhaled deeply and then continued, the smoke puffing out of his mouth and nose as he did so.

"One of the fleeing bombers, with a Seafire right on its tail, set a course which took it straight along the Brixton Road." He paused for a moment to watch himself carefully tap cigarette ash onto the floor beside him, before turning to pin me once again with his piercing, blue-eyed stare.

"It was during this chase over Brixton Road that the Heinkel pilot, without regard for the civilians beheath, decided to shed his bomb load.

I noticed the Commander's face suddenly take on a grave expression. Just as suddenly, my feet turned to ice.

"One of those bombs," he went on: "A thousand pounder, to be precise, landed directly on a house, number two hundred and thirteen, destr..."

...It was a sound like the roaring, rushing of a giant waterfall filling my head and shutting out the rest of the Commander's words. I have only the vaguest recollection of what happened thereafter. I seem to remember the ice-cold that had clutched my feet, now spreading upwards like an inverted avalanche to engulf me entirely. I remember standing up and shouting out something like, "No, no. Not my Mum and Dad," or something like it. I am pretty sure that the Commander was saying at the same time, something like "No-one could have given their lives in a nobler cause" or some shit like that, before things started to go black. It was a blackness filled with pinpricks of light; a blackness accompanied by an ever-louder roaring of a giant waterfall.

The very last thing I can definitely recall, is hearing the Commanders voice shout: "He's going. Grab 'im. He's going." I also vaguely remember arms being thrust under my armpits from behind.

After that, the blackness closed in.

Chapter 4

THE NEXT THING I remember was opening my eyes to see a swollen-eyed, tear-filled Aunt Sarah standing at my bedside holding my hand. My first thought was, 'why is she here and what the hell is making her cry?'

And then it hit me.

The effect was not as one would have imagined; of me being pitched headlong into a tidal wave of horror, sadness, fear and desperation. What happened was a huge guillotine came crashing down on my brain, severing at a stroke all normal feelings and reactions from my conscious mind. I was suddenly in a crazy half-way world, one half numb to all emotion, the other half refusing to accept what had happened and expecting my parents to come walking into the room at any minute.

As I sat myself up in this strange bed and leaned forward to allow my Aunt to tearfully plump up the pillows behind me, this odd, brain-numbing unreality began now to completely enshroud me. I guess I felt rather as a ghost would feel finding himself in a roomful of people he can see and hear, but cannot contact in any meaningful way, nor can they contact him in any tangible fashion.

(Strangely enough, barring one too short, magically magnificent episode in my life, it is something that I have never quite been able to rid myself of. I have it at this moment as I sit here, shaded from the dazzling, humid, heat of the early afternoon Cuban sun.)

A male voice cut into the blackness of my feelings of my numb nothing-ness.

"How are you feeling son?"

It was my Uncle Harry, speaking from where he was sitting, over near the bedroom window on the other side of the room. I looked across at him: small, thick-set, and as always, in a dark, three-piece suit, a white, tight-collared shirt and dark conservative tie. He was looking at me, his normally expressionless face now over laden with sadness and sympathy.

Hitherto, all my previous contacts with him had been only of the fleeting, distant type, typical of what one would expect from a young, music-orientated, fun-loving kid when he meets with a rich, serious and seemingly remote business man, who, in any case, was rarely at home whenever my Mother and I came to visit. I should and would normally have been surprised to see the look of genuine, grief-stricken concern on his face, because it was the kind of deep human emotion that I never had associated with him. But in my present mental and emotional state, all I could summon up was the kind of mild, detached interest one gets watching animals in the zoo.

I answered him as best as I knew how.

"I don't know Uncle," I said. "But... I think I'm alright."

For some reason, unfathomable to me at the time, this reply brought on a whole new flood of tears from Aunt Sarah.

"Oh, my God, my God," she sobbed softly as she leaned over to kiss me, her tears leaving cold wet patches on my cheek.

Then, after staring at me for a while, her face contorted with suffering, she asked me the archetypal question, posed by Jewish women of young boys, down the ages.

"Are you hungry?"

Normally, I would have said 'yes please', because my Aunt Sarah was a helluva good cook. Normally, I would have also tried to cheer her up like I used to do with my Mother, whenever I thought she was feeling sad. But there was nothing normal in this situation. But like I said, I was totally bereft of any feelings either for myself or anyone else.

"What time is it?" I asked.

"It's just after half-past ten" my Uncle said, after consulting the gold fob-watch he had taken from his waistcoat pocket

As cold winter daylight was streaming in through the bedroom window, I knew it had to be ten-thirty in the morning.

"D'you mean I've been here all night?" I asked.

"Yes my darling. They gave you a sedative to make you sleep." My aunt said in a voice thick from crying.

"I wouldn't mind a cup of tea," I said.

My Aunt clapped her hands together in front of her ample bosom:

"He wouldn't mind a cup of tea," she repeated gushingly to no-one in particular. It was as if the experimental operation on "Son of Frankenstein" had worked and he could now actually speak. Then, to me in a voice dripping with sympathy. "Certainly my darling."

She all but ran across the bedroom floor in her fervour to get to the kitchen, turning to me just before she disappeared out of the bedroom door:

"And while I'm at it, I'll just make you a few slices of toast and some scrambled egg and tomato."

She disappeared, only to reappear almost immediately to add "And I'll make it with real eggs, not that powdered rubbish." I couldn't help noticing how the very idea of cooking me up a breakfast seemed to have cheered her up.

Once she was out of the room, my Uncle said "We'll have to get you some new clothes Jake. You've got nothing to wear apart from what you came here in." Then he added, "I don't suppose you know if your Father had any life insurance?" I had no idea what he was talking about. So I just stared at him. He must have suddenly realised by my uncomprehending expression, the insensitivity of his question because he raised his hand, saying "Ach, this is no time to talk of such things, is it Jake my boy? I'm sure that under the circumstances, I'll be able to get some extra clothing coupons and then, when you are feeling more like it, we'll go out in my big new car and buy you a whole pile of new clothes. Would you like that?"

"Rather," I said. I did my best to sound enthusiastic although looking back on it, I cannot believe that my state of emotional anaesthesia went unnoticed by him. I was also finding it very awkward to affect a rapport with someone who had hitherto never taken any interest in me. But everything was so unreal to me I doubt if I would have been able to make sense of anything.

I leaned heavily back against the deep pillows to stare at the ceiling and try to get each event that had taken place since stepping off the bus at the Oval until I blacked out. But, as each incident popped into frame, so my mind would instantly move on to something else.

It was like a jumbled jazz solo, notes and chords running and blurring into each other, lacking shape and substance.

My Uncle's voice dragged me back into the numb, meaningless reality of the present. "Well Jake," he said, standing up and looking again at his gold fob-watch, "I've got some work to do. You know my boy, no matter how bad things are, you must never let the grass grow under your feet." He quickly crossed the carpeted room to the bedroom door, opened it and just before leaving, turned to me and said "Chin up my boy. Keep fighting. I'll be back in a couple of hours."

Aunt Sarah must have been coming up the stairs at the same time with my breakfast, because I could hear the hushed murmur of whispered conversation outside the closed door.

Then, she came in carrying a large, white, wooden tray with enough food to feed Glen Miller's AEF band, including the vocalists.

"Now sit up and have your breakfast my darling" she said in a voice dripping with sympathy as she came towards me. Setting the tray down over my legs, she watched contentedly as I polished off the entire meal. As I drank down the final dregs of my tea cup, she said "Now I want you to have a nice hot bath. Leave all your clothes outside the bathroom door so that the maid can wash and iron them. Meanwhile, Hylda Kleinman, you don't know her, but she has a son about your size, is going to lend me some of his clothes for you to wear just until you feel ready to go shopping with me." I nodded blankly and got straight out of the bed, surprised for some reason, to see that I was still fully dressed. The sight of my clothes gave me a kind of weird sensation. It was as if they were from another world, another existence; from a yesterday's world where life had form, identity and meaning. Now, neither the food I had just eaten, not the large, hot, bath that followed, gave me any pleasure. It was as if I had become a born-again zombie. I was conscious of but one thing; I could not think about my parents. As soon as my mind turned to them, some mental mechanism would automatically activate and bounce me into another line of thought.

On that first day of being entirely on my own, so to speak (because even though Uncle Harry and Aunt Sarah were kind and loving, they could never come anywhere near replacing the love and security of my own Mum and Dad), the only feelings I can remember were of alienation and unreality. The strange bathroom, the foreign feel of the fabric of the bathrobe which was several sizes too large for me, the strangeness of putting on someone else's underwear, socks, shirt, tie and a blue herringbone suit that fitted me, except for the sleeves which were a good two inches too short. Only the shoes were my own, and as I slipped into them I felt the kind of warm regard for them that a pair of scuffed, black leather lace-ups was never intended to engender in the wearer.

Once fully fed and dressed, I went downstairs to the kitchen where I knew my Aunt would be. I also knew that my cousin Ivan would be at college, so I had no-one else to speak with until then.

I found her in the breakfast room, which led directly off from the kitchen. She was sitting at the round breakfast table silently dabbing her tear-filled, swollen eyes, with a little white lace handkerchief. With her, also sitting round the table, were four solemn-faced women. They were silently watching my Aunt cry, whilst the maid reached over them in turn to refresh their tea cups.

As I came into the room she stood up and came over to hug me tightly and kiss me wetly on my cheek. The visiting ladies were staring at me in that concentrated way cats do when they see a mouse. I guess now in retrospect they were either trying to estimate either how I was handling my double bereavement, or maybe, they were just trying to memorise everything so that they could recount it in detail at their next bridge party.

With her arms still around me she looked up at me (I was already taller than her), and said, in a choked sort of voice. "I'm not just crying for you, but for me also. You have lost your Mother Jake darling, but I have also lost my only beloved younger sister." She turned her head to address the watching women. "Now, with my brother Louis dead, I have only one other member of the family left and that is my older sister, and she lives in Australia." She turned back to me. "So you see Jake my darling, to all intents and purposes. I also have no family left—except for you."

But in my emotionally numb state, neither her tale of woe, nor her tearful, heart-broken face made any impact whatever upon me. So I just nodded my acknowledgment of her filial state-of-play speech.

She unclasped me and clutching my jacket sleeve, pulled me over to the chair she had previously occupied.

"Come and have some tea with us," she said. As I sat down she yelled "Inga, bring another chair, an extra cup and some more tea please." Then, standing behind me, with her hands on my shoulders as I sat staring blankly at the milk jug, she said to the women "This is Eve and Ike's olav ha sholem, son Jake. For those of you readers who are not hip to Jewish religious custom, when you refer to someone no longer with us (shit I hate that expression: I mean 'dead'), they utter this imprecation, which simply means, 'Rest in Peace'.

"Jake darling," she said, introducing me to each lady in turn. "This is my friend of thirty-odd years, Cissie; this is my sister-in-law Pearl; my neighbour and good friend Rosie, and another of my very best friends who has come all the way from the Whitechapel Road, Golda.

Golda was fat, swarthy-skinned and oldish. (Mind you, everyone looks old when you are just twelve years of age). Looking at me with her dark brown eyes, she said, "I knew your parents well Jake. Eve, so pretty and full of life, Ike, always the life and soul of the party, always making jokes." She spoke slowly, with a toneless, flat, east-end-of-London accent. Then, Cissie, not wanting to be outdone in the eulogy department chimed in with "I was at their wedding you know. I'll never forget..." But I mentally switched her out.

To me at that moment, the very mention of my parents' names was like a dagger in my gut. Unconsciousness or, at the very least, mentally blocking out, is the mechanism humans instinctively use to handle deep, sudden shock. And these dumb, middle-aged broads were forcing me to come face to face with the one thing I needed to confront least of all; the reality of my parents' death. Listening to these four vultures pick over the bones of my Mother and Father's lives, tumbling over each other to top the other's reminiscences was finally more than I could take.

I leapt to my feet yelling at the same time "I can't stand you going on about my Father and Mother. Why can't you just leave it alone." As I ran from the breakfast room, back to the bedroom, I heard one of the women ask, "What did I say?"

Half way up the stairs my Aunt called out to me "Jake, don't be like that. Come back."

But I had to be on my own. Solitude seemed now to be my only refuge.

I slammed the bedroom door but could not find the key with which to lock it. I went and lay on the bed trying to force my mind to concentrate on whether I would now be sent to a boarding school or whether I would be sent to a local school. 'I know Mum and Dad would want me to keep up with my education', I thought. But even this accidentally self-induced reference to my parents drove me deeper into the nightmare of depression. I turned face down on the bed, pulling the pillow over my head in some vain hope that the dark suffocation of it would match and so in some way, ameliorate the dark suffocation of grief that was now starting to assume an ever-growing reality within me. I realise now that it was the beginning of my emergence from my short bathe in the river Lethe.

Not more than a couple of minutes could have passed before the door was pushed open and the pillow roughly pulled off me. I turned over onto my back to see my Aunt, pillow in hand, staring down at me, her face an even mix of panic and misery.

"What do you think you are doing?" she asked fearfully. "Trying to suffocate yourself?"

I made no reply. I just lay there, eyes firmly shut.

Now a female voice piped up from the foot of the bed. "It's no good feeling sorry for yourself Jake my boy. I knew your Father and Mother very well, and I know that they would not like to see you acting in this way." I opened my eyes to see who was speaking. It was the small, mean-lipped, peroxide-blonde, who had caused me to run back to my bedroom in the first place.

"Leave the boy alone Cissy," said my Aunt. "If he wants to lie here, then let him."

"No, Cissie's right," said Rosie, who was standing directly behind my Aunt. For some reason I can recall exactly how she was dressed. She was wearing a brown woollen dress, belted tightly at the waist, accentuating her titless top and her plump, saggy-arsed, thick-legged bottom.

"It's no good him lying about the place, feeling sorry for himself and..."

"Please," I pleaded over her nagging cackle: "Just leave me alone." But there was no stopping her.

"...And..." she went on, her voice growing louder as she spoke, "...being rude to ladies old enough to be his mother."

Now she moved up to my bedside, saying: "I never knew your parents but I am rather surprised that they did not teach you to show some respect for your elders and betters"

I said nothing. Misery, frustration and anger were building up inside me with every passing minute. I wanted to cry but was incapable of tears. The screaming that was going on inside me would have been better on the outside but I could just not bring it to the surface. I also had a strong desire to punch this woman who was standing over me, very hard on her powdered, large nostrilled nose. Only my upbringing stopped me from doing so.

Now it was Cissie's turn again. "Well, how ungrateful of you Jake. After all the kindness your Aunt and Uncle are showing you. If it wasn't for them, you would be in an orphanage right now. Aren't I right Rosie?"

But before Rosie could say anything, the dark and swarthy Golda came to my aid: "I think the lot of you should shut up," she said. "You're acting like a couple of coarse, goyische fishwives. Have you no feelings? Can't you even try to imagine what he is going through?"

"You are so right Golda darling," said my Aunt. Then, turning to where Rosie and Cissie were standing, she added, "Don't you two have any feelings of sympathy?"

"Sympathy? Sympathy" Cissie replied angrily. "If I didn't have any feelings of sympathy do you think I would have given two German Jewish refugee girls jobs? Believe me" she said self-righteously, "I would never have employed those two arrogant bitches except out of sympathy." Then she turned to me "And they've suffered a lot more than you will ever suffer, my boy. And they aren't moping around feeling sorry for themselves."

I got off the bed saying: "I am going to the bathroom and I am going to lock myself in until you have all gone." As I was making my way out of the room Golda moved across to me, her arms open and gave me a hug: "You are a nice boy Jake and I like you a lot," she said, looking straight into my eyes. "Don't take any notice of these silly, stupid women. They were only trying in their own misguided way to snap you out of your sadness." Then she added loudly, turning to look directly at Cissie and Rosie: "Only they were doing it far too soon." Then turning back to me she added "You'll be alright Jake darlin'. We Jews have had to endure nearly two thousand years of pain and suffering. We are the world's experts when it comes to handling the loss of ones nearest and dearest."

I pushed myself free of her encircling arms. "Look, I just want to be left alone," I said. "Can't you all just let me be?"

As I got to the bedroom door on my way to the bathroom, I heard Cissie say to my back, in a surprisingly sweet voice "Goodbye Jake. I only said what I did with your best interests at heart"

"Absolutely," echoed Rosie.

I could not bring myself to acknowledge this sudden change of heart. 'They can go to hell', I thought as I went out.

I stayed in the bathroom until I heard them clomping their way down the stairs. They were arguing away at what had gone on in the bedroom. I heard my Aunt saying "Of course it was worse under Hitler. But two wrongs don't make a right." As soon as I was sure the coast was clear so to speak, I quietly nipped back to my bedroom to lie on the bed again.

I must have somehow drifted off to sleep because I dreamed that I was standing next to our piano, watching and listening to my Father as he played Jerome Kern's 'They Didn't Believe Me', when all of a sudden, the cigarette that he always rested on the ashtray at the treble end slipped on to the keyboard, setting it ablaze. My Father did not seem aware of it, and although I was trying as hard as I could, I could not get my voice to work in order to warn him. I tried to run into the next room to fetch my Mother, but my legs were suddenly leaden and I could only move very slowly and ponderously. I turned to see my Father still seated at the piano, but now engulfed by flames. I was trying to yell, 'No, no, not my Dad, no, not my Dad'. But I could only mumble incoherently. Then I found that I was shaking from side to side uncontrollably.

I heard a voice at first soft, but getting louder saying, "Hey, hey. Hey, hey."

Suddenly I was awake to find my cousin Ivan sitting astride me shaking me. "Hey, hey," he was saying as I opened my eyes. "That was some dream you were having."

"Oh," I said waiting for my head to clear. "Yeah, it was a bad dream that's all."

Ivan got off me and went across to the dressing-table seat, on which he had left a pile of records.

"So, how are you feeling Jake?"

"Not all that great," I said quietly

I got off the bed and went across the room to look at the records more out of habit than a desire to know what was actually on them.

"Well, I've got some news for you Jake." He was speaking to me whilst studying himself in the dressing-table mirror and retrieving a small comb from the back pocket of his grey flannel school trousers, with which he carefully combed his hair as he spoke.

"I got my call-up papers today. I've got to report for duty in five days time."

"Christ," I said. "You're not old enough to be drafted are you?"

"I'll be eighteen next month." He'd done with the hair combing and was now unbuttoning his pants in order to tuck in his hanging-out shirt-tails.

I suddenly felt a bit better. Maybe it was because I had something other than my tragedy to think about. I also realise now, that knowing Ivan was worrying about something other than me made somehow made me feel better. When you know that someone else is concentrating on your worries, in some way it seems to magnify them. When they are concerned with their own problems, then your attention becomes focussed upon them instead, which is probably why the worst-off among us so enjoy burying themselves in all the endless problems and tsuris that are the basic substance of soap operas.

"Have you told Uncle Harry and Aunt Sarah yet?"

"Yep."

"How did they take it?"

"Not very well," he said after a pause. Now having completed the task of tucking in his shirt, he turned to face me.

"What with your terrible troubles and now this piece of news, things are not too happy in the Mother and Father department"

I had by this time taken Ivan's records over to the small armchair by the window to look at them, when Ivan said.

"I suppose you know that we all have to go to the cemetery this afternoon for a memorial service for your parents?"

"Oh Christ," I groaned. "Do I have to go as well?"

"'Fraid so."

I felt closer to Ivan than anyone else. We had been close for as long as I can remember. I will never forget the look of wonder on his face after he heard me play "St. Louis Blues" for the first time. I was seven years old then and he was thirteen. All that day he kept making me go back to the piano and repeat it over and again. Ivan always loved coming over to visit us. He adored the music that was always playing in our house, either on the piano or on records or the radio. Also, my Mother doted on him. His 'phone call to say that he was coming to visit, was the cue for my Mother to immediately start in to baking a large bread pudding, which she knew was his favourite.

His visits during the summer months would mean endless games of cricket in the garden, or going to the local cinema, especially if there was a Laurel and Hardy movie showing. In winter, or if it was raining outside, we would play draughts or sometimes, table tennis which would entail rigging the net across our dining room table, already bearing the scratches from previous games. Then we would play whatever records we had, which often brought great, heated arguments over such important earth-shattering matters as, whether Fats Waller was greater than James P Johnson, or Teddy Wilson had the edge over Earl Hines.

After Ivan reached the age of fourteen, he never grew any taller. He stayed at about five and a half feet, although he had broadened and thickened over the past four years. I was quite tall for my age. So, even though I was only twelve years old, I was already a little taller than him. In fact, he was becoming more like his Father every day. Not only were they the same size and shape, but, like his Father, he had become precise and orderly about everything. For example, I pretty soon discovered that the books on his bedroom book-shelf were set out in alphabetical order by author, not just by the first letter of the writer's surname, but where necessary, to the second and third letters. Also, he never left his clothes lying about, like I did. Everything was placed on hangers and put into the wardrobe, separates to the left and suits to the right.

But he had inherited his Mother's warmth of nature. All the time I lived with them, I never saw him argue with his parents, even though he would tell me privately how something they had said or done had upset him. When I would ask him why he didn't complain, he would say something like, "They're doing their best Jake. No point in upsetting them." The most he would do when he felt particularly aggrieved would be to go out of the house to 'walk it off'. This would, on occasion, take an entire afternoon, but he would not come home again until he was feeling back to normal.

Maybe that is why I liked him so much (I actually loved him, but I don't want you to get any wrong ideas). Also, my volatile temper would always be calmed by Ivan's calm reasonableness.

So, as we joined my Uncle and Aunt, to set off for the Jewish cemetery and the memorial service, which comes before the actual burial, my resistance to the whole idea was tempered somewhat by the knowledge that Ivan would be there alongside me to understand my feelings of pain and horror.

I am not going to write about the burial service, or the Sitting Shiva, a traditional Jewish requirement, that followed. This is not in order to save you, the reader, from any further pain, but rather to save me from the deep depression that can still sweep over me, when I cast my mind back to it. Suffice it to say, that when it was over, I was inconsolable.

Just to have to tell the Rabbi all the details of how I learned of the tragedy, let alone having to hear him spout it out all over again to a gathering of people, who in the main, were completely and quite naturally, insensitive to the fact that each spoken word was a stiletto-stab to my soul was bad enough. But the Sitting Shiva (which is roughly the equivalent of a Catholic Wake), really finished me off! I do not know to this day, what was the worst aspect of it. Was it the retelling, and thus the re-living, of my tragedy over and over again to worried faces who, just two minutes later were shouting over to my Aunt, "Lovely cake Sarah. Did you make it yourself or did you buy it?" Or was it the two cigar-smoking men discussing a business deal that was interrupted by my Aunt introducing me to them? Having shaken my hand, one of them said to me "Shame about your parents kid," and reaching into his trouser pocket, brought out a thick bundle of five pound notes, peeled off one and stuffed it into my jacket top-pocket and even before I could say 'thank you' (or, 'fuck you' which is what I should have said), they were back to their business discussion, as if I no longer existed. I just stood there not knowing whether I was supposed to wait for a chance to acknowledge the gift or go away.

I was thankfully rescued by Ivan, who took me over to meet one of his friends, although by then it had become too much for me. I had had it. I just wanted to be on my own.

But even when I escaped back to the bedroom which I was sharing with Ivan, it was no good. No sooner had I got into the room and sat on the arm of the little armchair by the window to look out on to the rain-soaked street, than the door burst open and a worried looking Aunt Sarah accompanied by Ivan hurried in to explain to me that I must be downstairs with the guests, because I was the sole representative of my parents and that it would be bad behaviour on my part not to be in attendance.

"I know how you must be feeling," Ivan said sympathetically, "But do my parents a favour and come back downstairs."

And so I went. And so it went on interminably. I even had to parade my borrowed clothes for Hylda Kleinman and some friends of hers. She noticed that the sleeves of the jacket were far too short.

"Good gracious, he must have arms like a chimpanzee," she told her friends, who fell about laughing, whilst I had to stand there and watch them. Then, just like the two business men earlier, I became invisible to their gaze, as they went on to talk about a shoe shop in Bond Street that had in stock, 'exquisite shoes, but I do mean exquisite'.

What I am so aware of now, but was too young and too damned depressed to understand at the time, was, that I was getting my first lesson in social politics.

Lesson number one is that we live in a fuck-you-Jack world. Even the doyens of the church look the other way and maintain a discreet silence about the homeless beggar-children of Rio de Janeiro, or the filthy and degrading slum-life in New York City's South Bronx, or in that charming area known as 'Chicago South Side' or in those countless other cockroach and rat-infested social cesspools that the great freedom-loving United States, denigrates millions of its citizens to live in.

Little wonder that this dispossessed and hopeless under-class turn to crime in order to try to get their share of those goodies the rich have in so much over-abundance. As a result, the entire western world (or the 'Free World, as the U.S. propaganda radio station that broadcasts to Cuba has the chutzpa to describe it), is becoming a six-locks-on-the-door, and if-you-got-it-don't-give-none-of-it-away society. The comic, Joey Bishop is credited with having come up with the line 'A friend in need is a pest!' He was probably too juiced to realise that his wonderful one-liner, exemplified the social morality of middle and upper class America (and Europe also for that matter).

When I finally was allowed to escape up the stairs to bed, sick with sadness, and benumbed by a sense of alienation I was too young to understand, I prayed for the first time in my life (but certainly not the last), to be allowed to die. It was as if I had become the filler in a nightmare sandwich.

As I lay there in the dark, listening to the distant rumble of the anti-aircraft guns, and thinking how good it would be if I could die in exactly the same way that my parents did, I heard the door gently opening. I turned my head to find that it was a smiling Aunt Sarah peeping in.

"Are you awake?" She asked in an urgent whisper.

"Yes."

"Everyone is in the shelter except you. Aren't you afraid?"

"Please Auntie, let me stay here and give God the chance to help me join my Mum and Dad"

She came over and sat on the edge of my bed. Gently stroking my hair, she said "I know how you are feeling. Believe me, I feel much the same way too. Never forget that your Mother was my sister, and I loved her almost as much as you. But we must keep strong. We'll get over it, you'll see" She kissed me gently on my forehead. "I know that we can't replace your parents, but we are going to try very hard. It is the least I can do for Eve."

But, barring the odd chink of hope provided by Ivan, who was due to join his regiment in a few days, my life was a bottomless, endless cess-pool of pure misery.

As I think back on it now, I realise that Ivan was very smart in his dealings with me. He would never mention my tragedy unless I brought it up, and even when I did, he always had some message of hope with which to cut through my hopelessness. I remember saying to him as we lay on our respective beds "I'm missing them more than ever. I'm starting to think that I love them now even more than I did when they were alive"

"Yeah, well that is understandable right now," Ivan would reply. "But you've got to believe me when I say that it will all fade into the past in a very short time."

"How can you possibly know that?"

"Have you ever known me to lie to you?"

"No."

"Well then, believe me now. I actually got a book out of the college library on this very subject and read it carefully, and it said that you will be over the worst very soon."

"I don't think I'll ever feel different to how I feel right now. I can't stop myself thinking about what they must have felt as they were actually being blown apart."

Ivan let a long minute go by before saying "Can you keep a secret?"

"Sure I can."

"Well," he got up and closed the bedroom door to underline the conspiratorial nature of the information he was about to impart. "In a few months you'll be having your Bar Mitzvah, and..."

"Christ, I don't want any Bar Mitz..."

"...and I heard my Father telling my Mother that he is going to buy you anything you want as your Bar Mitzvah present. And my Father is very rich Jake, and if he says it's anything you want, believe me, he means it."

"Hell," I said.

"So Jake my boy, you just work out what you want and tell me. I'll make sure that he gets the message. You can rely on that. So, start thinking about it."

"Jesus and how," I said, my spirits immediately perking up as I lay there concentrating on what fabulous present I would be getting.

Of course, the entire thing was almost certainly made up by him on the spur of the moment to cheer me up. Yet, for some reason, it always worked no matter how many times he pulled the same trick. But Ivan was not the only means of escape from my misery. Both my Uncle and Aunt were pulling all the stops out to lift me out of my trough of despair.

I still recall clambering into the back seat of my Uncle's big, shiny, black Buick to be taken to see a friend of his who owned a wholesale clothing business. It was situated in one of the many grubby, down-at-heel back streets that honeycomb the East End of London. Aunt Sarah had decreed that I must be fitted out with three suits, two separate sports jackets, three pairs of pants in grey, blue and brown, as well as a dozen shirts, some ties, socks, sweaters and underwear.

After a couple of hours at the wholesalers during which time my aunt tore the place to pieces to find exactly what she was looking for, and after making me put on and take off so many items of clothing that I was sick to death of the entire expedition, we finally got out of there. True, I had been fitted out to my aunt's satisfaction, but it had cost the warehouse dear. When we left it looked as it had been struck by a tornado. There were mounds of discarded shirts, sweaters, underwear, pants, suits etc., lying all over the floor. But we still not through with the shopping. On we drove to another part of this then predominantly Jewish, part of town. I watched my Uncle as he gently turned the big, limo into a narrow cul-de-sac with grubby, tenement houses running down one side, and on the other, a scrap-yard, followed by a bicycle repair shop, and next door to that, a tatty little kosher butcher. The end of the road where we had stopped was cut by high, khaki-green wooden double gates with three-inch metal spikes running along the top of them.

Uncle Harry got out of the car, and using his handkerchief to keep his hands clean, pulled a rusty chain that dangled down where the two gates met. I watched from the back seat as one of the big gates opened about a foot and my Uncle held a short conversation with a tall black man, after which he came back to the car whilst the gates were being drawn open to allow us to enter.

Once inside the concreted courtyard, we parked the car in the customers car park facing two single-storey brick buildings, one large and the other much smaller with a white painted door on which was a brass panel with 'Office and Enquiries' engraved on it.

Before we got out of the car, Uncle Harry told me about the man we were about to meet.
"His name is Chaim Rabinowitz. He came over here from Russia around the beginning of the century when he was just a boy. He started out with a broken down old pram in which he kept a shoemaker's last, his tools and his bits of leather. Every day he would go walking around the East End knocking on peoples doors asking if they had any shoes that needed repairing. With the pennies that he made, he managed to scrape enough money together to open a little shoe-repair shop in Hassel Street, just off the Whitechapel Road. A couple of years later he bought a very expensive pair of shoes from one of the most exclusive shoe shops in the West End. The very next day he returned to this same fashionable shoe shop with an identical pair of shoes, which he had made overnight in his back room. He told the manager that he can sell him shoes like these, including the name of the shop printed inside, for about half of what he is currently buying them in for. He used the same method of selling to all the other big-shot, expensive West End shoe shops, and within a couple of months he found himself with enough orders to start a factory employing about twenty men. Now, he is a millionaire with factories in the United States, Australia and God-knows where else. But he won't leave London. He says he made his fortune here and that the British are the salt of the earth and he wouldn't think of leaving, especially in this time of war."

"And," he said to my Aunt as we got out of the car, "now, he's doubling his fortune with the huge contracts he's got to make shoes for the forces."

We went in to the office building to find ourselves in a room filled with the deafening clatter of a half dozen typewriters. Set into the wall behind the flying-fingered typists, was a large, impressive, highly-polished oak door with a silver door handle.

Nobody took the slightest notice of us as we stood and waited. My Uncle suddenly turned to my Aunt and, spreading his arms out wide, shouted over the clatter,"How can anyone make themselves heard over this bloody row."

Just as it seemed that my Uncle was going to lose his temper, the door at the back of the office opened and a tall, elegantly dressed young man, motioned to us with his finger to follow him. We trooped out of the clatter of typewriters into the silence of a carpeted, light-oak panelled hallway.

"Good morning and welcome," he said as he offered his hand to my Uncle. "I'm Barry Prendergast, Mister Rabinowitz's personal assistant. I'm so sorry you were made to wait. Mister Rabinowitz will see you now. Just follow me please"

He spoke with the kind of accent that screams public schools and salmon and cucumber sandwiches.

We followed him down the hall, past an office door bearing the legend, 'Director, Latin-American Sales', followed by another saying, 'Director, USA sales'. My Uncle, who was walking in front of us, alongside Barry Prendergast, turned his head to us and said 'Fency-shmency eh?" Then speaking loudly enough for us all to hear he said to Prendergast, "I see you have separate sales directors for North and South America."

"We also have a Director for Sales covering India, another for the Far East as well as separate sales directors for the Middle East and Australasia"

"Oy," was my Uncle's single response.

By now we had taken a right hand turn into another hallway, wider and even more thickly carpeted, at the end of which stood tall, dark oak double doors with what looked to me like gold door handles.

Prendergast tapped lightly on the door before opening it and announcing us, rather like a butler in a Stately Home "Ahem. Mister and Missus..."

"Harry, Sarah. How lovely to see you. The great Chaim Rabinowitz rose from his chair as he was speaking and came towards us smiling broadly, his arms outstretched.

At that time the only knowledge I had about moguls who control vast manufacturing conglomerates, came from what I had seen in the movies. In my mind's eye I had imagined that I was going to meet someone with carefully combed iron-grey hair, a firm jaw, piercing blue eyes and dressed in an Edward Arnold suit. He would almost certainly be puffing a big cigar and be seated behind a huge desk with at least six telephones on either side of him.

This big shot was almost bald, barring a few strands of black hair on the top of his head appearing from under his black yarmulke and thick, grey, uncombed hair crowding his temples. His clothes were about as far away as you can get from the super-smart suits Edward Arnold wore in nearly all of his movie appearances. Chaim Rabinowitz was wearing creased, black trousers, with a matching creased waistcoat, from which the tassels of his tsitses (a kind of miniature prayer-shawl) protruded at the bottom, a white cotton shirt, buttoned up to the neck, and no tie. He was also very thin, with a small-boned frame, a long, thin face, an aquiline nose, a generous mouth and large, sad-looking dark brown eyes. When I think back on him now, I realise that had he have been an actor, he could have made a helluva good Don Quixote.

"It's been too long, far too long," he said as he embraced my Uncle and Aunt in turn. His voice was deep and resonant.

"I was then introduced to him. As he shook my hand he said to me "Your Uncle has told me all about your tragedy" Then, putting his hands on my shoulders and holding me at arms length, he looked straight into my face and said quietly, almost as if he only wanted me to hear. "Nobody knows more than I do what pain you are suffering Jake." He moved toward me and putting one arm around my shoulder, he motioned to my Aunt and Uncle to take the two upholstered chairs that sat facing his work table, for he had no desk.

He released me to bring over the hard wooden chair which was parked by the heavily curtained large window that was set into the wall directly behind his work-table. He set the chair down on his side of the table so that I would be sitting right next to him. I noticed that he was sitting on a hard chair just like mine.

He sat staring at me thoughtfully for quite a while, his fingers interlinked, forefingers steepled and resting just below his bottom lip. Then he said "Tell me, how old are you Jake?"

"I'm twelve and a half."

He turned to my Uncle and Aunt "May I speak just to Jake for a few minutes?"

My Uncle held the palms of his hands out towards him, nodding at the same time. Turning back to face me, with a long and thoughtful gaze, he said: "You know Jake; I was a year younger than you when I lost my parents. Only, it wasn't the Nazis who killed them: it was the Cossacks. Before my very eyes Jake, before my very eyes they cut them down with their sabres. At least, you were spared the horror of seeing your parents killed. I wasn't." He allowed a few moments to let that sink in before going on.

"I was returning home from visiting a good friend of mine..."

"So was I," I said, interrupting him. He held his hand up to stop me speaking.

"I had just turned into our little street when I saw a crowd outside my house. As I got a little closer I could see that it was a bunch of laughing, jeering, vodka-swilling Cossacks, and I had already learned to have the good sense to keep away from those sorts of people. So I ran down the side of the house I was standing in front of, which happened to be four or five houses away from mine. I ran into their back yard, then over the fences and across the other back yards until I got to the back door of my house. I opened it and went in. The first thing I saw were my two elder brothers. They were twins Jake, five years older than me. They were on the floor, tied back to back and bound hand and foot. They were both covered in blood, and..."

He stopped while he searched for the best way to phrase what he had to say. Even young as I was, I could see that he was still clearly upset by his recounting and thereby re-living the scene. When he did go on, the pain was visible in his eyes and audible in his voice.

"...I saw that they had been...mutilated...down there." He pointed to his genitals. Then, covering his face with his hands, he murmured "It is too terrible to describe." But after a few moments of tortured silence, he got a grip on himself, took his hands from his face and running them up and down his thighs, went on:

"Then, I heard my Mother give a terrible shriek from the direction of the front room. I ran to the door towards her to see my Father, bound hand and foot, being carried on the shoulders of four men, out of the front door towards the screaming mob outside. Behind him was my Mother. She was naked and a huge man was dragging her along by her hair.

I yelled, 'Mother, Mother'. Hearing my voice, she screamed out to me, 'Run Chaim, run for your life" Then another fellow walking alongside my Mother struck her in the face with the butt of the rifle he was carrying."

Chaim now seemed to be talking out loud to himself rather than to any of us. I looked across at my Uncle and Aunt who were to my eyes as clearly shocked as I was. Again, we had to wait while with a deliberate effort of will, he pulled himself out of his memory-world and back to the present. Turning to me his eyes wet with tears, he went on. "So Jake, I did what my Mother told me to do. I ran. I ran back to the room where my dead brothers lay, out into the back garden and then around the side of our house to where the crowd, was standing. Thank God, they didn't notice me. I suppose they were too carried away by their drunken blood-lust to bother with a little boy. As I stood there, I saw two curved scimitars rise above the heads of the crowd and then come flashing down. I heard a loud 'aah' from the mob as the swords did their murderous deed."

We again had to sit in shocked silence while he took a white, handkerchief from his pocket, shook it open, blew his nose, and then, while still wiping his eyes, he went on. "After that I just turned and ran as fast as I could. For some reason I ran to the house of a long-standing customer and good friend of my Father. I went to him because, firstly he was not Jewish, so the mob wouldn't come looking for me there. And secondly whenever he came to the house for a fitting, he was always smiling and friendly to me."

"What do you mean by 'fitting?" I asked.

"Didn't I tell you my Father was a tailor?"

"No," I answered.

"Oh, yes, he was quite a well known tailor. The wealthy land owners and all the top people from miles around used to come to our house in order to get a Moshe Rabinowitz suit."

I saw an expression of pride flit across his face as he said that. But it did not last long. As soon as he went back to telling his story, his face resumed its sombre expression.

"Anyway, this man whose house I ran to, I think worked for the government in some capacity or other. His name was Ivan Petrikov. I knocked on the large front door of his grand house. After what seemed a very long time, but was probably not more than a couple of minutes, a manservant opened the door.

'Please may I see Mister Petrikov?' I said.

This servant just glared down at me, 'What do you want to see him for boy?'

'Please' I said, 'tell him that Moshe Rabinowitz's son is here. Tell him that the Cossacks have murdered my Mother and Father as well as my two brothers'.

Do you know Jake, his face showed not a bit of sympathy. If anything, I think it showed hatred."

'I'll tell him about my experiences with Jimmy Abel and his gang.' I thought. 'He'll probably like that story'. But I decided to wait until he was finished..

"Wait there," the servant said, and he went away. About five minutes later he came back with a ten Kopeck note which he handed me, saying 'My master says to give you this. But he can do nothing more to help you. This is not a part of your ghetto. Jews cannot stay here'.

Still holding the note, I said 'But where can I go? They've killed my whole family'.

He just stared at me with a cold, hate-filled expression on his face. Then he said 'I thought you Jews had relations all over the place. Why don't you go and ask them for help, instead of bothering us?'

'All my Father's family live in Moscow and my Aunt Henrietta has gone to live in England.

Suddenly, the manservant suddenly reached down to grab my shirt collar and frog-marched me back down the driveway, through the big, front gate to the road beyond. Then, letting go of me and pointing with his long right arm, his forefinger outstretched, he said 'That way takes you south to England. Then he pointed with his left; and that way takes you north to Moscow. You can decide which of your Jew relatives you want to go and visit. Now be on your way and don't come back here'. Then he locked the large gate behind him, leaving me to stand and watch him walk back up the path to the big house without so much as looking back once.

It was only then that the truth started to dawn on me Jake. Suddenly I realised that I was all alone in the world. I started to cry and went on crying for a long time. But after I had cried myself out, I decided that I had to do something.

I knew that I could not go back to the ghetto because the Cossacks had, for some reason, decided to wipe out my entire family, which I reckoned, must include me. The chances are, I thought, that they are searching the ghetto for me at this very moment.

It was then that I made my decision. I will go to England and find my Aunt Henrietta and ask her to look after me. Of course, I had no idea how far away England was. I didn't even know where my aunt lived. I knew she was in London somewhere, and I figured out as I started on my long journey, that I will go to wherever the ghetto is in London and ask for her. I know it all sounds a little crazy now, but such are the dreams of young boys. Had I have known that it was going to take me over two years to get to this island, I would probably have gone back to our little ghetto and taken my chances with the Cossacks. So you see Jake, it turned out that my ignorance was all for the best."

He gave us all a little smile at that point, probably because he had sensed that the atmosphere, created by his sad and sombre tale, was a bit too heavy. He pressed a key down on the oblong box that sat on his work-table. Instantly, Prendergast's voice came through the little speaker inside the box.

"Yes sir?"

"Barry, bring in some tea for us all. And" he added, giving me a smile, "Bring in some chocolate biscuits for my friend Jake"

"You see what a nice man Mister Rabinowitz is?" said my Aunt.

"Yes I do," I said. And I genuinely meant it. Then I said to him "Please go on with your story sir."

"If you wish me to"

"Oh yes please" I said whilst my uncle and aunt simply nodded.,

"Y'know Jake, I could write a book this thick about my journey across Europe." He held his hands about nine inches apart. "In one way, my boy, you were luckier than I with your tragedy, because you have a kind and loving Uncle and Aunt to look after you. But in another way it is worse for you because it also means that you've had time to dwell on your tragedy. I had no family to run to. There was no-one to care if I lived or died. And believe me; I was brought close to death many times. But maybe, where I was luckier than you" and he pointed a forefinger at me, thick and coarsened by his long years of manual labour; "I was so busy just keeping myself alive, finding enough food to eat, enough water to drink, keeping warm when the weather was freezing, that I had almost no time to dwell on what had happened to my family." Again, he seemed to be looking inwards as he said "And even when each day was over, and I had finally found somewhere to sleep, I would be so exhausted that thanks be to God, I would instantly fall into a deep dreamless sleep"

Then, without any movement of his head, he just slid his large, dark eyes across to where my Uncle and Aunt were sitting, as he said "But sometimes the dreams came. Terrible dreams, vivid and real, that force you to relive things best forgotten." And shifting his gaze downwards to the carpet by the side of his chair, he murmured to himself almost inaudibly "My God. My God"

We sat unmoving, allowing the silence to honour his bitter memories. But after a short time, he continued with his story. (I too have had to learn how to shut myself off from the terrors of remembrance, although my method is different. He did it with the power of will. I do it with the power of good, strong Cuban rum).

"But Jake my boy, the two years it took me to get to this country were great teachers. I learned how to survive on next to nothing. I learned how to hide so that I could sleep without some other beggar robbing me of my few possessions while I slept."

As he spoke, he counted off on his fingers the survival lessons he had learned.

"And I learned to fight Jake. After you've been beaten up a few times, you learn that if you want to survive in the dangerous jungle of destitution, you had better learn how to protect yourself. But, equally importantly, I learned how and where to beg. That is how I met the wonderful Issac Burnberg.

I had got as far as Berlin. I was begging outside a Schul, just before the morning service, which was always a good time and place to earn money. I was singing the only song I knew in Yiddish, which was one my dear Mother used to sing to me. I had a card tied around my neck written in Yiddish which said simply, 'The Cossacks killed my entire family'. Sometimes Jake, this would get enough money to keep me going for three whole days or more. But no-one before had ever offered to let this filthy little beggar-boy stay in their house. Isaac Burnberg did. I remember him so clearly.

He was a shabbily dressed little man of man of maybe sixty or so. He stood there, hands pressed deep in his old, creased overcoat pockets, studying me as I sang. Y'know, most people just threw a coin into my hat as they made their way into the Schul. But not Mister Burnberg. He stood there: no expression on his face, but never taking his eyes off me as I sung my song. After I had come to the end of it and was picking up my hat to count the money I had earned that morning, he suddenly said: 'So, what's your name?'

'Chaim Rabinowitz', I said.

Now he came to stand right next to me. 'And how old are you, Chaim Rabinowitz?'

I turned to look at him. His face betrayed no emotion that I could see. 'I'm Twelve years and eleven months'.

'So' he said, 'You have to be Bar mitzvah very soon.How can you do that if you spend your life begging in the streets?'

'I don't need any Bar mitzvah sir,' I told him, 'I'm already a man.'

He took a step back in order to survey me from head to foot. Then he said to me:

'I'm sure that by you you're a man, but by me you are a Jewish boy and will remain so until you stand on the Bimah in the Schul and read your portion of the Torah'

I said nothing. I had already realised that this poor old man wasn't going to give me anything. So I just went back to counting and pocketing the money I had earned that morning, ignoring him as he stood there, slowing rubbing his unshaven chin and studying me thoughtfully.

Suddenly he took his hand from his face and pointing at me said 'No, no, no. It is no good at all. You must come home with me and work in my shop. And above all, you must study and take your Bar mitzvah like a man. After that you can beg your head off, if that is what you want to do. But now', and he took my arm in a surprisingly strong grip. 'Now you are coming home with me'. Then pointing down at my feet, which were wrapped in rags, because I had worn my shoes out months before, he said, 'And I'll make you a nice, strong pair of shoes to fit your big feet'.

Well, Jake, I let him walk me to his tall, thin and run-down old house. He had turned the ground floor into a little shoe-repairing shop, which you had to walk through to get to the stairs that took you up to the living quarters. As soon as we got up there, he yelled for his wife, whose name I remember, was Yetta. All the while he was telling her about me, and why he had brought me to live with them, she was looking me up and down in a most disapproving manner. I remember thinking Jake; 'this is some tough old bird. She won't put up with me for a second'. I was actually working out the best way of begging some food off them, before they threw me out, when she suddenly interrupted him; 'Yes, yes' she said. 'We'll hear all about it later. But first, he has to have hot bath. He looks like he hasn't had a bath in a month.

I could not believe my ears Jake. Not since I had begun my long journey had anyone offered me such a kindness.

'It is seven months actually' I told her.

Y'know she was horrified Jake. 'Seven months'? she yelled.. Oy weiss mir! Right my boy. You are going up stairs and you are going to have a long, hot bath, and you are going to scrub yourself clean. Then, when you appear from behind that layer of filth, and I see what you really look like, I'll make you a proper meal' Turning to my Uncle and Aunt he said "Harry, Sarah, I'll never forget that bath."

Then he turned back to me again: "After seven months of bathing in ice-cold streams without any soap, or maybe, washing down using a tap at the bottom of someone's garden, believe me Jake, lying back in that tin bath buried up to my neck in steaming hot water was more wonderful and luxurious than any bath I have ever had since'. As he leaned back in his chair, he seemed to have blocked us out of his mind, as he relived that luxurious experience. Then, after allowing himself a minute's joyful silent self-indulgence, he once again pulled himself back to rejoin the present.

'Anyway, I finally forced myself out of the bath, and covering myself in a large towel I went back down the stairs to the most delicious aroma of food being cooked. I found my way to the kitchen, where she was busily preparing the food.

'Now that's a bit better', said Mrs Burnburg as I came in. 'Now I can see what you actually look like'. She looked me up and down as I stood there in my bath towel. 'Mmm. Not too bad. A couple of proper meals and you'll look like any other boy of your age. Now go and sit at the dining table and I'll bring you in some food. 'Do you know Jake, I can still remember not only everything she gave me to eat that wonderful day, but also the taste of it'.

"So, what did she make for you?" asked Aunt Sarah, now that the story had come round to her pet subject; food.

"Well Sarah; by our standards the food she made was pretty primitive. You must remember that they were poor people. But after going without a proper meal for months and months, what she served up was to me, a banquet. She started with a large bowl of freshly made, piping hot barley soup. Then she gave me a plate of beef with vegetables, together with three thick slices of warmed black bread. And to top it all off, a plate of stewed fruit. All the time I was gobbling down this wonderful meal, and then mopping up the beef gravy with my bread, I was aware that she was following every mouthful I ate from the plate to my mouth. Then she brought in two large cups of coffee. She gave me my cup and sat down opposite me with her own."

'Isaac will be back in a few minutes' she said as she sat down. 'Meanwhile, you can talk to me. As I did not know what to say, I just sat there waiting for her to say something. She took a long swig of coffee and putting the cup back on its saucer, she asked me "So, do you feel better now that you have had a bath and some food?'

'I feel like I am going to burst' I said. 'You gave me more food to eat than I get in a week normally'. And then she leaned forward as she said..."

But his story was broken into by Prendergast entering carrying a large silver tray bearing a huge silver teapot, together with milk jug, and sugar bowl. Behind him appeared a young lady in a tailored blue costume, carrying a large plate of chocolate and cream cakes, which in tightly-rationed war-time Britain, was quite a rare luxury.

While the lady was serving and passing us our tea and cakes, I said to Chaim Rabinowitz:

"May I ask you a question sir?"

"Certainly," he said, smiling at me.

"How was it that you could speak to these people? After all, you spoke Russian and they were talking German. So how could you make yourself understood?"

Aunt Sarah swiftly moved in to chide me: "Jake, you mustn't doubt Mister Rabinowitz's word. If he says that he spoke to them, then that should be good enough for you"

"Nonsense Sarah," Chaim said. "It is a perfectly normal and reasonable question to ask. And," he said, tapping his right temple with his forefinger; "It shows the boy is a thinker."

Then, focussing his deep-set, large, dark-brown peepers on me once again, he explained "Y'know Jake, I had to walk from my village which was about twenty miles from L'vov, all the way through Czechoslovakia and into

Germany via Dresden. Of course, at that time Czechoslovakia did not exist. It was all part of the Austro-Hungarian empire. Now although Dresden is close to the German-Czech border, the German tongue was by far the most important language from say, Brno onwards. It also meant that I had been amongst German speakers for over three months before I arrived in Berlin. But I had learned to speak Yiddish as well, because I did most of my begging to Jews. They were naturally more sympathetic to my plight. In fact all my conversations with Isaac Burnberg and Yetta, his wife were in Yiddish.

He took a sip of his tea, which I noticed, was taken without milk and with a lump of sugar in his mouth, which, my Uncle explained to me later, was a typically Russian way to drink tea. Then, he carefully put his teacup on his table and continued. "Also, you must bear in mind my boy that I have a very good ear for languages. I speak eight languages fluently, and I can get by in three others.

Then, with the palms of his hands held towards me he said "Now Jake, if you will excuse me, I must speak with your Uncle and Aunt. I haven't seen them for at least," he turned to look inquiringly at Uncle Harry, "Two years?"

My uncle nodded as he said, "At the very least Chaim."

So I sat silently drinking my tea and eating the cake and chocolate biscuits, watching and listening to them as they proceeded to fill in the details of their respective lives and, sometimes scandalously, the lives of others. As I sat there, it suddenly hit me that I liked Mister Rabinowitz very much. As I think back on it, I realise that it wasn't so much that I liked him, as admired him. The way he had handled the loss of his parents seemed like an object lesson to me. So, as I sat on my hard wooden chair, polishing off the last remains of my chocolate cake, I now knew that I too had to grow up to be strong, rich and powerful like my new-found friend Chaim Rabinowitz. I also childishly believed that because we had both lost our parents, this single fact made us as if by rote, close buddies. How I could have ever believed that a twelve year old boy was now the close friend of a middle-aged multi-millionaire, I just do not know. But such is the mind of an impressionable or maybe, naive kid.

"Now," Chaim said suddenly, clapping his hands together and turning to me, "Jake, take off your shoes please." I had no idea why he had asked me to do so, but I obliged him. He looked at my feet for just a few seconds, before again buzzing Barry Prendergast on his intercom.

"Barry, get me three pairs of brown and three pairs of black, styles E.X one, two and three" Then after another quick glance at my stockinged feet, he said into the intercom; "Size six and a half, AB fitting.

"Right away sir," said the ever-faithful Prendergast, before adding "And those two men from the Ministry of Defence are here to see you."

"Tell them I'll be just a couple of minutes," he said. The moment he had released the key of his intercom I jumped in:

"How can you tell my shoe size by just looking?" I was genuinely incredulous at the seemingly endless ability of this man.

He smiled as he said, "If I couldn't do that after so many years in the shoe-making business, then it would be time for me to move over and let you take over Jake." Then, addressing us all he said, "After the shoes come up from the stores, I am afraid I will have to ask you to let me get back to running my business"

"Aren't you going to finish your story about how you finally got to England?," I said disappointedly.

"For heavens sakes Jake," my Uncle said. "Can't you see that Chaim is a very busy man?"

Chaim leaned over, gripped my arm and said quietly to me "Another time Jake my boy, when I have a little more time. I promise. I'll come to your Uncle's house and we'll have some more tea and cakes and I'll tell you stories that will make you hair stand on end."

There was a light tapping on the door, and in his response to his." Come," a man entered pushing a trolley carrying my six pairs of shoes, all carefully wrapped in shiny silver paper.

Chaim rose from his chair saying to the shoe-porter as he did so, "Thank you Jimmy," and after checking the invoice that Jimmy handed to him, he said "Take them down to the car park and wait for my friends. They will be along shortly."

Then, taking my Aunt's hand and putting his other arm around the shoulder of my Uncle, he led them to the door, with me following behind.

I was genuinely sorry to have to leave the company of this man. He had for the first time, since the death of my parents, given me a sense of purpose, hope and direction. But it was a sorrow lightened somewhat by the thought that he was shortly coming to visit us.

"It was lovely to see you two again," he said to my Aunt and Uncle. "We must not let another two years pass before we see each other."

My Uncle then tried to pay him for the shoes. "Ach, don't be silly Harry," he said with an airy wave of his hand. "The next time I want a nice piece of jewellery, you can make me a special price."

As I was leaving he shook my hand and ruffling my hair with the other he said "Wear the shoes in good health my boy." Then bending over, he whispered in my ear, "And keep strong, not only in your body, but in your mind also."

"Yes sir. Thank you sir," was about all I could think of in reply.

Once in the car and heading home, Aunt Sarah turned around to me from her front seat and said: "Well, what did you think of him? You know that he is a real multi-millionaire?"

"When are you going to invite him over for tea?" I asked. I was already starting to feel just a little bit lost without the strength and certainty of his presence.

"He'll never come to visit us," said my Uncle.

My heart fell. "Why won't he come? He said he would come and tell me about all his adventures."

"He's a big businessman son," my Uncle explained as he carefully manoeuvred his big car out of the yard where he had left it and back into the reality of the shabby, little back street. "He's got companies all over the world. He can't just walk out on all his responsibilities in order to have a cup of tea and a bun to talk with you about his past."

My Aunt must have spotted the look of deep disappointment on my face. She suddenly smiled reassuringly at me.

"Of course he'll come over and visit us," she said. "Don't you take any notice of your Uncle," she said, looking at him sharply. "Chaim seemed to like you very much Jake, and I am sure he will come to see us at the first opportunity. So cheer up" she added, looking at my Uncle with an unconcealed expression of warning in her eyes.

He must have got the message. "So nu, maybe he will come and see us," he said in a resigned voice.

Such is the nature of boyish optimism that I immediately chose to believe my Aunt. Now quite satisfied that I would be seeing good ol' Chaim Rabinowitz again within a few days, I spent the rest of the journey home deciding upon what I would talk to him about when we next meet.

In fact, for the first time since my tragedy, I was beginning to feel the first signs of desire to rejoin the human race. And it wasn't only due to my meeting with Mister Rabinowitz. Starting at my new school was now only a couple of weeks away, and I was actually looking forward to it. But at that time, relaxing on the large, comfortable back seat of my Uncle's Buick, it was Chaim's story that was occupying my imagination. And then a wonderful idea struck me. Chaim had said that he could write a thick book of his experiences since the death of his parents. Why don't I write down everything that has happened to me since the death of my parents? Not only that; I would keep a diary of everything that happens to me for the next year. And then I will write a book of my experiences. 'Hell', I thought, 'Mister Rabinowitz will be really impressed.'

That night over dinner, I announced to my Uncle and Aunt that I was going to write a book. My Uncle looked across the table at my Aunt, his face an even mix of bemusement and amusement.

"And when I have written it, I'm going to give a copy to Mister Rabinowitz. I bet he'll enjoy reading it."

"He might, but I wouldn't count on it," my Uncle said as he reached across the table to help himself to an extra slice of chicken.

"Don't say that Harry," Aunt Sarah said quite sharply. "He might love reading Jake's book." Then, giving him a knowing look, she added "And anyway, it might be extremely therapeutic for Jake to write down all his experiences and feelings." My Uncle stopped eating to look directly in Aunt Sarah's face. Having got the unspoken message, he suddenly pursed his lips and nodded a couple of times. Then turning to me he said "Come to my office after the meal, and I'll give you a writing pad and a pencil and you can start right away." Then, probably to avoid me seeing his amused look, he buried his face in the food.

What table conversation went on thereafter, I have no idea. My mind was completely taken over by what I was going to write. Looking back on it now, I guess it was an early, but cogent sign that I was really beginning to extricate myself from the horrors of my tragedy.

I even managed to enjoy most of New Year's Eve. In this household, Christmas was not celebrated. But it was all made up for on New Year's Eve. We had a dozen or so, guests of varying ages at our party, although none were as young as me. But everyone present seemed determined to have a good time and so did I. There were some patches of bleak despair and yearning for my Mother and Father, but these were off-set to a considerable degree by the presence of Ivan, who had wangled himself a three-day leave.

Even when the air-raid sirens went into their nightly warning wail, everyone formed into a paper-hatted queue and drinks in hand, danced conga-style into the air-raid shelter.

I waited until everyone had Auld Lang Syned themselves into the New

Year, before, feigning tiredness, I went to bed. (I was quite blasé to the thump of the bombs and the crash-bang of anti-aircraft gunfire. After I don't know how long, it had become a natural accompaniment to night-fall).

Also, as Ivan was home, I was sharing the bedroom with him once again, and I wanted some time on my own to write down what at that time, I felt sure were going to be the foundation stones of my book. As I scribbled them down, in my imagination, I was saying them out loud to a wrapt, enraptured Chaim Rabinowitz.

Little did I imagine that a week and a day later, life would once again, return to total shit!

Chapter 6

'It All Began So Well,
But What An End'

IRA GERSHWIN'S LYRIC says it all. At the outset everything was getting better by the day. Ivan was giving his maximum encouragement to my book-writing. He was happy to just sit on his bed seriously listening (or so I believed), while I walked around the room, yakking on endlessly about Chaim Rabinowitz, and how he is coming to the house, specifically to visit me, and how surprised and knocked out he will be, when I present him with my book. Also, I found myself getting interested once again in jazz. Ivan had brought home two recordings which he had got from a couple of black American soldiers he had chummed up with. The first record he played me was "Lady Be Good" by the Count Basie Quintet. I can never forget the great rush of pure pleasure which engulfed me as I listened to the great tenor saxophonist Lester Young reeling off two choruses of such might and majesty. And then, before I could absorb it all, he ran another disc, this time of the Basie big band playing 'John's Idea'. It was like food and drink for my hungry and dehydrated soul.

I was even getting the urge to go back to playing the piano. Since my terrible disaster, I had been unable to even look at a piano, let alone play it.

But this early dawn of my recovery, plus Basie's great piano playing, rekindled my desire to play again. Even Ivan's return to his battalion did nothing to dampen this new-found optimism. And starting school in a couple of days, and with it the promise of having some friends of my own age, was also helping me to feel a lot more positive and optimistic.

Then came my first day at The North London Secondary School. It turned out okay. To begin with, there was not all that much work to do. It consisted mainly of registering and filling in forms, one of which asked me to list my favourite hobbies and school subjects, etc. But I did get that old, familiar feeling of depression and alienation when I was required to answer the question contained at the top of one of the questionnaires, which was 'Please write full name and ages of both parents'. I had to write 'Both parents dead'.

What classes there were on that first day, consisted primarily of talks by the various teachers on what we will be studying during the current term. There was also a short welcoming address by the headmaster, who also told us how and where we must go in the event of an air-raid.

I did have to write one essay, but the subject was so interesting to me, it wasn't like schoolwork at all. I was required to write two pages about my favourite movie, my favourite kind of music and my favourite book. I also had to say why.

I cannot for the life of me recall what my selections were, but I do remember enjoying writing it.

During the morning and afternoon breaks, I managed to get into conversation with a few of the boys in my class, although most of them were too preoccupied with renewing friendships formed in previous terms to give me much of their time. But, from those I did manage to hang out with, it became clear that the main topics of conversation were, Joe Louis (who was referred to only as 'The Brown Bomber'), or the relative merits of the Spitfire, the Hurricane and the Messerschmitt 109. Coming from a school where the only cause of argument would be about the talents or relative beauty of various Hollywood film stars, seeing and listening to the quite fierce rows that erupted over fighter planes and heavyweight boxers, was strange and novel to me.

As to the girls, most of whom stood around in small groups on the other side of the playground, chatting and seemingly oblivious of us boys, I did spot one gorgeous looking baby, with long, large, dark brown eyes, a voluptuous mouth and dark brown hair, done up in ringlets. Even more exciting were her long legs, her proud arse and her quite prominent bosom, even though she was only twelve years of age, like the rest of us.

I kinda found myself crossing the playground (thereby thwarting a certain goal that was about to be scored by one of the younger kids in their all-important playground football game), just to be nearer to this beauty. After I had been standing and gawking at her for a couple of minutes, watching her and her two girl-friends secretively immersed in conversation, quite suddenly, all three of them turned in my direction and stared, expressionlessly, across at me. I smiled and waved a small and awkward hello, in the hope that I might get invited over to talk with them, and so get a chance to stand next to this pretty thing. But my smile and shy little wave was greeted with blank-faced incredulity, followed by them turning their backs on me to continue with their conversation, but with a couple of loud giggles thrown in, just to make me feel an even sillier fool than I already did.

Overall though, I enjoyed that first day back at school. Walking home that afternoon, I was happy enough to be going over in my head, Lester Young's saxophone solo on 'Lady Be Good' (which I had played at least fifty times), whilst trying to work out the actual notes so that I could try to play it on my Auntie and Uncle's's piano.

"Well, here comes my favourite schoolboy," was how Aunt Sarah greeted me as she opened the front door to me. I followed her into the kitchen, where she pointed to a huge pile of sandwiches: "Be a darling and carry that into the breakfast room for me."

I had no sooner set down the tray on the circular breakfast table, than Aunt Sarah entered bearing a large, freshly baked, Madeira cake. After setting it down, she yelled to the German Jewish refugee maid, "Olga, bring in two plates, some spoons and some cream." Then she sat down opposite me. Nothing was said until after the maid had done as she was bidden and we were alone.

"So nu?" she said, as she took a cake-cutter from the pocket of her apron and cut me a large wedge of cake.

"What do you mean," I asked.

Then she did a typically Jewish thing. She brought an invisible third party into the conversation.

"He doesn't know what I mean," she said to it. "He comes home after his first day at his new school, and I say nu? And he doesn't know what I mean."

"It was okay," I said through a mouthful of pudding.

Once again she appealed to her invisible friend. "It was okay he says. No mention of what he did. Nothing about what he learned, if he made any friends, if he liked his teachers. Nothing. It was just okay." Then she shifted her glare from the invisible to the visible; namely me. I dredged my brain for something to say.

"It was okay," I repeated desperately. "It was good. I liked it. As to making friends, I have arranged with one boy, Phillip something-or-other, that I'll meet him at the top of the road tomorrow morning so that we can walk to school together." Of course, I was wishing in my heart that it could have been that beautiful girl I was walking to school with.

"Good. You've made a friend. That is good." Then, as she put two corned beef sandwiches onto my emptied plate, she said "Next time I ask you a question, don't make me have to schlep it out of you like some butcher schlepping the kishkes out of a chicken."

I said nothing.

"Jake," she said, as she carefully watched me consuming the first of the sandwiches, "Wait and see what I have done to your room. You are going to be very pleasantly surprised."

But I was not all that interested in what she had done to my bedroom.. I was too busy figuring out how to discover the title of my beautiful baby's favourite tune, and learn to play it on the piano. At that time I didn't even yet know her name. I was determined to find that out from Phillip as we walked to school tomorrow morning. Provided, that is, I can get him off the subject of Spitfires.

"I'm going back to the kitchen," my Aunt said, using the table to push herself up. "Finish your tea and sandwiches. Then call me." At the breakfast room door she turned around and wagging a warning finger at me, said, "And do not go up to your room without me. I want to be there when you see what I have done."

"Can I take my food on the tray into the lounge and listen to a record while I eat?"

"You can," she said, half in and half out of the breakfast room door. "So long as you don't play it too loud: I can't stand all that banging jazz that you and Ivan think is so wonderful."

As I carried my tray down the hall towards the lounge, she shouted from the kitchen "And don't spill crumbs all over the place. Olga has spent all morning tidying up the lounge."

I sat down on the piano stool, put the tray on the walnut top of the Bluthner baby grand, and ate up my sandwiches and polished off my cup of tea in the company of the Benny Goodman trio, Count Basie and his wonderful quintet, Fats Waller and Art Tatum.

As I carried my tray back to the kitchen, to tell my Aunt that I was now ready to see what she had done to my bedroom, I was feeling better and happier than I had felt at any time since my tragedy.

"Right," my Aunt said, putting down the knife she was using to make lockshen. Then, cleaning her hands on her apron, she said almost conspiratorially "Now let me show you what I have done to your bedroom."

As we climbed the stairs, my Aunt, who was leading the way, said to me over her shoulder, "I went to a lot of bother to do this, so I hope you like it."

She held the bedroom door open for me to enter first. As I did so, she announced, semi-triumphantly "Well, what do you think?"

What she had done blew away my newly-found recovery in an instant.

Now, with the advantage of retrospection, I realise that all that rediscovered sense of optimism had nothing to do with coming to terms over the loss of my parents. On the contrary, I remember clearly that any thought of them brought on feelings of utterly hopeless loss and despair. Rather, any apparent improvement in my mood or outlook, was because over the three months or so since their death, I had managed to bury all thoughts of them so deeply into my sub-conscious, that I was able to get through my days without consciously thinking of them, even once.

But the sight of what my Aunt had done flung me onto a psychological helter-skelter, down and down through a black vortex of horror, depositing once more in my own, private, shut-in world of loneliness, yearning and alienation.

"It's lovely," I heard my voice saying, "But could I be left alone with it please, Auntie?"

"Of course you can darling," she said, backing out of the room and quietly shutting the door behind her.

Now on my own, I slowly looked again around the room.

What she had done was fill the room with enlarged, framed photographs of my parents. On the previously bare wall behind my bed was now my parents wedding picture, enlarged and set into a thin, gold frame. It was a full-length photo of two smiling, ecstatically happy people.

On the dressing table there were two separate, seven by ten-inch framed photos. One was of my Father, exactly as I remembered him, standing outside the little studio he had in The Bon Marche department store in Brixton. (I still have this picture). There he was in his smart, well-cut double-breasted suit, his grey homburg tilted slightly back on his head, a freshly lit cigarette dangling from his lips.

The other was of my Mother. It was taken in our kitchen, so I guess it was my Father who took it. She was wearing her apron which meant that he had caught her off guard and clearly in the middle of some cooking chore or other. Nevertheless, she had still managed to find the inspiration, to affect the typical pose of a twenties flapper, standing on one leg, the other crooked behind, one limp-wristed hand held beside her ear, the other at her side, her head tossed back and a joke come-hither smile on her face.

On the bedside table there was another seven-by-ten inch photograph, that I clearly remember being taken. It was at the beginning of October 1939. My Father had already received his Petty Officer ranking in the Royal Navy, but had just taken possession of his new uniform prior to his first posting. As he had about four hours to wait for the train that was to take him to his naval base, he, together with a good friend of his, who had enlisted at the same time as my Father, and who I knew only as Uncle Alex (although he was not related), decided to make a last-minute visit home. I was messing about in the garden when I was called by my Father to come to the front porch for a family photo. I recall how put out I was at having to stop whatever it was that I was doing, for something so unimportant as a photo, and it is clearly evident on my face. My Father, resplendent in his new uniform, is standing next to my Mother, smallish, plumpish and dressed in a flowered frock, with me standing between and in front of them. They are both half-looking at each other and smiling, both with a hand on my shoulders. I am half-staring, half-scowling straight at the camera. I remember Uncle Alex who was taking the shot with one of my Father's cameras, bent over, and underneath a black cloth that photographers always seemed to need in those days, yelling to me, "Smile Jake. Say cheese or something for Chrissakes." But I would not. I remember thinking 'Why the hell should I smile? I didn't want to be here in the first place'.

Everywhere I looked there were photographs of them. There were four small, oval, metal- framed mementos; my Mother with Uncle Harry, taking tea in the back garden: another of my Father, Mother, and Aunt Sarah standing on the beach at some seaside or other. Judging by their slimness, it was taken before I was born, because I cannot remember my Mother ever being so Sylph-like. My Father was wearing a one-piece bathing costume like Buster Crabbe used to wear in those old movies, and my Mother and Aunt Sarah were saucily attired in Mack Sennet bathing-beauty costumes. He was standing between them, his arms around both of their waists. There was another of my Father, with a four or five year-old me sitting on his shoulders. The fourth was of just the close-up heads of my parents facing the camera, heads pressed tightly together, but with their eyeballs pivoted in each other's direction.

The sight of each picture, as I slowly toured the room, was like a hand gripping the pit of my stomach ever tighter. Finally, I found it difficult to breathe and so I lay down on the bed and stared blindly at the blank white ceiling, grateful that my Aunt hadn't thought of sticking another smiling, happy, snap-shot up there. I was now once again completely and utterly gutted, spiritually and emotionally. The defensive screen that my unconscious mind had so diligently built up over the past few tortuous months, in order to block off my yesterdays from my todays had been torn down, and the sudden shock of seeing my beloved Mum and Dad again, so alive, yet so inanimate, was more than I could take.

My first thought was to take all the photographs down and hide, or even burn them. But I instantly dismissed it together with an added self-directed anger for allowing myself to even think of doing something so disloyal toward my parents.

I was also mature enough to realise that I could not, or indeed wished, to let my Aunt or Uncle know what a toll this parental picture gallery was taking of my psyche. This meant trying to act as if I was in the same positive frame of mind as was just an hour before, when I came home from my first day at school.

There was a soft knock on my door.

"Can I come in?" my Aunt's head appeared around the door.

"Of course," I said trying to make my voice sound normal and unaffected by my inner misery.

She came into the room and looking around, her fingers intertwined across her plump bosom, as if in prayer, she said quietly but with a facial expression that showed her complete satisfaction with what she saw. "Well, Jake darling, what you think of my handiwork?"

The hand that was hitherto gripping my entrails had now metamorphosed into a knife. But I tried all I knew to maintain a facade of normality "It's lovely," I said, trying to sound genuinely appreciative. I sat up on the bed and watched her as she slowly walked around the room, looking at each picture as if seeing it for the first time.

They were so young and full of life weren't they darling?"

The knife gave a violent twist. She came over to stand by my bedside and while looking at the wedding photograph on the wall above my head, said "Everyone loved to go to your parents house Jake. It was always so full of life and love and laughter. But you know that, don't you?"

Now the knife in my gut was ripping at me viciously. In my mind I was begging her to go away, but it was not to be. The torture had to continue.

"And there was always music playing. Ike was a lovely pianist you know." Now the knife moved upwards to rip into my heart." And your Mother Eve, always singing, always happy. Do you know, I can still hear her voice singing 'Look for a Silver Lining'. Do you know that Jake? I can still hear her."

Her own sense of euphoria seemed to be preventing her from sensing what I was suffering as she went on with the quiet destruction of my heart, soul and spirit.

"I can see her now; standing by the side of the piano singing, with your Father accompanying her. She had such a pretty..."

That was it! I could take no more. I leapt off the bed and bolted past her into the bathroom. As soon as I had locked the door behind me, I felt a bit easier. Even though the knife was still cutting at me, it had stopped the twisting and ripping which she had caused it to do with every word she uttered. For a while, I know not how long, I stood staring at the frosted glass of the bathroom window, wishing I could cry, or scream, or do something to express the deep, terrible yearning for my parents that the photos had once again brought to the surface of my conscious mind. But I could not.

There came the inevitable tap, tap on the door. "Are you okay Jake darling?"

"Yes Auntie," I lied. "It was just a sudden pain in my stomach."

"Oh, alright." Then, after a pause; "Jake, I heard your Uncle just come in. So when you are finished in there, come down right away. I'm sure he'll want to hear all about your first day at school."

"Okay." I said in as cheery a voice as I could muster. I waited until I could hear the thud of her footsteps going down the carpeted staircase. Then I sat down on the lavatory seat to try and think things through calmly. My Aunt and Uncle were showing me a great love. That was true. But it was too much love, and it was suffocating me. If I could not run into my parents arms, I did not want to run into anyone else's.

And then, what seemed to me at the time to be the perfect solution, hit me. I would run away. What I was running away from, I had no idea. But the idea of running just about anywhere seemed so much better than living in a house that continuously forced me to confront the problem of how to continue living without the love, support and guidance of my Mother and Father. So running seemed a great idea. Where would I run to? I could try to stay a few days with one of my school friends, Joey Segal maybe. 'But that would be no good', I realised. 'I'd surely be caught if I remained in London. No, it would have to be out of London, and preferably, out of England. But where? Who could tell me where to run to?' Then it hit me.

Why, of course: my best friend Chaim Rabinowitz. He would know. And he would understand. I immediately started to feel better. I had an escape plan. All I had to do was work out the details. 'I'll wait until everyone is out of the house. Then I'll go to my Uncle office and get Chaim Rabinowitz's telephone number out of the big, red leather-bound address book he keeps on his desk. 'I'll just phone him up and explain my problem to him. He will definitely understand and tell me exactly what I must do. He'll probably give me a job in the United States or somewhere'.

'That's it' I thought. 'Brilliant' I thought.

I was now ready to go downstairs and face my Uncle.

I found him in the drawing room-cum-library. He was sitting in one of the large armchairs, nearest to the coffee table, reading a newspaper.

"Ah, Jake. I was looking for you," he said putting down the paper and removing his pince-nez reading glasses.

"Yes. Aunt Sarah told me."

"Your Aunt told me you had a pain in your stomach. How is it?"

"Oh that. It's all better now."

He took his coffee cup from the table, drained it, and as he returned it to its saucer, he said "So, my boy. How did you like your first day at your new school?"

"It was fine Uncle" I said trying to find the right tone of voice to imply light-hearted optimism.

"Ivan will be phoning this evening and I'm sure he'll want to know how you got on."

I made no reply to that. I went over to the other armchair and sat down.

"Have you heard from Mister Rabinowitz yet, Uncle?"

"No. And I don't expect to. I've told you before Jake. He's a very busy man."

Then I had a smart idea. "It's just that I want to phone him and tell him that his shoes are very comfortable and to thank him for giving them to me."

"Commendable. Very commendable of you Jake" I watched him pick up his newspaper once again and carefully fold it in such a way as to make the article he wanted to read, more accessible. Whilst he was in the throes of his paper-folding act, I thought I would press my luck.

"It's just that I would like to phone him tonight," I said in what I hoped was a grown-up and business-like voice. "Tomorrow we get home-work and I might forget to do it if I don't do it tonight."

"Quite so" he said, having now got his 'Evening Standard' folded to his satisfaction. As he replaced his pince nez he said.

"I think it best if you write to him Jake. You would never get through on the telephone, and in any case, writing to him is a nicer thing for you to do."

Before I could even try to change his mind, he went on "I'll tell you what. Go and have yourself a cup of tea or a glass of lemonade with your Aunt. After that, we'll go to the office and I'll get you his address and I'll also give you some headed note-paper and an envelope. How's that?"

I could see that he wanted me out of the way so that he could read his paper. But I gave it one last shot." Maybe I should try to phone him. Just the once" I added hastily. "He may just speak to me."

It didn't work.

"No, that would be a bad idea. Come back here after you have had your tea and we'll go to the office, where I'll give you everything you need to write to him." He started to read his newspaper article, switching me out at the same time.

As I got up from my chair to go to the kitchen, I was thinking that once I had the name and address of Chaim's company, I could trace his telephone number through the phone book. 'It'll be a lot easier than getting into my Uncle's office and out again, unobserved', I thought.

Sitting here outside the 'Bar Cuba Libre', watching the silver stair-rods of rain bounce on the rutted road and run in endless rivulets toward the Caribbean, I am damned if I can remember why I felt it so vital not to be seen entering or leaving my Uncle's office. I could have dreamed up a dozen good reasons for being in there. In any case, neither my Aunt nor Uncle had forbidden me from entering it. I guess it must have been that I had seen too many movies, and felt that to get a telephone number out of a book that sat on my uncle's desk, without anyone knowing, was a caper for Boston Blackie or Nick Charles, and now, Hollywood's latest—and youngest—shamus, Jake Silver.

My tongue and throat were still burning from drinking the hot tea too quickly, as I tapped on the library door, before diffidently letting myself in.

"That was pretty quick," my Uncle said, observing me over the tops of his rimless pince-nez, his newspaper still folded exactly the same way as it was when I left. I just stood there saying nothing. After this picture of still-life-with-newspaper had gone on for a half minute or so, he suddenly put down the paper on the coffee table in front of him, and getting to his feet, said.

"Okay Jake my boy. Let us get you what you need."

I followed him into his office and watched him sit down behind his desk, and bring out a small sheaf of writing paper from the top right hand drawer. He placed them in front of him on a large leather-backed blotter. I put my hand out for him to give it to me, but he ignored it, saying "Let me show you something first Jake." He reached into a hitherto invisible pocket that he had sewn into the inside top of his tailored blue, pinstripe trousers, and retrieved a small pouch which he set down on top of my writing paper. Then, he angled the desk lamp, so that it shed a pool of concentrated light on the area of the desk where the pouch lay. He proceeded to open it with all the prestidigitation of a performer doing a card trick. As he did so, he said quietly "Come round here Jake. Stand next to me and take a look at this."

On the tissue paper were five sparkling diamonds. While I stared at them, he reached into another pocket, this time in his waistcoat, and again, rather like a magician doing the rabbit-in-the-hat trick, produced yet another piece of folded tissue paper, which he carefully and delicately unfolded..

"This is what we call a freak stone Jake. You see? It is deep blue, but it is nevertheless a flawless three and a half carat stone. These here," he went on, as he gently and lovingly caressed the other stones with the tips of his fingers, "These are all three and four carat pure-white flawless stones. Aren't they beautiful?"

I must admit that I was taken by the way they flared and glittered under the bright desk-lamp glare. Beyond that, they left me totally cold.

Are they very valuable?" I asked, as I too fingered them gently, just as my Uncle had.

He left quite a long pause before saying: "My boy, there are men who are making millions out of this war. These days, it seems to me that almost any two penny-halfpenny engineering firm can get government contracts worth hundreds of thousands of pounds in profits. And as to the big boys; well, they are making millions. So you see Jake, while our boys are giving their lives at the front, at the back, our industrialists are stuffing their wallets with money."

I watched in silence as he selected a medium-size Havana cigar and a cedar wood spill from the humidor on his desk. Then with an onyx-handled cigar - cutter, I watched him carefully circumcise the cigar, carefully remove the name-band and after lighting the spill with the desk lighter, I stared fascinated as he addressed and re-addressed the cigar with it until it was glowing brightly, giving off that aroma of sensuous luxury that only a Havana cigar can give. As I remember it now, this ritual was far more interesting to me than looking at glittering, but inanimate bits of stone.

As to what he was telling me about the fat cat-rats of the armaments business, frankly I was not remotely concerned. But I was smart enough to know that I was not going to get Chaim's address until after he had finished his tale. So, I just hung in there and looked interested

He blew out a couple of blue-grey smoke rings, leaned back in his over-size desk-chair, and continued "Y'see Jake, when you are making all that money you have to find safe places in which to put it, and where the tax man can't grab his pound of flesh. This is why diamonds are one of the best and safest investments anyone can make. He rested his cigar on his matching onyx ash-tray, and as he carefully returned the glittering stones to their tissue-paper nests, he said "And that is how your Uncle earns his keep—by selling jewellery to these greedy, bastards for the highest price I can get."

As he picked up his cigar again, he mused more to himself than to me "I suppose that makes me a war-profiteer as well. Well, sobeit. I mean, why shouldn't I get some of their blood-money, hey Jake? How else can I afford to pay the ridiculous black market prices they are charging for everything these days?"

"Could I have that address now Uncle, please?"

"The address?" He looked at me uncomprehendingly for a few seconds. Then suddenly, the penny dropped. "Oh, the address. Yes, of course." He scribbled it down on his note-pad, tore off the page and handed it to me, together with the headed writing paper, saying as he did so "There. Now off you go and write him a nice letter."

"Yes, I will Uncle. Thank you." I got out of the office as fast as I could, hoping he saw no hint of the guilt I felt for my deceit. Here I was doing my best to make my Uncle see me as a nice, appreciative, young lad, when in actual fact all I wanted was Chaim's address in order for him to get me out of this house and give me a job in one of his overseas factories.

Back in my bedroom, I started to feel better immediately. This was because I was on my own, which was all I wanted to be, since the shock of coming face to face with those damned photographs.

I haven't the foggiest idea of why Garbo 'vanted to be alone', but I certainly knew why I did. Dali did a painting called 'The Persistence of Memory'. I was the living proof of the accuracy of that title. Thanks to those fucking photographs, the memories of my parents had become so persistent, so alive in my head that memory had become the reality and reality nothing more than an alien intrusion.

As I walked over to my dressing table to put down the writing paper my Uncle had given me, I could not stop the sickening scrunch in my stomach at the sight of my Mum and Dad, smilingly dead, looking out from their picture frames. I grabbed the note paper with Chaim's address and went over to the bed to lie and stare at my Uncle's carefully handwritten note:

C. Rabinowitz Esq.,
Chairman,
Town Crier Shoes Ltd.,
43 Goldney Road,
London E.C.4

Such is the mind of a child, that as I lay there reading and re-reading the address, I was absolutely certain that Chaim would get me out of this Photographic House of Horrors and bring about my nirvana in some happy land far, far away.

So, when I went downstairs to get my dinner, it was with the vibrant, yet guarded elation of a convict who has discovered the way to escape.

Dinner was still a good half hour away according to Olga, the refugee-maid. So I went into the lounge with the idea of playing a couple of records. But all those pictures of my Mother and Father had recreated in my mind, such a close affinity with them that they had become alive again for me. Suddenly, I was possessed of a strong urge to play the piano, an urge allied to an over-whelming sensation that it would please them. I decided to play my parent's favourite tunes as some kind of recognition of their ethereal re-appearance.

I flipped the lid of the piano and started to play very quietly, 'They Didn't Believe Me'. As the tune unfolded, so this spiritual affinity with my parents strengthened. Crazy though it seems to me now, at that time, after I had played only a few bars, I could swear that my Mother's sweet, tinkly voice was singing along with me as she so often did in the past. Also, I had an uncanny feeling that my Father was standing behind me, watching me play. I almost expected him to lean over me and show me a better harmony than the one I was playing, as he had done so often. I became evermore transported by that old Jerome Kern standard. My hands on the keyboard seemed to have become the agents of my heart and soul as they tore the melody out of the Bluthner baby grand.

The spell was shattered by my Aunt's voice. "Oh, it's so lovely to hear you play Jake darling."

I had not heard her come into the room. But here she was, standing behind and to the right of me, fingers clasped across her chest smiling and clearly delighted that I was once again playing the piano. I finished the tune although it seemed suddenly pointless to do so. I stopped at the end of the chorus. She said "You take after your Father 'aleva sholem' alright. I think those lovely photos of your mother and father must have inspired you,"

I was in too much spiritual pain to speak. Then she said, "Now play something for me"

I said nothing.

"Do you know 'If You Were The Only Boy In The World?' I just love that tune. You know Jake, your Mother and I used to sing it as a duet whenever we went to parties."

I played it for her, my teeth clenched from pain, anger and frustration. It was as if my family had been snatched from me all over again.

But that night, in bed, surrounded by the almost alive, photographic mementos of my parents, and thinking about the strange, possibly psychic feelings I had experienced as I played one of their favourite songs, it suddenly hit me: the piano could be the medium through which could cement and confirm my closeness with my parents, rather than the pain I had hitherto expected it to bring.

I got a warm thrill of joy through my entire body at the thought that through the piano, I could make them vivid and relevant to my life again. It was like discovering a spiritual telephone line to my beloved Mother and Father. But I also knew in my soul that I would not be able to do it with other people present. I had to be on my own.

Before drifting off into a light, troubled and dream-filled sleep, another realisation came to me: that the only route for me, to bring me any kind of happiness or contentment, was by being left on my own with a piano.

For then on, I spoke very little to anyone. At every opportunity I would close myself into the lounge, and then try to close out the real world as I played my heart out. Sometimes, I thought I felt a spiritual presence, but it was too often dispelled by the maid bringing me in some tea and cake, or by the sound of my Aunties out-of-tune voice trying to sing along with me.

I of course knew, by the worried look on my Aunt's face every time she looked at me, that my new state of silent introspection was causing her a great deal of grief and pain, but try as I might (and I did try), I was unable to mask it from her.

And then my shitty little Sprite, ever sadistic, never averse to putting the boot in when I was down, decided that now was as good a time as any to add some additional pain to my already closed-up, shut-down life.

We were just finishing dinner. I had no appetite whatsoever. But trying to keep up some charade of normalcy, I had forced some food into me which had left me feeling sick and heavy. I had just one thought in mind; to get back to the solitude of my bedroom, so that I could lie on the bed and go over my plans for getting away from this house. But judging by the look on my Aunt's face, as she sat munching her way through yet another latke, I knew that if I just stood up and went to my room, she would undoubtedly follow me up and try to press me into talking about what is wrong with me, as she had done so often over the past few days, and which had been such a depressing nerve-wrenching drag for me.

So, I decided to sit it out and wait a half an hour or so before feigning tiredness and hopefully, being allowed to go to my room and be left in peace.

As I sat there half-listening to my Aunt and Uncle's dinner conversation, the front door bell rang. All conversation stopped as we listened to Olga open the door and have an indecipherable, short conversation with a deep-voiced man. After a couple of minutes, she came in to announce that there was a naval officer who wants to speak with Master J. Silver. I went out into the hall accompanied by my Uncle.

At the door was a naval lieutenant. He was big, beefy man with a dark, curly beard. He was wearing under his uniform, a cream, polo-necked Guernsey. Uncle Harry immediately invited him into the lounge and offered him a drink, which he declined.

"I've just come up from Portsmouth for a spot of leave," he told us in a sonorous, west-country accented baritone voice. "When I told my commander that I would be staying with friends at Finsbury Park, he asked me if I could deliver this parcel for him" Then turning his piercing marble-blue eyes in my direction he said "And you I take it, are," he read carefully from the label on the parcel, "Master J. Silver?"

I nodded, reaching out at the same time, to shake his proffered hand. He had a bone-crushing grip.

"It's nice to meet you Silver. Your late Father talked a great deal about you. I understand that you also play the piano."

"Yes, I do play a bit," I replied, hoping that my fake smile would hide the agony I was suffering from crushed hand syndrome.

"Well, I hope that one day you can play as well as your Pater did. He was a damn fine player. And, from what I am told, a damn nice chap"

"Did you know Ike very well?" asked my Uncle.

"Unfortunately no. He was on special ops and I was involved in something quite different and far more ordinary I am afraid."

As he handed me the quite large brown paper parcel, with Master J. Silver hand-written on it, he said to us both. "But I must tell you, those chaps who were working with him were damned shocked when they found out about the tragedy." Then he turned to look at me directly:

"You look like you are handling your tragedy in a way that I am sure your Father would have been proud." Then he added something like, "We've all got to keep our chins up until this ghastly business is over, haven't we?"

The theatrical unreality of such a cornball cliché left all conversation dead on the floor. My Uncle vainly tried to revive it with a "Are you sure I can't tempt you into having one for the road?"

But it was no good. We made are respective farewells (with me avoiding further painful damage to my hand, by avoiding any further handshaking), and after mutual good wishes for our respective futures, he was gone.

Aunt Sarah now made her entrance. Whilst my Uncle was giving her a quick rundown on what had taken place, she took the parcel from me. She waited patiently until he had finished. Then she said, "Well that is very nice." And turning to me she said, "So nu, are we going to open it here, or do we open it upstairs?"

"I would prefer to open it upstairs, please Auntie."

Whether or not she understood by the way I stressed the 'I' in my reply, to indicate that I saw this parcel as something personal to me and me alone, I know not. But if she did, she chose to ignore it.

"Okay," she said in a reasonable voice, designed to cover her determination to be present when the parcel was opened. "So let us go upstairs."

For some reason, the sight of the photographs as I went in to my bedroom did not have the same traumatic effect as previously. But the contents of the parcel did—in spades!

My Uncle, either out of consideration for me or because he was more interested in finishing his dinner, had chosen to stay downstairs. But the lady would not be denied. She had to be there at the opening ceremony.

She allowed me to tear open the brown paper to find a second brown paper wrapping, but with an envelope pinned to it. Even before I could unpin it, my Aunt was in position, on the bed, right up close to me, ready to read whatever was in this brown envelope with my name typed to the outside of it

It contained a handwritten letter from my father's commanding officer (which I still have). It read:

Dear Master Silver,

As Petty Officer 'Ike' Silver's commanding officer, I would like you to know that we thought very highly of your late father. Apart from his absolute dedication to the highly technical and dangerous job for which he was the first to volunteer, he was always cheerful and is very sorely missed by us all. His nightly concert on the piano in the mess was something we always looked forward to.

He also spoke of you with great pride. I understood from him that you are also a promising pianist.

I would like you to know that in petty officer 'Ike' Silver, you had a father of whom you can be justly proud. Even though he was with us for far too

short a time, he set standards as a serving officer, which will be sorely missed and long remembered.

This parcel contains all his effects.

Yours sincerely,

Tim Wilkinson. (Rear Admiral).

Station Commanding Officer.

My Aunt did not even wait for me to fold the letter back into its envelope, before tearing open the parcel.

I can't even get near to describing or explaining the resentment I felt as I watched red-varnished finger-nails ripping open the paper wrapping of something so deeply personal to me. It was bad enough having her lean over my shoulder to read what to me was a private and personal letter, but far worse was having to watch her tear into the last physical evidence of my Father's existence. This was a moment that no one had the right to share with me. But in those days my feelings made no goddamned difference. Back in 1942, a thirteen year-old kid had no rights. For me to tell a grown-up to keep their nose out of my private and personal business was unthinkable. So I was forced to assume the role of a simple bystander at the unwrapping of the last remaining personal effects of my own beloved father.

The first thing the busy, bejewelled, chubby, inquisitive fingers of my Aunt, drew from the parcel, was a blue, pinstripe, double-breasted suit, that I not only remembered him wearing, but went with him to the tailor for its final fitting. I remembered it well because, at the same time, I had a final fitting also, for my first suit with long trousers. I recall my Father being as careful and critical of how my suit fitted as he was of his own.

The purpose for our two new suits was so that we would cut a dash at the wedding of a friend of my parents. But week or so before this great nuptial event was due to take place, I came home from school to find my Mother sitting on the settee, her arm around a youngish, lady, with eyes swollen from crying. I had no idea what it was all about at the time. All I knew was what was what Mother told me after the lady had gone; the wedding was off. I didn't get to wear that suit for a good three months and then it was only because I was growing so fast that if I hadn't worn it then, I probably would have been too tall to wear it ever.

It is frightening how the mind can make one see things. As my Aunt held up the suit jacket, my Father suddenly seemed to appear inside it, so that it seemed to my eyes, that Aunt Sarah's hands were resting on my Father's shoulders rather than simply holding it up for me to see. A cold chill ran down my spine at the sight of him, quickly followed by a wash of disappointment and regret as he faded from my view.

"Do you remember him in this Jake?" my Aunt asked as she held the jacket admiringly at arms length. "He looked so smart in it" Then she added as she went over to the wardrobe to place it on a hanger; Mind you, he should have. That suit cost him twenty guineas you know."

But I by now was too emotionally screwed up to say anything.

The sight of this suit plus the memories it brought forth, compounded by the sudden appearance of my Father, only to be followed by his equally sudden evaporation into nothingness, was almost more than I could handle. I watched numbly as my Aunt laid out the remainder of the package on the bed: a pair of gold cuff-links, half dozen handkerchiefs, five pairs of socks, two pairs of black shoes, a small camera and a wallet. I managed to grab the wallet before my Aunt's acquisitive hands could reach for it. Inside we found a photograph of me, another of my Mother and one more of me and my Mother together.

Then, to my great relief, Uncle Harry called my Aunt for something which meant her having to go back downstairs..

Alone at last, I went over to the wardrobe to look again at my Father's suit. I carefully removed it from the wardrobe and lay it down on my bed. For no reason that I can recall, I decided to put the jacket on. Having done so, I went across the room to stand in front of the full-length mirror, to look at myself in it. It was of course, far too large for me and appeared to swallow me up. Once again, I got an uncanny feeling that my Father was inside the jacket with me.

I was about to take it off, when I felt something in the inside pocket. It was an envelope, inside of which was a photograph of him in his uniform, upon which he had written 'To my son Jake, from your loving Father' There was also a handwritten note addressed to me:

My Dearest Son,
Very soon I will be leaving to go on a difficult but necessary naval operation. I may be gone for quite a while. Just so that you don't forget what your old Father looks like, I would like you stick the enclosed picture of me on your bedroom wall.

PS. Help your Mother all you can. You are the man of the house until I get back.

Your ever-loving Father, Ike.

Standing there, staring at myself in the mirror, my Father's blue, pinstripe double-breasted jacket half-way down to my knees, his photograph in one hand, the note in the other, and surrounded by the familiar ambience of cigarette tobacco that hung around everything he wore, I started to shake. There may not have been a single tear drop to see on the outside. On the inside, I was drowning in them. And they weren't tears of sadness so much as rage over what had happened to him and my sweet Mother. For the first time I was not grieving over my own loneliness and alienation, although, God knows, I was up to my eyeballs in that. This time, it was grief, mixed with anger and frustration over the mad meaninglessness of my parent's deaths that was causing me so much pain.

And then, something amazing happened. As I stood there, staring at myself in the mirror, my reflection all of a sudden disappeared and my Father appeared in its place. There he stood in the mirror, wearing the same suit of which I was wearing the jacket. He had a half smile on his lips and he was holding his cigarette between his first and middle fingers. I could clearly see the smoke whisping upwards. He was looking at me appraisingly, as if he was just about to tell me something. For a minute we just stood there staring at one another. I was just about to beg my Father to help me, when I heard the door behind me open and he instantly disappeared to be replaced by my own reflection once more.

My Aunt came hurrying into the room and around the two beds to where I was standing, which was on the side farthest from the door?

"My God, what's happened?" she said as she took the photograph and note from my hands. Her face was an even mix of fear and worry.

"He was here you know," I said to her. "He just gave me the note and the picture. The moment you took the suit out of the parcel I knew he was here. He just did not want to appear with you in the room."

"Yes darling. I am sure you are right." Her eyes were filling up with tears as she gently led me towards my bed. "Now, lie down and rest. I'll go out of the room and let you speak to your Father all alone."

At that moment, I believed every word that I had uttered. How else could that note and the photo have suddenly materialised? How else could I have looked in the mirror and seen his and not my own reflection?

I lay on the bed, his jacket still enshrouding me.

"Would you like me to help you off with the jacket before I go?" My Aunt's voice was as soft and gentle as she could make it.

"DO NOT TOUCH THIS JACKET," I yelled. "Don't lay a finger on it" It was as if I had been put in charge of defending the Holy Grail.

"Yes, of course my poor darling. Of course." She bent over me as if to kiss me, then thought better of it, and quietly went out of the room.

Now on my own, enshrouded in his jacket, the picture and the note held tight with both hands against my chest, I felt sure that I could now talk once more with my Father.

"Oh Dad, it was marvellous to see you again." I spoke aloud to make sure he could hear me. "Are you with Mum? Can I speak to her as well as you?"

I waited in a breath-held silence for his reply. All I heard was a car pass by in the street below, and then an air-raid warden's gruff voice shout "Put that light out!," a phrase I had heard over a thousand times since the black-out began. But from either of my parents, I heard nothing.

"Please Dad, please. Say something to me." Again I waited. But my pleading was in vain.

I turned over on to my stomach and with closed fists, punched the pillow in rage. I could not understand why he would not speak to me. After, I had punched myself out, I just lay there trying to accept the pointlessness of trying to make any further contact with my parents. But then another thought struck me as I lay there, my face in the pillow, my fists still clenched on either side of me. 'When I was playing the piano, before my Aunt screwed it up by coming into the room, were not Mum and Dad in the room listening to me? Of course. Yes. That's it! I can make contact with them, but only through the piano'.

"Okay, Mum and Dad," I shouted, as I leapt off the bed. "I know how to talk to you now." I rushed out of the room, still enveloped in my Father's jacket, pushed past my Aunt, who had been standing outside my bedroom door, listening, and flung myself down the stairs, rather like a demented Superman, the overlarge jacket flying out behind me.

I rushed into the lounge, banging the lounge door behind me. and all but flung myself at the piano.

I began with the same song I had played previously for them, when I felt they were in the room with me. I played 'They Didn't Believe Me' quietly but with all the frills my unpractised hands would allow. All the time, I was looking up and around for them to materialise. But again, I was disappointed. Undaunted, I went into 'All The Things You Are', another of my parents absolute favourites and on which my Father had spent a good hour teaching me the harmonies. This time, I played it louder, shouting over my playing," Can you hear this Dad? See, I still remember all the harmonies." I played the chorus through twice, the second even louder than the first, all the while shouting over my playing, begging them to appear.

When that tune failed, I quite literally banged out 'The Man I love', another of their favourites. I played it as loudly and as rhapsodically as my as yet only half-formed talent allowed. This crazy, but absolute conviction that my playing the piano would somehow bring them back to life inspired me to play well above my actual ability. Over the years this has happened to me a number of times; where my fingers have taken on a new set of wings and my mind has soared into hitherto unexplored regions of invention.

But this was the first time it had ever happened to me.

I smothered the keyboard with love, grief, hopefulness, hopelessness: I cried out as I played, "Please, please, come back" Once I thought I heard my Mother laugh. I looked around in excited hope. But I saw no-one. Did I really hear her? Or was it merely the vibration of something in the room caused by my pounding on the piano? I never found out.

I must have played 'The Man I love' for about twenty minutes or more. I played over it, around it, on top and underneath it. I tore that tune to pieces in the vain hope of materialising my parents.

I finally stopped playing, heartbroken and exhausted. Why did I see my father when I put on his jacket, but now, still wearing it draped around my shoulders, and more than that, playing my parents' favourite tunes, had I not been able to summon them up?

I took off the jacket, and after carefully folding it over my crooked arm, went out of the room, past my Uncle and Aunt who had apparently been standing listening in the hallway and slowly dragged myself back up the stairs.

Back in my bedroom, I sat on the bed looking at the photo of my Dad in his naval uniform. Then, I got up and brought over the picture of my Mother camping it up in the kitchen of our now non-existent house. I held one in each hand, staring at them in turn.

And suddenly, all those tears that had been welling up inside me started to flow. All the feelings that I had carried inwardly, all the horror and pain, all the alienation and loneliness as well as the deep, deep longings of a thirteen year-old boy for his parents: all were transmuted into a deluge of tears. I wept uncontrollably and bitterly for I don't know how long. But when it finally, came to a finish, I drifted into a deep, dreamless sleep, probably from exhaustion as much as anything else.

When I next opened my eyes it was daylight. A bright winter sun was streaming its frosty brilliance through the curtained window. I also noted that the black-out curtains had been opened by somebody.

I leapt out of bed. I had no idea of the time, or even the day. Then the events of yesterday jumped into the frame of my consciousness and I suddenly felt weak. So I sat down on the bed again, whereupon I noticed a glass of milk and a plate of scrambled egg sandwiches on my bedside table. Resting against the milk glass was a card from my Auntie. It said 'In case you wake up in the night feeling hungry. If you want anything else, please call me'. Then, for no reason I could fathom at that time she wrote, 'We all love you very much' Your Aunt.

PS. Your father's letter etc. is on the dressing table.

It wasn't until I was in the bathroom that I realised that I was only in my underwear, which meant that someone must have undressed me whilst I was asleep.

I washed and dressed. It was while I was having my usual battle with my hair, which was strong and thick enough to do its own thing, regardless of any known comb and hairbrush, that I realised I felt a lot healthier, happier and more optimistic than at any time since my Aunt had set up the picture gallery. The previous night's long crying jag, must have miraculously unburdened me, although I didn't realise it at the time.

I checked my watch, which I (or whoever undressed me) had left on the dressing table. It told me it was ten-thirty. 'Jesus', I thought, 'school started an hour and a half ago'. I rushed out of the bedroom, down the stairs and into the kitchen. Aunt Sarah came hurrying over to me, and holding my face in her hands, she said "And how is my darling boy feeling today?"

"I'm alright Auntie. Listen, I've overslept. Can you write me a note for school? You know, make up some excuse for me arriving so late. Please Auntie."

As she poured some freshly boiled water into the teapot, she said "Stop worrying. It's all been taken care of. You are not going into school today.

Why not?"

"Because you've been sick, that's why."

As she brought me over a cup of tea she said "I've got someone coming to see you who is a specialist in what you are suffering from."

"But..."

"No, no, no" she said, cutting off whatever it was that I was going to say. Then, with a wagging finger "Your Uncle has gone to a lot of trouble to find this man, He's coming here to see you at three-thirty this afternoon and there is going to be no argument about it. Now drink your tea while I make you your breakfast."

I was sickened at the thought that I was now considered to be one sandwich short of a banquet, or, to be more exact, off my head.

"I don't think I'm very hungry Auntie."

"Did you eat the sandwiches I left by your bedside?"

"No."

She turned from her bread-slicing, to face me with an expression of Jewish-style shock and worry and disbelief in equal parts.

"You haven't eaten since dinnertime yesterday, and you're not hungry? Don't be ridiculous. You must eat your breakfast."

"But Auntie..."

"You want me to worry even more than I am already worried about you, is that it?"

"No, of course not. It's just th..."

"When Olga and I undressed you last night, I said to her, 'Look at him. He's a bag of bones'. So, my boy, I am going to put some flesh on those bones of yours." She went back to her pots and pans. She picked up a frying pan, then suddenly put it down and turning to me with a kind of mad scientist look on her face, she said triumphantly, "I know what I'll make you. I'll make you some porridge."

"Christ Auntie," I moaned to her back, as she disappeared into the scullery, "I don't fancy porridge. I don't even like porridge."

She came back laden with a large pack of the stuff, a medium size copper pot, a long, wooden spoon, as well as some other packets. Once she had plonked them all down on the table next to her gas cooker, she turned to me, and with her right forefinger six inches from her ear and pointing straight up at the ceiling said "But you have never had porridge 'A la Aunt Sarah'. The triumph in her voice, plus the fact that I did not want to upset her, forced me to give in.

"Okay, I'll eat the porridge," I said resignedly.

"And after you have eaten, you can go and play the piano. And I won't come in. I promise."

"Why do you say that," I asked her, as she emptied half the contents of the packet of porridge into the copper cooking pot.

"Because of what you were saying while we were undressing you."

"I don't even remember you undressing me. So how could I have said anything?"

"You kept saying things like, 'Leave me alone. Let me play the piano in peace', and things like that."

Once she had set down the thick, glutinous mess in front of me, together

with half a dozen slices of thickly buttered bread, she took the chair opposite me, and resting her cheeks in her fisted hands watched me eat (In view of the strict rationing of food in Britain at the time, I realise in retrospect that my Uncle must have had some damn good contacts in the black market.
Only in Buckingham Palace, Ten Downing Street and my Uncle's house was there such a luxuriance of food).

"You played the piano wonderfully, yesterday," she said, her eyes seemingly magnetically drawn to the movement of my spoon from plate to mouth.

I said nothing, preferring not to have to relive one single moment of the agony I had endured while I was playing.

"Your Uncle and I stood outside in the hall captivated. You should be on the BBC or the London Palladium."

Again, I said nothing. A long silence ensued, with her watching me finish off the porridge. As she poured for me the inevitable cup of tea that followed every meal, she said "If it is alright with the psych... I mean, the doctor, I want you to play every day. Apart from the fact that it will keep you in practise, I think it is good for your nerves."

`So, it is a psychiatrist I have to see', I thought. The only thing I knew about psychiatry was, that it was for the mentally sick. I did not remotely feel that I was a candidate for the funny farm, and my nerves were fine. In fact, as I sat there, my guts bloated from having put away enough porridge to feed the entire Black Watch, I was conscious of feeling better, stronger and more in control of my emotions than at any time since my tragedy.

But, at three-thirty precisely, the front doorbell rang. I was in the lounge playing records of various jazz pianists and trying to work out on the piano some of their harmonic tricks.

I stopped my playing to listen to the front door being opened and Aunt Sarah saying, "Oh, hello doctor, do come in." There followed a couple of minutes of inaudible, hushed, conversation in the hall, before the lounge door opened and my Aunt, followed by the shrink, came in.

"Jake, this is professor Scheinbaum." She spoke in an affected, bright and unconvincingly informal manner.

As I crossed the room to shake the prof's proffered hand, my Aunt, still using her phoney, gay voice, said, "And this is my nephew Jake, er, Jake Silver." As we shook hands I could not help noticing that he was smiling at me with his mouth, but calculatingly me with his eyes.

"Would you like me to arrange some tea or coffee?" Aunt Sarah said, still using her chintzy-cheery voice.

"No, denks verra much. Jake and I, ve talk on our own if you pliss."

He was a short, stout, man, with a roundish face and a thick neck. He had a thick, wiry, unkempt, black and grey beard, and a moustache that had crumbs of food stuck to it from his last meal.

His nose was large and bulbous and his eyes were small and black, made to look even smaller by his Franz Schubert-like tiny, round spectacles He also had the thickest pair of eyebrows I have ever seen. Some of the hair from them spiralled upwards almost half-way up his forehead, whilst the remainder sprouted thickly in all directions. You could have upholstered a small armchair with them. The hair on his head was thick and springy, and like his beard, was an even mix of grey and black. He had on a suit that looked like he had been sleeping in it for a week, matched perfectly by his crumpled, grubby shirt. As to his tie, it was so food-stained that I think if he had boiled it, he would have got a reasonable bowl of soup out of it.

My Aunt said, "Very well. I'll just leave you two alone now" and she tripped out of the room in a very un-Aunt Sarah-ish way.

As soon as she had closed the door behind her, the professor said "Now Jake, you sit dere," he pointed to the settee, "Und I vill sit here." He took one of the high-backed chairs and dragged it over so that he would be sitting to the side of me.

"Vell, und how are ve today mine poy?"

As I sat down on the settee, I said "I'm okay, thank you."

"Do you mean okay, because you are resolfink your problems, or do you mean okay because everyvun in dis house luffs you, or do you mean okay because you are sleeping better now, ya?.

I instantly did not like this man. I could not stand the way he was dressed, I hated his grubby beard and I loathed his eyebrows almost as much as the thick wads of hair that were tufting out of his ears. I also found his accent unpalatable. His guttural R's made him sound like Sig Ruman. This accent may have be okay for playing the part of 'Concentration-camp Erhardt', in 'To Be Or Not To Be' with Jack Benny, or playing the Nazi in 'A Night In Casablanca' with the Marx Brothers, but it did not work within the serious context for which my Uncle had hired him.

So I just replied "Yes," and proceeded to examine the shine on my shoes.

I was conscious of his stare, which went on quite a while before he broke it with a quiet, thoughtful, "Ach tzo."

Reaching into the inside pocket of his f'kakte jacket, he brought out a small scribbling pad with a fountain pen affixed to it with an elastic band. After carefully removing the elastic band, unscrewing the pen top, and searching for a clean page upon which to write, he said "Tell me Jake Silver, who did you feel clozer to; your Mudder or your Fadder?"

Suddenly, I was beginning to enjoy the whole thing, because I was busy fantasising that I was in a war movie, where I was the British spy being grilled by the Gestapo. "I felt close to them both, because I loved them equally, and I still do" I told him.

"Vere interesting," he said with sinister slowness, as he scribbled something down in his little pad.

"Are you sure of dis Jake? Normally, a boy vill feel clozer to his mudder, because deep down he sees his fadder as a threat und a challenge."

"Well I loved them the same" I insisted.

He looked at me intently. "You started your new school on Monday, yah?"

"Yes."

"Und tell me Jake," his voice had became silky and more intimate (for a Gestapo officer), "Did you find yourself vanting to be more among der poys, or being vid der girls? Both are quvite normal in a poy of your age, so you can tell me the troot."

"I enjoyed talking to a couple of the boys about cricket and fighter planes, if that is what you mean."

His eyes glittered behind his Schubert-like spectacles, as if he had uncovered some dark secret that had been lurking in my brain.

"Acht tzoooo" he said, as he wrote rapidly in his little pad. "So you prefer being vid der poys radder dan being vid der gals?"

"Girls don't know anything about cricket and they are not interested in aeroplanes" I answered.

"So you ARE more interested vid der poys?" he persisted.

I was not going to tell him about my being in love with a girl called Rene. I wouldn't have even told my parents about her, let alone Concentration-camp Erhardt. So I said nothing, unaware of the implication of my silence. In 1943, boys, except for those who boarded at our highest class and most expensive public schools, were generally ignorant of homosexuality.

While still scribbling in his note pad, the professor asked, in an off-hand way "Ven vass der first time you found poys more attractive to you dan gals?"

In my innocence, I tried again. "Look, girls don't know anything about Joe Louis and they don't know anything about the Mosquito or the Spitfire or any other fighter plane" And then I added, "And they don't know much about jazz either."

"But der poys do?"

"Yes."

"Und that is vy you like standing close to dem?"

"What do you mean, standing close? Do you mean do I fancy boys like they were girls?"

He stopped his scribbling, to stare at me hard. "Vell, do you?"

I was now starting to suspect that this man was out to lunch, bereft of his marbles, in other words, plain barmy.

"Do you mean like wanting to kiss them and stuff like that? That's silly that is. Boys kiss girls, not one another."

Like I said, I had never heard of homosexuality, and in any case I was just about as hetero as you can get. So this duologue seemed surreal to me.

Then he said another seemingly crazy thing, which annoyed me more than somewhat.

"Alright Jake," he said with more than a touch of disappointment in his gaze, his homosexual schtick having got him nowhere "Hef you ever been in luff vid a gal—apart from your own mudder of course.

I thought that I must have mis-heard his question.

"I love my Mother. But girls are different."

He gave me an indulgent little smile. "You do not understand der vorkings of der human mind. All liddle poys are in luff vid dere mudders."

"What, like wanting to cuddle and kiss them just like they are a girl friend?"

"Ja, of course."

I was now starting to be sure that this man was truly gone in the head. What he was saying seemed to me to be not only bizarre, but also nauseating. Furthermore, I saw it as insulting to the memory of my Mother. I started to get angry.

"I think that is absolutely stupid" I said. "And anyway, I don't want you to talk about my Mother any more."

His eyes now took on a penetrating stare. "Dis is very interesting. Vy do you get so upset at the idea of being in luff vid your Mamma? Und pliss Jake before you answer dis quvestion, tink about it a liddle."

As my anger grew, so did my hatred for this man. "I hope you don't mind, but I am not going to speak with you anymore. I am going upstairs to write a letter to a friend. Goodbye."

The friend I was going to write to was, of course, Chaim Rabinowitz.

As I started to remove myself from the settee, he suddenly shouted in a loud, Hitler-like voice, "You vill stay here pliss."

It was enough to stop me dead in my tracks. Then he once more reverted to his insidious, silky voice.

"Ach Jake (he pronounced it 'Chake'), you are such a liddle poy. Alright, ve speak about sumtink different.

I had not the slightest desire to speak to him about anything at all. So I just sat there, still smouldering about what he had suggested were my feelings towards my Mother.

"Do you dream Jake?"

"Sometimes," I replied.

"Tell me about der nicest dream you've had lately."

"I thought about it a while. I did not want to tell him anything anymore about my life, but this question did not seem to have any serious intent.

"The night before last, I dreamed about Linda Darnell. We were sitting on the settee in my house. I was just about to put my arms around her and kiss her when my Mother came in and spoiled it. But Linda whispered to me, 'We'll get together another time, I promise'. And then I woke up.

The shrink seized upon this silly little dream as if it revealed one of the darkest secrets of my innermost soul. He stared at me for a full minute, his face reflecting the flush of success, whilst at the same time he slowly rubbed his bearded chin, repeating "Ja, ja." Then he said:

"Dis Linda person; she iss a friend of your mudder's, no?"

I could not resist laughing as I answered "No, Linda Darnell is the most beautiful film actress in the whole world. Don't you know who Linda Darnell is?"

He chose to ignore my question, preferring to cling to his belief that my dream had some deeper truth buried within it.

Still writing furiously he asked "Und tell me Jake, were you happy or sad ven your mudder came betveen you and dis Linda person?"

"Sad of course." I did not tell him about the end of the dream which was all about trying to hide my erection from my Mother, which had been brought about by Linda's closeness, and the difficulty and embarrassment I had in doing so.

He stopped writing and leaning back in his chair, asked,"Und vat do you tink ze connection iss betveen your mudder und this Linda person?"

"None at all." I replied very firmly. "One is my Mother, and the other is the most beautiful girl in the world."

"Tch, tch, tch. Don't you see Jake; dis Linda person und your mudder are vun und der same person in your subconscious mind? You were really vanting to cuddle und kiss, as you say, your mudder. Dis Linda vass your mudder in anudder form, dat's all." I watched him as he scribbled away on his grubby little notebook. Was he being serious in suggesting something as stupid as this? His face was a picture of self-satisfaction. He looked to me like some kind of Teutonic Sherlock Holmes. All that was missing was him saying 'elementary, my dear Adolf'.

But, I was getting very needled by this suggestion that I wanted to make love to my Mother.

"Look, if you don't stop talking about my Mother, I am not going to say another word, no matter how hard you try to get me to do so. And that's final." And I truly meant it. I could not abide the love I had for my Mother being abused and distorted in this way. There was another long silence during which I looked away from him and he stared blank-faced at me. Then he started again:

"Tell me Jake" he asked, still silky voiced "Do you experience erections?" Before I could react, he went on, while pointing a finger at me. "Dis is quvite normal for a poy of your age."

"Yes," I said, flooded with embarrassment.

"Und do you...touch yourself down dere?"

"Sometimes," I admitted.

In truth, I had been 'touching myself down there' for more than a year.

"Ahaa," he said, as if I was the accused in a tense court-room drama, and Wolfgang Scheinbaum, the famous King's Council, had forced me to admit my guilt.

"So Jake, you do masturb...er, I mean play vid yourself. Das is gut. Das is gut Jake. Dis is just as I thought." He started scribbling again as he asked Und vat do you tink of vile you do it?"

"It's not so much what I think of," I answered awkwardly, "it's who I think of. I think of Anne Sheridan, and sometimes Joan Blondell and of course Linda Darnell."

"Aah, Linda Darnell. In udder vords, your mudder."

"No," I yelled, "NOT MY MOTHER."

I stood up and looked at this man, pure hatred in my heart, and probably on my face.

"I am going to my bedroom now, because I am feeling sick."

"Sometink you ate, maybe?"

"No, it was not something I ate. It was what you said about my mother that makes me feel sick."

He peered at me over the top of his little, round spectacles, a surprised look on his face. Then he affected one of the phoniest smiles of all time. This Kraut shrink had never been taught to smile, and he was just no good at it.

"Oh, dat?" Then he tried a Teutonic lunge at jocularity. "Ha, ha, ha, dat vas my liddle joke, ja?"

I stood staring at him. Then I said in as serious and earnest voice that I could muster, "Please professor Scheinbaum, never speak of my mother ever again."

I ran out of the door, and up to my bedroom. Jesus, I hated this sick, German gauleiter. Even as I think about it now, fifty-odd years on, I am sure that he was sicker than any of his patients, and the last thing I needed at this difficult period of my life, was a sick-o psycho.

I would never have believed that any normal grown-up could be so interested in my childish dreams, nor that anyone carrying legitimate medical credentials would want to explore my masturbatory phantasies so thoroughly.

I endured professor Scheinbaum's psychiatry, twice a week for over three months. Every sex phantasy I had ever had was wrung out of me and minutely examined. Often, some casual remark I might make, far removed from the subject of sex, would be seized upon and given a sexual association. But I kept strictly to my word on one matter. Any mention of my Mother and I got up from the settee, walked out of the room, and upstairs to my bedroom.

How I managed to maintain a good standard of schoolwork, and make a few friends as well, when I was continually in a state of either depression or rage, brought about by my bi-weekly mental strip-searches, I do not know. I suppose it was proof (although I had no knowledge of it then), that the healing and annealing processes of time were beginning to take their effect.

Psychiatrists, to whom I have since spoken about this portion of my life, have usually smiled indulgently and explained that the improvement in my mental and emotional condition was as a direct result of this psychiatric treatment and not in spite of it. I remain totally unconvinced. I have great sympathy with whomever it was dreamed up the phrase 'Anyone who goes to a psychiatrist, should have his head examined!'

Finally, on the twenty-sixth inquisition by Concentration-camp Erhardt, came the big bust-up.

He started off this session by announcing that today we will examine everything 'we' have discovered over the past three months. I resented the use of the word 'we'. It implied that I was a willing party to all his sexual gobbledygook, when in fact, the absolute opposite was the truth.

He consulted his note pad as he spoke: "Jake, ve haf discovered dat you are resistant to the idea dat you haf sexual feelings for your mudder." He riffled through a few more pages. "Also, dat you vere embarrassed to haf erections in front of her, und so you created dis Linda Darna person as a substitute for your mudder."

"Firstly sir" I said, trying to hide my anger and embarrassment as much as I was able, "The name of the film star is Linda Darnell. She has nothing at all to do with my Mother, who I love in a different way entirely. Secondly, as you know, I will not have you speak about my mother in this way. So, I am going upstairs to my room. Good afternoon sir."

I started my walk out of the room, exactly as I had done at least six times previously after he had made what were, and still are to me, disgusting associations about my relationship with my mother. But this time as I stood up to head for the door, he leapt up off his chair and grabbing hold of my upper arm as hard as he could, he forcibly pushed me back down on the settee. I got straight up again and started my walk towards the lounge door, but he got past me to stand in front of the lounge door, as if guarding it, his fat little legs planted firmly about a foot apart.

"No, mine poy, today I don't let you valk out of dis room." He tried to keep his voice friendly but his cold, grey eyes told another story.

"Let me out of this room." I spoke slowly and quietly. For some reason, whenever I am truly angry, I always talk quietly. And I was as angry now as I had ever been – before or since.

"No Jake. Today you face your true self before it is too late."

I went over to the coffee table near the settee. I picked up the heavy, glass ashtray. Holding it threateningly in my hand, I went back to within a yard of where the professor was standing.

"Let me out of this room. Now if you please." I said it as menacingly as I could, but my threat simply bounced off this sick-o psycho.

"You vill go back to the settee und you vill sit down. IMMEDIATELY" As he yelled this last word his face reddened, and for no good reason, I noticed the veins standing out from the sides of his thick hairy, neck.

That was when I let him have it with the ash tray. I hurled it at him with all the strength I could muster. It caught him a glancing blow just below his left cheek bone causing an inch-long gash. It also caused him to stagger away from the door, the back of his hand covering the bleeding wound. As he did so, I darted out of the door and up the stairs to my bedroom, slamming the door and locking it in case he was following me. I hadn't been in there for more than a couple of minutes, before I heard a turning and twisting of the door handle, followed by hard banging and my Aunt's voice shouting "Jake Silver, open this door this minute. Do you hear me?"

I unlocked the door and they came in. My Aunt entered first, rage writ large across her face, with Der Shrinko, behind her. He was dabbing at the cut on his face with an already bloodied handkerchief.

"How dare you do this," my Aunt yelled. "How dare you throw something at the professor? I will not put up with such behaviour. Do you hear me? Now, say you are sorry to the professor and maybe he will forgive you. But whether he does or not, I certainly won't for a very long time."

She was angrier than I had ever seen her.

"Well," I mumbled shamefacedly, "I will apologise if he will stop saying I want to make love to my mother."

That clearly knocked her back on her heels. She let a couple minutes of stunned silence go by before saying in a mystified way "Where in heaven's name did you get such a crazy notion. The professor would never say a thing like that."

"Oh yes he did. And he keeps on saying it." Now it was my turn to start yelling:

And he can't talk about my mother and me like that." I walked over to the bed and sat down heavily and, I hope determinedly. Aunt Sarah turned to the Kraut Shrink: "I am so sorry professor Scheinbaum. Jake has been through a very nasty time. If you will explain to me what you were trying to get across to him, I am sure that I can straighten everything out." She proceeded to give him her sweetest smile.

The professor, still holding his handkerchief to his face, said "I vas merely trying to get him to start to come to terms vid his problems by explaining that it is kvite normal for a poy to subconsciously vish to have haf sexual relations vid his mudder, just as it is for a gal to vish to make luff vid her fadder. Dese are vell known facts since Siegmund Freud disc..."

"Are you suggesting that I wanted to sleep with my Father?" She quietly asked, the smile now frozen on my Aunt's face.

"Ya, of course. All of us, ven ve are liddle babes . ..."

"So professor, you did tell this boy, that he er, harbours sexual feelings for his mother?" She sat down next to me on the bed and placed a protecting arm around my shoulders.

"It is a vell known fact madame. The poy-child harbours resentment towards der fadder for having sex vid der mudder, because he..."

My aunt stood up and while observing her own hand as it smoothed down the front of her dress, said in a quiet voice "I think I have heard just about enough professor Scheinbaum." She rested her hand gently on my shoulder as she went on: "Jake is thirteen years of age. It is a difficult time under the best of circumstances, because it the crossover point between boyhood and manhood. In Jake's case it has been made as difficult as possible by the dea... er, by what has happened to his parents. I expected you to help him through his problems, not make them worse."

The professor stood looking at my Auntie with the kind of smile a prize-fighter reserves for when he has been caught with a painful punch. Of course he tried to fight back, but anyone who knew my Aunt could have told poor old Professor Scheinbaum that in this kind of verbal battle, he is going to be out-punched and out-classed. When it came to verbal fisticuffs, Aunt Sarah was a class act. But, like many a punch-drunk pug, he just did not know when to throw in the towel.

"I can assure you madame, dat it is a vell documented fact, dat ven ve are young, ve all haf sexual feelings for our mudders and fadders..."

My Aunt interrupted him by raising her hand, rather like a policeman does to stop the traffic:

"I think we have heard enough from you professor Scheinbaum. Did you feel this boy had not enough troubles that you had to add to them by making feel guilty into the bargain? And how did you try to do it? By accusing him—and me for that matter—of harbouring some of the most disgusting and degrading desires I have ever heard! You may well have had these shabby, shameful, feelings for your mother. Having heard the filth that you have spoken here this afternoon, I have no doubt that you did. I can even understand your desires to burden somebody else with your guilt. But to take advantage of a young boy who has already suffered a terrible ordeal, I find that quite unforgivable."

Now it was the turn of Herr Sicko-psycho to get angry. With his fore-finger not more than two inches from his ear, and pointing toward the ceiling he said in his best Heinrich Himmler voice:

"I vill not be spoken to in dis vay. Madame you haf insulted my prof..."

Ignoring his protests, she stopped him in his tracks by turning to me and asking; "What other things did this man want to know from you?"

"Nothing much. But he did keep asking me questions about sex and stuff like that."

"Like what?" my Aunt wanted to know.

I was getting embarrassed all over again "About which girls I wanted to kiss... and... other things.

Aunt Sarah now ashen-faced, turned to the professor.

"You were trying to probe the sexual desires of a thirteen year-old boy?" Then pointing to the bedroom door, she shouted; "I want you to leave this house this minute. I believe you are a sexual pervert."

He made some mumbling attempt at a protest but the fight was over. Before he could come up with any kind of counter argument, she yelled very loudly, "Just get out of my house now, this very instant!"

As they went down the stairs I heard her, still yelling at him: "I will be speaking to my husband about this, the moment he gets home. He may decide to call in the police about what you have been saying to that boy."

Then I heard the front door slam.

A few moments later she was back in my room. "Jake darling, I cannot tell you how sorry I am for putting you through all the horrors you must have endured at the hands of that man." She sat down heavily on my bed. "We were told that he was such a clever person. Oy, what a mistake, eh Jake?"

"And how," was all I could think of saying.

Then her face broke into a mischievous smile as she said to me; "Your Uncle is going to be pleased as punch with you for throwing that ashtray at him" She got up off the bed and then bent over me to kiss my forehead. Then she added; "Believe me, he would have got a lot worse than a little cut on his cheek, if he had said those things to me."

She made to go out of the room, but stopped at the doorway to say; "And your Father would have been proud you too for what you did Jake."

She went out, only to pop her head round the door a few seconds later; "And so would your dear Mother."

"Maybe they did see what went on," I replied.

She looked at me pensively' "Maybe they did. Who knows?"

Chapter 7

Over the next three months or so, life bedded itself down into a predictable but acceptable groove.

I found myself evermore able to come to terms with life sans parents. I remained withdrawn and introverted (to some extent, I am to this very day), but I was evermore able to take the ups and downs of life without instantly wanting to run to my mother and father. I could even make it through the night without trauma.

School was a piece of cake. I found the work easy to do. As the most important requirement was an ability to remember what the teacher said, and as I had, and indeed still have (when I am not too juiced), a superb memory, I was forever getting top marks in my class. This, combined with my quiet and indrawn behaviour, got for me the reputation of being the class super-brain.

Best of all, I had found myself a couple of school friends who I converted into jazz fans. That happened as a result of my bringing them home and, over lemonade and bread pudding, introducing them to the sounds of Count Basie, Duke Ellington, Artie Shaw, Benny Goodman and Meade 'Lux' Lewis, the king of boogie-woogie pianists. They were especially impressed with Lewis's style of piano playing. Then to their wide-eyed astonishment (because I had never told anyone at school that I was even interested in music), I sat down at our Bluthner baby grand, and laid out a few choruses of boogie-woogie, which happened to be one of my musical specialities. As a direct result of their word of mouth, almost overnight, everyone in my class became aware that the 'brain' was also a hot-shot piano-man, or piano-boy to be more precise. All of a sudden I was getting invitations to parties.

The first I attended was at the home of one of my newly-converted -to-jazz friends, Peter Harris. Everyone seemed to be having a great time except me. Try as I might, I found it impossible to open up enough emotionally. I went through the motions of course, but, in truth, there was an invisible screen between me and life. I could see it going on in front of me, but was unable to reach out and touch it. I could and did laugh, talk and even joke with my school buddies, but all the while, it was as if I was in another dimension of time and space. I was ever the observer, never the participant.

And if that wasn't bad enough, Renee Cohen, my beloved Renee, whom I had been in love with since my first day at this school, came to the party with her boy friend. They sat across the room, she on his lap, her arm around his neck, kissing, nuzzling and licking the side of his neck, face and ear. Then she kissed him full on the mouth for so long that some of the boys started kidding her about it. "Look out for his tonsils," one of them shouted. "Be careful or he'll break all his fly buttons," another shouted, to massive raucous laughter from everyone. I too faked up some sort of a laugh, even though I was sick with jealousy and adolescent frustration.

Fortunately, by this time, I had learnt that by throwing myself totally into piano-playing, I could sublimate a great many of the traumas and sadness's of life. Also, by pretending that I had to stare intently at the keyboard, it got me away from what to me were the awful responsibilities of having to come face to face with people of my own age.. Of course, like most pianists, I didn't really have to look at the keys. I knew perfectly well where they were. But, as they say, the face is the mirror of the soul, and I was fearful of my face revealing what was really going on inside me. If for no other reason, that in itself was enough to be thankful for my pianistic abilities.

Over and above all that, the piano was holistically therapeutic for me. Pushing down those ivories was my passport and first-class ticket to another world, far removed from the self-induced loneliness and alienation of this one. Just a few jazz licks and there I was, instantly transported to the Golden Land of Hip Happiness.

Forcing myself at last, to look elsewhere other than at Renee Cohen and her writhing antics with her boyfriend, I noticed that there was a piano in the corner of the room. It was a large upright with family photos sitting on the top of it. Sitting on the closed lid was yet another 'necking' couple. (God, how old fashioned that word seems nowadays). I noticed how their feet were intertwined on the piano stool. At that moment they were engaged in a marathon kiss. I waited until they had to come up for air, before asking them if I could get to the piano. They looked at me strangely at first, before yielding their love-seat to me.

I opened the warmed piano lid and went into my carefully worked out arrangement of 'Over The Rainbow'. Slowly the hubbub and laughter died away, and a hush fell over the room as everyone started to gather around the piano. After I had closed down that tune with a long arpeggio, everyone clapped and cheered.

Jesus, I felt good! Wow! Somehow, the applause temporarily removed the invisible screen. It was as if, like Lewis Carroll's Alice, I had managed to break through the looking glass back into the real, fun-loving world with my school-friends.

Now I swung into my own interpretation of 'Honeysuckle Rose', which was loosely based on the Fats Waller and Joe Sullivan recordings, but with a few of my own improvised choruses thrown in. More enthusiastic applause. I decided to end my short recital with my latest piece de resistance, 'The Honky Tonk Train Blues', a number which has now become a boogie-woogie classic. When I finally rolled that old Honky-tonk train to a halt with a long, G-seventh double-handed tremolo, everybody went wild enough for me to be able to turn and face my audience with a sense of confidence and a feeling of belonging, something excitingly novel to me. Right in front of the clapping, whooping crowd, so close to my right hand, that I could have reached out and touched her, was my darling Renee Cohen. She was smiling and applauding as much as the rest of them, but I saw in her eyes a look of calculating re-assessment. It was as if she was thinking 'If this kid is going to be the school new social success, maybe I should give him a break after all'. But whatever thoughts she had about me at that moment had the shortest of shelf lives. Five minutes later, I found her outside on the carpeted staircase, lying on top of her boyfriend wildly kissing and necking.

In retrospect, I guess that the best and most curative thing for me at that time, and which might have lifted me out of my isolated and introverted world, once and for all, would have been having a girl friend, but no way and no how could I get one. Regardless of the fact that my piano playing was getting me invites to parties and teas with various members of my class, I could make no headway with my sex life. To start with, I had the hots for only one girl, and, after her amorous performance at Peter Harris's party with her thick-haired (probably with brains to match), boy friend, I had given up any thoughts of success with her.

There were other girls I fancied of course, but unfortunately, they were not interested in the attentions of Jake Silver, amateur pianist, professional nebbish. Due to my withdrawn remoteness, girls understandably, but quite wrongly concluded that I was antipathetic to any kind of emotional relationship with them. Being unaware at that time of the true reason for my failure with girls, I concluded that it had to bc that I was simply ugly and unattractive.

I can remember studying myself in front of my bedroom mirror in order to see if there was anything I could do to improve or maybe, disguise my appearance. I had grown quite a lot over the past year. I was now not more than a couple of inches off six feet tall. I had thick, black hair that grew a good three of four inches straight up from my scalp, before it would deign to bend over. It was also resistant to all known combs. Any attempts I might make to bring it under control invariably ended with a semi-toothless comb. I looked for the entire world like a tall, bony, pale-faced kid, standing underneath a misshapen busby. No wonder in the game of boy and girl, my score was big, fat, zero. But, as they say, you can get used to anything. At least, the boys in my class, probably because they were less sensitive in terms of human relationships, seemed unaware of my introversions and treated me as one of them.

Like I have already said, my life had settled itself into a reasonable pattern. Every night after dinner, I would practise the piano for two hours. Then, I would polish off my homework and, after that I would hit the sack – except for the two nights per week, when I had to visit our local Rabbi in order to learn my portion of the Torah for my coming Bar Mitzvah.

Rabbi Eli Korn was a large man of, I guess, about seventy years of age, although when you are just a thirteen year-old kid, most grown-ups look seventy years of age. As I remember him he had a square, grey beard and he always seemed to be wearing the same black suit. He might even have been good looking in his younger years. I guess he was what one would call an 'imposing' man: tall, with straight, aquiline nose, and a high, straight forehead, thick grey hair, and behind his round horn-rimmed spectacles, piercing, black eyes.

His study where I had to report for my instruction was in his apartment next door to the Synagogue. It was a long, oblong-shaped room, with floor-to-ceiling book-cases crammed with books of all sizes lining every wall. He usually sat in a large armchair which he completely filled with his big, heavy body.

I was always ushered into the Rabbi's study by Mrs. Engelmann, his housekeeper. She was a small, extremely thin woman of around fifty years of age. As I followed her down the narrow hallway that led to the study, I would always be fascinated by the jerky way she walked.. Aunt Sarah told me that it was due to some drunken Nazis smashing their way into her house in Munich, dousing her young husband with petrol, and then setting him on fire, leaving him to perish in screaming agony, whilst they gang-raped her. Then, presumably in order to slow down her efforts to get help, they broke both her arms and legs with their rifle-butts. That happened in 1938.

Friends did manage to smuggle her out of the Third Reich, to Paris in order to get her bones re-set, but it took more than a month to organise, by which time she had deteriorated to such a degree that the French surgeons were unable to return her to complete physical normality. After that, she came to Britain and moved in with a cousin who lived in Hull, a small town in the north of England. Suddenly, just a couple of months after her arrival, she suffered a complete mental breakdown as a result of the delayed shock of what had happened to her husband and herself. She was visited in the mental hospital every day by Rabbi Korn, who was then the local Rabbi for the area. He, more than anyone else, gave her the moral, spiritual and loving support which gave her reason to go on living. When the Rabbi decided to accept the Rabbiship of a Synagogue in north-east London, Clara Engelmann asked if she could stay with him as his housekeeper.

She would tap lightly on the study door three times. This would always be answered by the Rabbi's deep voice saying, "Come in Jacob, come in." As ever, he would be in his big armchair, always reading from a large, black leather-bound tome.

He was also the only person who insisted upon calling me by my biblical name. When I asked him to call me Jake like everyone else, he replied "There is no such name as Jake, except in those childish Hollywood cowboy films. But the name Jacob; that is a name to be proud of." Then, wagging his finger at me, he added, "And as I want you to grow up straight, smart and intelligent, not like some ignorant cowboy, I must address you as Jacob" Then he would point me over to his big old desk, where I would find a scroll of the Torah opened at my Bar Mitzvah portion.

My problem was that at that time, I had no regard either for the Torah, or Judaism, nor indeed, for God. As I sat at his desk, awaiting his instruction, he would always start with the same kind of banter.

"And how are you today, Jacob?"

"Okay, I think. About the same as ever." On one particular evening however, which was the third anniversary of my parent's death, I decided to tell him of my true feelings about what I saw as nothing more than a ridiculous ritual. So, as I sat staring at the strange, mystical looking, Hebrew lettering, I said: "Honestly Rabbi, I think all this Bar Mitzvah business is a waste of time. I really do."

I spoke to the back of his armchair, the Rabbi facing away from me. But I heard his deep-voiced reply.

"Jacob, everything in the Jewish faith has been tested for thousands of years. If it were a waste of time, as you claim, it would have fallen by the wayside a long time ago."

"But Rabbi, all this stuff I have been reading, about how His name shall be glorified and exalted and stuff like that. Why should I be expected to exalt and glorify a God who allowed my parents to die?"

Rabbi Korn got off his chair and turned it to face me. Then, he took off his glasses, polished them and sitting down again he said "Wrong Jacob. The allowing of Hitler into such a position of power was man made. There are some inherently evil people on this earth my boy. And when evil people get into positions of power, they create openings for their evil friends to obtain powerful positions also."

"So why doesn't God do something about it? He's supposed to be all-powerful. Why didn't God destroy Hitler and Sir Oswald Moseley? No, He chose instead to destroy my parents."

There was a deathly silence in the room. I suddenly became conscious of the regular tick coming from the large, ornate mantle-piece clock. I watched the Rabbi as he completed the cleaning of his spectacles, and their careful replacement on his broad face. Then he said.

"So. You hold God responsible for what happened to your dear parents. Is that it in a nutshell?"

"Well wasn't he? I mean, after all, if He can't stop bombs falling on nice, good people like my Mum and Dad, then I don't see any reason why I should honour and exalt him."

"You know young man; there are many holy men in this world who would have thrown you out of their offices for taking the Lord's name in vain, as you have this evening. But I am not going to do so. Because I realise that if I were a boy of your age and if what has happened to you had happened to me, I suppose I could possibly feel exactly the same as you do. But in order to provide you with an answer as to why God allowed your parents to be killed; well, I would have to know how God thinks. And I don't. No-one knows that."

"But you are a Rabbi," I persisted. "If you can't explain God's motives, then what is the point of being a Rabbi?" He fished out a large fob-watch from his waistcoat pocket, studied it and then put it back.

"You know, at this time we should be doing nothing but concentrating on your Bar Mitzvah portion. But I can see that you are really troubled by your relationship with God, and it is more important that we straighten that out, than it is for you to sing the entire Torah."

He got up again and crossed the room to drag a large, engraved, heavy old mahogany chair with leather covered armrests, to a position in front of, and not more than three feet away from, his armchair. As he sat down again, he said, whilst looking directly at me and pointing to the chair at the same time:

"I am going to do my best to help you. Come and sit over here."

In truth, I was not very interested in what he had to say. As I recall it, my feelings were, "My Aunt and Uncle are very anxious that I get my Bar Mitzvah. So nu, I'll be Bar Mitzvah. But to me it was just a load of religious clap-trap.

On the other hand, for no reason I can remember, I liked Rabbi Korn a helluva lot. Maybe it was because he was always kind, always patient with me. Of course, at that time, I was too much of a self-opiniated little shit to realise that the Rabbi was displaying the first and most important law of wisdom: humility.

As I moved over to the chair facing him, he leaned his large-boned frame back into his armchair, crossed one leg over the other and began:

"I told you a couple of minutes ago that I was incapable of divining God's motives, and you then asked me what was the point of my being a Rabbi. I am going to tell you. Because we cannot understand His motives, it does not mean that God doesn't speak to us. So now you are thinking, 'When and where does He do that?" Am I right?"

I nodded.

"I thought so. You are a bit young to understand the full import of what I am about to say, but you must try"

Even though I really wasn't that interested in whatever it was that he was about to tell me, I nevertheless adopted, what I hoped was an expression of serious interest, more out of my liking for him, than anything else. He never took his eyes off me as he spoke.

"In order that this world doesn't eventually destroy itself, a social order has to be created whereby man can live with man" He wagged his finger as he went on "And not only that. Man must learn to understand that in order to bring this social harmony about, he is no more than another jig-saw piece in the huge puzzle of life. Every animal, every plant, every tree; they are all part of the same total picture. We must learn to appreciate and treat with respect, even the earth beneath our feet, because it is all part of Life. Everything in nature is inter-dependent upon everything else. Unless we can learn to understand that, there is no hope for a properly civilised society. Now how and when did we come to know of all this? I will tell you. God told us through Moses. Whether or not Moses saw God in person, or whether an invisible God simply dictated it to him, like a boss giving a secretary a letter to write, who knows? And it isn't important anyway. All we do know is, that after his meeting or whatever it was, with God, Moses was able to give the world the most important and inspired piece of writing in the history of mankind. Out there in the desert, Moses wrote down six hundred and thirteen laws, which lay down exactly how Man shall live peaceably with Man and how mankind fits in to the totality of life on this planet. And that is what Judaism is all about Jacob. Because He chose to give His message to the world through the Jewish people, we have the enormous responsibility of setting the world an example by living within these God-given rules, or Commandments, call them what you will. Then please God, the others will follow our example and we will be able to create a world order in which the things that happened to your parents and millions of other good people, will never happen again.

Now, if you want to help bring this about, you must be a good Jew. To say, ' I don't believe in this or that' or, 'Why did God do or not do something or other' does not matter. You are a Jew whether you like it or not. And being a Jew, you have been chosen to take on the enormous responsibility of living within the rules given to us by God, through Moses. This table of Commandments is called the Torah, which comes from the Hebrew word Yarah, meaning to instruct. And it is my role as a Rabbi to teach you these laws and help you to live within them. And you can start right now by singing me that part of these laws which will be your Bar Mitzvah portion."

Just as I was about to start, he held his hand up: "And try to remember Jacob, just how important the words are that you are singing."

Chapter 8

MY BAR MITZVAH turned out to be a big social occasion. Someone or other had told a Jewish weekly paper about me. They ran an article headed, ' 13 year-old Orphan Piano Wizard'. Then it went on tell of how I lost my parents in the Blitz, 'when just eleven years old'. The article then went on to say how every day, I go through the few mementos of my parents, which is all that I have to remember them by, and how I cry myself to sleep every night. It ended, 'Jake's sole ambition is to join the RAF and become a fighter pilot in order to get his revenge on the Luftwaffe, for what they did to his parents'.

As to going through mementos of my parents every night, or any night for that matter, this was just a load of crap. For the first year after their deaths, even thinking about them was enough to send me spiralling down into a pit of despair, let alone examining tangible reminders of their deaths. The only thing I carried on my person to remind me of them, was my Father's cigarette lighter. After my Bar Mitzvah I also carried their photographs, because among my Bar Mitzvah presents was a leather wallet, with two oval sections cut out for this purpose.

But no matter how inaccurate the article in the 'Jewish Chronicle' was, and regardless of the fact that it was largely a work of fiction, it was enough to ensure a crowded Synagogue on the day. I also received double the warmth and enthusiasm my performance deserved. There was so much sympathy running for me that day, that I could have got up on the Bimah and sung 'Stop Your Ticklin' Jock' and got a rapturous reception.

Over the next week, there were photographs in the local newspaper and also the next issue of Jewish weekly of me shaking hands with Rabbi Korn, and another where I am standing between my beaming Uncle and Aunt. I was even interviewed on a BBC radio programme called 'In Town Tonight' or a similar title, in which I closed the show with my version of 'St. Louis Blues'.

But once again, my miserable motherfucker of a sprite must have decided that things were rolling along just a little bit too smoothly for young Jake Silver. Said Sprite knew just how important and indeed therapeutic, my piano-playing was to me, so he decided to put a stop to it—and this is how he did it.

As a result of my BBC appearance, I was invited to perform in a charity concert for war orphans. The Master of Ceremonies was Tommy Trinder, a very big stage and film star at the time. He got me to show the audience my Dad's cigarette lighter. Then, as he took it from me to place on the music rest of the piano I was about to play, he wise-cracked in his broad cockney "Ooh knows, maybe your Farver is 'ere to listen to you play. And after 'es 'eard you bangin' abaht, 'e might need a fag!" The audience fell about with laughter, just as if he had come up with a truly funny one-liner.

I began by playing 'The Man I Love' and then segued into Irving Berlin's 'All Alone', I did not want to play either of these tunes but both Mister Trinder and the concert promoter thought it a good idea, for pathetically obvious reasons.

It was during my next number, which was a quasi-serious version of 'All the Things You Are' that it happened.

I found myself unaccountably drawn to looking at my Father's cigarette lighter while I was playing. For reasons I cannot fathom to this very day, I was simply unable to drag my eyes away from it. It was as if I was hypnotised by that small, silver object sitting on the lowered music rest.

Suddenly, I found myself suffused by an odd, eerie feeling. All of a sudden, I knew my Father was very close by. I could even smell that so familiar tobacco aroma that always came off his clothes. Even odder, I was playing in a way unfamiliar to me. Everything was suddenly completely effortless for me. It was as if the responsibility for pressing down the right notes had been taken from me. I was also using chord shapes that my Father used but not me.

The smell of tobacco got stronger. It was now as it used to be, when I would stand next to him, watching him play, the inevitable cigarette perched on the ash-tray that was placed at the treble end of the piano where I would be standing, so that the cigarette smoke would be strong and acrid in my nostrils.

As I listened to my hands playing (for I was no longer in conscious control of them), I dragged my eyes away from the lighter, down to my hands. I suddenly became icy cold with shock at what I saw. They were not my hands. They were my father's hands, replete with the nicotine stains just below the top joints of forefinger and middle finger of the right hand. It was him playing, not me. The cold sweat of panic and fear poured down my face and soaked through my shirt. Medical experts have since assured me that I was suffering from some kind of a post-traumatic hallucination. That may be so. But at that time, it was as real to me as the rum I am drinking as I write this.

Blind with panic, I just stood up, slammed the piano lid shut, grabbed the lighter and ran. I ran off the stage, past an open-mouthed Tommy Trinder, past the evening-dressed man and woman who were waiting to go on after me, out of the stage door, and on and on, down and across Lord knows how many streets until I was too breathless to run any further. Only then with my heart pounding like a Buddy Rich drum solo, did I dare look at my hands again.

Thank God, they were once more my own.

But I could not stop myself from inwardly trembling. Whether or not I was the victim of my own tortured memories, or whether it was some kind of spiritual practical joke dreamed up out of the sick sense of humour of my spite-filled Sprite, I will never know. But on that night, as I wandered the rain-swept streets of West London, looking for a taxi, I was trembling from top to toe from the after-shock of something that had been very real to me indeed.

Due to my being asked to play at very short notice, and further due to the fact that Aunt Sarah and Uncle Harry were already committed to going to some big-time dinner at The Guildhall, my Uncle had given me enough money to travel to and from the concert by cab. Sitting in the back of the taxi, as I made my way home, still tense and perspiring from the memory of being metamorphosed into my Father, I tried to think the 'happening' through. Whether or not it was because of my mental state at the time, I do not know, but as I sat there in the back of the dark, unheated taxi, looking out at the drab, bombed-out, unlit streets, I slowly became sure it was my piano-playing that was at the root of it all. It acted like a Ouija board at a séance. I became sure that the piano was the medium through which my parents could be summoned, intentionally or otherwise. And, whilst the idea of having the means to summon up my late Father (so far, barring one highly debatable tinkle of laughter, my mother had not shown herself in any tangible way), was a thrilling one; the thought of being really taken over by him in some eerie, ectoplasmic way was a very different matter.

I of course still loved my parents very much indeed, and still suffered spells when I ached and yearned for them. But it was now over two years since their deaths, and I was developing my own individual personality, self-pitying and self-opiniated though it undoubtedly was. But I had come to believe by then that I could stand on my own two feet and face the world. Whilst I was still a victim of my complexes, I was also learning to be the master of them. And anyway, it is one thing to love ones parents: it is a totally different kind of jazz, when it comes to joining them in some Bram Stoker, 'undead' kind of way.

So, by the time the taxi driver broke into my thoughts with an, "Ere we are, young feller-me-lad," I had made up my mind.

I was going to have to give up playing the piano.

I knew how much I was going to suffer from this decision, but being alive and being me and not sharing my innate individuality with anyone else, even my own Father, seemed more important than playing jazz on the piano.

I came into the house to find that my Aunt and Uncle had not yet returned home from their big time social occasion, nor did they do so until after I had gone to bed. So it was not until the next morning that I saw Aunt Sarah.

I decided not to tell them anything about my out-of-body experience the previous night. To start with, they may have concluded that I was still in need of psychiatric help and I had had my fill of that kind of schtick. I also reasoned that as I was not going to play the piano any more, the likelihood of any recurrence was extremely remote.

"So how did it go? Were you a big success?" she asked while pouring me the inevitable large, steaming cup of tea. I was about to reply when she yelled, "Olga, make some French toast for my maestro nephew will you please? Then, as she handed me the tea she said "So nu, why aren't you answering me? How did it go?"

"It was fine," I mumbled.

And how was that Tommy Trinder? He's supposed to be such a big shot, but I think he's stinks.

"He was okay."

Olga wheeled in the usual Sunday breakfast fare on the two-tiered trolley and after manoeuvring it as close to the table as possible, went out of the room.

"Where's Uncle?" I asked, as I watched my Aunt transfer the breakfast food, from the trolley to the table.

"He's already eaten and gone out to meet somebody." As she put the scrambled egg in front of me she said, "My, you're talkative this morning. You are asked to play at an important charity, with all the gunsa muchas (which is Yiddish for big shots), of show business appearing, and all I can get out of you is a half a dozen syllables, and even they are mumbled."

"It was good. It was a big success. Honest."

She watched me silently and carefully for a while as I ate, before deciding to give me the benefit of the doubt:

"Maybe you're a bit tired. You'll tell me later, when you feel more like it. Alright?"

"Yeah fine" I said, trying to hide the relief that I was feeling at her not giving me the expected third degree.

"Now let me tell you about our fency-shmency night." I feigned a greater interest than I actually felt, as she told me about her meeting with the guests of honour, the Duke and Duchess of somewhere. "They came over to speak to your Uncle and me, while we were all having drinks before going in to the main hall for our meal" she explained.

I found myself watching how her eyes danced with amusement as she sat, elbows on the table, her cheeks resting upon her fisted hands, as she recounted the encounter.

"He had such a 'faw-faw' way of speaking, you could barely understand a bloomin' word the man was saying. And as for her, she really got my back up. She spoke to me, and everyone else for that matter, as if we were her personal servants, the stuck-up bitch. Do you know what she said to me?"

As my mouth was full with toast and tea, I just shook my head.

"She stared through her lorgnette at the Mogan Dovid on the gold chain I always wear around my neck. 'Oh' she said, 'Isn't that something Jews wear?' I told her it was called a Star of David. 'David' she repeated 'Wasn't he the fellow who murdered someone or other in the Bible?' 'Yes, your Highness," I said. He slew Goliath, an evil man, twice David's height and three times his weight. But, King David also built the city of Jerusalem.'

`Are you a Jew?' she asked me.

`Of course', I said, and I fingered my Mogan Dovid as I said it. Then guess what she did?

"What did she do?" I asked.

"She picked up her lorgnette again which she had dangling around her scrawny neck, and leaned forward to examine my Mogan Dovid. Then she raised up the damned thing to examine my face, like I was some sort of a specimen you kept under glass or something. And then, after she had completed her examination, she suddenly straightened up and said, 'Hmm.' Believe me Jake, that is all she said. And then, without another word, she turned her back to me and walked over to another group and started talking to them. I swear it was for all the world, like she had never seen a real, live, Jew close up before, and now having met one, she chose to study me like I was some sort of a rare, insect or something. And after that," she snapped her fingers, "She just dismissed me from her mind. Bloody stuck-up cow"

I put down my tea cup. "I would have thought, knowing you, that you would have given her a bit of a mouthful for treating you that way, Duchess or no Duchess." My mind was actually much more involved with my own troubles, regarding what had happened the previous evening, but by pretending an active interest in my Aunt's story, I was hoping to put off the inevitable grilling I felt sure I was not very far away.

"I was just about to go over to her and give her a piece of my mind, but your Uncle stopped me. He whispered in my ear 'Don't worry Sarah. That little insult will cost them a couple thousand quid'. Of course I asked him how? He told me that through one of his Christian sounding companies, I think it's called Henderson and Smedley Antiques, or something equally as daft, he is selling the Duke an antique diamond and emerald bracelet. 'I'll just add two thou' to the price"

"But she still insulted you," I persisted, determined to keep the topic of our conversation on her problems and off mine.

As she stood up to clear the now emptied plates back on to the trolley, she said "Listen boychik, at two thousand pounds an insult, believe me, she can insult me all day long."

"Thanks for breakfast Auntie," I said as I stood up. Now I am going back upstairs to do my homework. Can you see to it that I'm not interrupted for a couple of hours?"

She gave me a big wet kiss on my cheek. "Work in good health my darling I've got to phone my friends now and tell them about last night.

And so began a new routine for me. It also signalled the beginning of a period of my life where happiness or joy was as foreign to me as the planet Mars. On a good day, all I felt was pretty miserable. On a bad one, well, if you have seen Munsch's painting "The Scream," you'll know what I mean when I say I felt like the screamer! On my very worst days, I seriously considered suicide as the only way out.

In general, I forced myself to concentrate on schoolwork, which resulted in my always being the top of my class. But the depressing aura of introversion that hung around me caused me not only to be shunned by girls. It even altered the chemistry of my relationships with my male school friends. These were rapidly being scaled down to casual acquaintanceships, which I was powerless to do anything about. Now that I no longer played the piano, the invites to parties or other social occasions dried up. So, the hours outside school were spent either doing homework, or reading books on my new-found favourite subject, which was Modern History, This had been brought about by a need to try to understand how my parent's killer, Adolf Hitler, had been allowed to become so powerful in the world.

Of course I tried very hard to disguise my feelings from my Aunt and Uncle. And I reckoned at the time that I had succeeded, because than treated me as if I was perfectly normal and healthy. They even accepted without a word, my excuse for not playing the piano anymore, namely that doing my school homework was more important and that there was so much of it now, I had no time for playing. As I think back on it now, I reckon it was quite simply that not knowing what to do about my sudden mood-shifts and my isolating myself in my bedroom for hours on end, they just decided to do nothing and see if I could dig myself out of my doldrums.

Finally, I could not take it any more. I went back to playing the piano again. As I sat down on the piano stool that first time, just staring at those black and white keys, I knew that I did not give a shit whether my Mother, Father, or even Jesus Christ tried to get inside my body. I was back with my darling piano again. And this time nothing will part us ever again.

Now that I was back to playing every evening after school again, my Aunt decided to get me a piano teacher. So every Sunday morning, was spent with me being forced to do finger exercises and play terrible bits of corny music, with similarly corny names like: 'Dancing In The Daffodils', or, 'The Waterfall', etc. Finally, out of desperation, I asked her if I could play something a little more interesting, as I was losing interest in her piano lessons. She then let me have a go at playing some Bach two part inventions, on condition that if they turned out to be beyond my ability, I would go back to her original regime. At first, I found them almost impossibly difficult. But within three months or so, I was able to get through them all with a reasonable degree of fluency. By the time a year had passed, I was able to play not only the Bach two part inventions, but also, his three part inventions, as well as quite a few Chopin Nocturnes and Mazurkas.

After practising the pieces I had to have ready for my teacher, I would spend another hour or so working on how to incorporate the musical inspirations of these composers into my jazz playing. One thing I realised only too clearly as I struggled to include Bach's contrapuntal approach and Chopin's hugely technical compositions into my jazz improvisations; if either of them had played jazz piano, even the mighty Art Tatum would have had to look out for his crown.

Chapter 9

By the time I was seventeen, I had matriculated with very high marks, my piano playing had improved enormously, and, now that the war was over, my cousin Ivan was home and naturally, wanted his room back. So it was arranged that I would go to Durham University.

Of course, it wasn't as simple as that. Nothing ever is for me. In fact, I had to work damned hard to get them to let me go.

By this time, things had reached a stage where I was desperate to get away and be on my own. Even though I was well through the early traumatic stage, the effect of the death of my parents had left me the legacy of a mental attitude which did not seem to improve with my growing maturity. I had become a kind of schizoid. I could laugh; I could experience anger and love. Indeed, if I remember rightly, I exhibited all the usual ups and downs that every seventeen year-old experiences. Or, rather, half of me did. The other half of my psyche just seemed to look on, coldly, unemotionally and unconcernedly.

And it wasn't always a fifty-fifty division. Sometimes the ice-cold, totally negative, Zombie-like side took over totally. When that happened, I just wanted to be alone to sleep or walk the streets, often for hours on end.

At other times, usually when I was alone, playing my beloved piano, and playing really well (which happened too infrequently), the positive, zestful, ebullient, seventeen year-old kid would take over completely, and I would feel great and whole. And it didn't end when I got up from the piano. This positive half of me could, and did dominate, often for hours on end.

But, even when I was feeling pretty good I was ever aware of that cold, emotionless other side of me lurking in the shadows of my inner self, watching the other half of me go through the motions of normality, seemingly waiting for the opportunity to take me over.

Most difficult of all was hiding my real self (or maybe, selves), from everybody, especially Aunt Sarah and Uncle Harry and, hardest of all, Ivan. And the continual strain of trying to pretend that I was just like them, and that everything was just Jake (to make a lousy pun), was becoming an evermore onerous burden. Should I drop my guard for even a moment and let the negative side of me show out, a worried frown would immediately crease my Auntie's face and she would come over to me and looking deeply into my eyes, say in a voice dripping with sympathy and worry; something like "Are you alright my darling?" Which was a silly question, because the sheer asking of it, meant that she had already decided that I was not alright. So whatever I replied, she would busily and infuriatingly try to make me feel better. She could or would not understand that when I was in this state of mind, a cheerful, "I know, I'll make you a lovely cup of tea and give you a slab of bread pudding. Jake darling," had the exact opposite effect to the one she intended. Sometimes, when I was clever enough to find an excuse to get out of the room, and go upstairs to my (and now Ivan's) bedroom, and try to drag the positive side of my personality to the fore, by sitting as still as I could by the window just watching life go on in the street outside, Aunt Sarah, should she come into the bedroom for some reason and find me doing so, would invariably interpret it as, "Oh, my God, you look so sad and lonely sitting there." Even while I was objecting, she would be shouting to Ivan, "Ivan, come and talk to your cousin. You've been away for two years and you don't even want to talk to your cousin who's missed you so much." Then Ivan would have to stop whatever he was doing and reluctantly join me for a forced conversation that neither of us needed, nor wanted.

Worse still was my awareness that my Aunt was trying so hard to keep me happy and even tempered. Even when I was bursting with annoyance at her for trying to force me in a direction which was anathema to me because of my moodiness at that time, I had to bottle it up because I knew that she was genuinely trying to help me, even though she was getting it abysmally and irritatingly wrong.

So when it was decided that I should go to University, I jumped at the chance. The problem was, that post 1945 and the war being over, many young men were returning from their stint in the armed forces, intent on improving their lot by taking higher education courses. This resulted in a large and apparently unexpected influx of new applicants for university places.. So the nearest higher educational facility that had any room for someone wishing to study Modern History was Durham University, which for some unfathomable reason was not in the county of Durham, but in Newcastle upon Tyne in the county of Northumberland, two hundred and eighty-odd miles north of London. This was a thrilling thought for me. It meant that at last, I would be far enough away from this loving, luxurious suffocation to do my own thing, whatever that was.

My letter of acceptance from the University was greeted by my Aunt with a flat,"Don't be ridiculous! Of course you are not going there. How could you take care of yourself? You've never washed or ironed a shirt in your life. And who is going to cook good kosher food for you, up there in the middle of nowhere?" Take my advice, learn the jewellery trade. Let your Uncle teach you."

But at that time, the most important thing in my life overriding all else, was the desperate necessity to get away and be left to do my own thing. I tried everything I could think of, to persuade my Aunt to let me go to Durham University. (My Aunt was the only real obstacle in my way. Uncle Harry and Ivan, whilst they weren't exactly ecstatic at the thought of my being so very far away, were nevertheless comfortable with it. But they weren't so dumb as to openly back me against the iron-willed authority of 'She Who Must Be Obeyed'.

I developed what seemed to be a hundred absolutely brilliant reasons why I should be allowed to go, but all were knocked down by my Aunt. "You are not going anywhere where I can't look after you, and that is final." She seemed unshakeable in her crazy belief that I would either starve to death or walk around looking like a tramp, in dirty unpressed clothes, and then get arrested for being a vagrant. Then, she would press her cheeks with both hands, like 'Cuddles' Zakall used to do in the movies, and wail, "Oh my God, just think of the shame of it; my darling nephew lying in jail, being mistaken for a tramp!"

And then, quite by chance, I found how to get my way. It was quite simple really. The idea came to me one rain-drenched Sunday morning. Ivan had gone diamond buying with his father when the plan hit me. I immediately went down stairs to waylay my Aunt in the kitchen where she was busy with the Sunday lunch.

Casually crunching a biscuit I found on the tea trolley, which must have been left over from her mid-morning tea ritual, I said, in a calm voice: "Y'know Auntie, the more I think about it, the more I realise that I am not cut out for academic life."

"So," she said, with quiet satisfaction, "You've at last given up all that crazy nonsense of going off to some f'drekische town in the middle of nowhere to learn about modern history" She spat out the words 'Modern History' with all the contempt she could muster.

"I am glad to see that you are at last coming to your senses."

"Yes," I said, "I've decided to become a professional jazz pianist."

And I really meant it. I had to find more time to be on my own and be responsible for my own actions. So, I reckoned, if I cannot go to University, and by then I had given up all hope of changing my Aunt's mind, the next best thing was to try and get a job in order to earn enough money to allow me to live on my own.

What I was too young to understand at that time, was the great store set by all Jewish families on the importance of education. Admittedly, the thing was to study to become primarily a doctor or a lawyer, or secondarily, an accountant. But even if a Jewish boy decided to read something as far out and alien to a Jewish family as English, or even Modern History yet, well it was better than nothing. At the end you still come out with a degree, right? So Mamma can still brag about her prince of a son who is not only the handsomest thing on two legs, but also has A DEGREE.

Aunt Sarah put down her cup and staring at me, her eyes a mixture of rage and horror, said in a voice of quiet, frightening menace:

"What do you mean; you are going to be a jazz pianist?"

"What do you mean saying what do I mean? If I can't study Modern History, then I am going to become a jazz pianist. That's what I mean." I kept my eyes focussed firmly on her hands cutting up the chicken. I may have had some courage, but I didn't have quite enough to look her straight in the face.

She put the carving knife down excessively carefully. This was followed by a terrible silence while she slowly and carefully smoothed down her pinafore. Then the storm broke.

"Is this what I brought you up for? Is it not enough that I worked my fingers to the bone, sweating and slaving, so that my darling younger sister in heaven, olava scholem, can say 'Well done Sarah, my dearest sister. I know how you have sweated and slaved to raise my son for me. I know what you have gone through to make sure he is trained to live a decent, respectable Jewish life'." As she said these words, she held her hands as if in prayer, her gaze concentrated heavenward. Then she lowered her eyes to glare angrily at me.

"And now" she said, pointing at me with her stubby little forefinger. "You not only break my heart, but also the heart of your dear Mother in heaven by having the chutzpah to say to me that you are going to throw everything away to sit pounding out a lot of nonsense in some disgusting gin-swigging and God knows what else, night club. This is a life for a nice Jewish boy?"

I was about to reply, but she would not let me.

"And how much money will you earn being a piano tinkler? Flumpence a week, that's what you'll earn. And tell me, what nice Jewish girl will want to marry a boy who is up all night playing for a load of drunks and curuvers?" (In case you don't know, 'curuver' is the Yiddish word for prostitute). This was my opening. I was not at all impressed by her 'your-dearest-mother-in-heaven' jazz. She had used that too many times in the past. Almost every time she wanted me to do something I did not want to do, she had pulled that gag. But here was the opening, and I was going to exploit it.

"So what else can I do?" I moaned. You won't let me study and now you won't let me earn a living the only way I know how." I tried to look as sad as I could.

A long silence went by, before she said "If I let you go to that fershtunken University in that Godforsaken town, will you promise to give up all this silly rubbish about becoming a jazz pianist?"

"Yes," I said, hoping that I was not revealing by any look or inflection in my voice the glow of triumph that was now starting to course through my entire body.

"Gott sedanken," she sighed. "At least with a University degree, I can find you a nice well-off Jewish girl to marry and settle down with."

And that is how it was that a few of months later, I found myself, heart thumping with excitement, on the train to Newcastle-upon-Tyne. I was even travelling first class, thanks to the largesse of my Uncle, who, just as I was boarding the train also slipped a couple of five-pound notes into the top pocket of my best blue, pinstripe suit, which I was wearing for the trip, saying conspiratorially as he did so "Don't tell your Aunt Sarah"

"Thank you very much," I replied as co-conspiratorially as I could. This was after an incredibly long fifteen minutes of standing on the cold, filthy, Kings Cross station platform, assuring a red-eyed, tearful Aunt Sarah that I would keep my promise to write and telephone at least once a week. For the umpteenth time she told me that I can reverse the phone charges if I like, "But I must hear your voice once a week." Then there was the man-to-man handshaking from Ivan: "Don't forget kid, if you are not happy up there, just jump on a train and come home." Then he added in a brave but hopeless attempt to lighten the tense and worried atmosphere that hung in a pall over us; "After all, I've put up with you for all these years, so a few more won't kill me."

I affected a smile whilst trying to at the same time to shuffle imperceptibly backwards towards the train. Then Aunt Sarah, in a voice choked and hoarse from crying chimed in with "And I want to know what your room is like and what you are eating every day."

"Don't worry about me Auntie" I said cheerfully "In any case you've given me enough sandwiches to last me for the first week at least."

Uncle Harry who had bought me a new shaving kit and expensive hair brush as a going away present, shook my hand and, to my considerable embarrassment, gave me a sudden, short bear hug, saying as he released me, "let me have your address as soon as you can, so that I can post you some money each week." And then with a warning wagging finger; "And when you get it, keep it safe, so that you don't lose it. And one last thing," he put his hand on my shoulder," If you get into any trouble, let me know immediately. Don't try to handle it yourself."

At that moment, as I angled my eyes down to look at them (I was by then, just over six feet, a good five inches taller than any of them), I suddenly realised just how much I had grown to love these three people

"I'd better get on board" I said, bending down to pick up my two cases, in order to hide my face and thus my feelings from them. I have since learned the hard way, that when people who love each other have to part, the most painless way to do it is to just kiss or something, and split. If you don't, the atmosphere gradually becomes unbearable as you stand by the train or plane just staring and smiling at each other, everything having already been said. But I was not aware of it on that chilly October morning and neither were they. So after a scramble between Uncle Harry, Ivan and myself over who will carry my bags on to the train, and after they were safely stowed on the rack above my head, and after my Uncle had given me his 'Times' to read, they reluctantly got off the train, but still did not go. Instead they stood outside my carriage smiling at me in that I'm-smiling-even-though-my-heart-is-breaking way that people do when their loved ones are off to the front line or about to risk their necks in some worthwhile, but foolhardy endeavour.

And so we stared and blew kisses and after more stern, but mimed instructions to me to keep in regular contact, the pointless, wordless, interplay was thankfully broken up by the guard's shrill whistle. As the train slowly started to shunt and puff its way along the platform and out of the station, the last words I heard Aunt Sarah shout through the ever growing distance between us was, "We love you very much." I poked my head out of the train window and waved to them, standing in a little knot, looking for some reason, lonelier than me, as they waved back, until the train took a half-bend and they were no more.

I must admit that as I settled back in my seat, my sense of elation and excitement was now intermingled with a feeling of missing them and just a little of insecurity. But it soon passed. I was at last, on my own to do as I pleased. I took down one of my two cases from the rack above me, and got out the book I had chosen to help me with my studies, or so I thought at the time. I recall it was a book about the rise of Nazism in Germany, although I can no longer remember the title or the author.

But I could not concentrate on it. The even mix of excitement and trepidation wiped out any thoughts of Hitler and the Nazis. From this moment on I realised, I was no longer a boy, but a young man. I was wearing my new suit and I had twenty pounds including the tenner that Uncle Harry had pushed into my top pocket.

And so Jake Silver, sophisticated young man-about-town, left his book on his seat and picking up his London Times, sauntered down to the dining car for his mid-morning coffee and cake.

"And what can I get for you young sir?" The waiter was an oldish man, thin, wrinkled and balding and possessed of a strong cockney accent.

After ordering my coffee and cake I proceeded to peruse my newspaper, just like a real grown-up.

"There you are sir. Coffee and cake just like you ordered." I watched the waiter as he carefully laid out the cup, the saucer, the coffee pot, the milk jug, the sugar and finally the plate carrying the thick slice of Dundee cake.

"That'll be two and six please" the waiter said.

I took one of the five pound notes out of my pocket and gave it to him. He looked at the note with horror. "I ain't got change for that. Ain't cha got nuffink smaller?

"I'm afraid not" I said, in my best grown-up voice.

Taking the five pound note he said, "Cor!" while throwing his eyes up to heaven at the same time, before hurrying off down the lurching carriage to organise my change. I poured my coffee and whilst munching on a piece of cake tried to read 'The Times' like real grown-ups do, but I found it too utterly boring and dull. So I stared out of the window, but all there was to look at was the monotonously endless, drab-green grassland, with what to my city boy's eyes looked like the same set of cows occupying every field. I remember thinking, 'God what a lousy life it must be for a cattle farmer'. In fact, I still do.

Having quickly lost interest in the boring cow-ridden landscape, I took to studying my first-class fellow-passengers. There were not more than a dozen of them in the entire long carriage. Opposite me were four army officers who, going by the array of stars and crowns and crossed batons on their shoulders, were very senior officers indeed. They were all drinking brandy and they were all very seriously pissed.

I shifted my gaze on to the couple sitting two tables further up. This was a far more interesting scene. The man seemed to me to be about sixty years of age. He had a fat belly and a thick red neck supporting a large, florid face, topped off with thin, flaxen hair combed sideways across his broad cranium. He seemed to be unable take his rheumy, bloodshot eyes off his companion's cleavage. She was, I guess, about thirty-five, going on nineteen, heavily made up, with long, dyed red hair set into a sort of Rita Hayworth-like hairstyle. They were sipping champagne, that is, when she wasn't kissing him on his nose, mouth, or leaning right over to kiss and tongue the ear farthest from her, thus bringing her beautiful, big boobs to within an inch of his face. Every so often he would whisper something in her ear which would cause him to roar with laughter, and her to feign shock, followed by peals of girlish giggles. I just could not get over the way she looked into the watery, bloodshot eyes of this fat, old, unattractive man, with love and adoration all over her slightly hard but not unattractive face. With tits like she had, she could certainly have done a lot better than this old fart. I was even fancying her (or maybe just her tits) myself.

The waiter came back with my change. As he banged it down on the table in front of me, he said in a harassed voice; "'ere's yer change. Four pahnd seventeen and six." He stood next to me, swaying, as the train, now at full speed, rocked this way and that. Whilst I was carefully counting it, fully conscious of my Uncle's admonition to be careful with my money, one of the officers across the way, suddenly remembered that he had ordered some more brandies that had not yet arrived.

"Wherzh our demned brandy, you little cockney toad?" He had an angry red face, with eyes to match.

"I'm so sorry generule, I've 'ad to go all over the train to get 'is change."

Now, having checked the money that the waiter had slammed down on my table and found it to be correct, I put it all in my pocket, leaving a sixpence for a tip.

"Is tha' it?" The waiter said, pretending shocked surprise.

I nodded.

He put the small, silver coin into the palm of his hand, looked at it in disgust, and again said, "Cor!," and again flung his eyes heavenwards as he did so. Then, he hurried off to get the brandies for the heavily-oiled officers over the way.

As I looked across at the four sozzled, senior officers, one of them belched very suddenly and very loudly, to hoots of laughter from the other three. Then one of them bet him a pound he couldn't belch the word 'Bulawayo', to even more guffaws from them all. My attention was drawn back to Fatso, the Lover-boy, who at that moment was trying to tickle his girl-friends nipples with a rolled-up five pound note. She was pretending to fend him off amidst her peals and his roars of laughter. I found myself coming round to thinking that if this is how grow-ups behave, then I was not yet ready for adulthood. I decided that I preferred the tranquillity of my own carriage. I got up and folded the paper, ready to take my leave. As I was doing so, my eye latched on to the heading above a small article at the bottom of the page. It read:

> **Shares fall on Founder's death**
> Late last night, it was announced that Mr. Chaim Rabinowitz, founder and Chairman of Town Crier Shoes, had died peacefully in his sleep. Mister Rabinowitz had been rushed to hospital the day before, after suffering a heart attack in his office. Shares in 'Town Crier Shoes' fell by sixpence on the announcement of his death.'

I was shocked and sickened by the news. Thinking about him as I sat alone in my carriage, I became saddened and not a little outraged that such a kind, good, and decent man, who had overcome such tragedies and tribulations, could be valued at sixpence a share! I felt a deep sense of revulsion that I was part of a system so damnably ravening, so utterly possessed by Mammon that even human life is valued, or rather, devalued, in monetary terms. It seemed so long ago since I had written my letter to him begging for a job overseas to which he never replied.

Chapter 10

ABOUT TEN MINUTES OUTSIDE Newcastle-upon Tyne, we ran into a torrential rainstorm. I got out my showerproof which had been carefully folded underneath the packets of sandwiches which Aunt Sarah had squeezed into every available corner of my suitcase. As I put it on I could not help but notice that I now possessed a raincoat smelling faintly of smoked salmon and rye bread.

There was now one other passenger in the carriage with me. He had joined the train at Darlington, for the last leg of the journey. This man was quite clearly a gentleman of substance, judging by his immaculate Saville Row-cut dark brown suit, his beige, cut-away collar shirt, his green and brown silk tie and crocodile-skin ankle boots.

As the train slowly creaked and grumbled its way across the Tyne Bridge, he got to his feet to put on the fleecy-lined weather-proof that had been resting on the unoccupied seat next to him. I watched him as he carefully buttoned it right up to the neck.

"You look very well prepared for the weather," I said to him for no particular reason other than it was what I thought grown-ups did on trains. He looked at me blankly as I sat there in my light raincoat, designed for spring showers in London.

"Have you ever been to Newcastle before?" he asked. He spoke in a huntin' shootin' and fishin' 'eccent' that goes with having a country seat and all that jazz.

"No. I've never actually been of north London before, I'm afraid." I replied.

As he reached up to the luggage rack to take down his black leather overnight bag, he said quietly:

"I rather thought not." Then sliding open the carriage door, he disappeared down the train.

In London, the month of October is viewed as early autumn. In Newcastle, on this afternoon of admittedly the last week in the month, it was akin to the kind of weather you get in Chicago in February! Now I knew what the toff on the train meant. I had no sooner got both my feet onto the platform before being struck by a blast from an icy cold, flat, bleak wind, the force of which made my eyes run and my face sting. It did not take me long to realise that I needn't have bothered to have brought along my raincoat. This vicious razor blade of a wind forced the fine, ice-cold, needles of rain straight through it, and on through my new blue suit, my shirt and even my underwear. And that was even before I had reached the taxi-rank that stood in the forecourt of the station! All I can remember now of that first sight of Newcastle, as I stood shivering in the taxi queue was of being surrounded by grey granite buildings, as bleak and soulless as the weather.

Twenty teeth-chattering, drenching, miserable minutes later I finally got to the head of the taxi queue, to board the very next cab that came along., It turned out to be an unheated 1938 Wolsey saloon car, masquerading as a taxi. As I tumbled into the musty smelling back seat, hugging my suitcase tightly to my body in a fruitless attempt to gain some warmth from it, I told the driver to take me to the University. No sooner had we set off than he said to me:

"Weer yer from lake?"

"London," I replied through my half-frozen lips.

He studied me for a while through his rear-view mirror, as I sat shivering and huddling over my suitcase.

"Aye," he said. "It's a good bit coowalder oop heyah than it is doon sooth."

It took me a while to work out what he had said, but after I had done so, I replied "A good bit colder? I've never been so cold in my life." Even as I was speaking, I was wondering if he was having as much trouble understanding my accent as I was having with his.

"Divn't worry, me bonny lad, you'll get used to it." He said cheerily.

I fished out of my inside jacket pocket the now soggy piece of paper that had the address of the main entrance of the University written upon it.

"I have to get to the main entrance, Kings College, College Street, near the Haymarket," I said.

"Ah naw wheer it is man. Divn't bother on." He said as he cleared the condensation from the windscreen with a dirty, nicotine-stained hand.

Ten shivering minutes later I was walking through the main portals of Kings College. I must have looked like shit as I approached the porters lodge.

I know I felt like it. The residual rainwater, trapped in my thick thatch of hair was now running simultaneously down my face and the back of my neck. My shirt, so immaculately pressed by Olga, was now just a soggy white rag with pink undertones due to it being stuck to my skin. My raincoat was dripping water straight down into my shoes, so that I squelched as I walked.

Surprisingly, the porter seemed completely oblivious of my soaked-through ice-man-cometh condition. After checking and finding my name on the clip-board he had in front of him, he said as he handed me a printed form, "Fill that in and take it to the Registrars office over there." He pointed to an office door with 'Registrars Office' printed on it.

Having filled it in to the satisfaction of the middle-aged lady behind the counter in the Registrars Office, she wrote something down on a card and then something else on a piece of headed stationery. Handing them to me she said, "This is the address of your lodgings and this is your appointment card to meet your Modern History tutor, tomorrow morning at nine-fifteen. Be at the porters lodge at ten past and someone will take you Doctor Cabot-Smith's study.

As I was squelching out of the door she said to my back in a bright cheery voice, "And welcome to Kings College."

The porter told me how to find the address of my lodgings. After having drawn me a map showing how to get there, he looked me up and down before saying, "But before you go lad, you look like you need to warm yourself up with a cup of tea or something," and he directed me to 'The Union' which turned out to be the central meeting place for the students.

It was a noisy and buzzing room alive with the energy and excitement typical of a first day of term. I pushed and squelched my way through the laughing and yelling-to-one-another crowd, up to the bar, and got myself a large, over-strong mug of tea, served from a huge metal teapot by a skinny scrag of a girl, who had a local accent thick enough to cut with a knife.

"Wun cuppah tea. That's lake tuppence pet," she said as she pushed the steaming hot mug across the counter to me. I was tempted to say, 'It's not like twopence pet. It IS twopence pet!' but I said nothing. I was far too wet and miserable to be bothered with pointless banter. And so clutching my big suitcase with one hand, whilst holding under my arm the smaller bag full of Aunt Sarah's probably by now soggy, rain soaked sandwiches whilst carrying the steaming mug of tea in the other, I pushed and jostled my way to a small, unoccupied table in a corner of the room. I was aware that students of both sexes were looking across at me, but I refused to make any eye contact with them, until finally, they lost interest.

Even now, in retrospect, I cannot say with any certainty why I did not wish to get involved in this seemingly happy social scene. I know it was due in part, to the fact that I saw myself as ugly and therefore utterly resistible to people of my own age. But being soaking wet, freezing cold and feeling as much at home as an alien from another planet didn't help very much either. So I just sat there sipping my tea, secretly digging the girls I found attractive and enjoying the feeling of warmth returning to my limbs.

I drained the last dregs of my tea, and then checked my watch. It was half past five. I decided it was time to check into my new residence, before it got too dark, and I get myself lost in this grey, miserably depressing town.

As I set out for my new lodgings I noticed that the rain had ceased. Unfortunately, the ice-cold, gusting gale had not. So by the time I found my new 'home' my already soaking clothes had all but turned to ice on my body leaving me trembling with the cold.

My so-called 'Hall of Residence' turned out to be a very ordinary three-storeyed terrace house in a rather grubby, run-down side street. I found the front door ajar, so I went in to find myself in a narrow, depressingly dimly lit, hallway. Climbing up against the left wall was a staircase and straight ahead was, I guessed, a kitchen, because there were a few boys in there, drinking some beverage or other, as they laughed and chatted together. On the right hand wall, half way between the kitchen and the front door was a green-painted door with a plaque on it saying 'Caretaker. Private.' Next to this door, and thumb-tacked to the wall, was a typed piece of paper, naming the new occupants together with their room and floor numbers.

My room was on the first floor. I immediately climbed the creaky, threadbare-carpeted staircase to unpack and settle in. I noticed that there were four rooms on this floor, including my own. Each door had fixed at eye-level, two four-inch parallel slats of wood set about six inches apart, each bearing the name of the occupant.. Above, was a small sliding panel which, if slid one way, revealed the words 'Not In'.

My room turned out to be the first one, as you turned right at the top of the stairs. I cannot describe what a kick I got out of seeing my name up there on the door. To a visitor, it read simply, 'J.Silver'. But to me it said 'J.Silver, grown-up individual, able to stand on his own two feet and make his own decisions'.

I tried the door and finding it unlocked went in. My new 'home' was a room about twelve feet square. Against the wall to my left was an old writing table with chair to match. They were both made out of deal or pine wood, and the ink-stains and cigarette burns all over the table's surface evidenced the heaven-knows-how-many students who must have previously stayed here. Set in the middle of it was a small table-lamp with a pink, torn, clip-on lampshade. Beyond the table and next to the narrow bed that ran down the far wall, was a small dark wood, cupboard, with double doors at the bottom and a draw above. On top of it was a Bible with my door key lying on its tea-stained and cigarette burnt leather cover. The wall opposite the door comprised an ill-fitting sash window which rattled and moaned every time the wind gusted. The window ledge was dripping water from the rain which had started up again, adding to the puddle that was already there. To the left of the window, at the foot of the bed, was a decrepit, old (and I do mean old), chipped pink china wash basin with tall, matching jug. It was set on top of brown, boxwood, chest of drawers. Against the wall to my right was a two bar electric fire and next to it, a wardrobe that looked like it had been rescued, none too carefully, from rubbish dump. On the floor, in the middle of the room, was a threadbare old rug, upon which sat an armchair, with the tapestry armrests worn through to the wooden frame and about two inches of a rusted spring spiralling up through the worn-out, flattened cushion on its seat. Sitting on it could give you splinters and haemorrhoids at the same time! The flowered wallpaper was old, stained and faded, which was in a way fortunate, because when in the full flower of its newness, wallpaper such as this could easily drive a fellow to drink and maybe even worse! The room was 'illuminated' (if you will excuse the expression) by a single forty-watt bulb hanging shadeless and bare from the middle of the ceiling, designed I guess, to bring out the true shittiness of the place. Above the door was a coin-in-the-slot electric metre.

I took off my soaking raincoat and went over to the bed to test it for comfort. I found that it had the kind of mattress a monk doing penance would have adored. It went so well with self-flagellation and the sackcloth-and-ashes schtick. Beneath this mattress was a bedstead which rattled at every move. I was reminded of the, old erotic blues lyric: 'I'm Gonna Ride You Baby 'Til the Springs Cry on Yo' Bed'. This bedstead cried riderless. I opened the two doors of the bedside cupboard. It contained nothing except an old, cracked chamber pot. In the ink stained drawer above, I found, at the very back, an envelope addressed `To the new inmate'. I tore it open and found a letter, written in florid hand-writing. It said:

Dear Inmate,

Welcome to Belsen-upon-Tyne. Herewith a few tips to help you enjoy (ha-ha), your stay.

1] POKING. This a male-only concentration camp. Being found with a member of the opposite sex in your room can be punishable by being sentenced to having to spend the rest of your entire life here. (If you are a homosexual, you can of course, roger any male you like in complete safety). But should you be determined or desperate enough to risk all, and smuggle a lass into the room (preferably blindfold, because the sight it is almost guaranteed to destroy the libido of any but the randiest female), do so at four o'clock in the afternoon, when the caretaker takes his afternoon snooze. The only part of this room where one can enjoy a fuck, free from bed-rattles and tell-tale, squeaks of the floorboards, is on the floor directly in front of the wardrobe. DO NOT FUCK ANYWHERE ELSE. Believe me; I have checked every inch of this room. And very importantly, get the little lady out of the building before 5pm., by which time the Gauleiter has woken up and is on his daily inspection tour.

2] BEWARE OF THE CLEANERS. They may try to get you to think of them as room cleaners. Do not be fooled. In fact, they are robbers and spies. They will come to do your room every Tuesday and Friday morning. If you have any valuables in the room, remove them, because if you don't, they will. Also, any suspicious objects, such as a hair pin, or, heaven forbid, an article of female underwear, are immediately reported to the Gauleiter/caretaker. Do not try to buy their silence. They will take your money and report you anyway. The arrangement between the cleaners and the caretaker is unshakeable and immovable. They have full thieving rights in return for their spying activities. So, be warned.

3] SUNDAYS It is advisable to go to church on Sunday mornings, or dress as if you are going, regardless of whether you are Christian, Jewish, Moslem, Hindu, Bhuddist, or like me, you think that religion is just a load of shit. The reason for this is, that if Mister (or Herr), Milburn, our Gauleiter/caretaker, believes in your piety, he will lend you a key to the kitchen so that you can get yourself a nightcap, should you get home late. (The kitchen is locked every night at 9pm sharp). Also, providing he feels that the warmth of Jesus is upon you, he might even take a telephone message for you. As the only telephone in the building is in his flat, this could be important to you. Equally importantly, he will turn a deaf ear to your radio or gramophone being played after 10pm., which is the official switching-off time in this concentration camp.

Mr. Milburn is a conscientious Catholic. Indeed, one could even go so far as to say that Mr. Milburn is a fucking Papal maniac. And, like all religious madmen, anyone who is not a Jesus freak is by definition, untrustworthy, anarchic, idol-worshipping and a communist—in other words, downright evil. Such a person would definitely invoke the Gauleiter displeasure. Unlike his haloed, water-walking Son-of-God, Herr Milburn does not love his neighbour as himself. In fact, he will go to considerable lengths to make life a living hell for you, if you do not declare an undying devotion for the Virgin and Her impossible offspring.

Lastly, my fellow sufferer, you should know that after about a year in this dreary hole, it is quite usual to contemplate suicide. Bur before you are found dangling lifelessly from the end of your pyjama cord, think on this: In three years or so, you will have finished your journey through this place and be free to go anywhere you please. Everything that happens to you thereafter, no matter what it may be, will seem sweet and enjoyable when compared to this. And also try to remember that nothing can happen to you here that Hitler did not try first, and even Belsen and Auschwitz had their survivors. So good luck.

(Signed) James Gibbons (previous inmate of this room and survivor)

I arrived at the porters' lodge sharp at ten minutes past nine the following morning. Prior to that however, I had my first inkling as to the truth of James Gibbon's valedictory letter.

I was jolted awake at about 7am., by somebody in a nearby room banging out Glenn Miller and his band playing 'Moonlight Serenade'. I have always loathed the corny pseudo-jazz sound of the Miller band. At seven o'clock in the morning, I found it almost impossible to stomach.

But it got me out of my lumpy, rattling bed, and into a freezing grey-black, overcast morning, that I was to learn is only too typical of late autumn weather in this city.

I was shocked to find that there was only one lavatory and one bathroom to each floor. I subsequently found out that this was quite luxurious by local standards. Some of the places where students were living (if you can call it 'living'), had just one bathroom and one 'John' for the entire building!

The lavatory and bathroom on my floor, faced one another at the opposite end of the hall to where my room was situated.

There was already a queue of half dozen or so boys, waiting to use both amenities. Those lining up outside the bathroom were holding their pink, china jugs. Two or three were already fully dressed, two wore wearing old, torn dressing gowns covering old torn sweaters which they had on over their pyjama jackets Two were covering their pyjamas with their overcoats, whilst one lad, in socks, underpants, and a short-sleeved shirt, had resorted to wrapping the threadbare carpet from his room about him to retain some body-heat against the damp, bone-chilling, cold that hung in the air like an unseen ghost.

As I approached them in my new, silk dressing gown, bought for me by my Aunt as a leaving present, one member of the queue, a tall, thin, sickly looking fellow, with a prominent Adam's Apple, removed the cigarette dangling wetly from his lips and turning to me, said in a broad Yorkshire brogue "Hey, Noel Coward, this queue is strictly for people needing a shit. If you only want a piss, do it out of the window. You can water the plants at the same time."

"That is if his John Thomas doesn't turn to ice and snap off" said the short ginger-headed Welshman in front of him.

Being completely unused to ribaldry of this, or any other kind, I just smiled weakly back at them.

After about twenty minutes standing in the line, sickened by a frozen cocktail of excrement stink, mixed with cigarette smoke and body odour, all accompanied by the music of Glenn Miller (whoever it was perpetrating this music, must have had every record he had ever made).

I said to the student in front of me "Christ, I hate Glenn Miller."

"Oh, I don't know," he replied. "It goes so well with waiting to have a shit, don't you think?"

I later found out that he was a music student who loved only Baroque music to the exclusion of virtually every other kind.

After a difficult time in the lavatory (because the door was being banged upon continually by someone who was apparently desperate), I moved to the bathroom. And that is exactly what it was; a bath room. In other words, a room containing a bath and nothing else. There was no covering on the floor; no wash basin, or towel rack; just an old stained bath. Over one end stood a copper geyser, upon which was a note written in the caretaker's spindly hand, saying: 'Students wishing to take a bath must give two shillings to the caretaker <u>before</u> doing so. Failure to do so may result in bathing privileges being taken away. Also, please dry off either standing in the bath, or in your own room. <u>DO NOT</u> dry yourself off whilst standing on the bathroom floor, as water will leak into the floor below. This is an order' (Signed:) W. Milburn. Caretaker.

I went back to my room, fished out the required two shillings from my pocket, went down the stairs and knocked on the caretaker's door. It was opened by a tall, gaunt and almost bald individual, about four inches taller than me. His complexion was of the kind of papery paleness that instantly reminds one of death. He had pale, blue sunken eyes, with cheeks to match. He looked like an escapee from a horror movie.

"Yes?" he said in a surprisingly high, light voice.

"Good morning, mister Milburn," I said. "I wish to take a bath, so here is your two shillings."

Behind him, at the end of his hallway, I could see the obligatory oblong painting of the Virgin Mary looking down at the baby Jesus, cradled in her lap.

"Are you one of the new students?"

"Yes I am."

"Well, in future, never come down here in such a state of undress. On this floor you must always appear properly attired."

"Do you mean that I have to get dressed in order to come down here to pay you, and then go back upstairs to get undressed all over again in order to take a bath?"

He looked down on me with contempt. "The other students give me their two shillings at the beginning of each week, so that they can take their bath whichever day it suits them."

"So you'll want me to give you fourteen shillings at the beginning of each week. Is that it?"

His eyebrows shot upwards a good inch in surprise, making his horror-movie face even more horrific.

"Are you telling me that you want to take a bath every day?"

"Yes, if it alright with you," I said in as friendly a voice as I could find.

His facial expression now became an even mix of shock and condemnation.

"I believe that those who wish to bath too much are sinners. You wish to wash away your sins, do you not?" I noticed he was trying to give his voice a doom-laden quality. I decided to ignore it.

"Mister Milburn, here is your two shilling piece. I am afraid I am in rather a hurry."

"You need to go to church and pray to the Blessed Virgin for forgiveness. Only then can you..."

But by then I had bounded up the stairs and into my room in order to grab a towel prior to taking my bath.

Chapter 11

"I HAVE AN APPOINTMENT with Doctor Cabot-Smith at nine fifteen."

The hall porter looked at me with mild interest. "You are mister...?"

"Silver. Jake Silver."

He took a clipboard off its hook on the wall and studied it.

"Mister Silver, Mister Silver," he repeated under his breath as he scanned through it.

"Ah, here we are. Would it be Mister Jacob Silver sir?"

"Yes, But everyone calls me Jake."

"I'll make a note of that sir, in case someone leaves a message for you in that name rather than your real one." I said nothing.

"Will you follow me sir," he said cheerily, as he raised the counter-top that had separated us, and headed off briskly, with me following, up a couple of flights of stairs and around a couple of corridors, until we came to a door with a gold plated plaque and engraved into it: 'A. Cabot-Smith. Ph D'.

"Here we are Mister Silver sir," he said brightly and immediately marched off. I stage-whispered a 'thank you', but he was obviously in too much of a hurry to get back to his post, to acknowledge it. Before knocking on the doctor's door, I checked that my tie was straight and that both my jacket and flies were buttoned. Then I gave the door a respectful tap, tap.

"Entah," shouted a voice in an accent typical of an army officer.

Doctor Cabot-smith was sitting behind his desk as I came in. He looked nothing at all like an army officer. For those of you who know your movies, he looked a lot like Vince Barnet, about fifty years old, short, tubby, a scrubby little moustache, and sad eyes with an almost bald head above.

From what I could see of him above his desk, he appeared to be impeccably dressed in a double-breasted charcoal-grey suit, light beige shirt and a tightly-knotted dark tie bearing the motif of some college, club or regiment.

He rose, stretching out his hand and leaving it there until I had crossed the highly polished parquet floor and shaken it. Then he sat down again and consulted his diary, saying as he did so, "You are Mistah..."

"Silver" I said.

"Ah, yes," he said, after having traced my name.

"Please take a seat." His manner of speech was a classic of clipped British correctness. He pointed to a hard backed chair by a highly polished coffee table that was set along the wall to his left. After I had sat down, he came over to occupy the other seat. I noticed he had a slight limp.

"I trust that you are settling in alright and that your accommodation is satisfactory?"

"Thank you doctor. It's fine."

"Excellent," he said. He set his intertwined fingers on the table. I noticed how carefully manicured his fingernails were.

"I've ordered some coffee. I trust that is in order," he said with a well practised little smile.

I nodded.

"Even though you will not have to attend your first lecture for a couple of days yet, I have always found it helpful for me to get to know at first hand, so to speak, those that it is my honour to instruct. So, to start with, tell me what drew you into wishing to read Modern History?"

"When I was eleven years of age sir, I was orphaned by a bomb that killed both of my parents and totally destroyed our house, together with everything I owned," I told him.

He sat impassively, silently waiting for me to continue; so I did.

"It fostered within me an ever-growing need to know how such a universally agreed madman as Hitler, was allowed to be in control of Germany."

He continued to sit silently, as if expecting me to go on. But I had nothing more to say. So, after a half a minute or so, of silence he suddenly leaned back in his chair and looking up to the whitewashed ceiling and with fingers intertwined across his chest let out a long "Yessss"

This time it was I who sat silently waiting for him to continue. He returned to his former position with finger interlocked in front of him on the coffee table.

"Don't get me wrong mister Silver. I am not insensitive to what you must have suffered. But to offer up your parent's death by a Nazi bomb as your sole motivation for taking this subject is, I am afraid, a pretty insubstantial one." I watched him as he rose from his chair to go over to his desk and collect a clipboard, with which he returned.

As he sat down he said "Your Modern History course will cover the period from immediately after the French Revolution, up to the present day. It is not my intention to even consider the period from 1916 onwards, until you are well into your second year. So, I must ask you; what the motivation will be for your first eighteen months with us?"

In truth, I did not give a stuff about what happened to some greedy motherfucker of a King some hundred and fifty years ago. Monarchy was never my bag, and what happened to some French King then, or what happens to Monarchy now for that matter, was, and is, a matter of profound indifference to me. I find the concept of Kings, Queens, Dukes and Duchesses et cetera, just one big load of horse shit! Of course in those far-off days, I did not think in such bald terms. It took years of bad living, years of pain and years of mixing with the wrong people to learn the art of expressing myself in such simple and direct terms. So let us leave it, that as I sat there facing Doctor Cabot-Smith, my interest in the French Revolution was vague, almost to the point of non-existence. But I was damned sure that this was not the time to pass on that kind of information to the good Doctor.

"I think I am motivated Doctor, by the concept—in my opinion at any rate—that all the terrible things which have happened in the historical period you mentioned, occurred as a direct result of human error, greed or even stupidity. Judging by the little I have read about the world's reaction to Hitler's reign from 1935 onwards, it seems to me to have been so utterly short-sighted as to cause me to wonder what thinking processes apart from self aggrandisement, motivate most politicians. And as I doubt that politicians have changed that much since the French Revolution, I am hoping that by obtaining a broader and deeper view of our past, I will obtain a greater understanding of the present and future actions of Governments."

You will realise from this glib, ad lib piece of oratory, that I was the possessor of what Americans call a 'smart mouth'. It was a talent that was to get me out of, but also into some very nasty scrapes later on in my life.

In this instance it worked very well. As the good doctor carefully laid his clip board on the table in front of him without having written anything on it, he said "I think that is an excellent and if I may say so, an unusually perceptive basis upon which to study our subject."

At this point the coffee and biscuits arrived, and after some stilted small talk during which, I told him about my love of jazz, and he tipped me off as to where the largest record store in Newcastle was situated, no sooner had the coffee been drunk and the biscuits munched, he briskly rose from his chair to return to his desk and it was back to business.

As he sat down he said "I look forward to watching your progress here Mister Silver. I am sure that if you really buckle down and work hard, you will enjoy this course very much." I nodded back at him, I hope, encouragingly, which I doubt he noticed because he was too busy rummaging through the top drawer of his desk, clearly looking for something.

"Ah, here we are," he said, bringing out a green file, and passing me a sheet of paper which he had extracted from it, said "Here is a list of books you must get from the University library. Read them in the order I have set them down on this list." I took the list off him and as we shook hands he said, "I have enjoyed our little chat and look forward to seeing you the day after tomorrow. Goodbye."

I let out a long sigh of relief as soon as I got out of the Doctor's study. As I closed the door behind me, I noticed standing in the hallway the next student scheduled to see the Doctor. As our eyes met, she gave me a quick smile and I gave her a tiny nod. She had a long shapeless body, laughably short legs and thick, round glasses the convexity of which, made her look like Elisha Cooke Junior. This was one ugly looking chick.

As I made my way back to the porters lodge, to ask the way to the library, I said out loud "Shit. Jake Silver, what the fuck have you got yourself into (or words to that effect)? Fortunately, there was no-one around to hear me.

I collected the six books that I was required to read and lugged them back to my room. I started to read the first one, but found events which took place back in 1789 boring and uninteresting. So, I left the French peasantry to their Liberty, Equality and Fraternity thing, to take a stroll through the main square of Newcastle, called, if my memory is correct, The Haymarket, and then on down it's main thoroughfare, Northumberland Street.

As I sit here in the heavy, humid heat, of a Havana afternoon, how far away it all now seems. Between my life here, and Newcastle upon Tyne then, lies a tattered, shattered, landscape, overlade with the skeletons of impossible dreams and hopeless hopes: of Promised Lands which turned out to become deserts of despair, and horizons of bright expectation turning out to be little more than pitiless, bitter mirages.

On this, my very first stroll through the centre of this cold, grey city, I had some good luck. I came upon a shop, which not only sold pianos, but also had a studio with a grand piano for hire at two shillings and sixpence per hour. I also found the record store that Doctor Cabot-Smith had told me about. It had in stock not only a reasonable selection of jazz records, but a table radiogram for sale on the hire-purchase at ten shillings a week. As Uncle Harry was sending me ten pounds a week allowance, which was a fortune in those far-off days, I could easily afford to buy the radiogram, a half dozen records and book the piano rehearsal room for as long as I liked.

When I returned to my room to settle down and read about all that French Revolutionary jazz, I was feeling pretty damn good. Just the knowledge that within ten minutes walk of where I lived there was an available piano, caused my spirits to rise in a way I could never explain.

For the next six months or so, my life settled into a routine pattern. No matter how much reading or writing I had to do, every afternoon at five o'clock, I would check in to the piano studio and practise. After the first couple of weeks I came to an arrangement with the shop-owner that for two pounds ten shillings per week (payment in advance), he would give me my own key to the studio, which I could get into through the fire escape door from five o'clock onwards every evening, and play as long as I pleased.

During this same period, although I made no friends with anyone in my Modern History faculty, I did get myself a couple pals; one taking a degree in Music and the other in medicine. By sheer coincidence, both were Jewish. The musicologist was called Meyer Chulinski. I remember how he laughed when I suggested that even though it was a nice name, it would be even better if he could lose about ten minutes out of it. The Doctor-to-be had the far more accessible name of Harold Landing. Physically, they were complete opposites. Meyer short, weedy, narrow-shouldered, and with hand-knitted hair, a pale, washed-out skin colour plus round, horn-rimmed spectacles for his myopia. Harold on the other hand, was almost as tall as me, certainly six feet at least. He had thick, blonde, straight hair, a sensuous, Victor Mature-like mouth, and was given to fat, which he fought very hard by going to a gym twice a week.

We all loved music. I taught them to dig Duke, Basie, Tatum and jazz in general, and Meyer introduced us to the never-ending wonders of Bach, Bartok, Ravel and a host of other great classical music composers. What the Glenn Miller lover down the hall made of all this wild, wonderful music pouring out of my room, I never found out.

Harold introduced Meyer and me to cigarettes, good movies, together with the names of their entire casts, right down to the bittiest of bit players. He also showed us the right way to chat up ladies, because he was a ladies man. Actually that is a bit unfair to him, because in truth, Harold was THE ladies man! He possessed such sheer animal magnetism, that within a few days of meeting some chick (in some cases, it was just a couple of hours), she would all but beg him to take her to bed. For two sexually screwed-up guys like Meyer and I were, this uncanny sexual talent seemed far more magical than Jackie Teagarden, Benny Goodman, John Sebastian Bach and Igor Stravinsky all rolled up into one!

Harold did fix me up with a few odd dates, but half of them were intent on simply using me to get closer to Harold, and the other half were mostly the type who acted like they were nymphomaniacs when there were a lot of guys around, but who, once you get them on their own, suddenly assumed the persona of frigid frozen virgins. In the dozen or so dates I had during my first six months in Newcastle, I got little more than pecks on my cheeks, sometimes on my lips, and a whole load of, 'I-really-do-like you-Jake-but-I'm-just-not-in-the-mood-tonight' kiss-offs.

And then, completely out of the blue, I got lucky. And not just sexually: it was far, far more important than that, because it changed the entire course of my life.

Chapter 12

TO KEEP THE FAMILY SWEET back in London, I phoned once a week without fail. I usually made the call on Thursday evenings, because that was the nearest to Shabbat, which of course, starts at sundown on Fridays and lasts until sundown the next day. Even though my Aunt and Uncle could not be described as religious by any means, Aunt Sarah did harbour a belief in the importance of Shabbat, and did not welcome phone calls on the Sabbath. (Non-Jewish readers should know that for religious Jews, it is absolutely forbidden to use the phone except in the direst of emergencies during this period).

So on Thursday nights I would ring home to wish the family 'Shabbat Shalom' and reassuring Aunt Sarah that I was well and healthy, and that on Friday nights I always go to a kosher restaurant to eat (a complete lie. I don't believe there was a kosher restaurant in Newcastle at that time), and that I missed her very much. I said these things because I knew it would make her feel happy. But there was another reason why I phoned so diligently.

The one time I did not make my regular Thursday phone call (it was because I was out on a date with one of Harold's cheek-pecking lovelies), my Aunt got so worried that she phoned the Principal of the University in Durham at ten o'clock at night yet, to ask him to pop up to Newcastle (about sixty miles away), to personally make sure that I was alright and in good health. When he point-blank refused, and went so far as to challenge her sanity, she gave him a terrible telling-off, going so far as to accuse him of anti-Semitism. Apparently she also told him that he had no regard for the welfare of his students and that I might have been murdered in my bed for all he knew or cared. The upshot of this crazy contretemps was embarrassing and severe carpeting for me the following day. Thereafter, I never missed my weekly, usually Thursday night call home. On this particular Thursday, after I had gone through the usual promises to my Aunt regarding eating kosher food, and my brilliant state of health, etc., Ivan came to the phone.

"Boychik, are you still practising the piano?"

"Everyday. Why do you ask?"

"Did you see last week's Melody Maker?"

"I don't even know if it's even on sale up here, so I couldn't have seen it?"

"Listen, there's a big story in it about a 'Young Jazz Musician of the Year' competition. It's big and it's country-wide. It's going to cover all kinds of categories like best big band and best combo and also the best solo instrumentalist."

"So?" I said.

"So, I've entered you in the competition."

"You've what!?"

"Listen Boychik, you are better than all of them. You're gonna win. Believe me."

"Ivan, I can't just walk out of my studies and come to London to play at some amateur competition. Quite apart from what the college would say, can you imagine how Aunt Sarah would react? She'd go potty and you know it."

"You've got it wrong kid. You don't have to come to London. I've entered you in the North-East area heats. It is only after you've won up there that you have to come to London"

Suddenly I felt very nervous. "Look... I don't think that I'm ready to enter a competition yet."

"Listen to me. I've already bet my father a pound that you win your local area heat. Believe me Jake, when they hear you do your Fats Waller and Art Tatum stuff, you'll walk it. I promise."

So I filled out the forms, when they arrived, and for the two weeks after, up to when the first of the heats took place, I added an extra hour to my practising schedule.

Winning the first two preliminary heats was easy, not so much because I was that good. Rather, it was because the other solo entrants were so lousy.

Now, I was in the area finals. This was a much bigger deal, because it comprised the best new talent from all over the North-East of the country. Fortunately for me, it was to be held in Newcastle, which meant that there was no travelling involved. Unfortunately for me, it was to be held on a Saturday, which meant that Ivan could not be present, because it is forbidden to travel on the Sabbath, and Ivan was a good Jewish boy.

The contest was to be held at the Northumberland Galleries, a huge barn of a place but considered to be the top dance hall in the area. I rarely went there even though half the University could be seen there every Saturday night. My reasons for not going were twofold; firstly I hated those corn-ball arrangements of Glenn Miller that comprised eighty per cent of the band's repertoire. And secondly, I hated dancing. But there was a very good piano there.

Normally, the hall opened for dancing from 8 o'clock until midnight. On this particular occasion, there would be a break from their strict tempo nonsense between 9.30 and 11 o'clock to allow the contest to take place. The entrants consisted of three traditional jazz bands, in which teen-aged kids kidded themselves and sometimes, the audience, that they could recreate the music of seventy year-old black jazzmen from New Orleans, which is about as far away, socially and weather-wise, as you can get from cold, grey, white-skinned, Newcastle upon Tyne. The other two groups competing, were two Benny Goodman sextet sound alikes, only they didn't. Only clarinet players with the courage of fools try to emulate the great Benny G.

The only other person in the Solo Instrumental section was a guitarist who was allowed a rhythm section to back up his three pieces. He tried to play in a style that was a mixture of Django Reinhardt and Charlie Christian, only he did not possess enough technique to pull it off. Also, he was far too nervous to do justice to what talent he had.

I, on the other hand felt completely relaxed, To start with, I have always had an ability to close myself in mentally, so that I can give whatever I am doing, be it studying or playing the piano, maximum concentration. I think I developed this knack shortly after the death of my parents when I had to force myself to concentrate on whatever I was doing, simply in order to save myself from the agony of thinking about them. Also, the moment I heard the applause as I came on stage, followed by that magically pregnant silence as the audience waited for me to start, I knew that I was going to enjoy myself. And I did.

I started off with the Honky-Tonk Train Blues', which for all you squares out there is a specialist boogie-woogie showpiece with an almost hypnotic appeal. The applause at the end was loud and long. Then, to a dead quiet audience (all performers know that a silent, non-coughing audience is a sure indication that they are enjoying themselves), I played my version of 'Body and Soul'. I played the first sixteen bars out of tempo with lots of Tatum-esque arpeggios and frills. Then into a slow, bluesy tempo for the rest of the chorus, followed by two improvised jazz choruses, then up a half tone to D flat, to play out the bridge and the rest of the tune in semi-classical style and finishing with a virtuoso double-handed arpeggio. At any rate, to eighteen year-old Jake Silver it was a piece of virtuosity. By real virtuosos, it was probably just a piece of worthless tinsel.

But it was sufficient to elicit heavy, respectful applause from the audience. Then I went into my latest showpiece, which was the result of a solid month of practise. It was my approximation of the Art Tatum version of 'Tiger Rag'. By 'approximation', I mean that I got as close to it as anyone, barring possibly Vladimir Horowitz, could have got. Indeed, only a callow kid, such as I was, would have had the chutzpah to take on this work of death-defying difficulty.

I received a tremendous ovation after I had finished and had stood up to take my bows. In retrospect, I realise that all the cheering and clapping I received merely meant that not too many in the audience could have ever heard the actual Art Tatum version.

Anyway, I won the North-East individualist award, which meant that I was to go to London, all expenses paid, to compete in the national finals.

Once I had collected my little cup and certificate, presented to me by George Chisholm, the brilliant British jazz trombonist, and waved to Meyer and Harold who I could see cheering their heads off, I left the stage with but one thought in mind: to phone Ivan and tell him the good news.

I knew that Shabbat was over, and that therefore it was okay to phone home. But my watch told me it was 11.30, and I knew that Ivan, like his parents, goes to bed at around 10.30. But hell, I had won and it was all due to Ivan. So I took a chance and phoned. I had to hold on for so long that I was just about to replace the receiver, when I heard Ivan's voice:

"It's me. Jake."

"I knew it would be you. That is why I am answering the phone. So tell me?"

"I won."

"Did I not tell you, did I not tell you," he shouted down the line, his voice full of excitement and genuine joy. Then I heard him turn to someone and say: "It's Jake phoning from Newcastle. He won. He did it."

This was followed by a pause, after which my Aunt, to whom Ivan had obviously been speaking, came on the line. She was a lot more circumspect.

"So you've won. I'm very pleased for you my darling. Now no drinking with all your university cronies. I know what goes on. You go straight home to bed now. It's very late, and I want you to be fresh in the morning so that you can continue with your studying."

"Auntie, it means that I will be getting a free trip to London next month to compete in the finals. So I will be seeing you soon"

I felt sure that the 'I'll be seeing you soon line' would really grab her. I was wrong.

"So what are they going to say at the University when you tell them that you are stopping your studying for a few days so that you can enter some Tom-fool competition?"

"It takes place on a Saturday Auntie. I never have a lecture on a Friday," I lied, "So I can come to London on the Friday and return on the Sunday in plenty of time for my next lecture."

I had to wait a while before she said, "Do you promise that whether you win or lose at this competition nonsense, you will continue with your studies and get your degree?"

"I do. And with this competition out of the way, I'll work even harder. I promise."

That was of course, a classic example of the 'give-them-what-they-want-to-hear technique, a system that has been practised on parents by their teen-age children down the ages. It is almost invariably successful, as it was on this occasion.

"Well," she said, relief clearly evident in her voice, "In that case, congratulations. I must admit that I am sorry that you have to ignore Shabbas (which is an old-fashioned pronunciation of Shabbat), in order to perform at this damn-fool competition. You are getting more like your Father (olav ha sholem), every day. He never observed Shabbas either. Nevertheless Jake darling, I can tell you that there is one happy and proud man in Heaven tonight, and that man is your Father. And I am sure, your Mother also. So, maazeltov. I'll see you here in a month's time. Now let us both go and get some sleep." And she put the phone down.

I was just about to head back to the side of the stage where I knew Meyer and Harold were waiting for me, when woman of about twenty-five to thirty years of age cut into my path.

"Hello," she said, she said smiling. You're Jake Silver, am I right? You just won the award."

"Guilty on both charges," I said.

She was about five feet six inches tall, and of indeterminate build. This was because she was wearing an overcoat, admittedly unbuttoned, but not open enough for me to see if she had nice tits or anything, which is so important to an eighteen year-old kid. She had auburn coloured hair, tied back with a ribbon. She was attractive rather than classically beautiful. She had a nice mouth, even teeth and was almost bereft of make-up, which was pretty unusual in those days. She instantly reminded me of Susan Haywood, the film actress.

She reached into her small, black handbag and brought out a card, which she handed to me, saying as she did so "I'd like to talk to you about becoming your representative." She spoke with an accentless accent, definitely not from the North-East of England.

I looked at her business card. It read: 'Janine Gregson', and then it gave her address and telephone number. "It is very nice of you" I said, "But I don't think I need any representation right now, because I am still at University and will be for another couple of years yet. And even after that, I don't suppose I'll be taking up music full-time anyway."

She looked at me with an expression of great sincerity.

"Look," she said, taking one of my hands in both of hers. "I am only interested at this time in your winning the national final. You are certainly good enough to win, but you need to present yourself better than you did tonight."

"How do you mean?"

She flashed a smile. Then reaching up to pat me gently on the top of my head, she said "To start with, we have to get you a smart haircut. Then we have to decide on your stage-wear, and, most importantly of all, how to act when you are on the stage, before a London audience."

"Look, Miss Greg..."

"Call me Janine." Then she put her fingers up to my lips to stop me from speaking. "Jake, I can almost guarantee that you will win this contest if you let me help you. If, and I stress if, you then change your mind and want to turn professional, you will need a representative to handle your business affairs, and I want to be that person. Now, whether you want to be a famous pianist or continue with your studies is for you to decide. But at least let me try to help you now."

"Well, er, I'm not too sure," I said hesitantly. I was flushed and excited with my success and I just wanted to relax and celebrate with Meyer and Harold. Now suddenly, some older woman pops up from out of nowhere, trying to force me into making decisions I was neither ready, nor in the mood to make.

She suddenly put her hands over her ears. "It's too noisy to think around here. What are you doing for lunch tomorrow?"

"Nothing much," I shouted over the house band that was now banging out 'In The Mood'. "There's not that much to do on a Sunday."

"Good. Meet me at my office tomorrow at around twelve-thirty, and we can discuss it properly over a meal." Then, taking a step closer to me and looking up at with her large, hazel-coloured eyes, she asked, "How old are you Jake?"

"I'm eighteen for another six months yet."

"Do you have a girl friend or anything?" I presumed that she had asked this question in order to invite her along also.

"No I haven't." I had to admit.

"I thought not," she said. I sensed a tone of satisfaction in her voice.

Then, rising on to her toes, she kissed me lightly and impersonally on my cheek.

"Congratulations again Jake. See you at half twelve tomorrow. And after giving me a big smile, she slipped away towards the stage door.

I found my way to Harold and Mayer who were waiting, as arranged by the side of the stage.

Harold as ever, had a girl with him. She was tallish, blonde, pretty, big-bosomed with long, shapely legs, bright shiny eyes and full, inviting lips.

Meyer immediately grabbed my hand and while pumping it wildly said, "What the FUCK are you doing reading modern history? You've Got to be a musician, hasn't he Harold"?

Harold, in that soft, husky voice of his that so turned on the chicks, replied "All I can say is; every Yiddishe boy should be as good at anything as you were at the piano tonight."

This piece of repartee was greeted with peals of laughter by his girl friend, who then further rewarded him by hungrily kissing and biting him gently him on his neck, just below his ear.

"Well what are we going to do to celebrate?" Meyer wanted to know.

"You'll have to count us out," Harold said putting his arm around his girl. "I have to get lovely Lisa here, back to her home in Whitley Bay by one o'clock at the latest, or her father, who, would you believe, actually waits up for her, will probably kill me. Isn't that true sweet thing? he asked, kissing her lightly on her eyebrow.

"Daddy does get so worried about me" she said huskily. But her voice and eyes told the actual truth, which was that she could barely wait to make out with the handsome Harold.

I pulled Harold over to one side. "How can you make out with this chick in that little clapped-out car of yours?"

He smiled and consulted his wrist watch.

"It's ten minutes to twelve," he said. "That gives me time to take her to a quiet little place I know in Jesmond Dene, have it away, and still have her back with her pappy in Whitley Bay by one-thirty at the latest"

"Don't give me that jazz Harold," I said. "That car of yours is too small to screw a midget in, let alone a nice big girl like what's-her-name from Whitley Bay."

"Maybe it is," Harold said slyly. "But she's got hands and she's got a mouth. Believe me, I'll do alright." He gave me a knowing wink and a nudge, and then segued back to his "Sweet Thing." Putting his arm around her he whispered something in her ear which caused her eyes to smoulder and her full, heavily lipsticked lips to pout. Without another word they both turned and headed for the exit, leaving Meyer and me staring enviously after them. Then we too left the Northumberland Galleries, to the accompaniment of the band playing yet another cornball Glen Miller arrangement to stroll through the chill night, along Newcastle's drab, empty streets, up to The Haymarket, Meyer all the while eulogising about how well I played. He even managed to find some similarities between some of my phrasing and Bela Bartok's, with whom I was completely unfamiliar.

Once at the Haymarket, we found a fish and chip shop still open. I did not want to eat because somewhere during our walk, I had reverted to my normal, abnormal self. Quite suddenly, whilst Meyer was yakking on about atonality or something, I split into two people, the one coldly and impersonally observing the other. The elation and the joy that had glowed within me just a few moments ago was now turning into a joyless folly.

Meyer, entirely unaware of my internal change of persona, insisting on me joining him for some fish and chips. Apart from the swarthy-skinned, thick-set Greek owner, there were only two other people in this drab, smelly, run-down, dingily-lit café. One was a taxi driver. The other, an ill-dressed, unshaven tramp glowered at us drunkenly as we came in. We hadn't been in there for more than a couple of minutes before he suddenly stood up and shouted in a broad Glaswegian accent,, "Fuck everybody," at the same time with a swipe of his hand, sweeping his plate of chips and bottle of tomato ketchup off the table, covering the floor with chips, broken glass and blobs and smears of sauce. Even before the Greek owner could throw him out, he tottered out the door under his own steam, glaring at Meyer and me as he staggered past. At the cafe door he turned round and pointing at us, yelled, "And fuck all fucking foreigners."

It was too much for both of my personalities who were grappling for power within me. So I made up a story about having neglected doing an important essay and leaving Meyer to his fish and chips, made my way home.

Once on my own, I found it relatively easy to handle my dual personality problem. I suppose it was partly due to the fact that I was older, but it was also because I was free to handle it in my own way. No more did I have to endure Aunt Sarah's worried face peering into my eyes. No more did I have to bear the additional burden of pretending that her 'I-know-what-you-need-a-lovely-cup-of-tea-That'll cheer-you-up' nonsense had actually worked. I had known for quite some time that when this dichotomic thing takes me over, the first requirement in controlling it and then killing it off, is solitude. I must be left on my own. So, having broken away from Meyer, I strolled back to my lodgings, feeling evermore in control of things and thinking of Janine Gregson, and what I would say to her over our lunch.

On my room door I found a note from the Gauleiter-Caretaker which I read sitting on my jangling, lumpy bed.

`It is now after midnight and you are still not back in your room. When you do finally return, please remember that it is now the Lords Day, and be respectful of it. If you have done anything that requires confession, please leave a note on my door. If not, be aware that it is against the rules to play any music or entertain any guests. Sunday is a day for quiet thoughts. Please show respect. (Signed), W. Milburn.

"Fuck him," I thought, as I screwed up the note and tossed it into the almost full paper basket under my writing table.

I settled down to read my free copy of the 'Melody Maker' that I had been given at the competition. I was conscious of my surprise at how quickly my negative alter ego had evaporated, leaving me once again to enjoy my own success, mixed with the elation of being on my own and answerable to no-one,- not even the ghoulish Mister Milburn.

Chapter 13

IT WAS 12.30 PRECISELY on my wrist watch when I rang the front door bell of Janine Gregson's 'office', which in fact was in the apartment where she lived. It was on the top floor of a smart, purpose-built block, in a clearly fashionable part of town, which hitherto I had not known existed.

She opened the door and I was instantly taken by the way she looked. It was quite different to my memory of her from the previous night. Her hair, that had been so tightly held back, had now been allowed to fall softly and naturally around her shoulders, making her look much younger. She was wearing a tight, dark green skirt, and a light green, excitingly thin, cashmere sweater. The ensemble showed off her tits and shapely bottom to advantage—my advantage.

"Hi, Jake, come in." She said, as if I was an old friend. I followed her into a large, long, living-room.

"Sit down anywhere. I've got to get back to the kitchen for a couple of minutes." Then she added with a smile, "I'm afraid you've arrived in the middle of an emergency in the culinary department."

"Take your time. I can wait as long as it takes," I said.

"You are a darling" she said, lifting herself onto her tiptoes to give me a quick peck on my lips before hurrying out of the room.

Being left on my own gave me time to look around the room. The first thing that hit me was that this little lady had three very valuable commodities; money, class and money. Apart from the huge, low, jazzy, black leather armchairs, the long matching sofa, the elegant coffee table, the cocktail cabinet, the large radio-phonograph with shelves above it containing at least a hundred records, there was, at the far end of the room, a Steinway baby grand and what's more, it was very new. What with the chandeliers and the large painting of a sexy female nude on the wall above the fireplace, had I but known about these things then, I would have been aware of it's similarity to one of those exclusive brothels that exist in Buenos Aires, which you can visit only if you know the right people.

Her head suddenly popped around the door. "Fix yourself a drink," she said, and was gone again.

At that time, I never took a drink on my own. Maybe at night, when I was on the town with Harold and Meyer, I would have a single shandy, but nothing more. To me, 'fixing yourself a drink', was something that William Powell or somebody did in the movies. It was no part of this eighteen year-old's life style. So I played the piano instead. It was a beautiful instrument, with a warm, rich tone, made even warmer by the deep-pile, wall-to-wall carpet.

Maybe it was because I was concentrating so hard on what I was playing, or perhaps it was the sound-deadening carpet, but I did not hear her come into the room. I did not even hear her 'fix herself a drink'. The first I knew of her presence, was the feeling of her hip against my back and then her hand resting ever so gently upon my left shoulder.

She was wearing some crazy, heady, bewitching scent, which was all but overpowering me. These days, I don't like my women to wear overly pervasive scent, because it interferes with the bouquet of my cigars. But back then, it was a wonderful, sensual intrusion into my consciousness. When I finished whatever tune I was playing, she walked over to the armchair carrying her cut glass tumbler, half filled with some alcoholic beverage or other. As she sat down, I was granted a flash of knee and thigh, due to the slit down the side of her skirt. Her legs were slim and shapely. These were pins that would turn on a male of any age, let alone this sexually frustrated teenager.

She must have been able to read the expression on my face and in my eyes, because she reacted to it with a coquettish smile. I remember noticing again how white and even, her teeth were.

"Come over here and talk to me," she said softly and slightly huskily, as she pointed toward the sofa on her right. I stopped playing instantly and took a seat on the sofa, placing myself where I could get the best view of her legs, which were now curled under her, affording me a view of her right thigh, as high up as the darker brown edging of her stocking-top.

"Don't you know it is rude to let a lady drink all by herself?" she said, getting up and crossing the floor to the cocktail cabinet. She reached in and took out a large, cut-glass tumbler, like the one she was drinking from and put it on the silver, oblong tray that was on top the cabinet. Then she brought out a bottle of scotch and a soda siphon.

"I'm going to pour you a whisky and soda" she said, as she half filled the tumbler with scotch and topped it up with a squirt from the soda siphon. As she carried the tray over to the coffee table she said, "If you don't like it, don't drink it. But for heaven's sake, hold it in your hand, if only to appear like a grown-up."

As she set the tray down, she joked, "I may even force you to smoke a cigarette as well."

I was so green in those days, that even though when she joined me on the long sofa, and sat so close up to me that to get any closer she would have had to be on my lap, and this on a sofa long enough for King Kong to have stretched out on, I still did not entertain the thought for one moment that she was sending me any kind of message. For no reason that I can now recall, I continued to cling to the idea that me being just a kid and she a middle-aged lady (when you are eighteen years old, I suppose anyone over twenty-five is 'middle-aged'), the only reason she had invited me to her pad was to help me win at the final of the competition in London.

I reached over to the table, picked up my scotch, took a sip and hated it. I tried to disguise the fact but failed.

"Keep sipping," she said, an indulgent smile playing on her pretty little mouth. "Eventually you'll get to like it." And then she added quietly, "Believe me, you will."

I was now starting to be very aware of the heat of her body pressing up against me.

"Can I ask you something Jake?" She lowered her head as she spoke, so that she was kind of looking up at me with those sparkly, brown eyes of hers. "Do you have a steady girl friend?"

"I think you've asked me that before." I said, taking a sip of scotch while she watched me rather like a cat does after it has caught the mouse, and is now just playing with it.

"No, I do not have a steady girl friend. I don't even have an unsteady girl friend."

"Why not Jake?"

I fooled a little with my drink in order to avoid her steady gaze.

"I guess I'm just not the kind of person that girls fancy."

She made no reply, leaving a heavy silence which I felt called for me to fill in. "I mean, let's face it. Clarke Gable I aint. And girls don't seem to go for the jazz I play on the piano. So," I took another sip of whiskey, before going on, "I am like that ninety-eight pound weakling in those Charles Atlas cartoons. I'm the Grady Sutton of Durham University. You know Grady Sutton? He's the guy in the movies who never gets the girl."

We both by coincidence put our glasses down on the coffee table at the same time. Then she half turned, so that she was facing me.

"You've never made love to a girl in your whole life, have you?" She spoke in a low confidential tone of voice.

Now it may be damned attractive for a young girl to say that she is pristine and untouched in matters of love-making; it is downright humiliating for an eighteen year-old boy to have to admit it. So I tried to disguise the fact by attempting to adopt a subtle, sophisticated air.

"Well...not really," I said meaningfully, hoping that by leaning on the 'not really' line, she would interpret it to mean that whilst I may not have actually fucked a girl, I have done everything else bar that one thing.

She said nothing. The air was now as heavy as the final moments before a tropical storm breaks. Then, quite unhurriedly, she reached across me and took my left hand and carried it towards her, pulling me round to face her by so doing.

"Have you ever done this before, Jake?" she said softly and huskily, as she placed my captive hand over her right breast. She kept her hand over mine which she pressed into her breast while moving it in a slow, circular action. I can remember even now the hardness of her swollen nipple pressing into the palm of my hand.

In my life, I guess I have fondled, or kissed five hundred pairs of tits or more. I have buried my face (and my cock), into breasts of every shape and size. But none gave me the total, mind-blowing, star-bursting, sexual rocket-ride that this first experience gave me. Tits still turn me on, especially those on a seventeen or eighteen year-old chick. There is a wondrous, weighty weightlessness, a resilient yet yielding quality about a young, full pair of boobs that can still give me a hard-on just looking at them—always provided that they are attached to the right face, hips, arse and legs. And I am saying that now, when I am approaching sixty-five. Back then, it was Shangri-La, baby!

Still holding her hand over mine, still moving it in a gentle circle, she leaned back against the sofa, and tilting her head backwards as if she was looking up at the small crystal chandelier glittering over our heads, said in a soft, pleading voice "Kiss me Jake. Please."

I leaned right over her and kissed her as best as I knew how. The only knowledge I had about kissing had been got from the movies. And in those far off days, the Hayes office did not allow open mouth kissing. Movie kisses were strictly confined to two people pressing their faces hard against each other with lips firmly closed.

So I was surprised when, no more than a minute into my closed-lipped, face-pressing kiss, she turned her head away suddenly thus breaking off all lip contact. She took her hand away from over my breast-fondling one and hugged me tight with both arms.

"Oh, you are such a kid," she breathed into my right ear.

Now, taking my shoulders in her hands, she held me off, about six inches from her face.

"Darling" she whispered, "Say aah."

I had not the foggiest idea why she would want me to say something that only doctors ask you to say. But I would have recited The Lords Prayer backwards, let alone say 'aah' just to be allowed to go on fondling those wonderful boobs of hers.

"Aah," I said dutifully.

"Now kiss me with your lips open like that." And I did. And as I leaned back against the sofa, my right arm holding her, my left hand continuing to enjoy the endless delights of her beautiful breasts, all time suspended by the flicking of her tongue in and out of my hungry mouth, I was sure that this was the greatest joy any man could experience. Silly me.

We were still flicking our tongues into each others mouths, when I felt her hand gently land on my thigh. Then, to my utter shock, and I must admit, wild confusion, the hand slowly and gently began to make its way up to my fly.

Very gently, she was undoing my fly buttons. Then I felt her hand reaching inside for my cock. But what with all the twisting round to kiss her and fondle her tits, the damned thing, having been in a violently stiff state since she originally sat next to me fifteen minutes ago, had now managed to get itself hopelessly entangled in my shirt front and boxer shorts. So whilst above the waist, we were still kissing wildly, and I was still passionately fondling her breasts and nipples, my hand now being under her sweater, below it was a very different story, as she vainly battled to extricate my inflexible cock from it's tangled prison.

But suddenly, and with all the bells of heaven ringing joyously in my head, I finally felt her hand around it, gently guiding it out of my pants and into the outside world. And then, with mind-blowing gentleness, and excruciating slowness, she started to run her hand up and down its entire length.

Suddenly, right in the midst of this wondrous experience she suddenly stopped. I opened my eyes to find her hands up the back of her sweater, unclasping her brassiere. Then, in one swift, graceful movement, she removed her bra and sweater simultaneously. Taking her own full, heavy breasts in her two hands, she held them out to me:

"Kiss them Jake," she said very softly, while looking down at them, "Kiss them for me."

She stretched her full length on the sofa to allow me easier access. I knelt on the floor beside her, with my by now desperate cock twitching and banging into the side of the sofa, whilst I, for the first time in my life (since I was a babe, at any rate), buried myself in the irresistible headiness of kissing, sucking, and tonguing a girl's breasts.

After a while she said breathlessly, whilst running a hand through my hair "Do you like them Jake? Are they firm enough for you?"

"Mmm," I said, not wanting to stop what I was doing. This was no time for talk.

Suddenly reaching down the side of the sofa, she took my cock into her warm hand.

"Let me see this big thing of yours." She said. And using my cock as a kind of tiller, she gently guided me off the floor and up on to the sofa, whilst pulling herself up at the same time, so that by the time I was sitting on the sofa, she was sitting next to me.

"Oh, it's quite beautiful," she said, looking down at it. And then she slid off the sofa to kneel in front of it, her face not more than an inch or two away from it.

These days everybody over the age of twelve seems to know about 'going down', or, 'giving head', or even 'fellatio'. But in those far off, heavily censored days, there were no means by which I could have learned about such things. Harold had made some veiled references to it, and once I had overheard a couple of my fellow students make some smirking remarks about Henry Miller's books, but it was to be another three years before I was to read his then banned, but now famous 'Sexus'. So, when she started to go to work on my cock with her mouth, I thought that Janine was doing the wildest, most unimaginably sex-crazed act ever! I also presumed that this was something she had just dreamed up in a moment of sexually inspired frenzy, and that no female had ever done such a thing before.

She went on and on doing the most fantastic, mind-blowing things with her mouth and tongue. Well sir, there is only so much that a young virgin boy can take. Suddenly, and absolutely out of my control, I knew that I was about to come. The idea of shooting off inside her mouth was unthinkable to me. In panic, I pulled my cock out of her mouth, but I could not control the overwhelming orgasm that was already on its way. I had managed to get it about four inches from her face before coming, massively and profusely, shooting seemingly endless jets of sperm all over her face, neck and even into her hair. It wasn't until my multiple orgasm had fired its final salvo that I opened my eyes and saw what a mess I had made of Janine's face and hair.

"Oh, Christ I'm sorry" I managed to mumble.

She knelt there silently, her eyes still closed. As I stared at her in embarrassed horror, my cock still ramrod stiff, all she said was "Was it good Jake? I mean was it as good as you thought it would it would be?"

"It was fabulous" I groaned. I wanted to take her in my arms and kiss her, but seeing my sperm all over her face, I decided to resist that particular desire.

She gave my still stiff cock a sort of friendly squeeze and said to it "What are we going to do with you?" Then she looked up to my face and asked "Will you always remember it Jake?"

"As long as I live" I said quietly, but sincerely.

Suddenly, she galvanised herself into action, jumping to her feet and grabbing her bra and sweater from where they lay beside me in a rumpled little heap." I must tidy myself up" she said. And without bothering to cover her luscious bouncing tits, she hurried out of the room. A second later her head came round the door.

"The bathroom is second on the left." And she was gone.

I was still sitting there, my cock still half hanging, half sticking out of my fly. Suddenly I was suffused with embarrassment at my condition and position, even though (or maybe because), there was nobody else in the room. I stood up, forced my cock back into my pants and buttoned my fly. Then, after taking a big swig of my whiskey I made my way to the bathroom, where I combed my hair, readjusted my now badly creased tie, rinsed my mouth out and took a pee. As I was 'readjusting my dress' as they rather euphemistically term it in public lavatories' or, more realistically, as I was about to shove my cock back safely within the confines of my underpants, I said to it 'You lucky little devil, you'.

I was still on cloud nine as I floated out of the bathroom and down the silent, empty hallway, back to the living room-cum-chamber-of-earthly-delights, when I heard Janine's muffled voice coming from some other room. She was saying, 'Yes, yes, oh YES', in a kind of grateful manner. I assumed she was on the telephone and had heard some good news.

I went back to the long couch, whisky in hand, and waited for her to get cleaned up and finish her good-news phone call. Even though I hated the taste of the whisky, I felt like I was a real grown up and everything, now that I had had my first sexual experience. And sitting there casually, whiskey in hand. I saw myself at that moment as Jake Silver, man of the world, sophisticated, done-it-all-before and ready to do it again. I was sure she would certainly want to continue from where we left off. I know I sure as hell did. As far as I was concerned I had now partaken of the hors d'oeuvres of love-making. Now it was time for the main course so to speak.

Having nothing better to do, I decided to wander across the room and give her record library the once-over. It found it consisted mainly of classical music, but well organised with little tabs dividing up the collection into orchestral, vocal, chamber music and solo recordings. In this last section, I found a disc of the 'Dans Macabre' played by somebody called Vladimir Horowitz. Meyer had already played me a recording of the full orchestra version, so I was naturally interested to see what this guy Horowitz could make of it on the piano. I had never even heard of Horowitz.
As far as I knew, Art Tatum and Teddy Wilson were the greatest technical wizards of the instrument. So, having found out how to switch on Janine's wide, walnut radiogram, I played this guy Horowitz's recording.

I just could not believe my ears! I had just experienced a wild, fantastic, sexual orgasm. Now, I was having a musical one. This cat Horowitz was beyond my wildest dreams. I played the disc three times over, and was about to play it a fourth time, when the door opened. But it was not Janine. It was a large-boned lady of about forty years of age, pushing a trolley containing a pile of sandwiches, a pot of coffee, and some plates and cups.

"Miss Grrregson vill be here shortly," she boomed. "You vill begin viddout her." She spoke in a deep, guttural, tuneless voice, with a strong Slavic accent. Actually, her face would have been perfect for Hungarian stamps. She had high, pronounced cheekbones, and eyes that slanted like an Eskimo. Her lips which turned down at the corners to give her a slightly cruel expression, were full and in some indefinable way, sensual. She was dressed in a white, short-sleeved overall which exposed her strong, powerful arms. She could have passed for a javelin thrower, or even a prison wardress. Her legs, from what I could see of them, were long, strong and muscular, and they were attached to broad peasant-like hips. She also had big, strong tits. This was one tough, hard cookie.

"Will Janine, er, miss Gregson be long?" I enquired as lightly and casually as I could.

"I dawnt knaw." I noticed she made no eye contact with me, choosing rather to speak with her gaze directed firmly on the trolley in front of her.

"And what is your name?" I asked in a voice that I hoped would project the image of a worldly but democratic, friendly-to -the-home-help, nice guy.

"Mathilde."

She kept her eyes and unsmiling face looking straight ahead, as she transferred the contents of the trolley on to the coffee table. Then she turned the empty trolley around and wheeled it out of the room looking dead ahead of her, her face expressionless like one of those Transylvanian peasants in a Dracula movie.

As I was expecting the wonderful Janine to walk in at any moment, I did not play the Horowitz again, but munched away at the sandwiches in expectant silence.

But she never came. I ate all the sandwiches, washing them down with two cups of coffee. Every five minutes or so, I would go across the room, open the door and peer down the hallway, but there was no sign of life. Once or twice I thought I heard her voice followed by some booming response from Mathilde. But they were too muffled for me to know what was going on. It was now over half an hour since I had seen Janine, and I was missing her. I even tried shouting her name down the hall, but all I got back was blank silence.

I was now starting to have funny feelings. Things were becoming eerily unreal. What with the weird, stone-faced Transylvanian and now this strange uncanny silence; it was becoming just a bit too much for me: like the scary bit of a horror movie when the sweet virginal heroine, clad only in a nightie, clutching a guttering candle decides to climb the creaking, old staircase to identify the strange noises coming from the attic above, which she had already been warned never to enter. All it needed now was for Bela Lugosi to materialise in the room, fangs at the ready. I decided to get out of there. I found a piece of paper in my pocket and was busily writing Janine a note when the door opened and she came in, Mathilde standing behind her in loyal attendance.

"I'm sorry I've been so long," Janine said, "Things have been a bit hectic back there." I noticed that as she said the word 'hectic' she flashed a look at her faithful Transylvanian. I was also aware that her entire mien had changed. There was no warmth either in her eyes or her voice. She was talking to me in the same way as when she first spoke to me at the Northumberland Galleries. I made myself believe that she was adopting this attitude because she did not want the hired help to know about us. So I cooperated with her by pretending to be business-like also.

"I quite understand," I said. "Would you like me to wait until you have more time, or shall I come back later this evening?" I felt certain she would understand what I was trying to get across. I felt positive in my own mind, that she was as crazy for some more love-making as I was.

"Unfortunately, I can't make it this evening," she said as coldly and impersonally as a Doctor's receptionist making an appointment with a patient.

"Would you be a dear and phone me tomorrow? I'm sure that would be the best thing." I was completely baffled by her coldness, but I clung on desperately to the belief that it was nothing more than an act to fool Mathilde.

She held open the living room door as if to say, this way out please'. My stomach started to churn from confusion and disappointment. "But what about you being my representative when I go to London?"

I was desperately searching her face for any sign of warmth or intimacy, bit It was a case of no dice, cold as ice.

"My being your rep...? Oh that." It was as if she had completely forgotten the reason why I came here in the first place. "Of course I want to represent you." She said, smiling with her mouth, but not with her eyes. Mathilde was now holding the front door open. "When you phone me tomorrow we will arrange to meet again and really get down to things."

My heart leapt. She said that she wants to 'get down to things'. I was sure she meant this sexually and that it had nothing to do with representing me. I left her apartment in the highest of teen-age hopes.

I chose to walk back to my room rather than get a bus, even though the dark, grey clouds above were once more delivering those thin, cold, needles of rain, so familiar to anyone who has spent any time in this north-eastern city. But it didn't bother me in the slightest. To paraphrase the tune, I had my love to keep me warm.

I needed to walk because I knew that what had happened to me meant a re-evaluation of my future; and walking, for some reason always helped me to think more clearly.

To start with, before Janine came into my life, I had decided to give up reading Modern History in favour of becoming a professional piano player. I still had not the foggiest idea what dark reasons lay behind seemingly civilised governments that would cause them to not only allow, but actually encourage Nazism as they did in the '30's. But the price of finding out was too high for me. I just could not summon up enough interest in the French Revolution to give it my best shot. I was likewise bored and uninterested with the goings-on in Britain during the reign of Queen Victoria, and I could not give a fuck about the 18th and 19th century industrial revolutions. And any minuscule interest I might have still possessed was rapidly dying, now that I had won the north-eastern area best soloist award.

But now everything had changed. I realised within five minutes of leaving Janine's apartment that giving up my studies meant leaving Newcastle. And leaving Newcastle would mean not being near Janine and that was now unthinkable. It also meant that I would have to get serious with my studies in order not to flunk my exams—and I was a long way behind. But, being near to the centre of all my sexual desires was now centre stage, and if it took not only reading, but memorising all those boring, shitty history books, well that was just fine with me.

But as I walked on through the chilling rain, I found my mind shifting on to the other cataclysmic, mind-boggling happening of the afternoon. This fellow Vladimir Horowitz could do things and draw sounds from a piano which went beyond my wildest dreams! The effect of hearing that record had been every bit as electrifying to me as the effect of Janine's fingers and mouth on my cock. 'If I could develop a piano technique as great as this guy Horowitz, then I could easily become the greatest jazz pianist in the world', I stupidly thought. I realised, it would mean that I would have to practice the piano harder than I have ever done in my life. But how to arrange these two hugely time-consuming occupations of reading modern history and finding the time to get in enough practise to be as good as Horowitz? And more importantly, how to do it and still have plenty of time left over to spend with my wonderful Janine?

By the time I had got back to my room, I had decided upon a schedule that only an idiot, or possibly, a kid in love, could consider rational. And I was more than a bit of both. The way I had it worked out, I would study Modern History from 7am. Until 3pm., after which I would immediately hurry over to Janine's apartment for a couple of hours of ecstasy. Then I would go to the music studio and practise the piano until say, 2am. This would allow me a good four and a half hours of sleep per day—providing I didn't take any time off for eating, peeing or taking a crap.

I wasted no time. I dug out my book of Chopin Etudes, ran down to the kitchen, grabbed myself a cup of tea, which I drank almost at a gulp, ran to the music studio and using my pass key to gain entrance on a Sunday afternoon, I spent the next five hours buried in the 'Winter Wind' etude.

Fired by my determination to become as good a piano player as Mister Horowitz and equally determined to do well enough in my exams to enable me to stay on in Newcastle, I managed to maintain my murderous schedule for the entire month leading up to my going to London for the final of the competition.

By that time, I had improved my piano technique enormously, thanks mainly to Chopin's Etudes and J.S. Bach's Preludes and Fugues. I had also caught up with my Modern History course. But I had lost a stone in weight, mainly from not having time to eat, and I had developed some rather interesting looking bags under my eyes. I may have even had some bags over my eyes!

But things had not gone to plan regarding my love life.

As we had agreed, I phoned Janine the morning after our many-splendoured afternoon. Even though I was thinking of her to the exclusion of virtually everything else from the moment I had opened my eyes at 6. 30 Am., I forced myself to wait until half past ten, before I walked down to the phone box to speak with my new-found idea of Heaven.

It rang a long time before the phone was answered.

"Ya, who is spikking pliss."

I recognised the unmistakable voice of the Transylvanian. I assumed my cheeriest, most light-hearted persona.

"Oh, hello Mathilde. It's Jake Silver. Do you remember me? I was at the apartment yesterday afternoon. Is Janine, er, Miss Gregson in?"

"She cannot spik vid you now" she growled. "She is getting rready. She has to go avay for a coppla days."

My heart crashed straight through the floor of the telephone box. But I hung on in there.

"Could I speak to her before she leaves? It's very important" I added, desperation in my heart, but I hoped, not in my voice. There was a pause followed by the unmistakeable blankness that comes from a hand being placed over the telephone mouthpiece. Clearly, she was speaking with Janine, before replying. "You vill phawn back in vun hour pliss" and she put down the receiver, before I could say anything further.

The depression that was starting to envelop me was now put on hold by the hope that I could speak to her within the hour. I went back to my room, to continue with my studying, but nothing I was reading was going in. I could not get my mind off Janine; the look and feel of her wonderful, thrilling breasts, the magic of her soft, yet urgent tongue against my tongue, not to mention my cock, and the sweet softness of her as she lay in my arms. I closed the book I was supposed to be boning up on, and tried to pass the forty-five minutes remaining before phoning her again, by writing to Aunt Sarah. But I was too tortured in mind and spirit to do even that. So, I went downstairs to the kitchen, poured myself some breakfast cereal and while munching it down, tried to decide how I should play things when I do speak to her.

My body was begging me to say, 'I must have you now, now, now. I am aching for your tits and your tongue. Not to have you in my arms is like dying'. But my head was telling me I was thinking like a lovesick idiot. 'Be reasonable' it was saying, 'just listen to what she has to say, and respond in like style. That is all you can logically do'. Meanwhile, my negative other self was now getting into the act, calling out over the top of the other two voices. 'Don't waste your time with the lousy little bitch. 'After all, it was she who found you after the competition. If she wants some more, let her come and get it. And let's face it; you were a damn sight happier before you ever laid eyes on her. In any case, she probably hasn't forgiven you for shooting all that sperm into her face and hair!'

After what seemed like hours of mental turmoil, the forty-five minutes were up. I had decided to let my brain rule my body and run the show. That is, if I was strong-willed enough to do so.

I found the phone box occupied by a young girl who was speaking whilst eyeing herself critically in the little mirror that phone boxes used to have in those days (and for all I know, still do). I decided to stand close up to the phone box door. In this way, she was bound to see me waiting, and hurry up with her call. And also, if another potential phoner came along, my standing by the door would guarantee me being first in line.

After what seemed like forever, she gave up looking into the mirror, to turn and stare blank-eyed and unseeingly at me all the while going on with her interminable conversation, which I noticed, consisted of her speaking almost all of the time. After I had been waiting for heaven knows how long, I started to rationalise: 'Maybe she is dictating the entire script of 'Gone With The Wind' to the person on the other end of the phone'. I tried to read her lips in the hope that they would frame the final 'Tomorrow is another day' line that ended the movie. But no luck.

I looked at my wrist watch; it was now almost half-past eleven and the Transylvanian had said that Janine was going out at about that time. I was desperate. I opened the phone box door and put my head inside. I came into the conversation where she was saying in a broad Geordie accent,

"So the little bitch cums oop to wa and..."

"...Excuse me, but I have a very urgent call to make."

"Well, you'll just have to bloody well wait woncha?" was her snappy come-back.

"Look," I said, my brain and mouth running on sheer desperation: "There is a man dying in Newcastle General Hospital, and they need the address of his wife, so that she can be at his bedside before he dies. I am the only person who knows it. Every minute counts."

She eyed me disbelievingly at first. But I maintained my dead-pan expression, until she decided to give me the benefit of the doubt. "How long will you be?"

"Only a couple of minutes. Even less if it's too late and he has died while you were talking on the phone."

That did it. "Well, if it is a matter of life and death."..., then she spoke to whoever was on the other end of the phone; "Look pet, I'll ring yer back in a few minutes. Turah well."

As she vacated the phone box, she said to me, "Ah hope you're in time like."

I looked at my watch. It was eleven thirty-five.

"So do I" I replied. And I meant it from the bottom of my heart and soul.

But I wasn't. "She has already gone," Mathilde growled.

"Oh no" I groaned. Then in a desperate plunge at some sort of optimism "Did she leave any message for me?"

I distinctly heard her do the hand-over-the-mouthpiece-trick, again. It was a long wait before she came back on the line. "She left a nawt to say she has wrriten you a letter." And again she put the phone down before I could say another word.

The letter arrived the following morning. But not before I had spent the rest of the day oscillating in mood from broken despair to high optimism, based on the proposition that if she can be bothered to write to me at all, then she must surely care about me.

But the night was torture. I could sleep only fitfully, and when I did. I had strange nightmares. One I remember was Janine lying in my arms on the floor near the wardrobe, which, according to the previous tenant's note, was where the only creak-free floorboards were to be found in the room. She was, naked from the waist up. I had murmured to her, "Take off all your clothes," and she had whispered in reply,"Okay Jake darling." Just as she was wriggling out of her skirt, I saw on the floor, not six inches away from where she was lying, a huge, black, hairy, tropical spider. I flung my arms around her to roll her over me to the other side, so that I would be between her and the giant, evil-looking arachnid. But, as in all authentic nightmares, I was too late. Before I could make a move it leapt, landing on the back of her neck. I yelled, 'Keep still; keep still' as I tried to tear it off her neck with my bare hands. It was my own yelling voice that thankfully woke me out of it. In fact that night was filled with nightmares, until I was too scared to sleep anymore, and spent the rest of my allotted four hours of sleeping time reading and trying not to think about Janine.

The following morning I found her letter in the little wired box that was fixed over the letter box of the front door. It was a good half hour, before I could summon sufficient courage to open it. I was sure this was the kiss-off,—the 'Dear John', the 'it-was-lovely-to-know-you-but-it's-all-over' letter. What I was not sure of, was how I would handle this rejection. And so I kept putting off the moment of cold, dread truth, written in her own hand.

It was only after having shaved, bathed and dressed, that I threw caution to the winds and picked up the lavender coloured envelope. A faint echo of the perfume she wore on that single, fateful, afternoon, when she temporarily made me immortal with her kisses, wafted from it.

Inside was a hand-written note on a single sheet of lavender-coloured paper.

'Dearest Jake' it began, 'I am really sorry that I have been unable to get together with you again. At the moment I am so busy that I do not know when I will next be able to meet with you. I did enjoy our wonderful afternoon together, and I look forward to seeing you again as soon as is possible. Please believe me when I say that. Unfortunately, it doesn't look like I will be able to be with you again until the night of the final in London'.I turned the page over.

'You are a wonderful pianist Jake, and I am sure that if you play as well as you did in the local heat, you will walk away with the prize.

Win for me Jake. Win so that I can be doubly proud to represent not only a wonderful guy, but also an acclaimed jazz pianist.

As ever,

Janine.

Have you ever seen a guy shot out of a canon? That was me at that moment. I had been shot into a cloud of pure ecstasy. I carefully re-read the letter. Then I put it back in its envelope and carefully pushed it into the inside pocket of my jacket. I would never be depressed again. It was like a doctor's prescription. 'When depressed, take one dose of the enclosed letter and you will feel better immediately`. 'Win for me Jake'. That's what she had said. Wow! I felt like a knight at a jousting tournament. I would win, by Jesus I would win. And then the hand and heart (not to mention the body), of the fair maiden would be mine.

I was far too elated to study. I strolled, or rather, floated down to the College Union, where I celebrated by buying myself the biggest breakfast I had so far eaten since arriving in Newcastle. I sat there eating and grinning and nodding to anyone and everyone who caught my eye. I was glowing with radiant happiness. I even gave a friendly wave to the gambling card players a few tables away, who were always at the same table, always playing cards for money. Heaven knows how, when, or if, they ever did any studying.

I knew now that winning in London was the most important thing in my life. Nothing else mattered. When I returned to my room, it was not to start my required essay on the Economic and social conditions in Britain and Europe 1910—1914. It was to draw up a short list of song titles from which I would decide the programme that I would perform at the London finals.

But just a few days later, and with still almost three weeks to go before the final competition, my mood had undergone a profound change. Now, I was consumed with depression and doubt. Janine's letter, which had imbued me with such joy, was now causing within me a maelstrom of bewildered apprehension. Why couldn't she see me? After all, no matter how busy she might be, she has to sleep. So why couldn't we meet at midnight or even later, if that was the only time she was free? The more I re-read her letter, the more I was bothered by its wording. There was not one mention of love in the entire thing. It was full of phrases like 'it was wonderful to see you' or, or assuring me what a 'wonderful guy' I was. But where was the 'I can't wait to be in your arms 'bit? Even ending her letter 'As ever' had no clear meaning. 'As ever' what? I kept asking myself. As ever' I love you? Or, 'As ever' I think you are a pretty good piano player? The more I thought about it, the more her letter assumed the quality of a backing track. Everything was there but the actual melody and lyric.

I had to see her and get this whole thing sorted out.

I tried phoning her on several occasions. But each time I would get the Transylvanian telling me in her guttural, booming voice, that 'Miss Grregson iss nawt in', or 'She iss avay'. And each time, before I could ask anything else she would bang down the receiver. I grew more and more desperate with every passing day. It was now quite clear to me that whatever 'Miss Grregson' put in her letter to me; she did not want to see or hear from me again. I was determined to get my 'love life' (if you will excuse the expression), sorted out once and for all. I decided to go and see her.

I arrived at Janine's apartment at around lunch time on that rarest of all days in Newcastle, a cloudless, windless, sunny day. As it was the middle of the week, and if she is as busy as she claimed to be in her letter, then she would not be out of town visiting anyone.

It was quite a while before the front door was opened by the inevitable Transylvanian.

"Yes?" she said, eying me stonily with her flat, grey, eyes.

"Hello" I said crisply. I had decided to sound as business-like as possible in the hope that I would get a better reception than the friendly approach had so far got me.

"Would you tell Miss Gregson that Jake Silver needs to see her for a few minutes? And would you tell her that it is very important."

"Miss Grregson ees not here"

"I see. Well, may I come in and leave her a note?" I started as if to enter the apartment, but was stopped in my tracks, by her large, coarse hand pressed against my chest.

"Naw vun can come in viddout Miss Grregson's telling me it is alrright"

"Oh, but surely you know me. I just w... "At that moment I heard a thump from somewhere inside the apartment, followed by a voice, clearly Janine's, saying, "Oh shit." She said it quietly, but there was no mistaking the owner of that voice. It was Janine.

"And who was that?" I asked accusingly.

Nothing on her face or in her eyes changed. Only the tone of her voice was a little more rasping and threatening.

"I heard nussing," she snarled.

"Oh, come on now," I said in exasperation.

But before I could say anything else, she slammed the door on me. I thought of kicking at the door, or maybe sitting on the doorstep until someone opened it. But the first idea seemed to me to be too crude, and I had too much pride to resort to the second. So I went back down to the street, where I enquired from a lady with a shopping bag where the nearest stationer's shop was. Having found it, I bought a writing pad and some envelopes. Then I went in to a little café, two shops away, ordered myself a cup of tea, and while sipping it, wrote Janine a note, pleading with her to let me see her. I also wrote that if she wants to call the whole thing off, I will understand, but I would rather she came right out with it and said it to my face, rather than leaving me in my present limbo of unknowingness.

Having folded it into one of the envelopes, I walked back to Janine's apartment-block, intending to push it through her letter-box. I was not more than a couple of hundred yards from the apartment's entrance, when I saw her. She was with a young girl. They were both getting into Janine's car, which was parked in the street.

'Janie wait` I yelled, running as fast as I could towards the car. By the time I reached it, they were both inside and Janine was in the process of starting the car. The windows were up, so I had to shout to make myself heard.

"For Chrissakes, what's going on?" She looked wonderful. She was wearing a dark blue polo-necked sweater, with a thin string of pearls adorning her neck. She gave me a big smile and winding down the side window not more than an inch, said

"Sorry Jake. In a big hurry. Gotta go." Then she kissed the top of her middle finger, waggled goodbye with it, revved the engine and was gone.

I went back to her apartment and left my note, as if I had never seen her. A few tortured days later, I received her reply:

Jake Dear,

You must not torture yourself so. As I have already told you, I will be in London to be present at what I am sure will be your victorious night. Afterwards, we will get together, I promise, and everything will be made alright. I really do have very warm feelings for you.

Win for me. See you in London after the contest.

As ever,

Janine.

I read it a couple of times and then, in bitter exasperation, crumpled it up and threw it away. I was sick of all this ducking and diving. What kind of relationship did she want? I knew for sure what kind I wanted, and it wasn't this. I was not interested in a correspondence course of definite maybe's. As I threw the crumpled-up letter across the room, I thought; 'fuck it. If she contacts me, all well and good. If not, then the hell with it. '

In retrospect, as I sit here warmed on the outside by the hot Cuban night and on the inside by the even hotter Cuban rum, thinking about how it was in those far off days, I have to smile at how important it all was to me at the time. I also realise that all that 'fuck her', and 'the hell with her' jazz, was completely phoney. Underneath all that macho, don't-give-a-damn stuff, I was still clinging to the belief that Janine and I would at last be interlocked in a magnificent victory fuck, immediately after the competition in London.

By the time I boarded the train that was to take me back to London, I had rationalised how things stood for me. Top of the list: I have to win, for two reasons. Firstly, if I lose, then any chance I may have of fucking Janine will go out of the window. I mean, who wants to fuck a loser? Secondly, if I do win, maybe she will come across. But if she doesn't, then she will never know what she missed, and that, I reckoned, will bother her, every bit as much as she has bothered me.

But I was nevertheless totally screwed up emotionally as I sat there blankly staring out of the train window, watching the drab-green landscape slip by.

I had ducked out of college three days earlier than I really should have. This was not only so that I could enjoy a little more time with my family who I was now missing, but also because I had to get away from a town in which everything reminded me of Janine. As I had not heard any more from her after that enigma of a letter, I did not know what to think. Did she love, or even fancy me? Did she think I was too young and callow for her? Maybe there was some other older guy she was really was crazy about. 'After all' I reckoned, as the train rocked and rolled its way southwards, 'that would be logical. I am only eighteen and she must be at least twenty-five. Maybe she had looked upon me as nothing more than someone to wile away an afternoon with, whereas, in reality, she had some older man with whom she really was in love. The only thing I was sure of was that I wasn't sure of anything as far as Janine and I was concerned.

I was travelling back to London on a first class ticket, even though the competition organisers had only sent me a voucher representing a third class rail fare. Because of the money Uncle Harry had sent me every week, and what with my expenses being so small, I had managed to save sixty-odd pounds, which, barring the five pounds I had paid for my fare, was now sitting thickly and snugly in my trouser pocket. Just in case Janine did want to pick up where we had left off, I wanted to be able to show her some of the joys of the big city. I wanted her to see me as the kind of suave, high roller that Sheldon Leonard or Ray Milland was in the movies.

Of course I wasn't even sure that she would show up at the concert, let alone do me the additional honour of allowing me to fuck her. So, I reasoned, by taking on the Sheldon Leonard role right away and travelling first class, I might find myself in a carriage with some Lana Turner look-alike debutante, who would instantly flip for my sophisticated, worldly charm. But that just ain't my kind of luck! The only other person in my carriage turned out to be an old lady who could read a book and knit at the same time.

I got to thinking about Aunt Sarah, Uncle Harry and Ivan. Naturally, I was dying to see them. But there were drawbacks. To start with, just the thought of their house disinterred long buried memories of my parents. Even then, almost seven years after their cruel and untimely deaths, the very thought of them immediately caused a wave of depression to wash over me.

So I shifted my thoughts on to the loving but suffocating atmosphere in the house, and Aunt Sarah who had to know every last detail of everyone's personal lives. 'I better not tell her anything about Janine', I thought. 'Shit, she'll hit the ceiling if she finds out I have a non-Jewish girlfriend'.

'But then', I rationalised regretfully, 'one orgasm does not a girl friend make'.

And what if I do win the competition? How will I tell my Aunt that I am giving up my studies to become a professional piano player? 'Christ, I'll have to be careful what I say', I thought. I smothered any further worries by thinking of how Ivan will react to the great new jazz records I had collected whilst I had been in Newcastle. I wondered what he will make of all the new, great jazz performers, who were knocking me out at that time. Had he yet heard the incredible Charlie Parker, or Dizzy Gillespie or Bud Powell? Maybe he will prefer the cooler school of players like Lee Konitz, Stan Getz or Lennie Tristano? I drifted off to sleep thinking about which of all these fantastic players I will play to Ivan first.

I awoke just as the train was chugging and puffing its way into Kings Cross station. You may think it crazy but having been missing my family like crazy and having been looking forward so eagerly to seeing them again, all at once I found myself tensing up at the thought of surrendering my freedom to the iron reign of Aunt Sarah. But, as I brought down my two bags from the overhead rack, I said to myself' 'It's only for four days, so be all sweetness and light. Do whatever they ask and make them feel good'.

I was damned glad I had the foresight to buy everyone a present. That, I was sure would get me off to a good start if anything would.

As I followed the old lady who was so expert at doing the read-a-book-and-knit-at-the-same-time trick, off the train, I kept repeating to myself 'It's only for four days, it's only for four days'.

Walking down the platform, re-accustoming my ears to the noise and bustle of London, walking slower than usual to put off the moment of meeting a fraction longer, it suddenly struck me that it really was for only four days. In all honesty, I felt sure that I very little chance of actually being considered the best new soloist in the whole of Great Britain. So, it was all down to four days of being Mister Sweetness and Light, coming nowhere in the competition, returning to Newcastle to continue with my studies, and also definitely taking up Harold's offer to fix me up with one of his cast-off sweeties. That is, unless Janine actually does gives me a break.

I was in the act of telling myself to fix the happy grin on my face, when I saw them coming towards me.

I had forgotten how much I loved them. All that shit about it only being for four days vanished in an instant. God, I was glad to see them, and judging by the looks of pleasure on their faces, they were equally so.

And as we stood there on Kings Cross station, oblivious of the noise, blind to the scurrying porters and the criss-crossing passengers, Aunt Sarah beaming from ear to ear, hugging me tightly and me hugging her back, Uncle Harry, looking a little older than I remembered him, gripping my arm and saying 'Welcome home my boy, welcome home' and Ivan, who had now taken control of my bags, standing next to me, smiling with such genuine and sincere pleasure, I actually felt tears of joy starting to prickle the corners of my eyes. Only now did I realise how much I had missed them, and how deeply I loved them. The Mafia are right about one thing: family is THE most important thing in life. When the chips are down, the only people you can rely on and trust for sure, is Family. There is no other love like it, and I feel sorry for anyone out there who does not know it.

Little did I know then that within a shortish period of time, I would be walking away from them, never to see them again.

We walked towards the car, my arm around Aunt Sarah, Uncle Harry walking a little ahead of us, car keys in hand and Ivan walking alongside of me carrying my two bags.

He said,"Do you know, I think you've got even taller than when I last saw you."

"He may be taller, but he's a bag of bones," said my Aunt predictably. "And he looks like he hasn't slept for a month," she added, her face suddenly taking on an expression of concern. Then she added "Gott se danken, you got here in time. Another couple of months and you would have faded away."

We all piled into the car, which was a Lincoln Continental, I think.

"Do you like the car?" my Uncle asked proudly.

"I should say," I said.

"I only got it last week. A Yank colonel about to be restationed back in the States, owed me a bundle of money he didn't have. So, I took the car in part payment."

Ivan whispered to me, "Say something nice about the car. Dad's crazy about it."

"Wow, Uncle" I said, "This has got to be the best car I've ever been in."

He beamed with pleasure, whilst Ivan gave me a nudge and a conspiratorial wink.

"I hope you are hungry," Aunt Sarah said. "Olga and I have been slaving in the kitchen to make everything you like. So, mister Bag-of-bones, you had better eat it all up and not upset us."

It was like I had never been away. I knew what they were going to say even before they said it. Ivan wanted to know what I was going to play in the competition. Aunt Sarah made me promise that whatever the outcome of 'this f'dreckisher contest', I would go on with my studies until I got my degree. "I've got a wonderful and very wealthy girl to introduce you to. But not until after you've got your degree," Then Uncle Harry wanted to know in some detail how my studies are progressing, and went on to tell me that he has been speaking to some very big-time people and the moment I have completed my studies, they have some big plans in the pipeline for me, "But we'll discuss that tomorrow after you have had a good night's sleep, which frankly, you look like you need," he said. Clearly, the four hours sleep per day that I had maintained for the past month must have been showing.

Getting out of the car to walk up the front garden path into the house did cause me a few moments of regressive depression, but the distance between myself and the deaths of my parents was now far enough apart for me to rise above it and then put it out of my mind.

Once in the house, the first thing I did was to give everyone their presents. For Aunt Sarah I had brought a small but expensive vial of Tabac Blonde scent. I of course did not tell her that I chose this particular perfume because it reminded me of whatever it was that Janine was wearing on that fateful afternoon.

I had managed to get a pair of Cartier's gold cuff links for my Uncle, at comparatively little money. Meyer had been able to persuade his father, who was a pawnbroker, to let me have them for the same price he had paid, so they only cost me five pounds. Buying a present for Ivan was easy. I gave him two records of the then all-new Stan Kenton big band. At the time, most of the newest and best jazz records were not available in Britain. But my good pal Harold now had an American girlfriend called Meredith Something -or-other, and he fixed it with her to have her father send over any records I cared to order.

For Olga, I had bought a picture-book the title of which I have now forgotten. It was something like 'Berlin Memories', and consisted of photographic recollections of a Jewish photographer who had not only managed to escape from Germany and the Nazis, but also managed to bring his excellent and sometimes ghastly candid shots of life in Berlin with him.

After the inevitable cups of tea had been drunk, at Ivan's instigation I played some piano. I was careful to play only those tunes I knew my Aunt and Uncle would like. And then, to top it off, I flashed through a couple of Chopin Etudes. My Uncle actually clapped as the last notes of the 'Winter Wind' etude died away. My Aunt came over to me and kissed me, her face wet with tears. "Your Father, olav ha sholem, should have been here. He would have been so proud. And so would my darling sister."

The intense emotion of the moment was thankfully broken by Olga coming into the room to announce that dinner was now ready. I noticed that she was still clutching my present.

I have never been a food freak. I guess I like fine food and wine as much as anyone, but I am not one of those types who look upon food and wine as an alternative religion. As far as I am concerned, if all that is available is eggs on toast, it is okay with me. (In fact, thanks to the disgusting and shameful blockade of Cuba by the good old U.S of A., eggs on toast are already a big time meal here). And after having survived my year in Newcastle on a diet consisting mainly of sandwiches, and fish and chips, I was not ready for what I was about to receive.

There was enough food on that dining room table to feed the whole of Newcastle on Tyne! And what food! We began with some expertly home-made chopped liver, with wonderfully pungent rye bread on the side. This was followed by steaming hot bowls of chicken soup with kneidlach. And if you are not Jewish and so do not know what kneidlach are; well, tough titty! Get thee hence to a good Jewish restaurant and order some. Then maybe, you will start to understand why Jesus decided to be Jewish!

No sooner had these courses been cleared than they were replaced by two large salvers, one containing huge chunks, as well as slices of, roast chicken. On the other there was a mountain of freshly made salt beef (or corn beef if you are an American). There was also a third tray, on which there was a wonderful Jewish delicacy, helzel. For the side dishes, there was a choice of roast or mashed potatoes, compote of vegetables and stuffed marrows.

Even though I ate only half portions of everything, I reckon I got through more than I had eaten in any one entire week of the previous year.

When I dared to suggest that I had eaten my fill, the look of horror, combined with disappointment on my Aunt's face caused me to recant at once.

"Don't say that" she pleaded. What about the lockshen pudding? I made it especially for you"

"Of course I'm going to eat the lockshen pudding Auntie," I assured her. "No matter how full I am, how could I resist your lockshen pudding?"

I was of course, lying, but I could not, nor would not let her down. Every Jew knows that lockshen pudding, to be authentic, must be heavy. My Auntie's was heavy enough to require a fork-lift truck to lift it! Somehow, with a tremendous effort of will, I was able to consume an entire plateful. I was now so full that I just had to excuse myself. I came up with some nonsense about having been up all the previous night completing my college-work, in time to catch the train to London.

"You look like you haven't slept for a year," said Aunt Sarah. Then, just as I was staggering, leaden bellied, out of the room, she added to my astonishment "You barely ate anything. You are bound to wake up hungry in the night." Her face broke into a smile.

"I know," she said, "I'll get Olga to leave a dish of salmon sandwiches in the fridge for you. I know how much you love salmon sandwiches. And take a nice glass of lemon tea up to bed with you. It's good for your digestion."

As I tottered up the stairs, my tall glass of lemon tea in my hand, I muttered to myself, 'I may have lost a Jewish Mother, but I gained a Jewish restaurant instead'

Tired though I was, once in bed sleep eluded me. I just lay there staring up at the ceiling. Apart from the fact that I was horribly over-stuffed with food, I could not get Janine off my mind. I was busily depressing myself with what I considered will be the probable scenario, namely, that I would never see or hear from her again, when Ivan came in. As we lay there in our respective beds, I got him to talk about himself. At least it took my mind of Janine.

He started off with a surprising piece of news; he was engaged to be married. His wife-to-be came from a wealthy property owning Jewish family. He told me that she was two years older than he was, but, as he said, and with which I heartily agreed (I was thinking about Janine of course), that taking a wife older than you is no drawback to a successful union. I also learned that Uncle Harry had been diagnosed as having mild diabetes, and that he had been pretty sick before it was diagnosed. I was not told because both Aunt Sarah and Uncle Harry were so keen that I should continue with my studies untroubled by any news from London. He also told me that he was now in business for himself. He had two jewellery shops, one in the West End of London, and the other in Hatton Garden (which is the centre of London's precious stones business). He also had a diamond cutting workshop somewhere near Regent Street. Lastly, he told me that my Uncle had made some important contacts regarding my future, and which he would be discussing with me after the competition was out of the way.

"He says he wants your head cleared of all this competition stuff, so that you can give your full concentration to the plans he has made for you. And Jake, do what he says. He's got your best interests at heart, believe me."

As we lay there in the dark, unlit bedroom, I found myself becoming disturbed not only at what Ivan was saying, but also in the way he was saying it. In some indefinable way, he had 'grown up', which in Britain's screwed-up societal terms meant that he had sold out his principles for a free ride on the gravy train. Worse still, I realised that if I did win the competition and wanted to become a professional pianist, I could no longer rely upon Ivan to back me up in any of the arguments I will undoubtedly have with Aunt Sarah and Uncle Harry. Sure, he is going to be rich, rich, rich, but like so many other wonderful but weak people before him, his value to society will be nil, nil, nil.

So what with feeling nauseous from over-eating, the worrying uncertainties about Janine, and now this strong feeling that Ivan was joining, or probably had already joined the rat race, my first night in London was a pretty restless and depressing affair.

On the positive side, I was allowed, as I had requested, to be left alone to practise the piano in peace. And, barring the endless cups of tea that kept landing on the side of the piano, accompanied more often than not by large slabs of lemon cake, bread pudding, or, sometimes smoked salmon sandwiches, I was given all the time I needed to rehearse the four pieces I was to play at the competition. Strangely, I was not the slightest bit nervous about playing solo piano at the all-Britain finals, the reason being that I genuinely did not believe I had the slightest chance of winning.

In any case, the pieces I had selected were by now so well rehearsed, barring of course the ad lib jazz choruses that I could play them in my sleep. And I could not do much about the ad lib jazz choruses.. Either I was in a creative mood or I wasn't.

But I had genuinely enjoyed the experience of playing before a large audience in Newcastle, and was actually looking forward to doing it again in London.

On the Thursday morning before the competition, which was to take place on Saturday, having completed my practising workout, I went into the breakfast room to talk to Aunt Sarah. "Thank heavens the banging on the piano is finished," she said without looking up as I came into the breakfast room. She was sitting at the round breakfast table reading 'The Daily Mirror'.

"It's only for two more days Aunty, and then I promise I won't touch the piano unless you personally ask me to play."

As she poured me a cup of coffee from the percolator, she said "It beats me why you have to practise so much. After all, it's not like you are going to take it up professionally or anything,—are you?" She had suddenly looked up, her eyes boring into me. I decided to level with her.

"It all depends on how well I do at the competition tomorrow. If I win, which I have almost no chance of doing, well, I may consider it."

The room became clutched in an awful silence. Then it began.

"You'll consider it? You'll consider it? What do you mean, you'll consider it?" Her eyes had become like Laser beams.

"I'll consider it," I said, surprised at how sheepish my voice sounded.

Then she went into the routine so familiar to me when she is annoyed. She addressed the sideboard. "He'll consider it," she told it. "He'll consider living a poor, dirty, Bohemian life, running around with a bunch no-goods and lay-abouts. And this from someone raised in a good, clean Jewish house."

"Aunty" I said. She turned back from her conversation with the sideboard to glare at me.

"I'm only eighteen years old. Give me a chance to see what I want to do. After all, I've still got two years of studies to complete."

That seemed to dampen down her rage somewhat. She said nothing for a while, shifting her gaze from me to stare once more into her newspaper. When she next spoke, it was surprisingly, on another subject entirely. Still keeping her eyes on the paper in front of her, she said in a disarmingly off-hand way "Do you know that Ivan is getting engaged next month?"

"Yes," I replied, relieved that the heat seemed to have been taken off me. "I'm very happy for him," I lied. "So Aunty, what do you think of her?" My feigned deep interest was primarily to keep her on the subject of Ivan, and thereby off me. She tinkled the little bell on the table to summon Olga, and then whilst attempting unsuccessfully to fold up the paper she said "She's a wonderful girl. So sweet natured and kind. She is going to make Ivan a wonderful wife."

She gave up on the newspaper folding, choosing to dump the scrunched up mess of paper on the serving table behind her. Then turning back to face me, and stressing every word by tapping on the table with a fat, bejewelled forefinger, she said "And another thing,. She's absolutely loaded. Ivan bless him, will want for nothing." She tinkled the little bell again before saying:

"And do you know what her father is giving them for a wedding present?" I am sure the expression on my face indicated that I had not the foggiest idea what her father was giving them. I only hoped it did not betray the fact that I was not overly interested.

Now she moved into her finger-wagging routine. "A five bedroomed house in St, John's Wood, and a lovely flat in Cannes, and," and here her voice rose to a crescendo of victorious satisfaction,

"A motor boat"

She looked at me for some reaction, which I felt required to give.

"Gee," I said.

Then, in a completely matter of fact voice, she went on "Of course, as Irene's father explained to me," (so that's the rich bitch's name, I thought), "by putting everything in Irene's name now, they will avoid death duties. And even though her parents will be living with them, because after all, it is their home, there will be ample room for Ivan and Irene to have their own independence"

'Run Ivan. Run for your bloody life' was all I could think.

"I hope the parents won't complain when Ivan plays his jazz records," I said out loud.

I sat watching her as she demolished the rest of her coffee. As she put the cup down, she said.

"So nu, if the parents don't like it, then he won't play his damned jazz records. Let me tell you Mister Music-Mad, being a rich man and a mensch with it; that is what matters. Not a bunch of damned jazz records." She mustered into her voice all the contempt she could find, to say the words, 'jazz records'.

I was just about to make a pretty heated reply, but she held up her hand to stop me. "And" she wagged a forefinger as she spoke; "I've got a beautiful girl for you too. Two months younger than you are. A sweet, decent, respectable Jewish girl." Then she lowered her voice to a conspiratorial whisper "And her family are even richer than Ivan's in-laws."

"Auntie, I don't want to meet any rich girls. I couldn't care less about who's rich or poor. I just want to be left to get on with my own life."

"Oh, stop being a kvetch," she said impatiently. "Here I am thinking of your future and all you do is moan and groan. And you haven't even met her yet."

"Look, I am not interested in her right now, okay?"

She started drumming her fingers on the table, while looking at me intently. "You've already got a girl friend haven't you?" She said it quietly and disarmingly.

"Well...not really," I stumbled out.

She brought the sideboard into the conversation again." Not really he says," she told it. Then turning to me, icy fire in her eyes. "What do you mean by, 'not really`?"

"Well, I'm not sure how she feels about me," I stumbled out. "I mean, I think she likes me, but I'm not sure." I was already regretting not having lied about the existence of Janine. I can only blame my youthful innocence for opening my big mouth. Now, I found myself in the business of taking on a Jewish matriarch, which is a very frightening business indeed. Jewish matriarchs do not like it one little bit when their plans are thwarted. And, they will go to any lengths, short of murder to get their way. There are no Marquis of Queensberry rules when Jewish matriarchs fight. And I was about to be badly beaten. It began with the third degree.

"Is she a Jewish girl?"

"I don't know. I don't think so."

"So: she's a shiksa," she said, her voice rising to become an even mix of anger and indignation. "Some little totty with high-heeled shoes and blonde hair, I bet. Probably sixteen or seventeen years old, looking up at you with her watery, big, blue eyes. And you" she held an accusatory forefinger not more than six inches from my face, "You, like a mug, fell for it. Oy vey!"

She banged the heel of her hand against her forehead, her face showing rage and deep tragedy combined.

If I had been just a little smarter, I would have got out of that room there and then. But I was too dumb to know that eighteen year-old boys should not try to mix it with Jewish matriarchs. And this one was the Muhamed Ali of Jewish Matriarchs!

And yet, even whilst my inquisition was going on, so was my realisation of her uncanny similarities with my Mother. Every inflection of her voice, the hand movements as she stressed certain words, the way she moved her head, everything she was doing was causing vivid memories of my own dear Mother to come flooding back. Maybe, it was one of the reasons I hung on in there. If it was, it was a lousy reason.

"Firstly, she is not a blonde," I said. "She's got auburn coloured hair. And secondly, she is not sixteen. She is much older than that." No sooner than I had let the words 'much older than that' slip out, than I knew, by the look on my Aunt's face that I had made a fatal mistake.

"How much older than 'that'?" She said slowly and deliberately, but with undisguised menace in her voice.

"She's... a few years older than sixteen," I half mumbled, half stumbled, out. It was becoming like a Jewish version of Lady Bracknell's third degree of

Ernest, only this play was called 'The Unimportance of being Jake'.

"And how many years older is a few years older?' Thankfully, I got a little respite because Olga appeared. "I'm sorry Ma'am, I was polishing the silver. Did I hear you ring?"

All at once, Aunt Sarah's voice changed from cold anger to sweet reasonableness. "Would you get me a glass of whisky, Olga dear?"

"Yes, of course Ma'am," Olga replied. I had never known my Aunt to drink in the middle of the day, and judging by the look of surprise on her face, neither had Olga. As soon as Olga left the room, I said in some stupid, adolescent attempt to save myself from the discomfort of any more of my Aunt's cross examination:

"She really is a nice lady that Olga. How long has she been with you now?"

It was as if I had not spoken." How old is the shiksa?" And then in a voice filled with murderous threat, "And don't lie to me. I can always tell when you are lying. So, Mister Big-shot Piano-player, Mister Bohemian- Musician, HOW OLD IS SHE?"

Her sudden yelling destroyed any aplomb I might have had left.

"About...twenty-five to thirty," I mumbled out as indistinctly as I could.

"ABOUT WHAT!?"

I leaned forward to smooth out a non-existent crease in the table cloth.

"I think about thirty" I mumbled as softly as I could..

There was a frozen, deathly silence while Olga re-entered the room and set down the whisky my Aunt had ordered. She dismissed the German maid with a wave of her hand without ever taking her outraged glare off me for a second. As soon as Olga was out of the room, Aunt Sarah gave up being Lady Bracknell to become a Jewish Admiral of the fleet, issuing the order from the bridge: 'Turn all the guns on that pathetic, tablecloth-straightening schmock. Let him have it!'

"Thirty years old!?" She ground out through gritted teeth. Now her voice suddenly changed to heart-broken tragedy. "Thirty years old!? My lovely eighteen year old baby, who I raised and did my best for, out of love for his poor mother, is running around with some thirty year-old SHIKSA. Is she divorced, this monster?" Before I could even start to answer, she went back to the gritted teeth routine:

"Ooh, if I could get my hands on this scheming bitch, I'd give her something for taking advantage of an eighteen year-old baby." "She is not taking advantage of me," I said defensively but for no good reason, guiltily. "She's trying to help me."

But I didn't stand a chance. She decided to finish me off with a salvo of emotional torpedoes.

It began with her walking up and down the little breakfast room, her clenched fists pressed into her cheeks, rather like 'Cuddles' Zakall used to do in the movies and exactly what my mother so often did in real life. Suddenly she stopped walking and took her hands from her cheeks to rest them on the back of a chair. Then she said "And what do you think your dear, darling dead mother, olav ha sholem, would say, if she were here now?"

She took her hands from the back of the chair to press them together in front of her chest, as if in prayer, and looking upwards at the ceiling, tears running down her cheeks, she said in a voice of shocked sorrow "My poor darling sister Eve. Tortured in this world by Hitler's bombs, and now tortured in the next by seeing her only beloved son running round with a woman twice his age."

After a long, dramatic pause, she hit me with the big one.

"I dreamt of her last night Jake," she said as she wiped tears from her face with the back of her hand. "She was standing right there." She pointed to the small rug in front of the door that leads into my Uncle's study. "And she was crying Jake. Your Mother was sobbing. And I said, 'what's the matter Eve? Don't cry' But she went on sobbing Jake; sobbing her heart out."

Now her voice changed from broken-hearted to bitter recrimination: "And now I know why she was so heart broken. How can you do this to your Mother? I know you don't care about my feelings. But your own dear Mother Jake, how can you do it to her?"

She sat down heavily on the chair, burying her face in her hands. Bette Davis could not have played it better. It was more than I could handle. I was beaten and I knew it.

"Okay," I said. And going over to her and putting my arm around her heaving shoulders I whispered to her "I promise I'll give her up. Please stop crying Auntie. I won't ever see her again. I promise. Please stop crying now"

I pushed my handkerchief into her hands. As she gently dabbed her eyes with it, she said in a broken-hearted voice "If you ever see that scheming bitch again, you will break the heart of your poor mother. And if you do that I will never forgive you." Then, pointing her forefinger straight up at the ceiling, she added, "And neither will The Almighty."

She managed to inculcate into her voice a terrible finality of Biblical authority as she spoke.. She became a female Moses addressing not so much the Israelites, but THE Israelite. Me.

"Okay, okay," I said hopelessly. "I've said I'll give her up and that's a promise. In any case, I think she has actually given me the heave-ho already. But whatever, I promise I will give her up. Is that enough for you?" She searched my face for what seemed a long time before saying humbly, and with deep sincerity "Thank you Jake darling. I know you are doing the right thing. Your Mother can now be at peace once more. Thank you."

I watched her as she dabbed her eyes again. It had been a brilliant performance on her part.

Having won the argument hands down (although she failed to inflict upon me the guilt complex that was supposed to live within me for the rest of my life), she handed me back my handkerchief, and then, rather like a piece of elastic that had been temporarily pulled out of shape, she snapped back to her normal self. Reaching for the little bell on the breakfast table and ringing it furiously, she said "Where is that bloody Olga. She's never here when I want her" She got up from the table and went out into the kitchen.

I noticed that the whisky still sat untouched on the table. But it had served its purpose. It had simply been a stage-prop in an Oscar winning performance.

Chapter 14

TWENTY-FOUR HOURS LATER, one entire day since I had given my solemn promise to Aunt Sarah, that I would cut Janine out of my life, I was still unsure whether I intended to, or indeed was even capable of doing so. She was so intertwined with my sex drive that she and it had become one and the same thing. In my mind, giving her up was tantamount to giving up sex, which was unthinkable.

I also knew deep down, that were I to see her at the Lyceum on Saturday night, the only stand I could make against her would be with my cock! But I had also come round to the cold reality that the odds of her putting in an appearance were very small indeed. Of course, I still clung to the shreds of her promise that she would be there to see me perform, but in my heart I knew that something had caused her to re-evaluate our relationship.

I went upstairs to the bedroom I shared with Ivan, to find a parcel on my bed, with a note attached in Aunt Sarah's handwriting. It read 'Because you were making such a bloody row on the piano, I went out shopping. While I was out I bought you half-dozen shirts. I will not have you walking about looking like a tramp. Wear them in good health. I love you'.

PS. I have thrown your f'kakte old shirts away.

Whilst it was great having a pile of new shirts, I was also not unmindful of the fact that my Aunt must have gone through my belongings without my knowledge. I knew I loved her and that she loved me. I also knew she had a heart of gold. But I was nevertheless very put out at the thought of her rummaging through my belongings without my permission. Even though I was living a life of luxury here, it caused me to look forward evermore to getting out of this claustrophobic atmosphere and back to Newcastle where I could be my own man (or boy), again.

That same evening after I had bathed and shaved, as I did every evening whilst I lived in this house, I borrowed some of my cousin's expensive aftershave friction, followed by so much Brylcream on my hair that it finally surrendered without its usual fight and obeyed all the commands of my comb. Even though I had meant to reserve it for the competition, on Aunt Sarah's insistence, I put on my best suit together with one of my new shirts and a barely worn tie that Ivan had sent me for my last birthday.

I looked about as good as I could. I studied myself critically in the full-length mirror that was fixed to the inside of the wardrobe door. In my favour, I was tall, about six feet two inches. My hair looked good to me for the first time in its life. Actually, it looked terrible, but I had seen a movie with Richard Greene, who was known for his wonderful, thick shiny, hair. And tonight mine looked like his, which, if I had any idea at all, would have caused me to wear a balaclava!

What I hated most about my reflection was that I was painfully thin. I did have quite broad shoulders, but they seemed to be all bone. I had very little muscle anywhere as far as I could see. My face was thin and pale, making my brown eyes look bigger and browner than they actually were. As I studied myself, I came to the opinion that I looked like a ghost, but with nice shiny dark brown hair.

I already knew I was ugly. But tonight, for one night only folks, I rejoiced in my ugliness. Because tonight my Aunt had invited the girl whom she had decided I was to marry, to come around to the house to meet me. Just one look in the mirror had given me the confidence to be sure that Aunt Sarah's fiendish plan was doomed to failure.

One look at me and Miss Multi-Millionairess will develop an instant headache and make a dash for her solid gold Rolls, or whatever it is that the super-rich ride about in.

My thoughts were broken into by Aunt Sarah yelling up to me to came down and meet Ivan's fiancée, Irene.

Ivan had already told me how, after coming home from his business, he likes to pour himself a beer and play a few jazz records while reading the evening paper. He said it was his way of unwinding. The previous evening I had sat with him whilst the Benny Goodman trio and a glass of Barclay's beer soothed away the tensions of running his business.

Tonight it was to be different. Instead of me bounding down the stairs in time with Gene Krupa's drum beat, I was horrified to hear the slushy banality of Bing Crosby gurgling his way through 'Sweet Leilani' coming up to meet me on the stairs.

"Hi, come in Jake," Ivan said as I came into the room. I immediately saw that he was drinking tea, not beer. It went with the music perfectly.

"This is my Irene," he said. Then, turning to her he introduced me "Darling this is my jazz-genius of a cousin, Jake Silver."

"Ivan has told me so much about you," she chirped, as we shook hands. I instantly knew that I was never going to have anything in common with this chick as long as I lived. To start with, her looks were utterly boring. She was the same height as Ivan but too thin for my taste. Nothing bulged through the thin, dark-brown, polo-necked sweater she was wearing. And her bottle-green mid-calf skirt was incapable of flattering the sexless hips and bottom. Her legs were of average length, but spoiled by fat calves and thick ankles. Her face was thin with lips to match. What with her brunette hair tidied back into a bun, she was a monument to prim correctness. She was a classic example of what many mothers at that time brain-washed their daughters into believing was the correct way to look. I could almost hear it as I looked at her: 'Sit up straight Irene'. 'Hold you hands in your lap like this Irene'.' Don't do that. It isn't very lady-like Irene'. What distortions of femininity, what sacrifices of female sexuality and sensuousness have been imposed upon young girls by mothers, who, when they were young, were often far more sex-mad than their daughters will ever be. Thank you Lord for those chicks who are so naturally sexy, so innately born to be fucked, that even the most forbidding of mothers can do nothing to obscure their sweet lustfulness.

Irene was certainly not one of these. Irene was 'correct and sensible', and I cannot think of anything worse to say about anybody. Her hair style, her clothes, her schoolteacher-like shoes, no doubt bought from a shoe shop in Bond Street or Knightsbridge, bearing the legend 'Suppliers of shoes to H.M. The Queen', even her wrist watch and her two thin gold bangles were in keeping with her corny conformity.

"You like Bing?" I asked in a phoney, cheery voice.

"Oh yes. Don't you?" Her eyes were searching mine to see if she had said the right thing. Saying and doing 'the right thing' was clearly almost a religion with this female.

"I used to like him" I said in a off-hand way, as I sat down on the sofa; "But he sings such crap these days" Oddly, I seldom used the word 'crap' to describe something I did not like. Also, back in 1948, such a word was considered too rude to be used in polite company. But there was something so annoyingly 'naice' about this woman, that it was all I could do, not to have described this execrable record as 'a piece of shit'. It was obvious that even the use of the word 'crap' had discombobulated her somewhat. It caused her to sit down very suddenly and concentrate on her hand smoothing her skirt, while she recovered from her embarrassment.

My pleasure at having mischievously pricked the bubble of her respectability evaporated the moment I shifted my gaze to Ivan. He was clearly upset at seeing his fiancé's discomfiture and quite clearly did not know whether to tell me off or make an excuse for what had admittedly been a churlish piece of teen-age gaucherie. The sad and confused expression on his face filled me with immediate remorse. (As I think about it now and remember that all this upset and remorse was about my describing Bing Crosby singing 'Sweet Leilani' as crap, I shake my head in wonderment at the comparative innocence of the middle classes in those days),

"I'm so sorry if I upset you," I blurted out. "I really am sorry. The word slipped out before I could stop it." Then I added an "I'm sorry Ivan," as he went across to the radiogram to remove the offending record from the turntable. I did the only thing I could think of by way of expressing the sincerity of my contrition. I went to the piano and even though I loathed the tune, I played it as best I could, playing the tune with my left hand and decorating it with corny arpeggios in my right. As I did so, I said "This is for you Irene."

She smiled over to me, and, at Ivan's instigation came over to the piano to watch me play it with evident satisfaction.

I was thankfully saved from having to play a second chorus, by the door being pushed open by Olga, wheeling in a trolley bearing a large jug of lemonade, a few bottles of some fizzy drink and a half dozen tall glasses. She was followed in by Uncle Harry, and behind him Aunt Sarah who was talking away to another woman with whom she had linked arms. This beauty was anywhere between forty and fifty rears of age, with obviously dyed, blonde hair, carefully coiffured, in a sort of June Alyson 'page boy' style. Her face had the rock-like hardness of a chorus girl twenty years past her best. She was of medium height and obviously expensively dressed But all the money in the world could not buy clothes subtle enough to hide her waistless waist, or her titless tits. No amount of Parisian scent could disguise the aura of cold, calculating, soullessness that surrounded her. She gave the description, 'hard' new depth and meaning.

When I was introduced to her by Aunt Sarah I put my hand out to shake hers, but she did not bother to respond. Her thin, over-lipsticked mouth managed, very reluctantly, to open just wide enough to say 'hello'. At the same time, her cold, grey eyes surveyed me, rather as if I were an apartment block, for sale and she was standing on the opposite of the road taking in the entire building panoramically, in order to estimate if it was a good investment. I noticed the near-reverence in my Aunt's voice as I was introduced her to her; "This is Dora Elman. Jake, you must have heard of her husband, Mordechai Elman, the international banker"

"No, I'm afraid not," I said. Dora Elman's eyes flashed in momentary hostility at that, before quickly returning to their hooded, expressionless norm. Uncle Harry said, "I'm sorry that Mordechai couldn't come with you Dora. It's a while since we have seen one another."

"He's away in America 'arry. He's involved in a major investment there" She flashed a look in my direction to see if I was suitably impressed at that momentous statement. As it did not mean a thing to me, I just poured myself a glass of lemonade in the leaden silence that followed. I noticed that she had a hoarse, hard voice with the accent of a cockney who is trying hard to hide the fact.

I may not have been impressed with Mrs Elman's intimation of great wealth and importance of the Elman family, but, by the looks on their faces, Uncle Harry, Aunt Sarah and, I am afraid, even Ivan, most clearly were.

Irene was too busy smiling sweetly and holding Ivan's hand to have an opinion.

Dora went over to one of the armchairs and sat down.

"Would you like something to drink, Dora?" Asked Aunt Sarah.

"Yes, but something just a little stronger than anything you 'ave on that trolley."

Uncle Harry now swung into action.

"Tell me what you fancy Dora dear. I keep my liquor in the bar, in my office, but I can have brought in anything you wish. Your wish is my command," he said smiling and pleased with himself for have come up with such a clever bon mot.

"I don' blame you keeping it under lock and key," she said. "The way the youngsters take advantage of us these days, they must think we're made of money."

"You are so right Dora," said my Uncle with sickening sincerity. "So, what is to be your pleasure?"

"We'll go into your office in a minute 'arry. We can 'ave a drink there and leave the youngsters to themselves."

I looked quickly around the room. Dora Elman was sitting throne-like in the armchair calmly surveying us all, her face bearing an expression that said, 'As I am by far, the richest person in the room, it means that I am automatically entitled to be treated better and with more respect than those with less of the green stuff.' I looked across at my Aunt and Uncle and then Ivan. The way they were acting, I was sure that they would not only kiss Dora Elman's arse, but would consider it an honour to be allowed to do so.

I interrupt this narrative to ask: why is it that western society is so fucked up over money? Even if the poor person is, say, an acknowledged poet, someone who can pick up a piece of paper and a pencil, and seemingly pluck from the air, wondrous thoughts and set them down in wondrous language, and the rich man is just a dull, old banker, who has given nothing of any true value to society, and whose father and grandfather were probably equally dull old bankers who also created nothing but money for themselves, ninety-nine per cent of western society would be far more respectful and obsequious to the banker than to the poet. Until Britain, the USA and the rest of what is laughingly known as the 'Democratic Free World' realise that putting the obtainment of personal wealth above all other considerations is an unsustainable philosophy, they will steadily go downhill (as they are now clearly doing), and must eventually implode from the poverty and crime that such a system creates and encourages.

"I understand young man that you can play the piano," Dora Elman said to me in imperious fashion.

"I play jazz piano" I said, refilling my glass with lemonade.

"Can't you play classical music as well?"

"Well," I replied, "I do play it for practise, but there's this guy Vladimir Horowitz. I reckon that the world of classical music isn't big enough for the two of us. So I let him do the classical stuff and he leaves me to play the jazz."

It was meant to be light-hearted party banter. It fell like a lead balloon! Ivan did start to smile at what I had said until he noticed that Dora Elman's reaction was to sit staring, stone-faced. He quickly changed his smile into a cough. Irene, who was sitting on the armrest of Ivan's armchair, dutifully did her best by getting as near as she could to not being there at all. She just sat perfectly still, staring unblinkingly at a spot on the carpet about six feet in front of her.

"I thought only niggers play jazz," said the delightful Dora.

I could not let that pass.

"It may interest you to know that both Horowitz and Rachmaninov are great fans of Art Tatum, a blind black jazz pianist. And did you know that black people dislike intensely being referred to as 'niggers', Mrs Elman?"

"I should care what they like or dislike," she said, shrugging her shoulders and looking around for approval, which she dutifully got.

"Anyway," she went on, "let us hear you play some of your nigger jazz music."

"No," I said rising from the piano stool.

Aunt Sarah now got into the act.

"Come on Jake darling," she said pleadingly, "You must play for Dora. I've told her so much about your piano playing."

I was starting to lose my cool, at this point.

"I am sorry Auntie, but I will not play jazz music, which is the cultural heritage of the black people of the United States, for someone who refers to them as niggers. And that is final."

I knew not what angered me most. Hearing that frozen-faced rich hag refer to an entire race of people in such disgracefully derogatory language, or watching my family, whom I loved so much, dancing sycophantically to the jingle of money. I was of course, too callow to realise that this adolescent display of petulance was both ill-mannered and unnecessarily embarrassing to them.

The atmosphere became frozen and deadly.

"Well," Dora said, cutting into the heavy, frozen, silence, to look around her as she slapped her knobbly, arthritic but bejewelled hands on her thighs. Then she started to rise with a look on her face that said, 'That did it! I think its time for me to go'.

Aunt Sarah leapt in to save the situation.

"He's such a temperamental musician," she said with jokey sweetness. "He'll play later, when your Candy gets here."

And then turning to me with a smile on her lips but pleading in her eyes, she added, "Won't you Jake darling?"

I gave in. "Yeah, sure," I said hopelessly.

Uncle Harry took this as his cue to say in his cheeriest voice "Come on Dora, let us grown-ups go to my office for a nice drink and leave the young folks to their nigger music."

I understood why he had used that phrase and so did not hold it against him.

Once they had left the room, I asked Irene, "What did you think of that cow?"

She immediately looked into Ivan's face, I guess in order to find out what she was supposed to think of 'that cow'.

"You've really done yourself in with her Jake boy," Ivan said, his voice full of regret.

"Mmm," Irene said, gladly agreeing and nodding her head knowingly.

The doorbell rang.

"That'll be Candy," Ivan said, rising to answer the front door. Just before going out of the room, he turned to me and pleaded "For Chrissakes Jake, be nice to her."

I heard my Aunt running along the hall so that she can also be present at the door opening ceremony. I heard the door open and my Aunt say, "You look lovely dear." Then she came into the room clutching Candy's hand who was behind her, with Ivan bringing up the rear. It looked to me like my Aunt was pulling her into the room. I had returned by now to the piano stool and was sitting there nursing my lemonade, and wishing like hell it was whiskey, as my Aunt led, or pulled, Candy straight across the room to me.

"Jake darling, this is Candy Elman." While I got to my feet to shake her hand, Auntie turned to Irene; "Irene, this is Candy and Candy, this is Irene" Then she added, "And Ivan, you already know." Then, she added with a knowing smile: "Well, I'm going to leave you all to enjoy yourselves."

Just before going out of the door, she turned and said to Candy, "Be nice to Jake, Candy darling. He's so nervous at meeting you."

"Yeah," I said, now thoroughly sick of the entire evening; "I'm scared out of my wits. Auntie. Could I have a large scotch to steady my nerves?"

Before she could show shock and displeasure that her plans for me to marry this female had been wrecked by my displaying such dissolute tendencies, the Great Candy said "Ooh, what a good idea. Could I have one too please?"

Aunt Sarah gave a relieved smile. "Of course Candy darling. I'll send Olga in right away with a tray of drinks. I'm so silly, I forget how grown up you all are" And she hurriedly disappeared from the room.

Before I tell you what Candy Elman looked like, I should tell you, it is my contention that nearly everyone has a phantasy ideal partner. Of course, only the lucky few, even get to meet, let alone have an affair with, or marry yet, someone who fits their ideal image. So, should you meet someone who is, say, sixty per cent of your ideal, you will probably mildly fancy him or her. Should you meet an eighty or ninety percenter, the chances are that you're going to fall head over heels in love and probably get married. (Unless marrying money is your sole object. In that case, what I am about to say won't interest you in the least).

My ideal woman hasn't changed at all from back then, when I was eighteen, to this very day. (A little later on, I am going to tell you of a woman who was not just eighty or ninety percent of my dream woman, but a hundred and fifty per cent! And you'll also discover why it was through her that I now find myself stranded in Cuba, living the life of a drunken bum. But like I said, that is for later).

To start with, my ideal woman must be intelligent, knowledgeable and hip. She should be tallish, about five feet eight inches and preferably blonde, rather than brunette or red head. She would have a high, proud, intelligent forehead, a delicate, kissable nose, high cheekbones and full inviting lips over even, white teeth. She must never, ever, allow lipstick to get on her teeth. Red teeth may be a turn-on for Dracula but they are a total turn-off for me. She will have emerald green eyes, veiled by slightly hooded eyelids. Her ears must be shapely and not too big, and she should also possess a firm, little chin. Her complexion must be smooth and flawless. This pretty face would be attached to her body by a slim, elegant, neck. She must also carry her shoulders proudly, because I hate a sloucher. Also, slouching does bad things for a gal's tits. She should have a straight slim back and large, deep, firm breasts, with not over-sized nipples. She should taper to a waist, small enough to accent the swell of her hips. My Miss Perfect must have a firm, high arse. Floppy, dropped arses are another complete no-no for me. She will have graceful arms and smooth long-fingered hands. If she has vaccination marks, they must be all but invisible. I hate the sight of vaccination marks as big as tennis balls on any female's upper arm, which can be a very beautiful part of a woman. My dream woman will have long, Cyd Charisse-long legs. And they must be proportioned like Ms Charisse's legs and must also taper down to beautiful, kissable feet and shapely toes. One last thing. She will speak in a dulcet-toned, mellifluous, speaking voice. And that ladies and gentlemen, is my perfect woman.

Now I suppose, feminists reading this will be very outraged. They will be thinking 'Who the fuck does he think he is, being so picky and choosey about women?' Well, my reply to that is 'Who the fuck do I have to be, to be so picky and choosey about women?'

Having given you a brief (but you must admit, exciting), rundown on my ideal woman, let me now tell you about Miss Candice (Candy), Elman, the chick my Auntie thought I should, to use her favourite expression, 'settle down with'.

She was about five feet four inches in her high-heeled shoes. She had a small forehead above which was frizzy black hair, which looked like it had been combed with an egg-beater. She had dark brown eyes, the same colour as the large round frames of her spectacles, which kept sliding down her tiny, upturned nose. She did have nice lips and teeth, thank heaven, or she would have scored zero for face and hair. She was also plump in a bouncy sort of way. It was the kind of figure one associates with a senior girl at St. Trinian's. She was wearing a black knee-length dress, with white lapels, and a white sash pulled tight around her waist in a hopeless attempt to fool you into believing that she had a waistline. Her feet were too small and out of proportion to her calves and ankles.

Set against my ideal female, I would have scored her maybe eight out of a hundred. As I looked down at her from my six feet-plus angle, I found myself thinking 'Aunt Sarah must be out of her mind to think that I could settle down, up, or sideways, with this frizzy frump. I mean, how much can anyone love money?'

She did have a couple of things going for her. To start with, she was bouncy and bubbling with energy. After having said her hello's to Ivan and Irene, following up with something complimentary about Irene's sweater, she came back to the piano stool, where I was once more sitting, and taking my hand, pulled me over to the sofa, saying as she did so "Come and talk to me."

Ivan, upon seeing this, put his arm around Irene's shoulders and stood up, taking her with him.

"Listen you two, we have to go down to the shops and buy something for Irene's mother."

I saw this for what it was; a nice but pointless gesture to leave us alone in order to get to know one another better. I thought, 'he must be as crazy as his mother to think, even for a moment, that I would want to be left alone with this f'shtunkener looking chick!'

No sooner had they gone out than Olga arrived with a tray bearing a bottle of Johnny Walker Black Label, a soda siphon and some glasses.

"Oh, great," we both said, or words to that effect. Candy leapt up to pour the drinks. I noticed that she filled the whiskey goblets two thirds full of scotch and topped them off with the barest splash of soda.

"You really make a stiff whiskey," I said, as she brought the two drinks over and set them down on the coffee table in front of us. "That's not the only thing I can make stiff," she answered to my utter surprise. For this line alone, she immediately gained ten points and took one giant step forward in my estimation.

Having plonked herself down next to me, she reached for the two glasses, one of which she handed to me saying "A toast. Here's to living fast, dying young and making pretty corpses."

Then, again to my considerable surprise, she polished off the entire glass at one go, after which she immediately went and got herself a refill.

"I hear from Ivan that you are a shit-hot jazz pianist. ('And I had to apologise to Irene for using the word 'crap'. I thought. I was getting to like this girl more and more.)

"I try to be" I said. "Do you know that your mother refers to it as nigger music?"

She made no reply until after she had fished a packet Luckies out of her handbag, together with a gold cigarette lighter. Once she had lit up and blown the smoke above my head, she said.

"Mummy's an old bat. She never lets herself go. She smiles less than Buster Keaton."

'Another good line' I thought.

"Hey," she said. "I forgot to offer you a ciggie." She held out the pack to me.

In truth I had decided to stop smoking. Due to Harold Landing, who had introduced me to the habit, I was smoking about five cigarettes a day, back in Newcastle, mostly in the evening. But now that I was out of his sphere of influence, I had stopped. I had also decided on the train up to London, that the next fag I smoked would be after I had fucked Janine and not before.

But, as they say, that was then and this is now.

"Thanks," I said, fishing one out of the packet with my lips (which I thought was a very sophisticated, Hollywood thing to do), and lighting it with her Cartier lighter.

"Where is the old tart now?" she asked, and then took another huge swig of scotch. She noticed the look of surprise at the speed with which she could put away the booze.

"Don't try to keep up with me, or you'll end up under the table."

"She's with my Aunt and Uncle in his office." I said.

"I hope she stays there," she said flatly. Then she looked at her wrist watch. "Hell, I'll have to leave in five minutes"

She ground out her cigarette in the ash tray.

"Does Sarah know you smoke?" she asked me.

"No, she doesn't," I said.

She took my cigarette from between my fingers and as she carefully stubbed it out she said "Open your jacket pocket." I did so and she carefully poured the contents of the ash-tray into it.

"My old yenta of a mother doesn't know I smoke and I don't want her to find out. It's probably best that Sarah doesn't find out about you either. We've got to have our own lives Jake. And we must not let them in or believe me; they will go out of their way to screw it up for us."

"Jesus, you are so right" I agreed. This chick Candy was really something. She gave the impression that she was travelling at a hundred miles an hour.

"You know what I believe Jake?"

"What?" I said.

"I believe we are meant to have a good time. I'm a sensation seeker." She polished off her drink, and went across the room to get another. As she turned to come back, she said "I want to try everything at least once."

Sitting down real close to me and she said very quietly "Maybe you can tell me something, because you're in the jazz world. I and a few of my friends are mad keen to try smoking some of this marijuana. It's supposed to be great. We know jazz musicians smoke it. Can you get us some?"

I couldn't resist smiling at the idea that she thought me worldly enough to have connections with the drug scene. All I knew about marijuana at that time, was its mention in the titles of a couple of jazz records I had, one was Louis Armstrong's 'Muggles' and the other was I believe, Wingie Manone singing a tune called 'Dreamed About a Reefer Five Miles Long'.

"I'd love to help you," I said. "But I am not a professional jazz musician yet. I am still at Durham University reading Modern History."

"Shit, what a bloody bore. I only came over here because I thought you could help me."

She bounced to her feet. "I've go to go Jake. I've got to get home and change into something a bit sexier, 'cos I'm off to a party. In any case I'm dying for a smoke, so I better go somewhere Mamma is not. Come and walk me out to the car."

"I'm helluva sorry you have to go," I said, and suddenly I really meant it.

Her car was a new two-seater MG. "Wow, what a great car," I said and started to look inside at the dashboard.

"You are supposed to be seeing me off, not the car" She reached under the front seat and came up with a large woollen scarf which she proceeded to wrap around her neck. Then she said "Well, come and kiss me goodbye."

As I went to the other side of the car, where she was standing, she got up on her tip-toe, her face facing the sky, her eyes closed. I put my arms around her to kiss her and she gave me a lasciviously wet, open-mouthed kiss. As we went on kissing and tonguing, her hands, which had been on my back, descended to fondle my arse. Then, to my surprise, she put one hand on my rapidly stiffening cock, gave it a loving, friendly squeeze, saying as she did so, "Mmm," even while her tongue was still flicking into and out of my mouth. Then she broke off the fondling and kissing, whispered," You're alright Jake." and jumped into the MG and shouted to me over the noise of the revving engine, "Daddy is giving me my own apartment next month. I'll let you know the address once I know it myself. Daddy owns about a thousand apartments and I don't know which one he is going to give me."

Then she threw the gear lever into first, gave a little wave and over the noise of the revving engine yelled "I'll ring you" and shot off down the road.

I went back into the house very confused and extremely randy (or horny, if you are an American). As I settled down once more on the sofa to finish off my drink I was aware that I liked Candy very much, even though I knew that I could never be in love with, or even fancy her. 'But we might be good for one another at that' I rationalised. 'She's all energy and risk-taking, whereas I'm withdrawn and careful. She is very rich and I've got no money of my own'. It was starting to occur to me that together we made a lot of sense. 'And' I suddenly realised, 'we are both pretty ugly'.

Aunt Sarah came bustling into the room.

"Where have you been? And where's Candy?"

"I was just outside seeing her off."

She crooked a finger at me; "Come" she said. "Dora wants to talk to you. And Jake," she said pleadingly, as we walked out of the room together; "Be a good boy and treat her with respect."

She suddenly stopped me in the hallway and made a motion with her forefinger against her lips for me to be quiet. Then she whispered "What did you think of Candy?"

"I liked her very much," I whispered back.

"Good, good," she was smiling jubilantly.

We went into the study where Dora was seated in the big, brown, leather, swivel-armchair behind my uncle's desk, clutching her gin and tonic, her cigarette smouldering away in the ash-tray in front of her. Aunt Sarah took one of the smaller brown leather chairs facing her, saying brightly as she sat down "Let me have another gin Harry darling."

So, what did you think of my Candy?" Dora asked me, in a hoarse, gin-soaked voice.

After seating myself in the only vacant chair I said, "She's very nice Mrs. Elman."

She took a sip of her drink, and reached for her cigarette.

"More important," she began, but we had to wait to find out what was more important, while she took a large drag of her cigarette and with great care, flicked the ash into the ash-tray. Then she went on, smoke pouring out of her mouth: "More important," she said again, "is what Candy thought of you. And we won't know that until after I have spoken to her will we?"

I said nothing. But it hit me that Mrs. Elman was decidedly drunk.

"And where is Candy now?" she asked me.

"She had to leave in order to change her clothes to go to a party. And as far as liking me goes, Mrs Elman, she has invited me to visit her when she moves into her own apartment next month."

"Dora sat staring at me, the gin glass still resting on her lower lip, her expressionless, grey eyes very bloodshot. Then she moved the glass a couple of inches from her mouth to say, more to herself than anyone else:

"Over my dead body is she moving into 'er own flat."

Then, I rather stupidly said "She is over eighteen, Mrs Elman. Don't you trust her?"

"I trust 'er alright. It's nigger-loving piano players I'm not too sure about."

"Now wait a min—"

But she cut me off with a wave of her hand. "But that is by the way," she said. "Whether or not she moves into her own place is nothing to do with you. What is to do with you is that in the summer, beginning of July to be precise, we are taking a few people on our yacht for a Mediterranean cruise."

Aunt Sarah jumped in excitedly; "You should see their boat Jake. It must be the biggest private yacht in the world." She clasped her hands in front of her chest as she spoke, exactly like I remembered my Mother doing when she was eulogising about something.

Dora let her finish and then, while holding her glass out to Uncle Harry for a refill, went on.

"It may not be the biggest in the world, but it is the largest in Cannes, at any rate. Now young man," she swivelled her big chair around to face me directly, but being pissed, she swung round too far. When she stopped, she looked around in puzzlement because I was nowhere to be seen. When it did seep through her gin-sozzled brain what she had done, she very carefully swivelled it back until she did face me.

"If, and I repeat, if my daughter does like you, then you are invited on the cruise. But I warn you, there will be two or even three other boys on board who will also be trying to win her. So you are going to have to fight hard to get your hands on my Candy." ('You should see where she had her hands on me' I thought). "And even if she likes you the most, you will still have to impress my husband and me."

Uncle Harry, who had been leaning against the bar listening, his cigar firmly clamped in his mouth, his brandy snifter in his hand, now entered the conversation.

"Dora," he said, removing his cigar. "I and some of my friends have big plans for Jake."

I looked at him in some surprise, because, barring a passing mention in the car on the way home from Kings Cross station, he had made no mention of his 'big plans'. He saw the puzzlement on my face.

"I know you don't know anything about this yet, Jake." Then, turning to Dora; "I have decided to wait until this competition business is over before discussing it with him. But believe me Dora, when you and Mordechai hear of our plans, you'll realise just how good an investment Jake is going to turn out to be."

Aunt Sarah jumped in again. "And he's such a nice boy Dora. He'll make Candy a wonderful husband, believe me."

Dora, who had swung her chair round to face Uncle Harry whilst he spoke (and also to receive her refilled gin and tonic), and then swung it back a little to face Aunt Sarah whilst she spoke, now swung round to face me again. She gave me a long, drunken stare, before saying, whilst still staring at me "If he'll stop all this arty-farty nigger music nonsense, he might be alright. But anyway, I think Candy is looking for something a bit better."

I could feel my anger starting to rise with this nasty, drunken, old broad.

I raised my hand. "Now wait a min—" But again she cut me off by shouting over the top of me, while pointing with a knobbly, bejewelled forefinger.

"You keep quiet and don't speak until you are spoken to, young man."

She was now starting to slur her words a little.

"You have very bad manners, d'you, hic, know that? You should know better than to, hic, interrupt your elders and betters."

I could take no more. She had picked up her glass, but before she could get it to her lips, I suddenly stood up and reaching over the desk, very firmly pulled the glass out of her hand, spilling a few drops on my hand and on the desk. As I pulled the glass forcibly from her she drew back in fear. But I was too damned angry to give a shit about that. I never took my eyes off her as I set her drink down on the corner of the desk, furthest from her reach. With my hands on the edge of the desk to support me, I leaned forward so that my face would be as near to hers as possible. It wasn't as close as I would have liked due to the depth of the desk, but I was near enough to have to suffer her gin-soaked breath.

"There are a few things you should know, Mrs Elman" I said, doing my best to keep my voice level and calm. "Firstly, I do not like being talked of in the third person, as if I am not here in the room. Secondly, although I may get to like your daughter, Mrs Elman, because in the ten minutes or so we spent together, she came across as a nice girl, I would never marry her. So, you can kiss that idea goodbye. Frankly, Mrs Elman, Candy is nowhere near good looking enough to satisfy me. I'll go further Mrs. Elman, Candy is a very plain looking girl indeed. But even if she had looked like Lana Turner and had I been head over heels in love with her, I would have talked myself out of her, because of you."

She reached forward for her open cigarette case that lay on the desk in front of her, but I got there first, grabbing it and setting it down out of her reach next to her glass of booze. She started to say something, but I shouted her down, saying slowly and stressing every word. "You've drunk enough and smoked enough for one night. Now show the good manners to shut up until after I am finished."

For a moment, I listened to the stunned silence in the room.

"Do you know Mrs. Elman that your daughter refers to you as the Old Bat, and the Old Tart? In my opinion, to call you an old bat is being kind to you. As to whether you are an old tart, I neither know nor care. But of this I am sure; you are a nasty, gin-soaked, arrogant, ugly and miserable old hag."

She got to her feet, and swaying drunkenly, pointed a finger at me saying "How dare you. If my husband Morde—" But I cut her off, by first pushing her accusatory finger firmly out of the way and saying loudly over her rasping voice; "As to your poor, pitiful husband, I don't know whether to feel sadness for him or contempt for putting up with an old witch like you."

She fell back into her swivel chair, a stunned look on her face.

"You accused me of having bad manners Mrs. Elman," I continued. "Luckily for you, I actually have rather good manners. Or else I would have told you in very graphic terms, where you can stick your yacht and your money." She just stared at me in shock and disbelief, her mouth hanging half open.

"I am going out of this room now, Mrs. Elman, and I hope that I will never have the total displeasure of looking upon your drunken, dreary face again." Then I turned to my transfixed-with-shock Uncle and Aunt.

"Goodnight Uncle, goodnight Auntie," I said as sweetly as I could. I strolled through the thick silence to the office door. Before going out, I turned and throwing my arms outward in the 'Grand Guignol' manner of an over-the-top thespian, said.

I leave you in the company of the Daughter of Dracula. You had better get yourself some garlic, before midnight and the old bat turns herself into a real old bat and attacks your respective jugulars. Goodnight."

I closed the door behind me as quietly as I could and went directly to my bedroom. Fortunately, Ivan was still out with his beloved Irene, so I had the room to myself.

I lay on the bed, fingers interlocked under my head, staring at the ceiling. I recalled how I used to lie like this when I was younger, after my dreaded sessions with 'The sicko psycho'. Whether it was because that recollection invoked memories of such an unhappy period in my life I do not know, but it triggered something within me that caused me to start missing my parents all over again.

'Do they know, or even care how I am feeling?' I wondered. I suddenly needed them to know and care very much indeed. I desperately wanted their advice about what to do.

I tried to assess my present predicament, I had no girl friend. The only one I wanted had sent clear signals that she did not want to know about me. Without her, I was not interested in returning to Newcastle and continuing my studies. Also, I was beginning to realise that I had almost certainly screwed up my relationship with the only people in the world I loved, namely, my Aunt, Uncle and Ivan. I felt pretty certain that the little performance I had given downstairs would earn me the telling off of the century, and that it was a serious possibility that my Uncle would cut off my weekly stipend. Without any regular money, I realised, I could not go back to Newcastle. 'And what if they asked me to leave this house because of my disruptive influence? No, they would never do that' I reckoned. But could I go on standing the strain of living here? Even though I loved them, there was no doubt in my mind that we were growing apart. My sense of values was already fundamentally at odds with theirs.

And even Ivan had changed radically. He had given up Count Basie for 'Sweet Leilani'. He seemed to have given up being young in favour of becoming prematurely middle-aged and 'sensible'. But worst of all, it seemed to me that my cousin, whom I had admired for all of my life, had now sold his soul to some little schnipke of a girl, solely for money and security. All his aesthetic sensitivities were being anaesthetised in favour of selling glittery bits of stone, to boring, rich old people. Poor Ivan. I wanted to talk and dream and argue with him about jazz and great tunes and movies and such, as we always had in the past. But these days, his conversation appeared to centre upon the two most negative words in the English language; 'settling down'. 'You have to think about settling down Jake'. Or, 'once Irene and I have settled down' etc, etc. To me there was no duller concept than 'settling down'. And yet for Ivan, this seemed to be the most desired state. So, as I lay there thinking about my life, future and past, it all seemed black.

And what of my relationship with my Uncle and Aunt? Uncle Harry clearly believed that the acquisition of personal wealth takes precedence over virtually everything else. He had fought tooth and nail, for most of his life, in order to be counted among the 'wealthy'. He still runs around all hours of the day and night trying to buy or sell his wares. He will even endure insults—even anti-Semitic ones—to make another few thousand pounds. And he could never accept or begin to understand any alternative philosophy. Tonight, I saw him endure what must have been a very painful experience for him. My innately clever and reasonably well-read Uncle, my cultured and literate Uncle, cow-towing and obsequiously pretending to be friendly with a low, common, coarse harridan, in order to sell me off for money, in exactly the same way as he sells his diamonds.

I, on the other hand clung to what I believed were the theories of Karl Marx and Vladimir Ilyich Lenin. I wanted to see a redistribution of wealth based upon one's contribution to society, rather than what you can plunder for your own gratification in the financial markets. To my way of thinking, a great composer, poet, painter or dancer, were as great, although no greater than, a top industrialist or politician. In this way, society would reward Art Tatum, Lester Young, or Horowitz and Heifetz with the same amount of income as say, Howard Hughes or a Winston Churchill. All of them make equally important contributions to society.

Then I heard sounds from downstairs.

I heard aunt Sara's voice followed by Dora Elman saying something, followed by Uncle Harry's reply. Then I heard the front door open and, after a few more words, shut again.

'Here it comes,' I thought. 'Having sewn the wind, I am about to reap the whirlwind'. I began to steel myself for what will inevitably follow.

I heard Aunt Sarah coming up the stairs. There and then I decided that I would apologise profusely. I would even be prepared to say I was sorry to Dora Elman, if it would help in any way. I knew that I could not face upsetting and disappointing my Uncle and Aunt any more than I already had. But also, although I could not admit it to myself at the time, I did not have the courage to face what the consequences might be, if I did not back down.

The door opened a couple of inches. "Can I come in?" my Aunt said quietly, presumably in case I was asleep.

"Sure Auntie," I said resignedly.

"Well, she's gone." Her voice sounded happy and friendly. I opened my eyes. She was smiling broadly. I could not believe it.

"So tell me the worst" I said.

She sat down herself at the bottom end of the bed, next to my stockinged feet.

"Well, the shock of you really letting her have it, sobered her up, just like that," and she snapped her fingers. "She said that she had never been spoken to like that in all her life."

"Oh, Christ," I mumbled.

"Wait Jake. So then Harry says to her, 'Well Dora, I don't like to take sides, but you did push the lad a bit far'. Then she hands her half-full drink back to Harry saying, 'I don't want any more to drink thank you'. That is an unheard-of thing for Dora to do, believe me. And the look on her face; she was absolutely stunned.

"Oh, my Christ," I moaned softly.

Then Aunt Sarah took one of my toes and wiggled it. For reasons I could not begin to fathom, she appeared to be bubbling with excitement.

"Then Dora says, and listen to this Jake; then she says, 'Do you know I think I like that young man. He reminds me a bit of the way Mordechai used to be when he was young. He wouldn't take anything from anybody either. I think he's the first young man who's got what it takes to bring that madcap of a daughter of mine, into line'. Well, I looked across at your uncle and he looked across at me. We were both thunderstruck. Meanwhile Dora is going on 'Yes', she says, 'Your Jake is just the sort of boy I want for my Candy. She needs a bit of rough" Then, imitating Dora's voice and accent, she went on, 'e's got fire in his guts that boy 'as. Tell him tha' 'e'll be invited over to meet Mordechai'. Then Jake, she turns round to me and she says, 'Sarah, I think you may have found the answer to the problems I have been having with that bloody daughter of mine. 'I must go 'ome and phone Mordechai in America to tell him all about it.' Then she turned round to Harry and said, ''e really let me 'ave it didn't 'e 'arry?' And she was actually laughing. I, and I don't think anyone else for that matter, has ever seen her smile let alone look pleased with anybody. She's crazy about you. How's that for a turn up Jake?"

She wiggled my toes again.

"She can still go to hell as far as I am concerned," I said.

All thoughts of apologising were gone for ever. I was in the driving seat and loving it.

"Ach, Jake darling, don't be silly. You simply have no idea what a miracle you pulled off tonight."

Ivan came into the room. Having caught the end of what my Aunt was saying, he asked "What miracle did he perform?" He went across to his dressing table and started rummaging in it.

Pressing in her cheek with her open hand, rather like Jack Benny used to do, she said to his back: "Oh you should have been there Ivan. Your cousin gave Dora Elman such a mouthful, and she loved it."

Ivan froze. Then he turned around quickly saying as he did so. "What do you mean, he gave her a mouthful and she loved it?" His face was a picture of disbelief and incredulity. Then he turned to me; "What did you say to her?"

I sat up, pulling up my knees and interlinking my fingers around them.

"I just informed her that she was an evil, drunken old bat, and she was and she still is.

"And she enjoyed it!" my Aunt said, absolutely cock-a-hoop. "AND," she said loudly, her finger pointing to the sky triumphantly, "She thinks that Jake is the perfect husband for Candy, AND, the finger shot even higher, "She has invited Jake to their Grosvenor Square apartment to meet the great Mordechai Elman." And then she clasped her fingers together in front of her chest, as her voice changed from jubilant excitement to angry frustration.

"And he, the bloody fool, doesn't want to go."

"What do you mean, you don't want to go?" Ivan said.

"What I mean is, I do not want to go. And furthermore, I am not going to go, and that's final"

"He's not going to go and that's final," my Aunt repeated to Ivan, as if I had spoken in some obscure foreign dialect that required her to translate it back into English so that he could understand it. Then she apparently felt that the room door should be told separately, so she repeated it for the door's benefit. Then turning to glare angrily at me, she opened her arms wide and addressed the entire room.

"He's not going. Even though he is being offered on a plate, the opportunity to be a MILLIONAIRE." She yelled the last word at me in angry frustration.

"Ma," Ivan said quietly, closing the dressing table drawer at the same time, "Go downstairs and let me and Jake discuss it, cousin to cousin."

As she walked out of the room, she was saying to no-one in particular "Oy weiss mir, you do your best for them, and..."She finished whatever she was saying out of my earshot, because by then she was out of the room and had shut the door behind her.

"Where's Irene?" I asked, once we were on our own. In truth, I did not give a shit where Miss Sweet Leilani was, but I vaguely hoped that I could keep the subject off Dora Elman and the Elman millions.

"I've taken her home. She has to be up early in the morning and she wanted an early night."

Then he said, "Jake..." but I decided to beat him to the punch.

"I know what you are going to say, so save your breath. I am in no way interested in marrying Candy Elman, and I am even less interested in meeting or even clapping eyes ever again on her horror-movie of a mother.

Ivan went back to the dressing table to continue his search for whatever it was that he had failed to find at his first attempt. While he rummaged he spoke. "I have no intention of telling you what to do. All I am going to do is set out the facts as I see them, and then let you make your own decisions."

"Go ahead," I said, won over as ever, by Ivan's sweet reasonableness.

"I never had a brother," he said. "Well I did, but he died before I was born. So I look upon you as my younger brother, and as you know, I only want the best for you."

He gave up his search, closed the drawer, and came over to sit on the side of his bed, facing me.

"How long have you got left at college? Two years. Is that right?

"At the most," I said darkly.

"Okay," Ivan said, ignoring the implications of my reply. "So," he went on, "In two years time, you will have to go out and face the big, wide, world. Believe me kid, it's rough out there. Take me for example. I've been in business now for a little under eighteen months. In that time, I've lost a bundle of money buying fake golden sovereigns. They were brilliant fakes. The police said that they were the best they'd ever seen. Then, I had a crooked copper who came to my Hatton Gardens office and dumped some stolen jewellery on one of my shelves while I was out of the room taking a pee. Then the bugger pretended to find it and accused me of receiving stolen jewellery. He told me he was prepared to forget all about it for fifty quid a week. I was lucky Jake boy. My father knows a lot of important people. So he was able to save my skin, thank God."

He paused, presumably waiting for me to say something. I said nothing. So he went on: "So, what have I learned over the past couple of years? This is what I've learned. Go for an easy life Jake. Take me for an example. Irene's father is going into producing films, and he wants me to go into it with him. There is very big money in the film business. And imagine, one day you'll see a film that says in big letters, produced by ..."

"Do you love Irene? I interrupted him to ask.. "I mean do you love her for herself? I mean, would you marry her if she was poor and lived in a lousy part of town?"

He looked at me incredulously;" What do you mean? Irene is wonderful. Wait 'til you get to know her a bit better. You'll know what I mean then."

"Don't take offence Ivan, but you seem to put such a financial twist on the whole relationship. You seem to be talking about Irene like she is some part of an important business deal. I mean, what will happen if, after say, two or three years of married life with Irene, you really fall head over heels with someone? Knowing you, I am sure you'd never leave her; you'd just spend the rest of your life getting ever more bitter and regretful at what might have been. Mind you," I rationalised, "Then you could turn your own life into a big weepy movie. You could make a fortune out of your own misery. You could put at the end of the opening titles, 'Produced by Ivan the Schmuck!"

"What are you talking about?" Ivan said, raising his voice. "What makes you think I don't love Irene?"

"Well, you don't act like you do. You seem to have become so wrapped up in making money that you've killed off, or at least buried, whatever it is inside normal people that make them fall in love."

I suppose I was hitting out at the way I felt about Janine. I guess that I was also a bit bitter and maybe even jealous, because Ivan did have his Irene, whereas I had Janine only in my masturbatory phantasies.

After a long and thoughtful pause, Ivan said "Listen my boy; I am going to be very happy. Irene really is a wonderful girl. And I am going to make pots of money, and we'll settle down in a big house in Bishops Avenue in Hampstead and have a couple of kids and life will be great. Don't you want something like that too, Jake? I mean there is nothing to be ashamed of in wanting to settle down to a decent, respectable life."

"Do you know what I want?" I said. "I want to be playing piano in some famous New York City nightspot, and a guy comes over to me and says, 'Art Tatum is standing over at the bar and he wants to shake your hand'. To hear that single sentence would be worth to me more than all the money in the world plus all the houses in Bishops Avenue."

"And when you finished your gig" Ivan said, "You'll go home to your broken down, shitty little room in some shitty part of town. There is no money in playing jazz."

He walked over to stand looking out of the window, his back to me.. "In two or three year's time, you could marry Candy and have enough money to own the greatest jazz record collection in the country. You could knock yourself out playing great jazz on that big, brand new, Steinway concert grand that you've talked about and dreamed of. Christ Jake, with the kind of money you'll have, you'll be able to go to New York and hire the world's greatest jazzmen to play with you. Think about it. All your favourite players in the flesh to play with any time you felt like it. And you talk about Ivan the Schmuck. Well, that movie you mentioned won't ever get made. But, 'Jake the Schmuck' might be."

He turned round to face me. "Listen to me Jake. Who goes by bus, when there is a chauffeur-driven Rolls outside, waiting to take you anywhere you want to go? You've already done the impossible. You've made Dora Elman like you. This is a woman, famous far and wide for hating everyone, barring her husband and her daughter. And now, miraculously, she also likes you. If you get the thumbs up from Mordechai which you will, because Dora will talk him into it, well that is like being given a cheque for a million pounds. Use your cop kid."

I had to admit to myself that the way Ivan put it, it did sound very tempting.

"Look," I said. "Let me think about it. Okay? Anyway, you haven't mentioned Candy. Who says she wants to marry me? And then there is a very good possibility that old man Elman will not think as highly of me as the Old Bat does."

"But you promise you will think about it?" Ivan insisted.

"I promise," I said. For some reason, I actually meant it.

"With a bit of luck, the next time you say those two words will be when you are standing under the chuppa with Candy standing next to you."

"I can't understand why everybody wants me to settle down so soon" I complained.

He reached over to his bed and grabbed a pillow. "Schmuck, I don't want you to settle down. I want you to settle UP!" And he threw the pillow at me.

Chapter 15

By 9.30 the following morning, I was bathed, dressed and practising the piano. This was the day of the competition.

It was also Shabbat, and playing the piano is not allowed on the Sabbath day. Like I have explained before, although my Aunt and Uncle could by no means be described as religious, they did like to keep Shabbat apart from the rest of the week. I had and still have very little regard for the logic that says because the Lord rested on the seventh day, so should we. What evidence there is that He really did create the world in six days is pretty flimsy at best, not to mention that it flies in the face of contemporary astro/scientific thought. But even if He did do the entire gig in six days, then He must have worked pretty damned hard. So He deserved the break. But what earth-shattering deeds did we get up to that should cause us to identify with the Great One? But whatever else, it does prove one thing: the Jews invented the six-day week.

So I sat at the piano, practising away with a completely clear conscience. I was too wrapped up with myself and winning the competition to appreciate the enormity of the sacrifice my Aunt and Uncle were making in allowing me to desecrate their Sabbath in so noisy a fashion.

I practised and played without stopping until 2.30 in the afternoon. Whether it was out of some new respect for me due to the Dora Elman affair, or out of their genuine desire to want me to win the competition, I know not, but I was allowed to play on without interruption. Normally, apart from the constant bringing in of sandwiches or cups of tea, my Aunt's head would appear around the door at least twice to ask, how long 'the bloody banging and crashing is going to last'. Or, 'If you go on much longer, your hands will fall off!'

But today, it was different. For the first time I was allowed to properly prepare, mentally and physically, for the big night. After I had finished, I went up to my bedroom, put on my best blue suit and one of the new shirts that

Aunt Sarah had bought me; put another splodge of Brylcream on my hair, just in case Janine did actually show up, and came back downstairs to make my farewells.

My Aunt handed me a large brown paper package. "I made you a few sandwiches in case you are hungry," she said.

As I took them from her, I said. "I have left Ivan and Irene's tickets on the piano. Tell them to came and see me after the show." Just before going out of the kitchen door, I added "And tell Ivan to bring an extra handkerchief, because I'll probably need it to cry into after I come nowhere."

She came over to me and giving me a big hug said "You'll win. I know that your Father and Mother, olav ha sholem, will be there, right beside you, listening." Then, holding me at arms length, she said, her face very serious:

"I want you to promise me three things before you leave." She marked off each one, holding up the requisite numbers of fingers.

"One: whatever happens tonight, you will complete your university course—unless Candy wants to marry before you have finished, in which case we'll think about it again"

"I promise" I said.

Two: that you will have nothing to do ever again with that terrible woman who is old enough to be your mother."

Having one thing dead centre in my mind and that was getting out of this house, and out from under my Aunt's claustrophobic constrictions, I was prepared to promise anything.

I promise," I said.

"Good, good," she said searching my face to see if I really meant it. I managed to maintain the kind of dead pan expression of which any poker player would have been proud. I passed the test.

"And number three."

"Well?"

"Promise me Jake darling that you will telephone Candy and take her to the pictures or something. Poor girl, she has so few friends and hardly ever goes out."

'Jesus, if only you knew' I thought.

"I promise I will. But now Auntie, you must let me be on my way."

She got up on to her tip toes to kiss me on the chin.

"You're so tall," she said with parental admiration.

I nodded.

"You are going to make a wonderful husband for Candy. Now off you go and good luck my darling."

As she walked me to the front door she said "Just think, after you marry Candy, you won't ever have to practise the piano again."

I am sure my Aunt spoke that sentence in complete innocence. To me it was a sentence of death. The idea of giving the piano second billing to Candy Elman was chillingly unthinkable. At that very moment, any thoughts I might have had about marrying Candy were killed stone dead.

I put on my overcoat, bought for me three years ago, and which was now a couple sizes too small for me.

"'Bye Auntie" I said waving without looking back as I marched briskly down the driveway, into the street.

I heard her addressing the air. "He doesn't tell me he needs a new overcoat. He just goes out looking like a tramp" I neither turned nor acknowledged her parting shot, but kept on walking.

The bus from Upper Clapton to Trafalgar Square took about an hour, so that by the time I actually found the Lyceum, and discovered where the stage door was, it was only a couple of minutes before five-thirty, which was the time I had been told to be there for a sound balance. Having shown the stage-doorman my credentials, he directed me to the dressing room. I opened the door to find myself in a large, noisy, cigarette-smoke filled room, full of laughing and talking musicians.

It soon became apparent to me that each competing group was chatting only among themselves and the friends they had brought with them. There was no conversational interplay between the competitors whatsoever. Beneath the veneer of cheerful conversation, I sensed an atmosphere of extreme nervous tension. But even so, they did have one another to talk to and try to relax with, whereas I, being a solo performer, was on my own. I tried to make contact by smiling at everyone who looked my way, but it was as if I were invisible. All I got for my comradely smiles were cold, unseeing stares.

I was starting to feel like a complete schmuck. I had just decided to get out of this room and stand somewhere on my own, when the door opened and a middle-aged man came barging in. I watched him walk to the far end of the room, grab one of the three, hard, wooden chairs that were facing some cracked and stained mirrors and drag it to the centre of the room, bumping out of the way anybody who had been standing in his path. Then, he stood up on it so that he could be seen by everybody. He clapped his hands together loudly, shouting in a hoarse, coarse, cockney baritone. "Righ' then, righ' then. Can I 'ave a bit of silence, hif you please."

He was about five feet seven, thick-set, and with an alcoholic tan. His neck was too thick for his shirt, so that he had to leave the top button undone. Over his shirt he had on an old, creased jacket. He looked like an escaped barrow-boy from Covent Garden fruit market, which was just around the corner from where we were. He talked like one too.

"Righ'. Let's see if we're all 'ere." While the conversations around the room were quickly dying, he was removing and unfolding a sheet of paper from his jacket side pocket. He smoothed it out and starting reading from it.

'Ull City Stompers? He glared about him. A group of unkempt characters standing on the far side of the room shouted through the haze of their cigarette smoke. "Okay."

The man on the chair wrote something on his sheet of paper.

"Righ'. Nah, the Geoff Arlington sixtette."

The group, standing to my right, shouted a tutti "yes".

"Jack Grant and 'is band? There was a silence. Then somebody yelled, "Not here."

Again the man on the chair, wrote something on his sheet of paper

"Sax of a Kind?" he yelled out. One tall, thin guy standing near me said "We are all here, but the others are out having coffee."

The man on the chair bellowed belligerently; without looking up from the paper he was writing on; "Well, anyone 'oo aint present," he looked at his wristwatch, "Wivvin the next fifteen minutes, and ready to play, don't go on." Then he looked up from his creased piece of paper to glare about him, his red complexion getting even redder, matching his bloodshot eyes, his neck seemingly thickening at the same time.

"The Greene-Smith Quartette" he yelled angrily, for no apparent reason.

"All here," they shouted immediately and nervously.

The quasi fruit-seller screwed up his eyes as if trying to make sense of the next name.

"Jake...Slivver?"

"Jake Silver," I said.

Suddenly, for the first time the other musicians acknowledged my presence by staring at me, rather than through me as they had done up until now.

"My name is Jake Silver, not Slivver," I told him again.

"Okay, Mister Lah-Di- bloody-Dah." We all stood in silence while he laboriously crossed out what was written and wrote my name correctly, saying each letter out loud as he did so: S,I,L,V,E,R. Then, turning to face me, he said.

"Jake Silver. Is tha' better, Mister Lah-di Dah?" This drew a few strangulated, embarrassed titters from the assembly.

I have to admit that compared to his accent, and all those around me, I did have a bit of a la-di-dah way of speaking.

Bossman on the chair stuffed the piece of paper he had been reading from, back into his pocket.

Then he drew another piece of paper from the other side pocket of his jacket.

"Righ'. We'll do the sahnd check in the same order as you will appear in the show. First, Geoff Arlington Sixtette. Then the 'ull City Stompers. After tha,' Sax of a Kind', and then Mister Lah-di-dah, Jake Silver. After tha,' the Greene-Smith (pronounced Smiff) quartette, and Jack Grant and 'is band to close the show. Alrigh'?"

A thin, bearded chap of middling height, who I had noticed earlier, because of the huge Sherlock Holmes pipe he had been smoking, spoke up, with a strong, north of England accent.

"I think we should close the show, because we already have a reputation."

"And 'oo are you?" the man on the chair said, in a voice charged with belligerent challenge.

"We're the Hull City Stompers, man."

The expression on the face of the boss-man was one that should be reserved for when you are told that you mother is a whore.

"Nah listen, 'ull bleeding' City Stompers," he yelled, his face bloating and reddening, his voice hoarse with rage, "You might' be fuckin' Jesus Christ up there in 'ull city, wherever that may be.. But dahn 'ere in the Smoke, you're nuffink. Fuckin' nuffink. Un'erstan'?"(If you are not a Londoner you may not know that 'The Smoke' is cockney for London).

Then, glaring at us all in turn, he said, the veins on his neck standing out, rope-like; "I'm puttin' on this bleeding' show, not you lot." He turned his snarling face towards the Hull City Stompers, who were now huddled together, white-faced and worried: "You'll go on where I say and when I say. Or you can bugger orf back to bleeding' 'ull. Go' it?"

There was complete, frozen, silence in reply.

Boss-man, still glaring angrily about him shouted "Anyone else wanna be Mister Bleedin' Clever?"

Stunned frightened silence was his reply.

"Righ then. Geoff Arlin'ton`, sahnd check."

This was to be the first of hundreds of times when I have encountered insensitive and ugly rudeness from jazz promoters, in marked contrast to their classical-music counter-parts. Back-stage at a classical concert, one will almost always find that the promoter is well-spoken and respectful of the performers and especially of any visiting virtuosi or conductors. These are often, and indeed, usually, addressed as 'maestro'.

In the good ol' USA, and, from what I remember of the post 39-45 war British jazz scene, jazz-club owners and promoters, usually act as if they are gangsters (in the USA they are often the real thing). They treat jazz musicians like shit. I once played a club date in New York City, where I was a huge, but I mean a big, big hit. The audience demanded that I play encore after encore, so that I, together with the bass player and the drummer were on for a whole hour longer than we were contracted to play. When we finally got off the stage, dripping with perspiration and exhaustion, the applause still going on I said to the cigar-chomping club-owner, "We went over great hey?"

He took the cigar out of his fat mouth, and without even looking in my direction said in his Italo-Noo-York accent, "So what do you want? D'you want me to suck your dick because you got a little applause?" Then turning to jab me in the chest with the two fingers that were holding his cigar, he said "Did you make me any extra dough? No. Because they were so mother-fuckin' busy listening to you, they didn't order any mother' fuckin drinks. Jesus," he said, shaking his head in disbelief, "You fuckin' jazz people kill me." And he walked away. The bass player, an oldish, black guy with many years experience of playing in places like this, put his arm around my shoulders and said "Don't get upset baby. It's the jazz life, that's all."

But here, in the Lyceum, it was my first taste of the 'jazz life'.

As I stood in the wings of the large stage, waiting to be called for my sound check, I said to boss man who was standing next to me "It would be nice to know your name."

"What for?" he said aggressively.

"So if there is something I want to ask, or for any of a dozen reasons, I can call you by your name." Then I added in a semi-joking way "After all you know my name, so why shouldn't I know yours?"

He pushed his fat, red face so close to mine, that apart from the strong stench of whiskey on his breath, flecks of his spittle spattered my face as he spoke: "Listen Sonny-Jim La-Di-Dah, you're 'ere to play. This aint one of your 'ampstead tea parties. So just shu' up and get aht there and play. Alrigh'?"

Before I could say anything further, my name was called for the sound balance. As I went through my four pieces for the sound engineer, I found myself thinking about Candy Elman, and how 'settling down' with her suddenly did not seem such a bad idea after all.

As I came off the stage, having completed the sound check, an elegantly attired, thirty-five-ish year-old man came up to me and introduced himself. "Hello, I am Eliot Wilson, the emcee for the night. He was about my height, but a lot beefier than me. (Mind you, at that time, every one, possibly barring Frank Sinatra was beefier than me). As we shook hands, he added, "So if there is anything special you want me to say by way of introducing you to the audience, now is the time to tell me."

He had a quiet, mellow voice and was clearly well educated. It was also a great relief to be spoken to in a civilised manner. I gave him a few details of my life, such as my background and musical influences and what I was reading at University. I also told him that I had read all his reviews in the jazz magazine that was sponsoring tonight's competition.

"Drop into my office next Wednesday and you can be present when I listen to my review copies of the latest jazz releases."

My spirits immediately rose. Suddenly I did want to be a part of the World of Jazz again, and, just as suddenly, all thoughts of marrying Candy Elman evaporated.

When I returned to the communal dressing room, I found that apart from the musicians, a few girls had found their way in. They were laughing and flirting with three or four musicians I had not seen before. I later found out that they were from the house band.

My wrist watch told me that there was still a half hour to go before the doors were opened to the audience and a whole hour before the concert itself was due to start. As there did not seem anything better to do, I unwrapped the parcel of sandwiches which I had retrieved from my overcoat pocket. I had not yet got through the first mouthful of chicken sandwich, when a musician I had not previously noticed, came over to me.

"Hi man," he said, holding his hand out to shake mine. I transferred my sandwich to my left hand and shook his.

"I'm Bob Parfitt. I play the Joanna (cockney rhyming slang for 'piano'), with the Geoff Arlington mob."

"Oh, I see. My name's Jake Silver. I watched him as he crossed the room to grab a chair and return dragging the chair behind him.

"Yeah. I was listenin" to ya." He said as he sat down next to me. I noticed that his gaze never left the sandwich I was eating.

"Fancy a sandwich?" I said.

"Not half."

I gave him one.

"You couldn't let me 'ave two couldja? I aint eaten since last night."

As I was handing him another from my large paper bag, I heard my name being shouted by a scruffy old fellow who was standing at the door. I got to my feet.

"I'm Jake Silver" I told him.

"Note for ya' at the stage door." And he was gone. Why he did not bring the note with him I never found out.

It turned out to be a pink gently scented envelope. My heart started to bounce around even before I had ripped it open and retrieved the note inside. It was from Janine. I instantly recognised the handwriting from her previous and only letter to me, which I had read and re-read a hundred times before throwing it away.

Dearest Jake.

1] Walk on slowly and, before you sit down to play, acknowledge your applause with a short bow.

2] If you can, turn and smile at the audience every now and then, while you are playing.

3] After you have finished your performance, do not rush off the stage, as you did in Newcastle. Take your bows and wave to all parts of the theatre.

Jake, I know you are the best. Prove it to me by winning tonight.

Love,

Unowho

The envelope wasn't stamped, which meant that it had been delivered by hand. This could only mean that Janine is here and will be in the house when I play. I stood there letter in hand, wondering what I should do now. I was far too excited to go back to the dressing room and indulge in pointless chatter with that Parfitt guy. So instead, I went round behind the back stage drape, intending to see what went on at the other side of the stage. Half way across, I found a door in the back wall, behind which was an iron spiral staircase. At the top I found a hallway with three doors, set at regular intervals, running down both sides. The first was a small dressing-room, along the left hand wall of which were two mirrors surrounded by electric light bulbs. Opposite them wall was an old, faded chaise-longue. At the far end was a hand basin, next to a door, which I guessed, led to a lavatory. I sat down on the chaise-longe and thought about Janine (what else?), whilst doing finger and wrist-loosening exercises.

It all came down to one thing. I had to do the impossible and win tonight. In truth, I rarely make up my mind about anything. This is because most things seem boringly unimportant to me. For example, if there is an argument between Harold and Meyer, as to whether we should go to a pub or a dance, I let them argue it out and go along with whatever they decided. I could not give a toss. But, on the extremely rare occasions when something is important to me, I become the most dedicated and motivated guy you can meet. And this was more than ever, one of those times. The knowledge that Janine, my Janine has come all the way from Newcastle to see and hear me perform, concentrated my mind wonderfully. All my tenseness, all my nervous energy was now melding into a fierce and concentrated determination that I was going to play my arse off out there tonight.

I went back downstairs to stand in the wings and watch the stage hands making their final preparations for the show.

A musician, I think from the Greene-Smith quartette, came up to me and said "You're Jake Silver, right?"

"Right," I said.

"Well, they've been yelling for you to go to the stage-door."

I felt my heart bounce at the thought that it might be Janine, waiting for me.

"Thanks," I yelled over my shoulder as I ran towards what I hoped was the realisation of my dreams. But she was not there. I told the stage doorman my name whilst still clinging to the thought that she had been there but got tired of waiting.

"You're bleedin' popular aintcha? He said. "I gotta bleedin' telegram for ya now."

As I took it from him a wave of apprehension crashed over me, wiping out all my previous optimism. I felt sure it was from Janine, saying she will not be coming.

I ripped it open. It said 'All our thoughts, best wishes and love are with you tonight. Wishing you every success. Harry, Sarah, Ivan, Candy and Dora Elman'.

I folded it up, put it in my inside pocket and instantly forgot all about it. If I was going to win, my victory will be for two people only: Janine Gregson and Jake Silver. Even Ivan, who had dreamed up the whole idea of me entering the competition, meant nothing to me at that moment. All I could think of was winning and then getting it on with Janine.

I went back to the chatter and raucous laughter of the dressing room. The first thing I noticed was that the paper bag that had held all my Aunt's sandwiches was now empty. I picked it up looking around me at the same time to see if they had been moved elsewhere.

One of the members of the Hull City Stompers shouted across to me in his thick northern accent: "Hope you didn't mind us finishing up your sandwiches matey. We reckoned you was such a rich bugger you wouldn't be bothered." Another member of the same band then got some forced laughter as he added:

"Anyway, you can always get your butler to make you some more cantcha?"

I was considering an appropriate response, when Boss-man, now clearly the worse for wear came into the room.

"Righ'. Nah listen up." He made his way to the centre of the room, and with his thick hands holding the back of a chair, probably to stop himself from falling down, said "When it's all over and the last band 'as finished, you all walk aht on to the stage and stand in a line at the back, while the awards are read out. 'Ooever is called, go forward an' get yer prize, an' then go back an' stand in the line again. Don't go orf the stage. Go' that?" He glared about the room, his eyes redder than the Russian flag. "An' no smokin' on or anywhere near the fuckin' stage. Unnerstan'?"

He took the silence to mean a tacit 'yes'.

"Righ', he said. "Oos on first?"

"We are," the Geoff Arlington Sixtette piped up in an almost perfect frightened unison.

"Okay. Go an' stan' at the side of the stage and wait until the MC 'as called aht yer name. Then go on smartly. Wunnuvver fing. Don't play too bleedin' long. After eleven o'clock, I 'ave to pay the staff double, an' I aint gonna do it. So I wantcha finished and ou' o'the the building well before then. Issat clear?" Again, he glared about him with the now familiar Neanderthal expression of belligerence occupying his red, sweating, face.

As the Geoff Arlington group gathered up their instruments and started to file out of the door, I shouted across to them, "Good luck." Geoff gave me a pretemporary nod. The other five, including the pianist whom I had fed, ignored me completely.

I did not know it at that time, but I had broken an unspoken rule of the British jazz scene.

The requirement, if you wanted to be 'on the scene man', was cool detachment. An extreme (although made up) example of the way you were supposed to act, might be:

Jazzman One: "Listen man, I think we should open the set with something cool, like 'Buzzy'.

Jazzman Two: "Yeah man. That's fine. Then, after a long pause: "Hey, have you heard? The Russians have just hydrogen bombed Scotland man. They say there's nobody left up there"

Jazzman One: (After an equally long pause), "Yeah. So I suppose the gig in Glasgow is out. Yeah, that's tough man. Hey, how about opening with 'Cherokee' in B flat instead?"

By wishing the Geoff Arlington Sixtette good luck, I had broken the 'Rule of Cool' baby. This meant that I was clearly 'uncool' and so, by definition, a square. As I was completely unaware of these social subtleties, I was completely at a loss as to why my good wishes had been received with such cold stares and icy silence. I guess the other musicians had me down as a rich, spoiled, square, who gets good luck telegrams and notes like some operatic diva. I see now that they had every reason to do so.

It was now clearly obvious to me that my presence in the dressing room was not desired by the other occupants. So I wandered out and stood in the wings watching Geoff Arlington do his thing.

It was a nice, polished little group modelled on the Benny Goodman sextette, except for Geof Arlington himself, who was trying to copy Artie Shaw rather than B.G. I had been listening for no more than a few minutes, when there was a hoarse whisper in my ear, accompanied by a strong smell of whiskey.

"You're no' on next. Wha' are ya doin' 'ere?"

"Listening" I whispered.

Boss-man whispered back "Well go listen someplace else will yer? This area 'as gotta be kept clear. So stan'somewhere else."

Finding myself with nothing to do and nowhere to do it, I went out and bought myself an evening paper. I leaned against the wall just outside the dressing room door, and read it from first page to last, all through the crash and blare of the early, traditional jazz sounds of the Hull City Stompers, followed by the group which called itself 'Sax of a Kind'. This group opened with 'In the Mood', followed by a Glen Miller-type version of 'Stardust'. Then they went into 'The Indian Love Call', made popular by Tommy Dorsey, and ended with 'The Jersey Bounce'. Need I say more? They sounded like escapees from a third-rate dance hall.

As I was on next, during their corny rendition of 'Jersey Bounce' (which, let us face it, aint the hippest melody ever written, whichever way you play it), I slipped into the men's room, not only for a pee, but also to repeat my finger and wrist looseners, and more importantly, to get my head straight and my concentration in line for my performance.

I got to the wings just in time to hear and watch 'Sax of a Kind' end their version of 'The Jersey Bounce' with a coda that had been lifted, note for note from the end of Glen Miller's 'Moonlight Serenade'. I watched while they took their bows to only moderate, polite applause. Then, they filed off the stage, passing me by without even a look of recognition in my direction. As they were doing so, Eliot Wilson, the Master of Ceremonies, had come on stage from the opposite wing applauding the previous act as he made his way to the downstage microphone. I watched as the stage went suddenly black, except for the pin-spotlight that picked out the tall, elegantly tuxedoed, Emcee. Then, in the blackness behind him, I watched four stage hands manoeuvre the shiny, black Steinway grand to the front and centre of the stage, raise the lid, set two microphones by the piano and file off. All the while, Eliot was introducing me.

"Thank you for 'Sax of a Kind'. And now judges, ladies and gentlemen, something that as far as I know is a first for this competition. We have a solo pianist. He has no rhythm section to help him out. But, in the tradition of Earl Hines, Fats Waller and Art Tatum, he is going to perform alone and unaided. So from Newcastle-upon Tyne, where he won the local Individualist Award, in the North-Eastern section of this competition, please show your appreciation for eighteen year-old Jake Silver."

I walked on to the stage slowly as instructed by Janine. The applause was polite and respectful. I bowed to the audience as per milady's instruction and sat down at the long Steinway grand. As the applause died away I heard Eliot say as he walked off the stage "Take it away kid."

Soloists in both jazz and classical music seem to fall into two distinct groups. The first will play up an absolute storm in the dressing room or rehearsal room, but sadly become so full of tensions at the sight of an audience, that they will fail to perform at anywhere near their best. The other type of soloist is very much the opposite. At a rehearsal his or her playing will often be perfunctory and uncaring. But once in front of an audience, a dramatic metamorphosis takes place. This type of performer is so in tune with, or even in love with the atmosphere of the concert stage that as he stands (or sits), before the myriad faces staring up at him from the auditorium, a strange cross-pollination takes place. He, somehow or other, can absorb the psychic energy of his audience and use it to fire his own creativity in such a way, that it will inspire him to perform not only at his best, but sometimes even beyond it. Fortunately, I belong to this latter category. No sooner had the spotlight picked me up as I made my entrance, and absorbed the polite applause that carried me across the blacked-out stage to the shiny, black grand piano, already bathed in a pool of bright light, than a feeling of cool, controlled command took me over. I felt suddenly vivid and vibrantly alive. So after Eliot had shouted to me to 'take it away'

I did no such thing. I just sat still for a moment, to savour the expectant hush that had now settled on the audience.

If this been a Hollywood movie, there would have been my Janine, sitting in the front row of the audience, and it would have been her presence, her smile, her magic, that inspired me to play more brilliantly, more soulfully, than I had ever done before. But that, ladies and gentlemen, is just so much Hollywood crap! A solo performance demands from the performer, his full, utter and exclusive concentration. That is why so many jazz soloists shut their eyes when they are improvising their solos.

This Hollywood invention that someone can play something creatively valid, whilst thinking about someone else, is too ludicrous to give it serious thought. Jazz is a totally personal statement. To play it well, you have to be able to reach into yourself, so that when you express sadness, or joy, or excitement or love in your playing, it is your own sadness or joy or whatever that you are giving musical wings to, and nobody else's. And when you take that journey into your own soul as all really fine jazz players have to do, there is no room for passengers.

My first offering was a popular tune of a couple of years earlier, called 'Stella by Starlight'. I enjoyed wallowing in the array of harmonic possibilities this song presented. At that time, to my knowledge, no jazz musicians were yet playing it, although as the hipper of you know, it has since become a jazz standard. But back then, I believe it possible that I was the first person to discover the jazz possibilities of this Victor Young classic.

I played the first chorus in the style (I hoped), of a piano concerto, replete with arpeggios (stolen from Chopin and Rachmaninov), and ending this first chorus with a massive, double-octave, fortissimo run from the top to the bottom of the keyboard. Then, suddenly much quieter, I went into the second chorus, one tone higher and in a Teddy Wilson cum Mel Powell swinging style, except that my right hand had become influenced by the Be-bop angularities of Bud Powell, rather than the mellifluence of the aforementioned Mel.

Then I took it up a minor third and wailed my way through two further choruses at a really fast tempo, before modulating back to the original key, for a reprise of the last sixteen bars of the piece, again played in concert style and ending with a long, complicated arpeggio that I had made up myself and which took me two weeks of practise to be able to play.

There was a moment of silence after I had finished. Then like a sudden tropical thunderstorm, huge, enthusiastic applause engulfed me. I stood up and bowed to all parts of the house, just as Janine had told me to do.

As I sat down again to play my second piece, which was 'Body and Soul', the hush that descended on the audience was of quite a different order to the respectful, but unresponsive silence in which my first piece was played. Now the silence was electric. The audience was digging me, and as every solo performer knows, there is nothing that can imbue one with such a sense of exaltation and exhilaration as having an audience eating out of the palm of your hand. It was as if this night and this audience had been created just for me.

After 'Body and Soul', I moved without stopping, into an introverted, reflective, first chorus of George Gershwin's 'Liza' before suddenly taking the next six choruses at breakneck tempo, in the 'stride' style of Fats Waller and Art Tatum. The applause was as deafening as a thousand hailstorms on a corrugated iron roof. By now the audience was so much on my side, that even my simple announcement, "And now, ladies and gentlemen, I would like to finish with my 'Tribute to the Blues'. Thank you," was greeted with enthusiastic applause.

I felt sure that I had never played as well as I did that night. The adulation I was getting was swelling my confidence to such an extent that I would, willingly have played on for another three hours. I played the Blues in every tempo and style I could think of, ending up with a few choruses of some fast boogie-woogie.

When I finally finished, the applause was intermingled with cheering, I suspect from Ivan, and those around him. I took my bows and left the stage, the clapping and cheering, still going on even after I was back in the wings. Eliot had to use all his expertise to quieten them down in order to get the next band onto the stage.

As I stood in the wings, mopping the drops of perspiration from my forehead, Bossman came over; I thought to congratulate me on my success.

"You was on five minutes longer than you was supposed to be," he hissed in my ear. I tolja we 'ad to be aht of 'ere by eleven."

"I couldn't help it," I whispered back. "The applause went on for longer than I expected."

"Well it shouldn't bleedin''ave," he hissed back inexplicably. I noticed that he was in a pretty precarious state. As he turned to walk away, he all but fell over.

Still feeling elated, and wanting to talk about it to somebody, I turned to head back to the dressing room, but found the Greene-Smith group standing behind me, waiting to go on next. In my excited, elated state, I broke the 'Rule of Cool' yet again.

"I went down great, didn't I?" I whispered happily.

The guitarist in the group gave me the smallest 'yeah' it was possible to give, whilst the rest of the group were suddenly busily examining their instruments.

The dressing room was now filled with the groups that had already played, plus a lot of friends who had come backstage to see them. The piano player from the Hull City band, beer bottle in one hand, a half full glass in the other, shouted across to me as I came in: "Fuckin' 'ell, you really tore the arse out of the piana, dintcha?"

I had no way of knowing whether this was meant to be a compliment or not. So I gave him the benefit of the doubt.

"Thanks," I said.

Then he added "I don't know what it had to do with real jazz, but you must've played about four million notes tonight."

Now the trumpet player chimed in, while carefully filling his glass with a second bottle of beer:

"Leave ' im be," he shouted to the pianist. "'es probably very tired after playin' all them notes and all 'is modern 'armonies. Then turning to me, he added "what are you doin' now son? Waitin' for some of your up-town friends" (and now he tried imitate a Noel Coward accent), so that you can all pop orf to the Savoy for a spot of suppah?"

"Look here," I said, angrily over the laughter his attempt at being funny had evoked. "It's not my fault if you cannot speak English correctly. Neither is it my responsibility if your knowledge of harmony is so elementary and puerile. And it is also nothing to do with me that your playing is so far behind the times, that even the two greatest protagonists of New Orleans jazz, Louis Armstrong and Sidney Bechet, stopped playing like that in 1924.

The trumpet player was about to reply when I cut him off. "My advice to you my friend, is to drop your attempts at being arrogant and know-it-all, and start listening to what is being played now in 1948, and get back to practising. You sound to me like you need it." I walked out of the room, fully aware that the other members of the band were holding him back from committing some sort of violence against me. As I left the dressing room, I all but bumped into Eliot Wilson who was hurrying towards the band room.

"Oh, hi," I said.

"Hello Jake. Listen, have you seen anything of the Jack Grant band? They are due on in about five minutes and there is no sign of them."

"Well, they are not in the band room, because I've just come from there. Have you asked the guy in charge? He may know where they are."

I can't find him either," Eliot said. He was clearly very worried. So I said.

"Can I help in any way?"

"Actually you can. Do you think that you could organise some sort of a jam session to close the show with? We can't close the show without some sort of a big finish"

"I'll try," I said.

"Well, we've got about five minutes at the most, to get it together"

I went back to the dressing room with Eliot following closely behind. I clapped my hands, just as Bossman had done, to get some attention.

"It's that fuckin' ponce again," I heard someone from the Hull City Stompers say. But I chose to ignore it. "Look, we have a problem. Eliot is going to explain it" Then turning to face the Hull group, I said I suggest we forget any bad feelings any of us may have, and pitch in and help out." Then I turning to Eliot, I said "You take it from here."

After he had explained the problem and suggested that we close the show with a giant twenty minute jam, everyone, to my surprise, agreed.

It all came clear after Eliot had left the room, why they had done so, when one of the saxophone players in 'Sax of a Kind' said to nobody in particular, "Well man, you can't say no to the most important jazz reviewer in the business."

By the time we were half way through this twenty minutes of jazz mayhem, we had three drummers all playing on separate drum kits and three bass players all playing simultaneously. Then, barring the bass players, everybody stopped while a 'battle of the basses' was fought, each bass-man trying to overtop the other, to the ecstatic enthusiasm of the audience. But this was as nothing compared to the audience reaction during and especially after the 'battle of the drummers'.

It all ended up with everyone playing for all they were worth. I was given the top end of the piano to play, which I did standing up, whist the piano man from the Geoff Arlington group played the middle section, and the pianist from the Hull City band rumbled about on the bass end.

Finally, after all this crazy cacophony had come to its thunderous climax, I heard the violinist from the Greene-Smith quartette say to somebody, or maybe, nobody "Jesus, that sounded like Dunkirk with a rhythm section." Maybe I was the only one who heard him say it. I was certainly the only who laughed.

It took Eliot Wilson a good five minutes to quell the cheering, clapping clamour of the audience to get them quiet enough for him to speak.

"Well, judges, ladies and gentlemen, I'm sure you will agree with me when I say that jazz is alive and swinging in this country" This was greeted with another few minutes of wild applause. Once again Eliot had to raise his hands high above his head to quell the enthusiasm of the audience, in order to go on: "With new young players of this calibre, I am quite sure...etc, etc.

But I was no longer really listening to what he was saying. I was too busy searching every face in the audience for the only face I wanted to see: the one sitting on Janine's shoulders. So, I only half-heard him introduce the managing director of the sponsoring magazine, an Edgar Someone-or-other. Even though I cannot remember his surname, I can remember that he was a short, fat man, with thick-framed spectacles, which kept sliding down the nose on his round, sweating face.

We musicians were now all standing in a line at the back of the stage, as instructed by Bossman, while the sponsor made his predictable speech, about how high the musical standards had been this year, and how hard it was for the judges to come to their decisions, "Except in one case," he added rather interestingly. He then called a young lady on to the stage, who came on pushing a trolley, bearing some scrolls, a tiny silver cup, and a foot-high silver statuette of a bowler-hatted man blowing a trumpet.

"Now," said Edgar Fatso. "For the judges' decisions."

The girl handed him a clipboard, which she had retrieved from somewhere or other.

Carefully reading from the clipboard, he said "Firstly, the most promising new musician." The young lady selected a scroll and handed it to him, whilst he announced the name of the recipient who duly came forward and shyly collected his just reward, to the accompaniment of loud applause from the audience.

After the penultimate award had been handed over (which, I remember, was given to the Geoff Arlington Sixtette for the best jazz combo), he said "And now we come to the big one; the coveted 'Young Jazz Musician of the

Year' award" At this point, the young lady handed over to him the last remaining object on her trolley, which was the silver, trumpet-playing statuette. He fondled and stroked it in a Freudian or phallic way as he spoke.

"Well, for the first time ever, ladies and gentlemen, tonight we have a unanimous decision from our judges. This award has, up until tonight, been awarded only after much discussion and even heated argument among the judges. But not tonight. Now, before I announce the name of our unanimous winner, can I ask you all to show your appreciation for our judges who have all worked so hard tonight?"

While they stood up and turned towards the audience, bowing in acknowledgement, I took a look down the line of musicians. Those who had already won something were smiling broadly and familiarly at the bowing and waving judges, almost as if they were members of their families. The rest were standing, white-faced and tense with expectancy.

And they were not alone. I was also in a state of tense nervousness. The way I saw it, if I win, then Janine, who must be in the audience somewhere (although my screening of the audience proved unsuccessful), would surely come to see me after the show, and reward me with every kind of sexual favour. But, if I lose, which I was worried would be the case (the guitarist in the Grant-Greene quartette had played some very fine solos, which I felt half-way sure had wiped out any chance I might have had), it meant that I would have to go back to the dreary, boring, onerous task of catching up on my studies, in dreary, boring, Janine-less Newcastle, the only glimmer of pleasure being the possibility of making out with one of Harold's cast-off blondes. And this was apart from the actual disappointment, embarrassment and humiliation of losing.

In my state of mind at that moment, the applause that the judges were getting seemed to go on for hours, instead of the couple of minutes I suppose it actually lasted. At long last, the clapping died down, the judges, a couple of whom were famous band leaders, resumed their seats and Fatso cleared his throat. By now, the tension inside me was so great that even though I was (I hope), retaining an external appearance of just casual interest, my heart was doing a rumba whilst my guts waltzed madly round and round.

"As I said earlier, ladies and gentlemen," said Edgar Fatman, "there was complete agreement among the judges as to whom should receive this award. ("Get on with it for fuck's sake," muttered the pianist from the Hull City band, who was standing next to me on my left). "We were all astonished at the maturity and clarity of vision of this young gentleman, who, we feel, has a very bright future. And so, ladies and gentlemen, this year's 'Young Musician of the Year' award goes unanimously and with our heartfelt admiration and enthusiasm to the brilliant young pianist from Newcastle upon Tyne, Jake Silver."

I was stunned. My first reaction was that I had not heard right. So I just stood still, not daring to move in case I had only imagined he had said my name. But all doubt was dispelled by Geof Arlington who was standing next to me on my right, who pushed me forward saying "Well done lad."

I collected my award with my left hand, whilst shaking Edgar Fatman's hand with my right.

He was at the same time trying to make himself heard over the excited clapping and shouted 'bravos' (which I felt sure was coming from the area where Ivan was sitting). I was too astonished, excited and thrilled to hear what he was saying, but it was something like "Congratulations my boy. You deserved it."

Then Eliot came back on stage leading the four judges. I shook hands with each in turn, while, the elated audience clapped and cheered. I remember one of the judges shouting in my ear over the noise, as we shook hands, "Come to my office on Monday morning. I want to represent you."

'Too late' I thought, but said nothing.

Then Eliot took my arm and led me to the down-stage microphone to say a few words.

"I am a bit too flabbergasted to say anything" I said. It was now my turn to speak while lovingly fondling the silver statuette. I thanked my late Father for passing on his talent to me, after which I thanked my Mother for putting up with my endless fumbling at the keyboard when I was younger. Then I thanked my Aunt and Uncle. And then I thanked my cousin Ivan, "Who is in the audience tonight and who talked me into entering this competition in the first place." I pointed to him and asked him to stand up, which he rather shame-facedly did, waving to acknowledge his applause. Then I added, "I would also like to thank my music teachers who taught me everything I know. Thank you Fats Waller, Nat 'King' Cole, Teddy Wilson, Bud Powell and the great Art Tatum. Also thank you Vladimir Horowitz for showing me what it is possible to do on the piano, although I will probably never get anywhere near to doing it."

I said that last bit to fool the audience into believing how humble I was. In truth, because of my callow ignorance, I had no doubt that I was going to develop a piano technique at least equal to the great Vladimir. Silly, silly, me.

What thrilled me just as much as receiving the statuette (which I sold for ten bucks, some years later, in New York City, when I was very broke), was the cheque for one hundred pounds that also went with winning.

Of course I did not mention Janine in my thank you speech. Had I have, Ivan would in all probability, mention the fact to Aunt Sarah, which, in turn, would have undoubtedly resulted in the proverbial shit uncompromisingly hitting the proverbial fan.

But this did not mean that Janine was anything other than front and centre in my mind. With this extra hundred, plus the fifty-odd pounds I was already carrying, I would show her that even though I may be younger than she is, I was now not only a grown up, but a big-shot grown up, able to show her the kind of good time that Melvyn Douglas, or any other of those effortlessly suave film actors gave their girl friends.

When I think back on it, I realise that at eighteen years of age, I knew far more about expensive dinners at the Brown Derby in Los Angeles, or romantic, rapturous evenings down Argentina way, or in pre-Castro Cuba, than I did about where to go in my own home town of London. This was for two obvious reasons; my love for Hollywood movies and my contempt for British ones. As a direct result, all my ideas on how to comport oneself with a girl friend were based entirely upon what I had gleaned from American movies. For example, at that time, had the opportunity arisen for me to meet a girl for a drink, I would in all probability, have ordered an old fashioned on the rocks, like William Powell did in the 'Thin Man' movies, even though I had not the slightest idea what an 'old fashioned' was. For a dinner date, I would have tried to emulate Claude Rains or Otto Kruger or the aforementioned Melvyn Douglas. This would have meant, among other things, always paying the bill (or cheque, as they called it), by pulling out a bundle of money as I was rising to leave, peeling off a few notes and throwing them down on the table without either checking the bill, or working out a suitable tip for the waiter. For a candle-lit supper, I would have taken on the persona of Don Ameche or John Payne or any other of those actors who seemed to spend most of their lives in a white tuxedo, on board fabulously luxurious liners wandering around the Caribbean.

So, as soon as I could get off the stage, I hurried back to the dressing room, to wait for Janine to show up, after which, I would immediately swing into my Hollywood act.

The scene in the band room was exactly as expected: elation from the winners and depressed frozen resignation from the losers.

I hadn't been in the room for more than a minute, when the door opened. Sadly for me, it was not Janine but Eliot, who came in to congratulate me and also to ask me to wait back for his photographer to arrive, "So that we can get some nice shots of you sitting at the piano."

I told him how we all have to be out of the building by eleven o'clock at the latest, which was now only five minutes away. "Oh," he said, clearly thinking out an alternative plan.

"Well, in that case, there is a nice little club we can go to. I know the owner very well. They have a nice, white baby grand. I'm sure he'll let me take a few shots down there."

The door opened, but again it wasn't the one I was aching for. This time it was Ivan hurrying over to me, arms outstretched, embarrassing me (and astonishing the other musicians), by shouting as he came towards me "Ge-e-eni-us." After hugging me, he shouted jubilantly "Didn't I say you would win? Didn't I say it?"

I introduced Eliot to him and Irene (who was standing about six paces away, in case by coming any closer it would be interfering), explaining at the same time, how it was Ivan who caused me to be in the competition at all.

Ivan, who had taken my statuette off me and after looking at it with awe, kissed it with a loud 'mwa' said laughingly to Eliot, as he handed it back to me, "He didn't think he was good enough. Can you believe that?" And then putting his arm around my shoulder and hugging me tightly, he added "Jake Silver. The greatest pianist in, in...well, Europe, at any rate, and maybe the world." Then he babbled on to Eliot how he always knew I was a going to be great.

"Even when he was only six years old, six years old," he said twice, to doubly impress the fact on Eliot, "I could tell..." etc., etc.

But by now it was obvious that he had lost Eliot's interest, and mine too for that matter. I was much too preoccupied with Janine's arrival, to be listening to Ivan's potted biography of my playing career.

'Surely' I thought, 'she's got to be arriving any minute now.'

Eliot turned to me, probably to stop Ivan's excited loquaciousness:

"Jake, if I am going to do an interview with you and get some photos, we really have to be getting a move on." Then, turning to Eliot and Irene he said, "You two are of course perfectly welcome to come along, but I must warn you in advance, that you will have to be quiet or just talk to one another quietly, while I do my interview and photo session with Jake."

Ivan, after consulting his watch declined, explaining that both he and Irene had to be up early the next morning. They left, but not before further embarrassing me by saying as he shook my hand with both of his;"Okay Jake. We're off. Don't be home too late. I'll leave you a door key in the flower pot"

Why that should have embarrassed me even one little bit is a complete mystery to me now. But it did, and it caused the predictable reaction from the unrewarded, angry, embittered, and now pretty drunk trumpet player from the Hull City Stompers.

No sooner than they had left the room, than he said in a pretend prissy voice "Mommy will give you a smack on your little botty-boo if you come in late." This was greeted with hoots of laughter by his friends. I was about to turn and say something nasty, when the door opened slowly. Again, my heart leapt as I waited to see her, my beloved, coming towards me.

But it was only the scruffy stage-doorman.

"Righ', he said. "I wantcha all aht of 'ere wivvin the next five minutes. 'Cos I'm lockin' up and anybody 'oo aint ou' of 'ere by then gets locked in. Righ?"

"I've still got my drums to pack up," said Geoff Arlington's drummer.

"Too bleedin' bad mate. If you aint aht of 'ere pretty bloody smar'ish, I'm lockin' up this 'ere door an' for all I care, you can sleep on your bloody drums"

He looked across at Eliot and me to see if we were amused by what he clearly thought was a brilliant piece of repartee. When he saw that we were not, he left.

"Don't worry," Eliot told the drummer. "I'll make sure you can get out of here." Then he said to me "You help him pack, while I go to the stage door and make sure it is kept open until we have all left." He turned as got to the door and said to me, "I'll see you at the stage door Jake. Then we'll get a cab to 'Jacks'. That's the club I told you about."

I offered to help the drummer put his drums away in their cases, but he insisted that it would be quicker if I left all the packing to him, so I went off to join Eliot at the stage door.

I could not resist making a detour to take a last look at the now empty stage upon which I had known so much triumph. It was very dark as I approached the wings, but fortunately for me, somebody switched on a stage working light which shed enough light to stop me bumping into all the paraphernalia that was now cluttering the side of the stage.

As I stood staring at the scene of my triumph, for no reason that I can remember, I turned round to take a last look at all the electrical gadgetry that control the footlights and the safety curtain, etc.

Behind an upturned box, with a thick coil of electric cable piled on top of it, I saw a human foot jutting out. I went over to discover that it belonged to Bossman. He was either very heavily asleep or unconscious, because try as hard as I could I could not get him to open his eyes, or even move a muscle.

When I got to the stage door, the first thing I did was look outside, up and down the dark, little alley, in the slim hope that Janine had chosen to wait outside for me. I answered Eliot's rather questioning stare by explaining that I was looking for my representative, who must have been unaccountably detained by something or other. Then I told him about Bossman.

"He's out cold in the wings." I told him. "I think he has had a drop too much," I added with all the wisdom and knowledge of my eighteen years.

"I wondered where Arthur Collins had got to" Eliot said. ('So that's his name' I thought).

Then he added, "I presumed he was somewhere checking the night's takings, or something. Anyway, we can't leave him there all night. We'd better go and get him up."

"Yeah," I echoed gratuitously. "We can't leave him there all night. He'll die from the cold, apart from anything else."

Actually what I was trying to do was encourage Eliot to do his boy-scout good deed for the day, because it kept us here in the theatre longer, thus giving Janine more time to show up, although, I was coming to realise that I was just clinging to a dream, and that even though I had won, she was still not coming to see me.

I stood behind Eliot as he leaned over Arthur Collins and pulled him by his hand, saying at the same time, "Come along, old son," but there was no reaction. He was out cold. Then Eliot took him by his shoulders and shook him quite hard. Bossman's head bumped from side to side on his thick bull-like neck, but there was no sign of consciousness. Eliot got down on his knees to crouch low over the unconscious figure to study him more closely. While he was pulling up his eyelids with his thumb and taking his pulse, he said "Y'know Jake, I was a medical orderly in the army and I would swear that this is not a booze-induced sleep." He stood up, staring thoughtfully at the heavy, unconscious shape, when the scruffy stage doorman came up to us.

"Are you still 'ere?" he yelled at us, even though he was not more than five feet away. Eliot tuned to the old man.

"Just let me have your torch a moment will you?"

"Nah, just a bleedin' moment..."

Eliot shouted him down. "Give me your damned torch man. NOW!"

The poor little fellow, reacted at once to the authority in Eliot's upper class accent, and immediately handed over his torch, together with a muttered "Sorry Guv."

Having been away from Britain for so long now, I can view its class problems objectively. Britain's poor and poorly educated (almost invariably one and the same thing), have had it bludgeoned into their brains, that they are members of the 'lower classes'. Having brain-washed them to believe this piece of arrant, arrogant nonsense, it is comparatively simple to then convince them that the 'upper classes' are therefore of a superior breed, who should always be respected and obeyed. Of course in order to make it work, this cunning but evil proposition has to be artfully fed to the masses, inside a heavily sugar-coated pill. Two of the main constituents of this smarmily sweet sugar coating are: 'the British lower classes are the salt of the earth, and are to be envied', when in truth, they are mercilessly exploited by the better off and better spoken 'upper classes'. The other crafty, insidious piece of crap, fed to them by an Establishment-controlled Church of England, is that 'the poor will inherit the earth'. Like hell they will! And if they ever did try to claim this inheritance, rely on it; the Establishment would, if necessary, call out the army to stop them, just as they did at St.Peter's Fields in Manchester or in Liverpool and many other places. And I doubt whether it would work anyway. If you dear reader ever get an opportunity to observe a conversation between a 'toff' and some impoverished fellow from the 'lower classes', you will, by simply noting the body language and the way one talks to the other, understand a great deal about the hopeless and probably incurable British disease, known as 'Class Consciousness'.

Eliot briefly shone the torch into one of Arthur Collins's eyes which he had again held open with his thumb. Then he stood up and said to the stage doorkeeper, as he handed him back his torch, "Stop whatever you are doing and telephone for an ambulance. This man is in a coma."

Before the door keeper could say anything, Eliot added, "And put all the stage lights on so that the ambulance men can see what they are doing when they get here."

"Trouble is. guv" the old doorman replied, "The public telephone is buggered and I am under strict hinstructions not to open the stage door after eleven o'clock at nigh' It'd be more than my job's worth to do that guv."

Without saying another word, Eliot walked very quickly to the stage door, with me right behind him, followed at a distance by the stage doorman. It was exactly as the doorman had said: the public phone was broken and the door into the stage doorman's little office was locked.

"Eliot said to the now very worried stage door man, "Are you going to unlock this door or not?"

The poor little doorman, torn between two conflicting orders was clearly struggling. for a way out.

"I've go' an idea guv," he said in what he hoped was a convincing manner. There's a public call box just a couple of 'undred yards dahn the Strand. It'll only take yer a couple o' minutes. That's the best thing to do I'm sure."

Eliot stared at him in disbelief. Then taking out his top pocket handkerchief, and wrapping it around his right hand, he said to me while nodding towards my statuette which had barely been out of my hands since I won it. "Let me have that for a minute, will you?"

I handed it to him.

"Now, stand well clear, Jake," he said, and using the base of the statuette, he shattered the two glass panels of the stage door keeper's cubicle.

"'Ere, 'oo the bloody 'ell d'ye fink you are!?" yelled the scruffy little man.

Eliot ignored him. He hand me back my silver, trumpet-playing prize, reached into the cubicle, and after dusting off the shards of glass from the telephone with his handkerchief-wrapped hand, dialled 999 and ordered an ambulance. Then he turned to the stage doorman, whose face was a mixture of anger, fear (probably for his job), and typically lower-class obeisance.

"Find something to cover Mr Collins with, and don't leave his side until the ambulance crew is here."

The little fellow was about to say something, but Eliot raised his hand to cut him off, saying with all the inbuilt authority of his accent and social background; "Do it now man. Right away. Off you go."

For all the reasons I have given earlier, the scruffy little fellow reverted to the subservience of his class."Oh, right away Guv. I'll look after 'im, don' you worry."

As he hurried off to carry out the wishes of his superior, Eliot called out to him: "Make sure he's kept warm." Then turning to me he said "Well, there's not much point hanging around here any longer. Go and get your things and meet me at the top of the alley, in the Strand. I'll get us a cab."

I collected my overcoat, wrapped the statuette in the evening paper I had bought earlier, and after one last despairing look up and down for Janine, walked up the alley to join Eliot. By now I had finally come to accept that even though she had sent me a hand-written note, Janine could not have been present at my hour of triumph. I reckoned that she must have got a friend or somebody to leave it at the stage door. As we climbed into the taxi, I could hear the tell-tale ting-a-ling of an approaching ambulance.

Eliot leaned forward and shouted to the driver, "Jack's, in Whitefriars Street, please." I took one last despairing look out of the taxi's tiny rear window, for Janine, but all there was to be seen was an ambulance turning into the tiny lane, leading to the stage door.

'Jacks' was a key club, which meant that each club member had his own key to the front door of the place. As no amount of banging on the dark, highly polished, mahogany panelled door would ever receive an answer, to gain entrance, you had to be, or be with, a key-holding member.

The club was half way down a terrace of elegant Georgian houses, and its entrance was so discreetly anonymous, that all but the most observant pedestrian would be completely unaware that he or she was walking past anything but a private and highly desirable town house. The only mention of the name 'Jacks' was on the shiny brass door-knob, in the centre of the door, where it had been engraved diagonally in tiny italic print.

Eliot unlocked the club front door, and I followed him into the small, but elegant foyer. On my right was a place to check your hats and coats, and facing me, a small rectangular, antique dark-wood table, upon which, lay an open ledger-like book, presumably for members and their guests to sign in. Behind the table, were heavy, dark red velvet, floor-to-ceiling drapes, drawn tightly together, so that the actual club itself was invisible? The other side of the foyer was furnished with a Regency period chaise longe and a rather ornate, high-backed chair, probably of the same period.

Eliot had already told me in the cab that the club's membership was almost entirely drawn from members of the press and, to a lesser extent, show-business folk. He explained that 'Jacks', being so close to Fleet Street and the Strand, this type of membership was virtually guaranteed.

Having, signed us both in, he pushed the drapes apart and I followed him down the four, wide carpeted stairs into the club itself. It was an oblong room, about sixty or seventy feet long and thirty feet wide. If you took out the area of the bar, which was on our left as we came down the stairs, and which ran the entire length of the room, I would guess there was around twenty feet of width in which to accommodate the fifteen or so small, round tables. There were also a couple of cubicles in the far right-hand corner of the dimly lit room, as far away as possible from the baby grand piano that was set diagonally opposite the stairs from which I had just entered, and which was glowing whitely and brightly in its own spotlight.

Sitting at the piano was a very handsome looking black guy, impeccably dressed in a white tuxedo. He was playing 'Aint Misbehaving' so badly, that I found myself wondering whether he was really the club's pianist, or whether it was just a club member who fancied knocking out a few tunes.

Eliot was immediately waylaid by a friend who, judging by their conversation, he had not seen for a long while. While they were renewing their old acquaintance, I took the opportunity to look around the room.

The bar area was quite crowded, even though only a couple of tables were occupied. Those hanging around the bar were of no particular type. There were old and young, thin and fat, well dressed (especially the females), and some men in shabby shirts and even shabbier sports jackets. At one of the occupied tables I noticed a heavily bejewelled, middle-aged lady with a good looking, young, pale-faced fellow at least twenty years her junior. She had reached across the table to hold his hand, her facial expression one of such an insatiable sexual hunger, that you could be forgiven for fearing for the poor guy's life.

Two evening-gowned, slim-bodied ladies who had been sitting together at the bar, beyond my line of sight, because of a group of laughing, middle-aged and half-pissed men blocking my line of vision, walked across the room to sit on the high two stools which had been set on either side of the piano. They sat listening as the piano player fought a losing battle with the harmonies of the 'The Song is You'.

Eliot finally broke free from his conversation to turn to me and say, "Grab one of the cubicles while I get us a couple of drinks. What do you fancy?"

I was tempted to order an old fashioned on the rocks, but decided that without Janine's presence, the Melvyn Douglas characterisation was the wrong one to adopt. I opted for David Niven instead. "A scotch and soda will do nicely thank you."

I sat in the cubicle watching Eliot, who was now laughing and talking with a group of men, while he waited to get served. The two ladies near the piano had now got off their high stools and were standing either side of the piano player, their long, white arms draped around his shoulders, their faces pressed closed to his.

I was overcome with envy. 'This is the life' I thought. 'Working in a swish, little club with great looking chicks draping themselves all over you. Wow!' I reckoned that this was just the kind of room that Art Tatum would play in. I thought; 'Who wants to study crummy history, when, with a bit of luck I could work in a place like this'. I got a rush of pleasure at the thought of

Janine coming into a place like this, and finding me playing the piano with two luscious, adoring, blondes hanging all over me. 'Then she wouldn't treat me in the off-hand way she is doing now; no sir' I thought.

Eliot was now heading my way, with a thin, medium-sized, middle-aged man, superbly attired in a suit that had Saville Row written all over it. Eliot, was bearing a silver tray upon which was a bottle of champagne and three flute champagne glasses. I stood up as they approached the cubicle. As I shook the outstretched hand of this immaculately suited man, Eliot said, whilst carefully setting down his tray of goodies: "Jake, this is Jack Montgomery, the owner of this little oasis."

Then Jack, in an accent every bit as immaculate as his suit, said "When Eliot told me of your success tonight, I felt it called more for a celebrative drop of the old bubbly, rather than just plain scotch."

We two sat down, leaving Eliot to wrestle with the champagne cork, which he eventually managed to get off with a loud pop, after which he filled our glasses to the brim with the sparkling brew.

This was the first time I had ever drunk champagne, and I was delighted by the way it danced and tingled on my tongue. The barmen appeared with an ice bucket, into which he buried the bottle, and after covering it with a napkin, quietly withdrew. I was feeling more grow-up than I had ever felt before.

Jack raised his glass. "Here's to you Jake. Wishing you success and hoping that Lady Luck will always smile kindly upon you."

After we had drunk the toast, and put our glasses down. Jack said to me; "You know, I love all that jazz music. Always have. I've still got my records of Louis Armstrong, Sydney Bechet and all those great jazzmen."

"Oh, they're the best," was my rather lame reply.

"Speaking of luck," Eliot said, "Bill Mather is over at the bar. In case you don't know, he is a very big-time press photographer. He gets his work in the Picture Post, as well as all the dailies. I told him about you, and he is quite willing to get the camera and lights out of his car and do a few shots of you while you are playing. That is," and he turned to Jack Montgomery, "If it's alright with you."

"Absolutely old boy," Jack replied enthusiastically. Then he said, "I know. Why don't we bring Reggie over to join us?

He got up and went across to the pianist and ignoring the two fawning ladies, said something to the 'piano player' (if you'll excuse the expression) which, judging by Jack's thumb jutting in our direction was clearly asking him to join us. Then he said something else which caused Reggie to look up sharply in my direction. This guy Reggie was without doubt a musical mass-murderer. While Jack was speaking to him, he was busily dismembering a beautiful tune, called 'Flamingo'.

Jack waited by the piano for him to finish off the tune (and I do mean 'finish off'), chatting and laughing with his two female devotees whilst he did so.

As I watched them, I thought; 'They may be beautiful but they have to be deaf!' Probably to take my mind off what was going on in the name of music, Eliot told me a little bit about Jack Montgomery.

"You'll like Jack, once you get to know him. After he came out of the army, where incidentally, he won a couple of medals for bravery under fire, he went to work for his old man in the City. His father is, or rather was, the chairman of one of the most prestigious stockbroking firms in Britain. But Jack found the work too unadventurous. So, to give his life a little more excitement, he decided to buy and sell shares on his own behalf, sometimes with his clients' money. This, in case you don't know it Jake, is a very serious offence indeed. By the time his father found out about it, Jack was heavily in debt. His old man had to find several thousands of pounds to cover his son's losses. So, he was chucked out of the firm, and shipped off to work on a tobacco plantation in Southern Rhodesia. Unfortunately, he got involved with the plantation owner's wife, which resulted in his being shot by her husband. Luckily for Jack, the bullet just missed his testicles, which he is sure the plantation owner aimed at, because it went through the fleshy part of his upper thigh.

After he had recovered from his near miss, his father brought him back home again, and handing him a cheque for five thou', told him that this money is all he is getting and that as of now he is on his own."

Not knowing whether Eliot was telling me something that was common knowledge, or some private gossip, I took a quick look around the room to see where Jack was, with the intention of warning Eliot off the subject should I see him heading our way. I finally spotted him sitting at a table, in what appeared to be serious conversation with a couple of well dressed men. So it was still all clear for Eliot to continue..

"Well, Jack took the cheque and waltzed off to Monte Carlo, where, in just three days at the gaming tables he did in the lot! In fact, he was so broke after his third night of gambling, that he didn't even have enough left over to pay his hotel bill. So he decided, it being three o'clock in the morning, that this was the perfect time to pack his bag and do a runner. Back at the hotel he decided to go to the bar and get a last drink, charged of course to his room account, which he had no intention of paying anyway, only to spot four men at a corner table playing poker for pretty high stakes. So our Jack strolls over, glass in hand, to watch the play. One of the players, who turned out to be kind of a titled English aristocrat, asked him if he would like to join the game. Apparently this young lord felt that his losses were due to there being an even number of players. 'Poker', he claimed, 'must always be played with odd numbers at the table, three, five, or seven players'. Even numbers wreck the flow of the cards, he believed.

Jack explained that he would love to join the game, but that he had done all his cash in at the casino, and could get no more until the banks open, which was of course, a lie.

But, this young, slightly sozzled English blood looks up at Jack and says"Did you serve in the army during the war sir?"

"Yes," says Jack. "I was a captain in an infantry regiment," which was actually the truth.

Then this English lord asks, "And tell me sir, are you staying at this hotel?" Jack said he was.

"In which case" says this aristocrat, "You are clearly a gentleman or you would not have been an officer, and you must have means, or else you couldn't be staying stay here.. So, I am prepared to advance you a hundred quid against your IOU. In any case, once there is an odd number at the table, I am damned sure my luck will change."

So, with the agreement of the other players, Jack took the money and joined the game.

I waited while Eliot brought out his silver cigarette case, removed a cigarette and lit it. While he was doing so, I took the opportunity to check that Jack was still in deep conversation with his two male colleagues. After blowing some pale blue cigarette smoke upwards towards the ceiling, he continued with his Jack Montgomery saga.

"In spite of all the bad luck he had been having at the casino, after a few hands, Jack found himself a few hundred pounds ahead. He thought that this was about the right time to quit, but decided to play out one more hand. The game they were playing was straight five card draw poker," which meant nothing to me at that time. But I nodded knowingly nevertheless.

"Jack was dealt a pair of Jacks. He exchanged his other three cards and got himself another pair of Jacks, plus an Ace. I don't know how much you know about Poker Jake, but holding four Jacks is the sort of hand that poker players will mortgage their houses and sell their wives in order to keep the betting going.

Again, I tried to hide my ignorance by nodding knowingly.

"Anyway, after the first few rounds of betting, three of the players had dropped out, and Jack found himself playing against just one other, who according to Jack, was a German. This fellow raised the bet to one thousand pounds. Jack did not have this kind of money to match his bet, so he asked the young English lord to back him. He took one look at Jack's hand and said, "My British friend thinks that you are bluffing, and so do I. In any case," he said, probably because he was a bit pissed, "I'll always back an English gentleman against bloody foreigner. So we will see your thousand, and raise you another thousand." The German chap said, "I will raise your two thousand to four thousand, and strongly advise you to throw your hand in." Then Jack said, "Regardless of what my friend may think of foreigners, I like you and to prove it, I am prepared to see your cards for four thousand."

The German laid his cards on the table, saying as he did so, "Four tens gentlemen," and reached forward to take the money, only to be stopped by Jack: "Sorry old chum, but I have four Jacks."

"Mein Got," said the German, or words to that effect, and fainted clean away."

I looked across the room to see that some more people had joined Jack and his two friends. So it was okay for Eliot to go on with his story.

"After splitting the pot with his backer, Jack went up to his room with a couple of thou' in his pocket. Later that morning, with all thoughts of leaving the hotel now banished from his mind, he was reading the racing page of a daily newspaper, over a cup of coffee, only to see that at Longchamps that afternoon, there was a horse running called 'Jack's Are Best'. He went straight out of the hotel and put a thousand pounds on it."

"Don't tell me," I said. "He lost it all, I suppose."

"Au contraire, mon ami. It came in at twelve to one. Jack eventually returned to London with over ten thou' in his wallet."

Again, I looked across to where Jack was sitting. to see that the group who had gone over to his table were now busily dragging him up to the bar. I also noticed that Bill Mather was setting up his lights around the piano.

So, while Eliot poured us both another glittering glass of Veuve Cliquot, he went on: "You may wonder how it is that I know all this about Jack Montgomery. The answer is that he told me. He thinks that his story might make a great book, and he wants me to write it. Frankly, I agree with him. The only thing stopping me is this awful feeling I have deep inside me that it will be a biography with an unhappy ending."

Before I could ask why, he held up a hand to stop me, saying at the same time; "But let me tell you the rest. When Jack came back to London, he of course had nowhere to stay, having been banned from the family home by his father. But, with all the winnings, bulging his wallet out, he took a suite at the Dorchester, while he looked around for an apartment to rent.

The very next morning would you believe, who does our Jack bump into in the foyer of the hotel, but the wife of the Rhodesian plantation owner who had all but castrated him. Over breakfast she told Jack the outcome of her husband's attempt at either trying to murder, or, at the very least, emasculate him. After Jack had been rushed to hospital, the police came to arrest the plantation owner. He was very drunk by that time, and decided that rather than go to jail, he would shoot it out with the forces of law and order, which resulted in what usually happens when someone indulges in gun-play them: he ended up dead. As a result she not only came into a very tidy sum of money; she also found herself the sole owner of a vast tobacco plantation, which she sold to a British tobacco company for a bundle of money. The reason she was in London was to sign the transfer deeds and collect the cheque. Even though she had brought her newest Rhodesian boy friend along with her, she and Jack once again became very close, and within a couple of weeks, after a whirlwind romance, they were married. She bought this town house, and furnished it to Jack's taste, as a wedding present for him. That should have been the end of the story, but Jack being Jack, he got bored with the normality of married life and started to spend more and more of his time and more and more of her money, drinking and gambling.

About six months into the marriage, Jack was walking down Whitefriars street, on his way home, when she zoomed past him on the pillion seat of a motor bike, driven by the boy friend she had brought with her from Rhodesia. She gave him a cheery wave as she sped past. And that was the last he ever saw of her."

"Christ" I said, as Eliot refilled my drink. Jack saw me look across at him, and held up a hand to me, with stretched fingers, to indicate that he will be another five minutes. Then someone at the bar said something funny to Jack, because he let out a loud roar of laughter.

"So," Eliot continued; "Jack found himself in possession of a lovely house, but with very little money in the bank, and no rich wife to top it up. He managed to borrow some money from a couple of wealthy friends and turned what was the Billiard room and the wine cellar (he spread his upturned hands to indicate that this is where we are), into this little watering hole. Incidentally, he called the club 'Jacks' because of his poker hand, and not because of his name."

"Does he miss her, now that she is gone?" I asked.

"Good Lord, no," Eliot said chuckling at the thought. "Jack told me that he now has everything he has always wanted: plenty of money, a lovely house, and a place where he can drink to his heart's content. And he can also entertain his friends without ever having to go outside the house."

"Here they come" I said, interrupting Eliot.

Jack had the piano player with him. "Sorry we took so long," he said as they approached the table. Then, holding his hand out in my direction he said "Jake Silver, meet Reggie de Courcy." As he said his name he put his arm around the coloured pianist's shoulders.

I stood up and we shook hands.

"Jack has bin' tellin' me that you have just been voted the best new young jazz musician. Congrats man." The musical lilt of his Caribbean accent was entirely new to my ears. I immediately liked it.

Reggie was, I reckon about thirty-five years of age, my height, and clearly had the physique of a Greek God. His skin was the colour of milk chocolate and his good looking face was European in feature, rather than African. If he could have played as well as he looked, he may even have given Horowitz a tough time.

As ever, in situations like these, the ensuing conversation was stilted and full of forced informality. Thankfully, it was broken up by Bill Mather coming to the table to say that he was set up and ready to roll.

As I stood up to go to the piano, Jack said to me "Do you know 'Smoke Gets In Your Eyes'?"

"Sure."

"Be a good chap and play it for me. I adore that tune."

As I got up to make my journey to the piano, Reggie said, a smile on his lips but a look of worry in his eyes; "Try not to show me up too much man." But when you are only eighteen tears old, and blessed with the kind of chops that were good enough to allow me to sail through Chopin Etudes and Bach fugues, and then throw into the mix the arrogance of youth, it is an irresistible pleasure to destroy other piano players. In fact, Art Tatum delighted in doing just that, all his life, let alone when he was young. (By the way, for any squares who may be foolhardy enough to attempt reading this book, 'chops' is jazz musician's slang for technical dexterity on one's instrument).

As I approached the piano, I saw that the two chicks were still sitting on their high stools on either side of the piano. I thought; 'This is going to be great. Playing the piano with these to two beauties perched on either side of me'. After adjusting the piano stool to suit me, I zinged out a couple of arpeggios to check out the piano.' Then I looked up to say hello to both of the females.

Man, was I disappointed!

"The 'beautiful' blonde turned out to be at least fifty years old! Even though she was trying hard to bury her wrinkled features under a mass of Max Factor, at close range it was only too clear that the wrinkles had won out.

The brunette was about the same age as her peroxided friend. They both could have modelled for some church-inspired Temperance League advert. It could have shown their faces in close up, with the legend written underneath; 'If you don't stop boozing, smoking and staying up all hours of the night, you'll end up looking like this'.

Although, I must admit, I could not stop myself from digging the tits on the brunette.

I shut them out of my mind as I went into Jerome Kern's, 'Smoke Gets In Your Eyes'. Maybe it was the warm intimacy of the club atmosphere, or maybe it was letting out all the tensions of the competition, or maybe it was simply the effect of good champagne, but I played at least as well as I played at the competition. My chops were tops and the inspiration flooded through my fingers as I played about six or seven choruses of the tune.

When I finally closed the tune down, I was surprised to hear loud applause. I looked up from the keyboard to find that quite a crowd had gathered around the piano. I also noticed that the two ugly sisters were no longer to be seen.

"Did you get the photos?" I asked Bill Mather.

"Not yet," he replied, as he tinkered with the positioning of his lights. "I was going to run off a few shots, but everyone started to gather round, and, in any case, I didn't want to disturb your concentration." Play something else, and this time, I will be shooting, so look up from the keyboard occasionally, will you?"

"Okay," I said quietly. But there was nothing quiet about me inside. In actual fact, I was bouncing inside with excitement at being applauded by real grown-ups in a swish night club in London, the capital of Great Britain. I felt like I was Art Tatum, playing at the 'Three Deuces' in New York City. (And I wonder what the story is behind that name).

Before I could commence another tune, Jack Montgomery pushed through the mob standing around the piano, many of whom were shouting request tunes at me. He put his arm around my back and said in my ear, "Thank you Jake, I don't think I have ever heard it played as well as that, and by the way everyone was applauding, neither had they."

"I gave him the 'shucks, 'taint nothing', shy-and-humble routine, before launching off into a very fast 'stride piano' version of 'Get Happy'. This time, Bill pushed everyone back, to give himself room to move around me as he took a dozen or more shots.

Jack was standing up to welcome me as I returned to the table. He grabbed my right hand and shaking it warmly, said, "By God, you really are an exceptional pianist." Eliot and Reggie were also applauding.

As I sat down to drink a freshly poured glass of champagne, poured for me by Jack, a fat oldish man in an ill-fitting, unbuttoned sports jacket, and a wrinkled shirt, which had burst open at the navel, appeared to stagger up from nowhere. He could have made a great stand-in for W.C Fields. All conversation ceased while he stood staring drunkenly at me at me for at least a minute, before saying, "Bloody marv'lush." Then he tottered off in the direction of the bar.

Eliot leaned over to me. "That, in case you don't know it, is probably the best crime reporter in the country."

"Jack put down his champagne glass after swallowing the entire glassful in one go, and turning to me, said: "I wonder if you wouldn't mind popping along to my office with me. I've got something I'd like to talk to you about."

"Sure," I said as we both got up. Jack, after excusing us both, said, "Follow me will you?"

I had to crouch low as I followed him through a small door in the wall at the back of the bar, which led into a storage room full of unopened boxes and crates, plus a table full of every type of drinking glass. At the far side of the room was a small lift, which took us up to the floor above.

"It's so much more convenient than climbing the bloody stairs," Jack said, as he slid the metal lift-gate open. "Especially when you've had a skinful," he added as he clicked open the lift gate and we stepped out into a carpeted hallway at the end of the which were tall and cream lacquered double doors. Jack pushed them open before taking a step back to allow me to enter first.

It was a large room, furnished mainly with antiques, although the large armchair that Jack sat me down upon seemed to be of a modern design. Then he crossed the room to what looked like a tall, Jacobean cupboard, but which turned out to be filled with bottles and glasses.

"Care for a spot of something?" he asked

"No thanks," I said. "I've already had three glasses of champagne, and I do want to get home in one piece."

"Well, how about a cigar?" He reached up to the top-shelf of the cupboard and brought down a highly polished ebony humidor. Again I declined. He selected a long, thin cigar for himself, and after the circumcision ceremony, which he performed with a pair of gold scissors, specially shaped for the purpose, he carefully lit the Havana. Then he poured himself a large scotch and with cigar in mouth, scotch in one hand and ashtray in the other, he made his way to the armchair opposite me.

"I suppose Eliot has told you how all this came about" he said. "If he hasn't you must get him to tell you. I believe he is even thinking of writing a book about it.

'That's not the way Eliot told it' I thought.

"About how you came to get this house and the club downstairs?" I said.. "Yes he did tell me, and if only half of it is true, then you have had quite a life."

He leaned back in his armchair, and I waited while he blew two perfectly formed smoke rings in the air. Then he said: "Jake, dear chap, there is just one main ingredient to living a full, fruitful life. And that is luck. All that 'working hard' stuff is just a load of nonsense. Luck is the thing my boy. And as you get older you learn that it only comes in fits and starts. The trick therefore is to ride your luck for all that it is worth while you are on a lucky streak, and be philosophical about it when Lady Luck does a runner."

He took a long swig of his drink, followed by couple of puffs on his cigar, presumably to give me time to imbibe the importance of his words, before saying "I could easily have ended in the gutter y'know. But I have been lucky and I've always played my luck, and I suppose I always will." As he dusted an imaginary speck of dust from his lap, he added quietly and introspectively, "And I'll probably end up broke."

Then brightening, "But who cares, eh?"

He stood up and taking his glass with him, returned to the bar for a refill. As he held the glass and decanter up to eye level, as if to observe the exact quantity to be poured, rather like a scientist involved in a carefully controlled experiment, he said "How do you feel about riding your own luck, by giving up your studies and coming to work for me at a new place I am opening in Belgravia? It'll be worth thirty-five quid a week to you plus a whole load of tips that you will certainly get from the kind of clientele I intend to have."

Now kiddies, for those of you too young to remember, back in 1948, that was a very big salary indeed. It was about three times as much as your average accountant would earn for breaking his head open adding and subtracting figures, for nine hours of every working day! And that was without adding in any money from the tips that Jack assured me I would be getting.

"We'll also give you dinner at the club, so that apart from finding the rent for a pied a terre, it will all be spending money."

"Can I think about it?" I asked, even though every fibre of my being wanted me to kiss him on both cheeks and shout out "Yes, yes, yes."

He returned to his seat opposite me.

"What are you reading at university?"

"Modern History" I told him.

He let a few moments go by, before saying; "I heard and saw the way you played downstairs. You have music deep in your soul Jake. You are no more a modern historian than..." I watched him search his mind for the perfect example of the non-historian..."Charlie Chaplin" (In actual fact, Chaplin must have been quite a knowledgeable modern historian, judging by his two movies, 'Modern Times' and 'The Great Dictator'. But I knew what he was trying to say, and I knew that he was right).

"You haven't forgotten what I said about Lady Luck so soon have you?"

"No, of course not."

"Well, my boy, Lady Luck has just offered you a leg-up onto the first rung of the ladder in the only career in which you will be truly happy. You have to grab the moment Jake. If you are lucky, you'll end up rich and famous like that Duke Ellington fellow. If you are not, well at least you played the game as best you could. You can look at yourself in the mirror and say, 'I didn't sit on the sidelines being some dry-as-dust historian while the game of life was being played out without me." He polished off his drink, and as he walked over to the drink-filled cupboard to pour himself yet another, he said "Next week I am announcing the opening of my new club. I'd like to put in that announcement 'Jake Silver the brilliant young pianist, voted 'Young Jazz Musician of the Year' will be entertaining nightly'. One other thing which may help you to make your decision. I have bought a brand new Steinway baby grand for the club. So, my boy, what do you say?"

As he came back to his armchair and sat down, I said "I would really love to take the job, I really would. And I am very flattered that you have asked me. But before I can say yes, I have to do two things: the first is to get the consent of my Uncle and Auntie, who have been like a mother and father to me since my own parents were killed in an air-raid."

"Yes, Eliot told me about that. It must have been damn awful for you. But you said that there were two things. What's the other?"

I told him about my meeting with Janine Gregson and how I agreed that she would be my representative. Then I went on to explain, without going into too much detail, that I was now not sure if she wishes to go on with our arrangement. "So," I said, "I have to return to Newcastle and find out."

Jack tipped a long, whitish lump of ash into the ashtray, while I went through my explanation. Then, fondling the half full whiskey glass in his lap he mumbled, as if to himself; "Janine Gregson, Janine Gregson. Hmm."

Then, quite clearly he remembered something. He carefully put his glass down on his small, round side-table, and said "This Janine Gregson, your representative: does she look a bit like Susan Haywood, the film actress?"

"Yes," I said. "Actually she does." I was astonished. "Do you know her?"

"Good Lord" Jack said quietly more to himself than to me. He was quite clearly amused at whatever it that he was thinking. He suddenly got to his feet; "Listen, my lad, I'm going to get myself a drink. And I think,—no, I'm bloody sure—that you'd better have one too. Because after I have told you what I know about this young lady, you are going to need one.

I was concerned about arriving home pissed. But I had to know what it was about my Janine that was amusing Jack so much. So I thought 'what the hell'.

"Okay, I'll have a whiskey and soda please."

Even as he was pouring out our whiskies, he was muttering to himself, "Janine bloody Gregson. So that is where she ended up. Good Lord."

The not knowing what he was muttering about was becoming more than I could take. As he came back with the two drinks, I said "For Chrissakes, what is it that you know about Janine that I don't know?"

"Wait a minute" he said. "If I am not mistaken, Bill Mather covered the Janine Gregson affair for the Daily Sketch or some newspaper or other. That was of course before he became famous as a press photographer. But I am bloody sure it was him."

He walked across the room to the white telephone that was sitting on the little Louis-the-something table near the tall, double doors. "Let's get him up here," he said as he picked up the phone. "Mack" he said into it, "would you be a love and ask Eliot and Bill Mather to pop up here for a drink? There was a pause, and then; "No, you don't have to. Eliot knows the way quite well. Thanks."

As he made his way back to his armchair, I said, "Come on Jack, what the hell is this all about?" I felt very grown up, clutching my glass of scotch and calling him by his first name.

As he sat down and retrieved his cigar from the ash tray, he said yet again, "So, she lives in bloody Newcastle upon Tyne."

"Yes," I said, interrupting his musings: "She lives on the top floor of a block of luxury flats in a very fashionable part of the town. I understand her father owns the entire block."

"Of course. That would be right," Jack said, clearly having remembered something else. "It said in the paper at the time, that her father was a big time builder and land developer, among other things. D'you know I think he also got into trouble for trying to nobble the judge. Got off with a severe reprimand as I remember."

"What is this case are you talking about? What had she done wrong?" Before he could, or maybe, would answer me, his attention was drawn to a slight noise outside which Jack recognised as the lift door opening and shutting. "I think it's them," he said, as he got up to open the double doors, and receive Bill and Eliot.

The next five minutes or so was spent in what was for me, frustrating chit-chat whilst Jack poured the drinks for his new arrivals, and helped them to bring over chairs and ash trays etc. so that we were all sitting in a semi- circle, Eliot who was sitting next to me, leaned over and whispered in my ear; "You played great tonight. Reggie doesn't know where to put his face, poor chap." But I was so consumed with Janine Gregson that this normally gratifying compliment meant nothing to me.

Jack clapped his hands, asking for silence. Once he had got it, he said "Y'know, I rarely find myself thinking back to my army days. But something Jake told me brought back very vividly the memory of that train ride I took to join my regiment."

He took a sip of his scotch and a pull on his cigar, during which, Bill Mather said "And I have a feeling you're going to tell us about it whether we want to know or not, right?"

Jack continued as if Bill had not spoken.

"For most of that journey down to Colchester, where my regiment was stationed, I was completely absorbed, as was half of Great Britain for at that matter, in reading about a court case, involving a well-to-do, young and attractive looking girl called Janine Gregson."

"Christ Almighty," Bill blurted out. "Janine Gregson?"

"Oh," Jack said, his eyebrows raised, "I see you are getting interested Bill old lad?"

"I should say so" he answered. Then turning to me. "Why. Do you know her, Jake?"

"As I was telling Jack, I think she is my representative. At least that is what we had arranged. But as she didn't turn up for the competition, I'm not too sure anymore."

I had not the foggiest idea of what Janine had supposedly done. But there was still a deep residue of love for her within me, and I felt myself steeling inside with determination to defend her honour whatever they tell me about her.

Then Bill Mather turned to me and said something so wildly unexpected, that I asked him to repeat it.

"What I said was; were you a virgin when you met her?"

"Er, of course not," I lied. Anyway, what's that got to do with anything?"

"Well," he said, leering across at Jack meaningfully, "If you weren't a virgin, then I damned if I know what she wanted with you."

I suddenly realised by the hotness of my cheeks that I must be blushing. I tried to cover it up by pretending I was angry rather than utterly embarrassed.

"Will somebody for Chrissakes tell what all this virgin business is all about?" I said loudly, and I hope, aggressively. But I could see by the indulgent smiles on the other faces, that they had seen through my pretended bravado.

"Relax Jake. All will be revealed," Jack said. "That's why I invited these two chaps up. But before I ask Bill to take the floor, I must beg you Jake not to get upset about anything you may hear. After all, there is no way you could have known about her because, you would not have been much more than ten years old at the time. But I can tell you this lad: it was the type of case that had it not been for the war, would have been a cause celebre for weeks and maybe months." He turned to Bill Mather.

"Bill, didn't you cover this case for 'The Sketch' or some other newspaper?"

"Not only 'The Sketch', he said. "My stuff was syndicated all over the world" He quickly polished off his drink, and as he handed the now empty glass to Jack for a refill, he said "In fact, it was the last case I covered, before I was called up into the Navy."

Eliot came into the conversation. "I remember a bit about it. But I'm damned if I can remember the details."

"I can, Eliot mate." Bill assured him. "This is not the kind of case you forget easily. In fact, had I not been called up for naval service, I was going to write a book about it."

As he took his second gin and tonic from Jack, he added "Matter of fact, come to think of it, I might still do it."

Sitting there clutching my drink, I was feeling angry, embarrassed, and silly, all at once. It evidently showed in my face, because Jack looking across at me said "I think it is time to put young Jake out of his misery and tell him what his musical representative did to earn her fifteen minutes of fame, as the saying goes. So Bill, the stage is yours. And tell us everything. I bet there was a helluva lot more to it than ever appeared in the press, what?"

Bill smiled. "Unlike many of the bets you've made recently Jack, this is one you could actually win."

"Now, now," Jack replied, wagging a pretend warning finger.

Bill took out his packet of Gold Flake cigarettes and after selecting one and then going through the usual ritual of tapping one end of it on the packet as if he was sending a short message in morse code to the remaining cigarettes, placed it in the corner of his mouth before lighting it. We all sat watching this ceremony in a seemingly semi-hypnotic stare. Then having lit it, and with smoke billowing from nose and mouth simultaneously, Bill began his story.

"Of course it was the kind of scandal that all newspapers love, but for tabloids like the 'Sketch' and the 'Mirror' it was food and drink. There is nothing readers enjoy more than the wealthy and privileged being involved in a bizarre scandal. Of course Dunkirk kicked it off the front pages."

Then turning to me, presumably because the other two were presumably hip to this part of the story, he said, "Janine Gregson was, and for that matter is, the daughter of the multi-millionaire, Sir Rupert Gregson. He's involved in shipping, importing and exporting, land acquisition, building and many other things. His wife at that time, Yvette, was a dancer at the Follies Bergere, when they met. They got married and had two children, the elder, Paul was killed at the beginning of 1940, when his spitfire was shot down, over France. Their only other child was a daughter, Janine, younger than Paul by three years. She was educated at either Oxford or Cambridge, I can't remember which."

While he stopped to take a sip of his drink and a pull on his cigarette, Jack said to him: "Come on Bill, let's get to the juicy part for Chrissakes."

Now it was Bill's turn to ignore Jack.

"Anyway" he continued, "After she had come down from university, she took a teaching job at an exclusive, private school, somewhere in Buckinghamshire. Our dear Miss Janine taught Fine Art to fourteen and fifteen year-old boys and girls."

I could not see where his story was leading, but still feeling annoyed at them for looking upon me as a callow virgin; I was determined to get some of this angst out of my system by defending her, right or wrong.

Bill took another noisy slurp of gin and another huge draw on his Gold Flake, before continuing.

"But she did something more than teach. Every week-end, she would at her own expense, take one or other of her class up to London for the day, where she would show them around various museums and art galleries." A strange smirk spread across his face as he added, "Or, so the children's parents and the Headmaster were led to believe."

After the pregnant pause which invariably follows that kind of a zinger he went on; "In retrospect, I suppose there were two pieces of evidence that might have alerted anyone of a suspicious nature, to the possibility that all was not what it seemed, except that there didn't seem to be anyone around of a suspicious nature. The first piece of evidence was quite innocuous. She would only take them to London once, and having done so, would refuse to take them ever again, even though parents would write to her, at the insistence of their sons or daughters begging her to take them again because they had enjoyed it so much. And the second piece of evidence, had anyone realised it, only they didn't, was the nickname given to her by the school kids she was teaching, which was 'The Virgin Queen'. It came out at the trial that they always referred to her by this name. Now we all know that kids give their teachers nicknames, but 'The Virgin Queen' was odder than most and like I said, I suppose a more astute and suspicious headmaster may have tried to find out the reason for such an odd soubriquet. But, at the time, nobody gave it a second thought. Meanwhile, our Miss Janine was taking one selected boy or girl up to London, almost every week-end, to sample the artistic delights that London, even in wartime, had to offer. Finally, after she had been in the job for about six months, one of the kids, a fifteen year-old lad, accidentally let the proverbial cat out of the bag."

I was more convinced than ever by now, that this tale was going to have some corny and trivial denouement. To me, at that time of total innocence, I could not even begin to imagine how a story of a teacher taking a pupil to London, at her own expense, could contain any serious scandalous overtones. So I listened on intently to Bill's story, because I was determined to defend the honour of someone who had probably committed some minor misdemeanour while doing all she could to help her pupils, and who, most importantly, I was still crazy about.

"It all began to break wide open," Bill went on. "When the lad went right off his food and just moped around the house. He showed interest in nothing except one thing; getting his parents to go and see Miss Gregson, and beg her to take their son on another visit to the art houses of London. The parents thought it a bit strange, because when they took him to the Tate Gallery, the lad, whose interest in art did not seem to go much beyond building model aeroplanes, was totally bored. So they were a bit mystified by his sudden love for works of art.

Anyway, one day this lad's mother was tidying his bedroom. While she was cleaning under his bed she found a discarded love letter her son had written to our lady Janine, in which he refers to the feel of her body, and the touch of her lips and the heavenly joys she had allowed him to experience on their never-to-be-forgotten day in the Capital. The discovery of this note by the parents caused them to question their son very closely indeed. And finally this parental third-degree became too much for the lad, and he spilled the beans.

Having taken the lad to London in her car to show him the British Museum, Janine told the kid that first she has to pop into her London apartment in order to pick up the mail, pay her housekeeper and attend to a few odds and sods generally. She then suggests to the lad that there is no point in him waiting downstairs in the car, and that he should come up to her flat with her and have some tea and cakes while she is busy. So she settles the youth down on the sofa but then appears to change her mind. She will join him in a cup of tea before she starts to attend to her business."

Eliot now broke in: "Christ Bill, this story is becoming as long as 'War and Peace'."

"Wait," Bill replied. "It gets juicier from here on. She orders a pot of tea from her big, tough Yugoslavian housekeeper. Now according to the lad's sworn testimony which we could only outline in the newspaper because of the pornography laws, while they are waiting for the tea and cakes to arrive, she asked him casually if he has a girlfriend. He said he did not. Then, according to the kid, she gets up out of her chair and goes to sit on the sofa, next to the boy, but right up close to him. Then, she takes his hand and as she asks the kid, 'have you ever done this before?' She puts his hand under her sweater and on to her tits. Incidentally" Bill added with a gratuitous grin, "From what I could see of them in the court room, she seemed to have pretty nice tits at that."

I was now starting to feel pretty sick.

"Then, according to what the boy told the court, they kissed, with her insisting on showing him how to kiss the French way, with open mouths etcetera."

"Lucky little fellah," Jack said quietly.

'Oh shit' I was saying to myself at the same time.

"Be that as it may "Bill went on; "After some more hanky-panky" ('what a stupid expression' I thought), "She took out his John Thomas (which, I thought, was an even sillier one), and then, and I can still remember the words used in the affidavit, she 'fondled his member'. Isn't that a silly description," he asked, looking at us each in turn.

'Not as silly as calling it his 'John Thomas', I thought.

"But to continue," Bill said after polishing off his drink and holding out his empty glass to Jack for another. "And again I quote from the affidavit, 'this was followed by Miss Gregson performing the act of fellatio', which means in simple language" he said, turning in my direction, "She sucked him off."

I nodded my understanding, while trying to stop myself from looking embarrassed which, judging by the benevolent smirks I was getting from the others was not exactly successful. I could only hope that my face just showed embarrassment and did not reveal the deep disillusion I was also feeling at having my dream of a loving and special relationship with Janine, shattered. At the same time, I was starting to hate myself for having been such a gullible, juvenile, idiot in the first place.

"Then, according to the boy's testimony, she apparently did an odd thing. Immediately after his orgasm was over, she asked him 'Was it great?' Was it as good as you thought it would be?' And then, no sooner than he told her it was the greatest experience of his entire life or something like that, than she jumped up to her feet, and hurried out of the room, leaving him on his own for a good half an hour. Finally, when she did return, she was a changed character. Suddenly, she was cold and business-like. She tells the lad that there are some important matters she must attend to right away. She then gives him some money to cover the cost of a taxi to the station and buying a train ticket back to his home. The boy said that he tried to kiss her before leaving, but the big Slav maid fended him off.

However, she did say that if he promises never to say a word to any living person about what they got up to, she will invite him back real soon."

By now I did not know who I hated more; Janine or myself.

Eliot asked, "Was it ever discovered why she felt it so necessary to rush out of the room in such a hurry?"

"Yeah" Bill replied. "And I'll tell you the reason in a minute. But to continue: The next person put on the stand, was a sweet, pretty little girl of fourteen. She told the court much the same story as the lad did; about supposedly going to visit some works of art, only to have to go to Janine Gregson's flat for some reason or other. The only differences between the two affidavits were that with the young lady, she wasn't offered tea or coffee, but champagne, which she had never had before, and which made her quite tipsy. In her affidavit, she said that Janine somehow or other, brought the subject around to boy friends and sex. Then she apparently lectured the kid on the importance of retaining her virginity. But then she went on to telling her confidentially that being a virgin need not mean depriving herself of sexual pleasure or satisfaction. She then confides to the kid that she too is a virgin but that she has a marvellous sex life. 'Would you like to know the secret?' she asks her. Naturally, the tipsy little fourteen year old lass says yes. So, Janine calls in her housekeeper and tells her, that Miss X—we were never allowed to know her name by the way—would like to see how she gets her sexual jollies. And right there and then, Janine and the housekeeper both strip off and there on the carpet, right in front of where the young miss is sitting, they give the girl a demonstration in the arts of lesbian love."

"Maybe that is why she is known as the 'Arts Mistress," Jack ventured to suggest. Everyone laughed, including me. Except that I wasn't laughing on the inside. I was too disgusted with myself for being so adolescently gullible. Also, if my memory serves me correctly, I was none too sure what "lesbian love" actually meant. Even while I was trying to it work out what it must mean, Bill was continuing with his little saga.

"After a while, according to the affidavit, Janine seduced the girl into making it a happy threesome. When it was finally all over, Janine swore the kid to absolute secrecy, telling her that if she keeps quiet about what went on, any time she wants more and even greater fun than she had that afternoon, it will be available. But if she talks, Miss Gregson will not only deny everything; she will also have her expelled from the school. The same stories more or less, were told by four other girls, and five boys, although we know there were more.

Then the defence called in a psychiatrist, who told the court that Janine's strange sexual proclivities were brought about by an incident which happened to her when she was fourteen, while she was on holiday with her mother in the south of France. There she met a lady artist who initiated her into the joys of sex in exactly the same way as she had done to her pupils.. He also said that there should be no deleterious effects on any of the boy pupils, although there was a possible danger that the girls could become either lesbian or bi-sexual."

"I don't know why they had to pay a psychiatrist to tell them that." Eliot said. "I could have told them that and it wouldn't have cost them a penny."

"What I can't understand," Jack broke in to ask, "is why she now wants to be in the musical representative business. I mean, if she has this penchant for young virgin boys and girls, she's got less chance of being struck by lightning on a sunny day, than of finding them in the music business.

Even though I was only too well aware of the answer, I tried to pretend that I was as perplexed as Jack seemed to be.

"I don't know the answer, I am afraid," I said. "But the next time I see her, which will be over the next few days, I'll do my best to find out."

"Anyway" Bill went on, "the case for the defence was that Janine Gregson had not caused anybody harm. In fact, her counsel claimed, that the only crime that she could be found to be guilty of, was giving pleasure. Now, to the oohs and aah's of those watching the case, Janine was put into the witness box. She told the court that it was her belief that the first sexual experience was of paramount importance to the emotional development of any young person. All she was trying to do she said, was to make sure that this first experience was strong enough to prepare these youngsters for a normal, healthy and enjoyable, sex life. She also said, under cross examination from the prosecution counsel, that it was her belief that sexual joy can only be carried to its ultimate peak, if one of the partners is experiencing it for the first time, and the other partner is an experienced lover, which, she admitted she was. She added that after the first time, sex with the same person becomes progressively more and more mundane.

"So how did it all end up?" I asked. Frankly, I was so sick and angry with myself for having fallen in love with love in such a childish way, that all I wanted was for this topic of conversation to come to an end.

"She got off from the main charge of corruption of a minor" Bill said. "But she was found guilty on the lesser charge of common assault. But that was only after her father promised the court she will be shipped off to a psychiatric sanatorium in Switzerland, and not released into society until she is completely cured. If my memory serves me correctly, the judge fined her one hundred and fifty pounds and bound her over for two years. On the other hand, there were some very good reasons to believe that Sir Rupert Gregson, had bribed the judge to accept the lesser charge, but there was never enough hard evidence to prove it."

Turning to me he said "But it is nice to know that our Janine is once again back in our midst, teaching boys and girls fine arts. Or to put it another way; teaching them the fine arts of oral sex."

Everyone laughed. I joined them by again faking some sort of a half-laugh, whilst at the same time my mind demanded that I probe, and thereby add to the pain in my heart, by asking; "The only thing you haven't told us is why she runs out of—er, I mean, ran out of the room immediately after she has finished her performance." (I could read in the eyes of the others, that my slip of the tongue had confirmed what they already suspected. But they said nothing, and neither did I.).

"Oh yes," Bill said. "That came out in the cross examination of Mathilde, Janine's personal maid. Apparently, after Janine left university, her father wanted her to have a personal maid who was also big and strong enough to act as a kind of bodyguard for her. Mathilde, who looked tough enough to be Joe Louis' bodyguard, told the court without any trace of shame or guilt, that when she went for the interview for her job, she fell in love with Janine at first sight, and how, within a few weeks of her appointment, her relationship with Janine had changed from personal maid to just about as personal a maid as you could get; she became her lover. She went on to say with actual pride, that although giving boys and girls their first taste of sex, was tremendously sexually exciting for Janine, it was to her and her alone that Miss Gregson ran to, for the actual act of sexual fulfilment that only she, the Great Mathilde, could give. Or, so she claimed."

'So that is why she ran out of the room' I said to myself. The whole scene came back to me in a flash. How, as I came out of her bathroom I could hear her voice saying, 'oh yes, oh yes.' The realisation hit me in a flash. 'Jesus Christ' I thought, 'that was her having an orgasm!' Being only a very young eighteen year-old, I was sickened at this realisation. Nowadays, it wouldn't bother me in the slightest. In fact, it would probably turn me on. But that was then, and this is now. And there's been a lotta livin' done in the intervening years.

Jack voice broke into my thoughts: "So, I guess that all one can say about Janine Gregson and her maid Mathilde, is that they lived a happy hand-to-mouth existence, what?"

It was during the laughter following this one-liner that I stood up.

"I've got to go I'm afraid," I said. I have to get home and pack my bag; I'm on the ten o'clock train to Newcastle. But Jack, as to your offer, the answer is definitely yes. I would love to do it."

"Splendid my boy," he said, as he too got to his feet. "We open on the first of December. Where can I write you a confirming letter?"

"Send it to me at the Faculty of Modern History at Newcastle University. But I will be back in London a good two weeks before the opening, so I can sign anything you want, then."

"That's fine with me old lad, and I know you are a gentleman and will keep your word. But, just in case Miss Gregson breaks her time-honoured routine and actually invites you back for a second time."... He was laughing as he said this, whilst I felt myself once more going red in the face... "I don't want you trying to get out of it." Holding his hand out towards Bill and Eliot, who were now also in the process of getting to their feet, he added, "Remember, I have got two witnesses here who heard you accept the job. Admittedly they are drunken witnesses, but they are witnesses just the same."

"You need have no worry Jack," I said. "I'll be there."

I was trying to smile confidently as I spoke, but my blushing embarrassment at the knowledge that they now knew I was a virgin, turned it into a very crooked and forced smile indeed.

Sitting in the back of the car that Jack had hired (at his expense), to take me home, I had time to take stock of my position. Now knowing the truth about Janine, and suffering the consequential humiliation of discovering that what I had thought was a wonderful and, to me at any rate, a shattering expression of a woman's love, was nothing more than the trigger mechanism to fire her own weird passions, my first reaction was that I never wanted to see the lousy bitch again.

I could not even stomach the idea of returning to Newcastle, because I had built up the 'affair' in my heart and mind to such a degree that the entire city was enmeshed with the feel and the scent of her.

(Sitting out here in Havana, sweaty from the heat of the night and just a little groggy from the grog they serve up in this bar, I look back on that eighteen year old Jake Silver with amusement and wonderment that the Jake Silver of then and now are one and the same person. No matter how grown-up I remember myself feeling at the time, in actual fact I was so goddamned wet behind the ears, that I should not have been allowed out without a nanny to look after me. I can hardly believe that I was such a hopeless romantic. Maybe it was my fucked-up practical joker of a Fate doing what he was so good at doing, and what he has continued to do all my life; placing something I want desperately with my reach, only to snatch it away just before my fingers can get a grip of it).

I forced myself away from thinking about Janine problem, only to turn my mind onto another, far more pressing and a damn sight more intractable one than she could ever be: how to tell my Aunt and Uncle that I am going to give up my studies and take a job playing thc piano in a drinking club. The very thought of standing before my Aunt and announcing this fact was so horrifying and terrifying to me that I did what I had traincd mysclf to do since the death of my parents whenever facing the truth became too unbearable: shut it out by falling asleep. I fell asleep.

The next thing I remember was the driver shaking me awake, and telling me that we had arrived. I looked at my watch. It was 3.20am. I was therefore surprised to see lights on in the house. As I walked up the artistically laid out brick tile path that leads from the gate to the house, the front door opened and Aunt Sarah, stood there in a black, lace dressing gown.

I was still climbing the stairs up to the front door, when she said in a hoarse, angry, stage whisper, "And what time of night is this to come home!?"

"I'm sorry Auntie," I whispered back as I walked past her into the house. "I honestly had no idea that anybody would be waiting up for me."

As she quietly closed the front door, she said "I was giving you another ten minutes and then I was going to phone the police. You've had me worried sick. Anyway, thank God you're safe."

I said nothing.

"Now go to bed" she said, adding "and we'll talk about it after you've slept it off."

Presumably, her 'sleeping it off' remark could only mean that she thought I was drunk, which was not true although I probably did smell of liquor. But I was too tired to protest. So, after creeping into my bedroom, in order not to wake Ivan and writing a note asking him to wake me at 8 AM, which I left on his bedside table, I quickly undressed and was asleep before my head hit the pillow.

When Ivan woke me, I sat straight up, only to find that a little man with a very large mallet, had somehow strayed into my head, and was now trying to get out by smashing his mallet against the inside of my cranium, regularly and incessantly.

I somehow forced myself out of bed and into the bathroom, where I conducted a fruitless search for aspirins. I washed as quickly as I could, after which I dressed in the same clothes that I had worn the previous night, packed my bag, and went downstairs. I had to take each stair down very warily and gently, because each downward step seemed to infuriate or panic the little fellow in my cranium, so that he banged irately and with an even greater ferocity. I was also aware that my mouth was as dry as the Sahara, and that it tasted of rotten leather – which is something I have gotten quite used to over the years.

I went into the kitchen to find Aunt Sarah, seemingly unaffected by having waited up half the night. She was busily making toast and brewing tea.

"Nothing to eat please Auntie. Just a large mug of tea" I said as I sat down at the kitchen table.

"Don't be silly. You must have something. With a hangover like you must have, you must line the stomach" As she pushed the four slices of heavily buttered toast across the table towards me, she added; "Not that you deserve anything. Coming in drunk at that ridiculous hour and worrying me silly."

I had two immediate problems; the first was whether to protest and insist that I was not drunk. This would mean that I had no justification for asking where the aspirins were and that meant letting mallet man continue to beat up my brain. The second and even more pressing problem more pressing problem was how to stop the normally enticing smell of toast from causing me to throw up. I decided to plead guilty on the first charge so that I could ask for some aspirins. It also allowed me to push the toast away from me as far as possible.

"No thanks Auntie, no toast" I said. "All I want is a glass of water, a large mug of tea and a couple of aspirins. After that, I must quickly pack and run for my train."

Then she upset the man in my head very badly, by yelling loudly for the maid to run upstairs and pack my bag for me.

"I've packed it already," I said very quietly so as not to upset my cranial neighbour any further.

She yelled again at the maid to go upstairs and unpack my bag and repack it properly. "And put in the packet of sandwiches that I made for my stay-out-all-night-drinking nephew. It's on the table in the breakfast room."

"The aspirins Auntie" I semi-whispered. "Where are they?" I spoke softly to try and keep any overtones of pleading and desperation out of my voice, but I think I failed. She set down the water and the tea at the same time. The aspirins thankfully followed shortly after. They were in one of the kitchen cupboards.

She watched while I took the aspirins and polished off the glass of water at one go. As I started sipping the tea she said "So now you've won the damn competition. I hope it you've got it out of your system for good and all and that now you'll settle down to your studying, please God."

This was the moment. This was my cue to tell her that I was going to give up my studies to be a piano player. It was now or never.

I decided on 'never'.

"Yeah" I said.

"When are you coming to London next?"

"I don't really know" I replied. "But I think that I have a few free days in the middle of November. So I will see you then." Little did she know that the next time she sees me I will have quit university.

Chapter 16

Sitting on the train that cold, drizzly morning, as it thumped and bumped and swayed its way north, I found it impossible not think about Janine. I tried to read, but Janine's face and tits got in the way. To block her out of my mind, I tried jotting down a list of things of things I had to do upon my arrival in Newcastle. One of the first things I wrote was, 'Write to Janine severing all arrangements, business and otherwise'.

The very writing down of her name caused me to shut out of my mind any thoughts, other than about her. So I shoved my pen back into my inside pocket, and while staring blankly at the thin lines of rain, as they raced, wind-blown, across the window of the speeding train, I tried to make sense of what I had learned the from Bill Mather.

To start with, apart from her obsession with virgins, which was something entirely new to me, I was equally puzzled by the idea that she had the same sexual feelings for girls as she showed for boys. Whether my ignorance of the existence of bi-sexuality was normal for an eighteen year-old boy, back in 1948 I frankly don't know. But without any access to what was considered pornography back then, plus the fact that it had never been mentioned in any conversation of which I had been a part, the idea of a female having sexual feelings for another of her own sex was an entirely new and mystifying concept to me. But lesbian lover or not, virgin lover or not, there was one thought front and centre in my mind: I wanted to see and needed to see Janine again.

But what if she refuses to see me? This was out of the question. There had to be face-to-face answers to my questions. Writing would be no good at all. After all, she has to tell me to my face why, if I was nothing more than some sexual cipher in her orgasmic cycle, did she bother to send me that sweet, loving note just before the competition? Surely this proves that she must have been thinking about me for weeks after that wonderful afternoon in her apartment? 'Maybe this lesbian thing is just a passing phase' I thought. 'Maybe deep down, she really had developed some genuine feelings for me'.

I held on to that thought for about two and a half seconds, before another took centre stage.

Shouldn't I just say, 'Fuck her and all who sail in her?' Seeing her again will almost certainly stir up feelings within me that I would be better off smothering to death. And anyway the chances are, that having Mathilde for a lover (whatever that meant. I had no real idea), the chances of her suddenly switching to me were, in all truth, too small for serious consideration.

I decided to do what I always do when important matters dictate two possible courses of action. I decided to do nothing. If she phones me to say that she wants to see me, even if it is only to congratulate me, well, then I'll make my decision.

Having resolved that problem, albeit in the most negative way possible I felt able to get out my pen again and continue with my diary for the coming few weeks. I wrote, 'send in a letter of resignation to the college'. I followed this with: 'Buy the sheet music of all the popular tunes and learn to play them. Also, practise for five hours of every day'.

I went hot and cold with trepidation, as I wrote next on my list, 'Work out a letter to Uncle Harry and Aunt Sarah explaining why I am leaving university'. I put this immediately out of my mind, by writing, 'phone Eliot to see if he wants to come to Newcastle to do the interview with me that we never got around to doing in London'.

Then once again, I found myself considering whether I should I put on the list, 'Phone Candy?'

'Yeah' I said to myself. Even while I was writing down her name I was working out my letter to Janine. 'Dear Janine' I'll write, 'This is to inform you that you are no longer my representative. Goodbye Virgin Queen. You have fucked too many little virgin boys and girls. Now, go fuck yourself.'

Whether I hated her more for fooling with my emotions or for causing me so much humiliation the previous night, in Jack Montgomery's house, I neither knew nor cared.

Chapter 17

Dear Doctor Cabot-Smith and Doctor Glass,

I regretfully must inform you that I will not be continuing with my studies. After much consideration, I have decide to let my heart rule my head and become a professional jazz musician. I would however like you to know that I have enjoyed my Modern History course very much.

I got a great kick writing the next bit.

As you may or may not know, I have recently won the 'Young Jazz Musician of the Year' award. This has resulted in my having received a number of tempting offers, one of which I have accepted. I only hope that I will be able to make a more worthy contribution to the world of jazz, than I ever would have made in the sphere of Modern History.

Finally, may I say that many of the things I have learned both in my lectures and in personal conversation with my tutor, Doctor Glass have been invaluable. I will remember and value them all my life.

Once again, thanking you for all the time and trouble you have both taken with me.

Yours respectfully,
Jake Silver.

I addressed the envelope, folded the fateful letter, into the envelope and set off with it to the university. I had decided to deliver it by hand immediately, thus eliminating any chance of a change of mind. I looked at my wristwatch; it was just four o'clock in the afternoon. I had been back in Newcastle for little over an hour. In that time I had caught a bus to my lodgings, collected my mail (two letters, neither of which were in those pink, scented envelopes that Janine uses, so I didn't bother to read them there and then, preferring to stuff them into my back pocket to read when I had more time), taken down two notes that had be pinned to my door, both of which were from Meyer, unpacked and written my letter of resignation.

After handing in my letter to the hall porter, I went into the students Union for a mug of tea and a brick-hard, dried-up, slab of Madeira cake.

I took the two letters out of my pocket and read them whilst munching and drinking. Neither had been posted, because there were no stamps on the envelopes. The first was from the proprietor of a new jazz club opening in the nearby town of Wallsend on December 15, asking me if I would play there on its opening night. Further, the writer was offering me the princely sum of five pounds to do so. Considering that the average pay for a jazz musician in a local jazz club was one pound ten shillings, this, I suppose must be called 'big money'. Then came the sentence all jazz pianists dread, and which I have had to read in some form or other, a thousand times or more, in my professional career; 'Unfortunately the piano is an old upright, but I am told it is playable'. One of life's great mysteries is why jazz and night club owners don't seem to see anything wrong in asking a jazz pianist to play on a clapped-out, beat-up, old tin can of a piano. If a trumpet or sax player arrived at his club with their instruments so beat up that they could barely play, the club owner would have plenty to say about it, believe me! But only too often, the poor old piano man is expected to make a heap of shit sound like a Steinway grand.

The other letter was from a reporter on the 'Journal', the local daily newspaper, asking me to phone him tomorrow morning, in order to arrange an interview. I put that one back into my pocket. The other letter I screwed up and threw away on my way out of the college.

That night, I saw Harold and Meyer, for celebratory drinks. I was gratified to see how enthusiastically they greeted my decision to quit Modern History and return to London as a full-time musician. Harold was even kind enough to drive me to his house and arrange with his father to cash the cheque for the hundred pounds I had been awarded for winning the competition.

But when I left them that night to go back to my lodging house, it was with a deep feeling of regret at the way the chemistry of our close friendship had changed almost as soon as they learned of the new direction my life was taking me. Try as I did to maintain the facade that nothing had changed, and that we were still as close as the Three Musketeers, the balance of the friendship had altered profoundly and permanently. Even though I was not leaving Newcastle for another couple of weeks, it was as if I was already a visiting celebrity in the company of a couple of local students.

I got back to my lodgings to find a note from the Gauleiter/caretaker telling me that 'a Mister Eliot Wilson phoned to say you must phone him when you get in, no matter what time that is. His home phone number is HAM 9697. He said you may reverse the charges if you wish'.

Then he had added; 'Please make sure you understand that I consider the use of the telephone on the Lord's Day quite immoral. I trust that you will not allow such an occurrence to happen again'. W. Milburne. (Caretaker)

How I was supposed to stop anyone phoning me, I never quite understood.

Having no small change with which to make the call, I phoned Eliot reverse charges. I'm glad I did, because the purpose of it was to do the interview over the phone that we had been unable to do at 'Jacks'. It took over an hour. After it was done, Eliot asked, if he came to Newcastle, could I arrange for him to meet Janine

"Why do you want to meet her?" I asked.

"I don't only write about jazz, Jake. I might be able to write an article about her that I could syndicate world-wide. That is important for me, so do your best and let me know."

"I'll try," I lied, "But I doubt whether she will ever speak to me again after the letter I have sent her.," which was also a lie. I did actually write her several letters severing all my relationships with her. I wrote her a nasty, accusatory one, another sarcastic and acid in tone, and yet another, pleading with her to give me one more try. But no sooner had I written them than they were torn up and thrown away. For reasons I can no longer recall, whilst I did not wish to have anything more to do with her, the very idea of putting it in writing was just too irrevocable for me. In that adolescent dream world in which I guess spent half my life, I suppose I still retained deep down the crazy notion that there was still a chance she would phone to ask me to come and see her.

"Look Jake" Eliot said, "See if there is anything you can do for me. I'd really appreciate it."

I promised, that I would, although I had no idea as to how to do it.

Returning to the hostel after my telephone call with Eliot, I found the front door had been locked and bolted from the inside. I had to bang loudly on the door for quite a while before the outraged caretaker opened it.

"I am not putting up with you people coming in any time you choose" he said.

But this was different Jake Silver to the one he had previously known. This was Jake Silver the important piano star who gets interviewed by the press.and who is on his way out of this shitty little town, to return to fame and fortune in the big city.

"Firstly, I had to give an interview to a columnist on a very important magazine," I told him. "Secondly you knew I was going out because you left me the note telling me about Eliot Wilson's phone call. And thirdly" I told the Gauleiter's astonished face," It is now"—I checked my watch—"Half-past midnight, which means it is no longer your beloved Sabbath Day, so I don't have to keep it holy any more. If you don't like the time I get in at night, tough. Take it up with the university. But in future, if you know a student is out, leave the bloody door unlocked. Then you won't get disturbed will you?"

I pushed past him and his shocked face to go up the stairs to my room.

"I'm not putting up with this," he said after me.

"Go haunt a house," I shouted back as I shut my door.

I lay in my lumpy, rattletrap of a bed, reviewing all the pros and cons resulting from the decision to give up my studies. Once in London, I realised that I would have to give top priority to finding myself a furnished room. I certainly could not go on living with Aunt Sarah and Uncle Harry. To start with, the late hours I will be keeping, would disturb their lifestyle too much. Then I found myself mentally tip-toeing into the minefield of telling my Aunt and Uncle about my decision to quit university. But I still could not face even thinking about it, so I shifted my thoughts on to the far more enjoyable possibilities of picking up some great looking chicks at the club, and making out with them.

This again underlined to me the urgent necessity of having my own little furnished room or flatlet. After all it is no good thinking about having a girl in your life if you have nowhere private to do all those things you want to do so badly with her.

Suddenly and unaccountably, my brain flipped over to thinking about Candy Elman. I actually did like her, I realised. When I think about it now, I suppose it was her wild, uninhibited, outgoing personality that was just what my withdrawn, introversion needed. I had to accept that I didn't fancy her physically in the least, but then I got to remembering how she had kissed me and grabbed my cock at the same time. I was sure that she would come across for me, even if nobody else would. Suddenly, I found myself giving second billing to the fact that I did not really fancy her. Top of the bill was given over to the dictum of that great sage of bygone days, who had coined the immortal phrase, 'A fuck is a fuck'. I decided to phone her the very next night in order to try and keep her hot for me.

It was just as I was drifting off to sleep that I had a blinding flash of inspiration. It was so brilliant that I resolved not to wait until evening, but to phone Candy the very next morning. Suddenly, she became far more than just a friendly fuck. In a flash she had become the key to all my problems with Uncle Harry and Aunt Sarah. I drifted off to sleep, fully clothed, but happy and contented.

When I did rise, at nine o'clock I had all the 'amenities' (if you'll excuse the expression), of the house at my disposal. As the other students were already at university by this hour, it meant that for the first time since I had been here, I could actually take a crap in peace! I also took my time about bathing and dressing, so that it was almost ten o'clock before I made my way down the stairs of the hostel, only to be met by the ghoulish-white face of the gauleiter, at the bottom of the stairs. Hate and resentment plastered all over his parchment-pale face.

"What time do you call this?" he demanded to know. But I was in too much of a good mood to be bothered or intimidated by him.

I carefully studied my watch.

"Since you ask" I replied, "I call it five minutes to ten. What time do *you* call it?" I pretended to be really interested in his reply.

His eyes narrowed with repressed rage, Jimmy Finlayson-style as they followed me out of the hostel.

First off, I phoned the reporter on the 'Journal' and arranged to meet him in the bar of the Station Hotel at 12.30 and then have lunch together.

I knew it would not be hip to call Candy until eleven o'clock at the earliest. As this left me with about an hour to kill, I strolled down Northumberland Street to 'Tilly's', one of Newcastle's smartest, up-market cafes, for a pot of tea and a toasted bun. I was no more than half way through my little repast, when I heard female voice say, "Could we have some more tea please miss. We've been waiting quite a while now."

It was an unmistakable voice. I turned around to see where she was sitting. Janine was just three tables away. Her companion was a pretty, fresh-faced girl of around sixteen. They were talking so intently that even though I stood up to see them better, they remained unaware of my presence.

I knew that I had to go over to their table, even though I had not the slightest idea of what I would say when I got there. I felt all my feelings of resentment, plus the painful memories of my humiliation once more rising to the surface. But I could not help noticing how good she looked as she sat there. Even though I now knew that I was watching a spider in the act of cleverly enticing yet another virginal fly into her parlour, I could not help myself from thinking what a great looking spider she was. Even as I approached their table I was hating myself for still fancying her so much.

She was sitting, leaning slightly forward, her left elbow on the table, her head resting lightly on her forefinger and thumb. She was saying, as I got to the table,..."Of course, Surrealism and Dadaism are far more a social statement than..."

As I was approaching her table from a twenty-past-four angle, she was not aware of my presence until I said, in as casual and friendly voice as I could, "Hallo Janine."

She turned suddenly to face me, her face showing shock and surprise, as if I had returned from the dead. Then it turned into an icy smile.

"Oh, hello Jake" she said coldly. At least, that is what her mouth was saying; her eyes were saying 'Goodbye Jake'.

I stood there looking at her, not saying a word. I was not trying to psych her out or anything. I just could not think of anything apposite to say, and anyway, I was still trying to reconcile that face, that body and those legs with what I now knew about her. And so I stood, and she sat, both of us staring at one another in a cocoon of frozen silence, whilst little Miss Soon-to-be-had, looked in mystification, first to me, then at Janine, and then back to me again.

It was Janine who finally broke the icy, numb silence. "I'm sorry I couldn't be in London for the competition. Did you do well?" She asked in that formal, distant way a casual acquaintance might, when asking if one of your more distant relatives is keeping in good health.. As I watched her lips framing the words, I could not help myself from thinking that they were the lips that had helped to give me a sexual high I had never known before—or since.

"I won," I said, still not knowing whether I hated or loved her.

"Well, congratulations," she said. "We really must meet sometime soon Jake. Then, you can tell me all about it. Why don't you phone and speak with Mathilde. She'll tell you when it is best to come up for a drink. Unfortunately, at the moment I am involved in discussing this young lady's future artistic career, so I trust you will excuse us."

I was already annoyed, admittedly more with myself than with her. After all, nobody forced me to swallow all that pink, scented paper 'win for me Jake' shit. It was me who was the callow schmuck, who, in spite of all the facts staring me in the face, had gone to London, clinging to the belief that if I won, like some gallant knight at a jousting contest, my Lady Guinevere would take me to her bed.

But this kiss-off, which she had just given me, as if I were a bothersome child being told to run along and play somewhere else, added an extra dimension to my annoyance. It added anger to it. I was angry at the thought that I was not considered important enough to even be introduced to her miss Soon-to-be-had. I was even angrier that she saw me as being no different from any of those fifteen and sixteen year-old schoolboys and girls she had been using and dropping, like a used Kleenex after you've blown your nose in it. Well, I was no snot-nosed school kid. No sir. I was the winner of a national competition! I was now a real grown-up with a real, high paying job and all. Furthermore, I had a hundred pounds in my pocket, so I was rich. You never saw Cary Grant, or any other of those suave, wealthy Hollywood men-about-town, being dismissed in so casual a fashion, did you? And neither do you treat the new and improved, big-time Jake Silver like a piece of shit. You show respect.

I can see it now all too clearly that I was little more than a typically arrogant, adolescent know-it-all. It is the only excuse I can offer for what I did then.

"I had a drink with an old friend of yours," I said casually, completely ignoring her request for me to get lost.

"Oh yes?" she said, her voice (and her eyes), now granite-hard. "And who was that?"

"Bill Mather." I met him at 'Jacks'." Turning to little Miss Virgin, who had been looking from Janine to me and back again in complete mystification, I explained: "That's a night club in London" I felt sure that saying this would make the kid realise just how sophisticated and grown-up I was.

"I've never heard of him," Janine said. But I could see she was beginning to show signs of nervousness.

"Sure you know him," I said confidently. "He's a photographer now, but he used to be the chief crime reporter for the 'Sketch'. He certainly knows you at any rate, because he told me all about your 'five minutes of fame' as he called it. That was when you were in the dock at the Old Bailey for seducing little boys and innocent little girls. Girls of about her age." I indicated the shocked little girl with my thumb. Janine was staring at me aghast and open-mouthed with either horror, or rage, or maybe both.

"Yeah," I went on airily. "He was quite surprised that you were back in England. He thought that you were still safely under lock and key in a sanatorium for the mentally sick, somewhere in Switzerland. He told me to tell you that he would like to come to Newcastle and interview you, because he wants to write a book about you and your lesbian servant Mathilde."

Janine managed to put up a show of composure, but the croak in her voice gave her away. "Come ahem, along. We're ahem leaving dear," she said to the girl as she stood up. "We don't have to listen to all this nonsense do we?"

The young miss started to rise, but tentatively and uncertainly. She clearly did not know whether to do Janine's bidding, or run for her life.

"Don't let me drive you two away," I said, faking a pleasant, friendly innocence. Then, turning to the little girl, who was fumbling with her gloves, obviously in a state of panic and confusion, I said "You don't have to worry about Janine. As long as you make it a point never to go to her apartment, or anywhere else where you could find yourself alone with her and her Hungarian lesbian bodyguard and you'll be perfectly safe."

Janine's sweet face had now taken on a deathly-white hue. "You... you... bloody bastard," she said quietly, but from the very depths of her being.

"That's a bit rich coming from you after the way you took me for a ride" I replied.

As she stood buttoning her black, Persian lamb fur coat, she added, "You just don't care how much you hurt people do you?"

"You can say that after the way you used me and then ignored me? Janine, you have just won yourself an extra ten points for chutzpah" I said, relapsing automatically into the Yiddish vernacular of my Aunt.

"Come dear," she said, ignoring my last remarks and taking hold of the little girl's hand. But the little girl, shocked disbelief in her tear-filled eyes, pulled it away and ran out of the café.

"Good girl," I shouted after her.

"I hope I never, ever, see you again" Janine said to me over her shoulder as she too started to walk out of the café.

"What shall I tell Bill Mather?" I shouted after her.

She neither turned nor made any reply.

As I watched her walk out of my life, the waitress came over with the bill. "Who's going to pay for everything?" she asked me.

"It'll be my pleasure," I said shoving a pound note into her hand.

Before closing this little chapter, I would just like to say to Janine Gregson, if she ever gets to read this: I am sorry kid for the stupid, childish, and nasty way I acted. I had no right to interfere in your life, baby. As Frank Sinatra is reputed to have said, 'We all have to do whatever it is that gets us through the night'. I only hope you found lots more willing youngsters to pleasure yourself with, and in return, give them their single moment of joyous discovery.

Chapter 18

Leaving Tilly's, I checked the time. It was a couple of minutes before eleven. I found a phone box and rang Aunt Sarah, mainly to get hold of Candy's telephone number. It turned out to be a very unpleasant and awkward five minutes, the reason being that I had to tell so many lies. As I grew older and wiser it became clear to me that your parent's advice 'always tell the truth' is just so much crap. Now I know that it is far better to lie to someone you love, if telling the truth causes them too much pain. But way back then, when I was at eighteen, I was comparatively new to the business of lying, and I found it a depressing and uncomfortable experience. I lied when I assured her that my studies were going well, and that I was phoning from a call box in the university, between lectures. I lied again when I said that the reason I could not phone her the previous evening to tell her that I had arrived in Newcastle safely (which I had promised her faithfully to do, but had forgotten clean about), was because the phone box near my lodgings was broken. I told her another lie when I pretended that the only reason I wanted to phone Candy was because I missed her. (Maybe that was only a half lie. I did actually miss giving her another chance to fondle my cock). I had to invent yet another whopper, by pretending that the reason I will be returning to London in about ten days time and staying for four of five days is to give the university authorities the time and opportunity to repair some war-time bomb damage, which is now giving rise to some structural problems in the main lecture hall. How I managed to dream up so many crazy lies on the spot I cannot recall. I suppose it was out of desperation.

Sickened though I was to have to be so dishonest, it was somewhat offset by the knowledge that my lies had made Aunt Sarah very happy. As far as she knew, not only was I working away happily at my studies, but her matrimonial plans for Candy and me seemed to be bang on course..

As for me, overriding all else, was the fact that I now had the Elman's telephone number. As I waited for the trunks operator to connect me, I said to myself, 'Time to put your plan into action Jake Silver'.

"Hello, who's speaking please." I immediately recognised the tough, hoarse, voice of Dora Elman.

"Hello Mrs Elman. This is Jake Silver" I said as pleasantly as I could. "I wonder if it's possible to speak to Candy please."

"Oh hello Mister Big-shot. I thought after winning such an important competition, you would be too high and mighty to speak to us mere mortals."

"No, you've got it wrong Mrs Elman. It was that I got home very late and I had to be on the ten o'clock train the following morning. This is my first opportunity to phone"

"Well congratulations anyway, Mister Bigshot"

I had no idea whether she was trying to be nice or sarcastic with this 'Mister Big-Shot' reference, but I said nothing.

"I am running out of money Mrs Elman. Can I speak to Candy please."

"Hang on. I'll see if she wants to speak to you."

I heard the rattle of the phone being put down, followed by Dora bellowing; "Candy, telephone call, you lazy cow."

Another phone was picked up, and Candy came on the line. Her voice was all crinkly and croaky from having just woken up (or maybe, from having too many cigarettes the night before).

"Who's that?"

"It's me. Jake Silver. I'm phoning you from Newcastle."

"Oh Jake. I think I was just...what's the number you are phoning from?"

I told her.

"Put the phone down and wait. I'll call you straight back."

A couple of minutes later she was back on the line to me.

"Sorry I had to do that Jake darling. Now I am speaking on my own private telephone. The old bat listens in when I use the other number. Her voice changed to being kittenish and sexy. "I'm so glad you rang Jake, because it means that you must be thinking about me. I think about you a lot. D'you know that?"

I let a few seconds go by, before saying in the most conspiratorial voice I could come up with, "Listen, can I tell you a secret?"

"You know you can, sugar."

"I'm giving up my studies and returning to London. I can't take it up here any more. I want to see more of you Candy." I said, adding a little kvetchy misery to my voice. "So I am giving it all up to be back there with you."

"Ooh," she said, in a voice drenched in delight.

"And there's another thing."

"What's that Jake?"

"This is deadly secret Candy. I have taken a job playing the piano in a very exclusive little club in Belgravia. This way, I'll have money of my own so that I can rent my own flat, and we can be together as much as we like."

After a long pause she said "Jake, you know I would love that. But your Aunt Sarah would never let you get away with it. Don't you know that?"

"Yeah. But with your help, I think I have a way around that problem. Will you help me Candy, please?"

"You know I will if I can. But I don't think..."

"Listen" I said. "I'll be leaving here in about two weeks, maybe less. During that time, I want you to visit my Aunt, and say that you can't stand me being so far away from you. Say that you want me down there in London all the time. Say that you have spoken with me about it, but that I won't come back to London and continue cadging off my Uncle and Aunt. Tell them that I want to have a job and earn my own keep. And then push home how much you are impressed by that. Say some shit about how much you admire me for wanting to stand on my own. I'm pretty bloody sure that if my Aunt thinks that my taking a job will make you happy, she'll go along with it."

"Do you really think so Jake? Do you really think I could talk her into it?"

"If you tell her that we want to be together, and that the only way it can be done, is to let me be a man and stand on my own two feet and take a job. I'm pretty sure she would buy it. Oh, yeah, and add that you are sure your father would appreciate that as well."

"Jake." Her voice took on a serious tone. "Tell me the truth. Do you want me to do this so that you can take a job in a night club, or do you really want to see more of me?"

I lowered my voice in the hope that it would sound more sincere and also more sexy: "Look Candy, I'm mad to see more of you, but I want it to be on our own. And that means I have got to have my own place. And that means I have to take a job to pay for it. But I think about you a lot" I lied, "And the scene I conjure up is not exactly you and me taking tea in my Aunt's front room. It is a little more...intimate than that. You know what I mean. If I can get my own place, we can be alone as much as we want, baby."

She was cooing sexily with delight; "Do mean that you are prepared to give up all of your studying, and take a job, just so that you can afford a place where we can be on our own?"

"That is exactly what I mean darling. But I can't do it without your help. Please Candy, will you help me?"

It worked. "Don't you worry about a thing darling. Leave Sarah to me. Phone me again in about four or five days. I'll have some news for you then."

"Give me your private number so that I can phone you not just about that, but about other things. I want to tell you about a few of dreams I had lately in which you were the star attraction."

The schpiel was a complete success. She was mine now. I felt confident that if anyone can pull it off, she was the one. Failing that, it was going to have to be done the hard way. But, I was absolutely determined that nothing and no-one was going to be allowed to stop me from renting my own pad and playing the piano professionally. From here on, life was going to be just one long jam session.

As I briskly made my way along Grainger Street, towards the Station Hotel, I was one happy kid. The freezing, soaking rain actually felt good on my skin. The drear, grey clouds above seemed to be smiling at me. Forgive the pun, but everything seemed to be just Jake.

Apart from the relief I was feeling at being able to leave it to Candy to eliminate all resistance from Aunt Sarah, I also felt deucedly clever and terribly sophisticated for having been able to wind Candy round my little finger (although for the next few nights I suffered serious pangs of remorse for so doing). I had loads of money in my pocket, a great job to look forward to, and now I was on my way to give my second press interview. I felt like hugging the world.

I got home that night to find a letter in my letter-cubicle, and a note pinned to my door. The letter was from Doctor Cabot-Smith, saying how sorry he was to lose me, and how much he had enjoyed our informal little chats etc. He then congratulated me on winning the competition, and wished me well in my career. The note was from the gauleiter to say that Jack Montgomery had phoned, and to phone him back that night at FLE 4646. The rest of the note comprised his usual warning that all students must be in by 10.30 every night etc., etc. I looked at my watch. It was ten o'clock. As I made my way to the phone box, I had a feeling that something had gone wrong and that the engagement was off.

So it was with pounding heart and sinking stomach, that I stood in the 'phone box waiting for the long distance operator to connect me.

The phone was obviously behind the bar, because I could hear the burble of conversation plus the odd bursts of laughter, as I waited for Jack to come to the phone. I could also hear Reggie de Courcy tinkling on the piano. 'Jesus, I wish I was there' I was thinking as Jack came on the line.

"Jake are you there?"

"Yes, I'm here Jack. I got a note saying to phone you."

'Now for the bad news' I thought, steeling myself at the same time.

"Firstly old lad," Jack said, "I posted your contract to you this afternoon, so you should get it pretty soon. When are you coming to London exactly?"

My heart, which had been pulled down into my boots with fear and trepidation, now bounced back and was thumping with relief and excitement.

"I thought of coming to London about ten days before we open," I said, feeling great about saying 'we'.

"Oh, then don't bother to post it back. Bring it in to me when you are back in town. Now to something quite different. What do you propose to do about your living quarters? Are you going to stay on living with your Aunt and Uncle, or what?

"No, I can't do that Jack. The hours I keep would disturb them too much. The first thing I have to do when I get back, is find somewhere to stay."

"Well, in that case I may have something for you. I have a young titled friend, who is going off with three of his mates on a round the world yachting trip He was telling me that he needs someone trustworthy to occupy his flat while he's away. I suggested you, and he said okay, providing I guarantee you, which I did. He doesn't want any rent, but you would have to pay the service charge which is forty pounds per month, plus seven pounds ten shillings per week for the servant who comes in every day. Eliot told me to tell you that the flat has got a piano. He thinks you will find that pretty important."

"So that means that this place is going to cost me a little over seventeen pounds ten shillings a week."

"Actually, if you add in electricity, water and gas, I suppose it will come to just a little over twenty pounds a week. But do remember old chap, that you will probably get that much in tips every week. And one other thing. It is right around the corner from the new club. You wouldn't be more than three or four minutes walk away. All you have to do is look after his flat and not indulge in too many wild parties, and the place is yours. So what do you say?"

I knew it was bloody expensive. In 1948, twenty pounds per week was far more than most people's weekly wages. On what I was being asked to pay out in rent, a man could keep a wife and a couple of kids quite happily. But it did have a piano, and it was near the club. And most importantly, it saved me the hassle of having to hunt around for a place to live.

"When could I move in?"

"It is empty now. You can take it from the day you arrive."

"Okay," I said. I'll take it." Then I asked; "Is it a nice place Jack?"

"I have no idea. I've never seen it. But he is titled, and know his family has money, so I don't suppose it'll be too terrible."

He waited for me to say something but I kept silent. So, after a pause, he said, "Look old chap, If you don't like it after you see it, as long as you go on paying the outgoings until I find someone else to take it on, you need not stay there for too long."

"Okay," I said. "I will definitely take it, whatever it is like. What's the address?"

He dictated it to me whilst I carefully it wrote down. He told me that he would pay out the rent in advance up to December the first, and would arrange for the front door key to be left at the porter's desk for me to collect upon my arrival. He added that if I move in before December the first, I would have to make good the rent he has paid out. This seemed to be fine with me.

As I strolled back through the chill night to my lodgings, I sang out loud the last lines of 'I Got Rhythm'. 'Who could ask for anything more, who could ask for anything more'.

Sleep was out of the question. I was far too excited for anything as mundane as that. I sat on the bed. Still in my overcoat, because the room was so cold, I read and re-read the address Jack had given me. Flat Eleven, Kings View Hall, Wilton Place, Knightsbridge. 'What would it be like?' I wondered. On the good side it did belong to somebody with a title. On the bad side, I reckoned that any friend of Jack's, will almost certainly be a gambler. For all I know he could have lost all his money. Although the address sounded good, I had no idea where this Wilton Place was. I reckoned it would probably be some f'dreckisher little pied a terre in some forgotten back street of Knightsbridge. 'But it did give me my own place, whatever it turned out to look like'. I thought. 'And it does have a piano, even if it is a lousy old upright. And anyway, after this' I said to myself looking around my squalid, shitty little room, 'after this, nothing could seem all that bad'.

For the next couple of hours, I sat huddled on the bed making a list of everything I was taking with me and what I was leaving behind or selling.

The only clouds left on my horizon, were to do with my Uncle and Aunt. Will Candy be able to sell them my alibi for quitting university?. 'Shit, she just has to' I half thought, half prayed.

I looked in my pocket diary, and found that November the fifteenth fell on a Monday. What if I were to tell my Aunt that I am not coming to London until the Sunday after that? That would give me six days in my own flat before I have to see them. If it turns out that I don't like the place, I can move back in with Aunt Sarah when I visit them on the Sunday. As far as she will know, I am just arriving from Newcastle, so it would not create any hassle. But what if it turns out to be a nice apartment? Well, in that case when I go to visit them on the Sunday, I will have to find a way of telling them the truth. As ever, I shifted my mind on to another subject, the thought of having to tell them being too fright-filled to contemplate. So I thought about whether it will be the very first night or the second that I invite Candy to visit me. I fell asleep smiling.

Three days later, I phoned Candy. In the meantime I had become a bit of a celebrity in my students' hostel. The reason for all this new-found fame was the printing of my interview, together with a photograph of me, in the local daily newspaper, 'The Journal'. A visit to the kitchen to get myself a cup of coffee, would invoke all kinds of gratuitous compliments from whichever group of students were present. The only one I can still remember came from the Welsh music student, who lived on the same floor as I did. "Gee," he told his two friends, "Just to think boyo, I can claim that I shat in the same shit-house as the great Jake Silver."

As expected, it was the cause of more nastiness from the gauleiter. As I left the hostel to get myself some breakfast, he stopped me.

"I've just read about you in this morning's paper," he said. "You surely know that this so-called jazz music comes directly from Satan?"

"No, I didn't know that," I said. "But I knew you would. You're so much closer to him than I am."

* * *

"Hallo Jake darling. I was hoping you'd ring me," Candy said huskily.

"And I was hoping you'd be in when I did."

"I don't go out every night Jake. If I did, my parents would make my life a misery. By the way, I told my mother that you'll be coming back to London and that you wanted to take a job in order to prove to Daddy that you are capable of keeping me in comfort. She was very pleased with you Jake. So you've got one friend in your corner at least."

'Jesus Holy Christ, what am I getting myself into here?' I thought. 'I've met her once and she's ringing marriage bells already.

"That's good," I said. "Did you also explain to her that the other reason for my coming back to London is so that we can get to know each other better?"

"No, I didn't" she said. Then in a husky, sexy, voice: "Because that's between us and us alone. And I am going to get to know you and your lips and your body and that great big thing of yours better than you know them yourself. And that's a promise Jake."

"Mmm. Sounds pretty good," I said, not being able to think of what you are supposed to say while being raped over the phone. "But you know, a lot of this depends on getting my Aunt to allow me to quit university, and letting me have my own place. Have you had any luck with her yet?"

I tried to make it sound as if the main reason for my calling her was to simply hear her voice, and that the Aunt Sarah thing was just by the way. I hoped she was not aware, that in fact, it was entirely the other way round.

"Well I have spoken to her," she replied. "And for all I know, mommy has also. The thing is Jake," she sounded as if she was pouting as she spoke; "She is willing to let you leave university and take a job, if it makes me happy, but she is insisting that you stay at home, where she can look after you."

"Shit. Shit, shit," I said. "She wants to treat me like I'm a baby. Christ, I look after myself up here. I'm not dying from starvation or anything. I may be suffering from sexual starvation, but that's quite another thing."

"I'll put that right for you, don't you worry," she said, going back to her sexy delivery. "Anyway, we've always got my car. You can do lots of interesting things in a car. Did you know that?"

I could see that all she was interested in was me. It was only of passing interest to her whether it was me in my own pad, or me in my Aunt's house, or in her car.. Her sole aim was simply to have me around, and she had succeeded in that by getting my Aunt to agree to my leaving university and taking a job in London. But that was not what I wanted. Right away I realised that she was not going to be of any further use in persuading my Aunt to let me live on my own. And having my own pad was far more important to me than dating, or even fucking Candy. I decided there and then it was better to tell her nothing about the flat I had already taken. I was damn sure that if I did, she would spill the beans to Aunt Sarah, and I did not want that. I alone now had to make the decision as to how and when Aunt Sarah would learn about it.

I was also sure that if I did stay with my Aunt, she would not stop until she had talked me out of being a professional piano player. I knew instinctively that within a few months she would have brain washed me into becoming what she would call 'a mensch', which simply meant becoming an acquiescent Ivan look-alike and think-alike. Also there was my Uncle to deal with. He had made 'big plans' for me. Well, I had made big plans for me also, and, it might seem to be ungrateful considering how wonderfully my Uncle and Aunt had looked after me since my tragedy, but things were now different. I felt I was grown up enough to decide my own future. And I was immovably determined that I was going to be a professional jazz pianist, and that I was also going to live my own life the way I wanted; to keep the hours I wanted, and to sleep with whoever I wanted without arguments, tears, or recriminations. And no Aunt Sarah was going to stop me.

So I said "Not in your little car darling." "And listen," I added. "Say no more to my Aunt. I'll handle the whole thing when I get down there. Okay?"

"Gee you're so masterful Jake, d'you know that?" She sounded excited at the idea, but I was simply fucking angry.

"Yeah," I said, having now lost all interest in the phone call.

"Listen Candy, I'll call you the moment I know the exact date of my leaving here. But I'm gonna be busy. So, I won't call you until I know. Okay?"

"Okay darlin'," she said kittenishly.

"I have to go now," I said.

"Kiss me goodbye then."

I sent a kiss down the phone and cut off.

I now knew that I was in for a torrid time with Aunt Sarah. But as I left the phone box I said to myself 'This is one argument I am not going to lose, whatever it takes'.

I set off to go back to my room, but the thought of sitting on the rattling old bed trying to work out how to handle the aunt and uncle scene was too depressing for me to contemplate. So I went to the pictures instead and saw a movie featuring Melvyn Douglas and Cary Grant, the title of which was 'Mr. Blandings Builds His Dream house'. 'And so does Mister Silver' I thought to myself as I passed my one shilling and sixpence over to the middle-aged peroxide-blonde cinema ticket seller, in her little cubicle.

Chapter 19

As I boarded the train at Newcastle Central Station, on that bright, sunny, but bitterly cold middle November morning, it was with the warm certainty which comes from knowing that nothing had been left undone. Last night, Harold and Meyer threw a farewell party for me. Of course I didn't get laid. Just a few kisses and a few fumbling gropes and that was all. The only chicks I fancied, even remotely, were as ever, dead set on making out with Harold almost to the exclusion of everyone else. Meyer and I as usual, had to make do with what was left over. But there was plenty to drink and we did have a lot of laughs.

Emotionally, I was a an even mix of excitement, trepidation and awareness that I was starting an entirely new life. Sitting there in the empty carriage of the stationary train, looking out of the window onto the drab, dirty station platform, observing the porters trundling their trolleys and yelling incomprehensibly to one another, watching passengers and those seeing them off, laughing together as they hurried past my train window, their eyes watery, their faces reddened by the icy wind; and then the sudden thought of me playing a shiny new baby grand in a warm, dimly lit, exclusive little club was wonderfully thrilling.

The previous Wednesday morning, I had bought myself a large packing case, into which I had put my table-gram, my records and classical music books. (The sheet music of the popular songs, I had with me, in my suitcase). I had also shoved into the packing case my trumpet-playing statuette as well as the various bits of bric-a-brac that seem to multiply by itself if you live in one place for more than a few weeks. I also arranged for a removal company to collect and deliver the packing case at the address, Jack had given to me. I had made it my business to say or phone my goodbyes to everyone I could think of, from the porters at the university, to Hazel, the fat lady who served at the café where I suffered my daily breakfast.

Also, I had practised assiduously for five hours every day for the past two weeks. So, my chops were in as good a condition as they could be. I had worked out my own transcription of a 'Porgy and Bess' medley comprising the four most popular arias from Gershwin's great opera. I had also memorised most of his other published songs, together with everything I could lay my hands on of Richard Rodgers, Cole Porter, Irving Berlin and a host more. So, as far the job was concerned, I was as ready as I could possibly be.

There was only one thing left undone. Something I knew was the right thing to do, but had put off because I could not face doing it: THE letter to my Aunt and Uncle. I knew it had to be written. Procrastination may be the thief of time, but it can also be the father to some pretty damn good excuses, and I had managed to talk myself into honestly believing that the time and place to write the dread letter was on the train to London. As if to prove that fact to myself, I had bought a new writing pad and some envelopes, specifically for this purpose. By so doing, it had allowed me and my conscience a two week holiday. Now the fateful moment had arrived.

So I "prepared" myself, in other words, I stretched the time before having to write the damned letter by a few more minutes. Firstly, I got out my pack of State Express 555 cigarettes and took as long as I could taking the cigarette out of the box, tapping the end of it and then very carefully (and very slowly) lighting it. Then I took all the time I could putting the pack back into my small attaché case, before extracting my brand new writing pad. I took out my Waterman's fountain pen, which I suddenly remembered had been bought for me by my Aunt, because 'you'll need it for your studies at university', which added a further pang to all the other pangs that had panged into my convoluted conscience, since I had made my decision to quit the Modern History course. Then, I carefully (and as slowly as possible) set the cigarette down on the ashtray provided, and finally began.

My Dearest Uncle and Aunt,

I am writing this to tell you that I have made a fundamental decision regarding my future.

I knew right off that this was too dictatorial in its approach. I tore the page out of the pad and began again.

My Dearest Uncle Harry, and Aunt Sarah ('that's already better', I thought).

I am writing this to beg your blessing for something I wish to do and upon which, I have set my heart.

Fortunately, I was forced to stop because the train had gone into the jerky huffing and puffing mode that seemed to be a routine part of steam trains leaving stations. But having once settled down to its steady 'how do y'do, what do y'know' rhythm, I could think of no other excuse not to continue with the letter. So I forced myself onwards. 'Even though I have not seen as much of Candy as I would have wanted, she does appear to like me and we have had many conversations on the telephone'...

I stopped writing to lean my head back against my seat, close my eyes and think about Candy Elman. My first thought was that I will have to be damned careful to avoid being compromised. I mean, it's was one thing to like and even fuck someone. But if the price to be paid was a presumption of marriage, then it was too damned high. I was not going to be inveigled into some crazy romance faked up by the female Boris Karloff, Dora Elman, just because she had taken a liking to me for having yelled at her. And as for Aunt Sarah, who, rather like the British aristocracy, thinks that to 'marry money' is the be-all and end-all of life, 'Well' I thought, 'brain-washing may work with Candy Elman, but it aint gonna work with Jake Silver. No sir'.

Then I got to wondering if Candy will be as good at 'doing it' as Janine. 'I bet she won't do it with her mouth' I thought. Then I wondered if I could teach her to do it. The very thought it gave me a hard-on, which I hope, I disguised from the middle-aged lady now sitting opposite me, by crossing my legs, plus a strategic replacement of my writing pad.

'Somehow', I thought, 'I've got to get her to my apartment. But before I do, she will have to promise me that she will not give my address out to either her mother or Aunt Sarah, unless and until I give her the okay.'

Then I got my head around trying to picture the kind of place I would be living in as from tonight. Jack had referred to it over the phone as a 'pied a terre'. 'So', I reasoned, 'it will certainly be something small, probably one room with a small kitchen and, I hope, its own bathroom. Shit, it's bound to have its own bathroom' I decided.. 'After all, the guy's supposed to be an Earl or something' But he is a friend of Jacks, which means he's almost certainly a gambler, so the chances are he's dead broke. Maybe that's why he's sailing around the world, or even just pretending to be sailing around the world; to avoid his creditors. 'Yeah, that's it', I thought, convinced that I had hit upon the truth. 'In which case, he will have either hidden or sold anything of value in his apartment. So it's a virtual certainty that it will be a run-down, shabbily furnished little pad, which led me on to thinking that a tatty, shitty apartment will not create the kind of ambience likely to encourage any girl to offer her body to me in. 'The only thing that ever gets laid in this kind of pad, is the table' I reckoned regretfully. 'And where is this Wilton Place for Chrissakes? Probably some depressing little back street in Soho somewhere'. I had no idea where it was. Neither had I looked for it in a street map of London. I only knew what Jack had told me; and that was to get a taxi from Kings Cross railway station. He had assured me that all London cabbies knew where Wilton Place was. 'I'll find out soon enough where this so called 'pied a terre' is, I thought, subconsciously steeling myself for the worst.

My erection having now receded, I once more got on with the business of the dread letter.

'Both Candy and I feel that unless we get together pretty soon, and on a regular basis, our lives will inevitably drift apart. So...'

The carriage door suddenly slid sharply slid open. "First call for lunch" shouted the uniformed attendant, and he slammed the door shut just as roughly as he had opened it.

That was it. Right away I closed the writing pad and put it back into my attaché case. I was not all that hungry, but going for lunch gave me a perfectly legitimate reason to stop writing a letter that I knew to be a load of balls. As I said before, I consider myself to be a good liar, but I did have a heavy conscience about lying to two of the three people (the other being Ivan), I cared about more than anyone else. So, it was a great relief to be walking down the train to the dining car, even if it did mean eating the kind of crap for which British trains are renowned. (Or at least, they were in those far-off days when I lived in Britain).

About an hour later, I returned to my carriage, feeling bloated and nauseous from the food. I had ordered roast beef and Yorkshire pudding. What finally arrived was a lukewarm, glutinous mess that I reckoned must have been originally pre-cooked by some firm of caterers called 'The Sadist Catering Corporation'.

Lying underneath the tasteless thick brown goo, there was supposed to be some roast beef! I finally located it with my fork. There were two slices of meat cut so thinly, that if they had been any thinner, they wouldn't have been there at all! This was accompanied by hard, shapeless little lumps, with blue-black patches on them, which the waiter assured me, were 'roast potatoes'. I turned them over with my fork. 'Oy vey' I thought, 'the guy who cooked this must have learned his skills in a Paraguayan gaol or somewhere'. To top off this gastronomic horror story was, 'treacle tart and custard'. At least, that is what it said on the menu. What it was in fact, mankind will never know—and maybe mankind is a lot better off! It looked a lot like that yellow stuff, which you blow out of your nose near the end of a bad cold. It was slimily covering something that looked, felt and tasted frighteningly ominous. As it lay there on the plate, I was reminded more than anything else, of one of those strange objects, usually found in a field by an unsuspecting child, in the opening scene of a B-picture, called something like 'Blobs From Outer Space'.

So why did I eat it and make myself feel ill? The answer, I realise now, is that Jewish boys learn pretty early on in life that not to finish a meal is something no Jewish mother can comprehend. 'So nu, why didn't you finish your meal?' 'Are you ill?' 'I'll have to call a doctor if you don't eat it all up' Or, 'you'll surely die if you don't eat up all your food'. 'You know what'll happen to you? You'll slowly fade away. Do you want that to happen?' Etc, etc. So, rather than face the inevitable third degree that follows leaving even the smallest scrap on the plate, Jewish boys learn to take the easy way out and eat it all up, whatever it is and whether they like it or not. And that is why I ate all that shit, regardless of how seriously it may affect my life span.

Once more back in the carriage, I reluctantly got the writing pad out of my case and settled down, determined now to finish the damned letter. Actually, I would have been better advised to look at the scenery as the train hurried through it, because never again would I look upon the face of the countryside in the land of my birth, although of course I did not know this at the time.

'So', I continued in my uneven scrawl, 'I took the decision, with Candy's agreement, to take a three months sabbatical from my studies, in order for us to see one another regularly'.

I was sure that the 'with Candy's agreement' line would make the relationship sound a lot more kosher than it actually was (or ever will be). Also, I felt that implying I would be returning to my studies in three months time would take a lot of the sting out of my Aunt's and Uncle's objections.

'Fortunately, I have been offered a job, which may not entirely meet with your satisfaction, but it is well paid and something I can do easily. This will allow me to see Candy during the day, which I know is better for her than being out too much at night' ('clever' I thought). 'It also means that I can have my self respect, insofar as I will be able to pay for our lunches and the odd show, without my having to ask Uncle for more money. It should also leave enough over to start repaying you for all the time and money you have spent on me. Of course, I can never repay you both for all the love and kindness you have shown me since the loss of my dear Mother and Father'. ('That'll definitely grab 'em', I thought). Then I went on; 'As I wish to be near my place of work, which is in the West End, I have found a little pied a terre, which will be better for me than staying with you, which I naturally would prefer, because as you have pointed out so often, walking the streets at night can be so dangerous By living near my workplace, I will not have to be on the streets for more than five minutes in either direction'

God, I felt terrible writing this utter crap. But I could think of no alternative. To start with, I had no idea where this place called 'Belgravia' was. I only presumed it was somewhere in the West End of London. Because Jack had said over the phone that it was not too far from the new club. At that time, all I knew of the West End was Leicester Square, because that was where the movie houses were.

Even as I re-read what I had so far written, I knew that within a few days of receiving it, they will have found out where I am living and working. Then one bright morning, they will all present themselves at my shabby little pad, not only my Uncle and Aunt, but also Ivan and his drag of a girl friend, whereupon I will be embroiled in the most almighty row, probably ending up with Ivan being made to escort me back to Newcastle so that he can plead with the Modern History faculty for my re-admission.

'No dammit' I thought. 'I don't care how much they yell and threaten. I am going to be a piano player and they just better get used to it'

Then a brilliant thought struck me. Tomorrow, I will go to one of the big stores and buy my Aunt and Uncle a super present. I will have the store send it to them, enclosing a card saying something like, 'I have had a great stroke of luck. Expect a call within the week. Do not phone me. I will phone you when I am ready. I love you. I'll sign it, bung a few kisses on the bottom, and leave it at that until I am properly set up in my new lodgings. Then, I will take them out to lunch, because I'll have plenty of money to do so, and over the lunch table, I'll straighten everything out. Perfect.

I tore up the letter and settled down to a nice little snooze, from which I did not awaken until we were not more than a couple of miles outside Kings Cross station.

It was raining heavily in London and I was getting soaked through as I stood in the queue for a taxi.

'This is exactly what happened to me when I arrived at Newcastle for the first time' I thought. But I noted that it was thankfully nowhere near as cold as it was then, or is now, up in the north of England.

"Where to guv?" the cabby asked as I clambered in to the taxi.

"Do you know a street called Wilton Place?"

"Blimey, guv, if I didn't know where that was, they wouldn't let me drive a bleedin' cab."

"Well," I said, as I wiped the rain water off my face with my handkerchief, "I need to find to find a place called Kingsview Hall."

"Don't you worry nuffink guv. We'll find it. It's only a short street anyway."

As we headed off into the dark, rainy, car-filled, rush-hour traffic, I started to feel good. In fact, you could say that I was starting to feel very good indeed. Jake Silver, ex-student, from Drecksville-on-Tyne, who had to climb through the student hostel kitchen window if he got home after eleven at night, and who had been just another member of the all-time small-time, was dead. Arise the new Jake Silver, man-about-town, who now works in the romantic world of night-clubs and who is seen only in the best places, dressed in the sort of clothes that Cary Grant or Melvyn Douglas might be seen in and having his very own pad (fuck how drab it turns out to be), to which he returns at two, or maybe even three in the morning. Yes sir, this is the life for me.

I leant back in the cab, peering out through the rain soaked window. I had not the foggiest idea where we were, but wherever it was, it was just fine and dandy with me.

Gradually, the brightly lit shop windows were becoming more imposing, the buildings far grander and the rain-soaked traffic, even heavier. As we crawled past Fortnum and Masons beautifully laid out windows, I asked the driver where we were.

"Blimey guv, you're in Piccadilly. Doncha know tha'?"

"I haven't been back to London for a long time" I said apologetically. "I've been living in Newcastle upon Tyne."

"Ge' ova you stupid, fuckin' bastard" the taxi driver roared at the driver of a car as we overtook it. Then his friendly, cheerful, cockney sparra' voice returned as he said to me "I 'ope you don't want me to take you back there tonight guv. The fare would be too big for me meter."

I laughed over-loud to let him think that I had appreciated his pathetic little joke. As I could not think of any snappy come-back, I just shut up and looked straight over his shoulder through the windscreen, at the rain-blurred mosaic of white headlights and red rear lights in front of us. I also realised that wherever this Wilton Place was, it was nowhere near Leicester Square. Suddenly, we turned off left into a side street comprising a mixture of obviously very high-class apartment buildings on the one side, and elegant neo-Georgian terraced houses on the other.

"Ere y'are Guv; Kingsview 'all. As he spoke he reached across to switch off his meter, which told me that there was eight shillings to pay. I gave him a ten shilling note and told him to keep the change. This must have been a helluva tip, because he actually volunteered to carry my suitcase into the foyer of the apartment block.

'Jesus, this looks very big-time indeed' I thought as we padded across the huge, thickly piled, circular, red and black patterned carpet that lay decorously upon the pink, marbled floor, and up to the grey-haired uniformed hall keeper, who sat behind a long, pink marble counter. He looked at me as I approached, like I was something that was daring to make his marbled domain look shabby. He waited until the taxi driver had dumped my suitcase, before speaking.

"Yes"? he said, his eyebrows lifting heavenwards a good inch as he spoke.

"Good evening," I replied cheerfully, pretending to ignore his imperious, superior, manner. "I understand that the key for number eleven is waiting for me."

"Number eleven?" He thought for a couple of moments, saying at the same time, "Number eleven, number elev..." Then the penny dropped.

Suddenly his voice became hard and accusative. "Wait a minute. That's the Earl of... 'ere, what's your name?"

He was of course exhibiting all the typically arrogant class-consciousness which has fucked up Great Britain so permanently. This fellow, a commoner like me, was clearly angered that I should have the chutzpah to enquire about anything to do with someone so grand and important as the noble Earl.

"Silver—J.Silver," I said, assuming as Noel Coward an accent as I could. "Jack Montgomery assured me that the Earl had left instructions for you to let me have his keys." His face took on an icy, suspicious stare as I went on speaking, trying to sound casual and quite used to the marbled luxury that was all around me.

"I'll be staying here for a while, whilst he is away. Keeping an eye on the place. Keeping it all ship-shape and Bristol fashion y' know." I was still working on my Noel Coward impersonation.

"Are you an employee of Earl Brackington?" he asked, narrowing his eyes suspiciously.

"Good Lord no," I said. "Surely you know Jack Montgomery? Viscount Montgomery, the Earl's best friend. He told me that everything was arranged for me to stay here."

The lie worked. The fact that I appeared to know not only an Earl but a Viscount as well, could only mean to this hall porter's class-ridden brain, that I was a 'nob' to be treated with the subservience due by someone from his lower social rank. His face now creased into a phony smile.

"Oh, yes sir. I remember now" he said with mock joviality. "The night porter, who doesn't come on until nine o'clock; did say something about that. Just a minute sir, while I look in his drawer."

He disappeared into a back room, whilst I drummed my fingers on the marble counter-top, feigning impatience, Franklyn Pangbourne style. (He was a wonderful Hollywood character actor). I was gratified to note that he was now addressing me as 'Sir'.

After what seemed a long time, but probably was not more than a couple of minutes, he re-appeared clutching a piece of blue note paper: "Ah, here it is sir, I believe." I waited while he read the note very carefully and slowly. Then for no accountable reason, he turned the note over and studied the blank side. Only after he satisfied himself that there was no secret message written on it, presumably in invisible ink, did he unlock the wall cupboard behind him and select a key ring from the half dozen or so that hung in a neat row on their respective hooks. He handed it to me with one chosen key sticking out from the rest.

"There we are sir. This one is your front door key. You see here sir; it has an eleven printed on it." I looked at it and nodded my confirmation that I had seen the number eleven on the key.

"That means number eleven, which is the number of the Earl's apartment sir. That is on the top floor sir."

Again I nodded.

"The other keys lock the interior doors, your own garage round the back, and two of them are for locking wardrobes. But apart from the front door key, I don't know which is which sir."

As I took the keys from him, I said, still doing my Noel Coward thing, "Thanks very much. I'm quite sure I'll be able to work out which key fits what."

As I bent down to pick up my suitcase, I heard him say "Er, just one more thing, sir."

He consulted the night porters note again before leaning across the counter as if to supply me with some secret information. So I to leaned forward to find out what it was.

Although there was not another person anywhere to be seen, he whispered. "The combination for the safe is under the carriage clock in the drawing room."

"Oh. Jolly good" I said hoping my face did not belie my amusement.

I made my way, suitcase in hand, across the carpeted and marbled foyer to the elevator. It was typically British, meaning it was very small, and rattled and groaned as it made its way to the top floor. Semi-dazed by my luck. I could hardly imagine what this number eleven would be like. But if it was half as classy as the foyer I had just left, I would be the luckiest guy in the world. Outside the lift was a thickly carpeted hallway. There appeared to be only two apartments on this floor, number ten was to my left and number eleven at the right hand end.

I let myself in through the front door, to find myself in a small upper foyer looking down onto a magnificent, octagonal entrance hall, the walls of which were panelled in light oak.

From where I was standing, which was just inside the front door, there were three highly polished dark wooden stairs leading down into it. Gracing either side of this small staircase were thin, black and gold coloured coiled metal banisters supporting handrails made of a dark green material, that looked to my inexpert eyes as opal. The entrance hall itself was lit by a small but exquisite chandelier set into a cupola in the white ceiling. There were also four tall, elegant standing lamps around the walls, all of which were lit, presumably to await my arrival.

In the middle of the hall was a black and gold-edged round table tesselated with tiny opalescent tiles of every colour, on which stood a statuette of a beautiful nude negress, supporting with her left hand, a water jug which she was carrying on her head. It appeared to be made of ebony, although the bangles on her arms and wrists as well as two thin bands around the water jug were of gold. The floor was pink marble overlaid with deep Persian rugs. On each of the octagonal walls were hunting prints, which turned out to be a matching set. On either side of the small upper foyer, where I was still standing, were gently concave matching light oak doors with small inlaid gold handles. Opening them, I found that both contained rails for coats etc., plus a wash basin and lavatory in matching black porcelain with gold fittings.. The lighting was concealed around the tops of the pale green walls. Running down the middle of each door was a full length, very pale pink mirror. Above both wash basins there were shelves with hair brush, comb, and an ornate phial which, if you pressed, sprayed some exotic perfume.

I went back to stand next to my cases not quite knowing what to do in this wonderland. I shouted, "Is anyone home?" But all I got was the sound of silence.

I went down the steps into the hall, and leaving my bags where I had set them down by the front door, went on an exploratory trip, around the entire pad. To say that I had fallen with my arse in butter would be one of the great understatements of all time! This was quite simply the most palatial residence I had ever seen. Why anyone would want to piss off around the world, and just leave it to a friend to find an occupant was quite beyond me.

The apartment was on two floors. The front door had led me into the upper level. Off to the left of the main hall was a polished and panelled mahogany door which I opened to find a dining room, magnificently furnished and decorated in Japanese style. On the large, round, black glass dining table set in the middle of this crazily opulent room, I found a large Japanese ornamented salver on which were slices of roast beef, veal and pieces of chicken. Next to that in a green lacquered bowl, was a green salad, next to which were two tall, thin, glass receptacles containing olive oil and vinegar respectively. The table setting was entirely in Japanese style, except for the wine glass, and, the silver stand supporting the ice bucket, which stood next to the table, and by the side of one of the six high-backed, black-lacquered dining chairs surrounding the table. In the ice bucket was an unopened bottle of Chablis with a corkscrew sticking up from the ice cubes surrounding the bottle.

Even though I was hungry, my desire to explore the rest of this paradise, overrode my hunger. I opened an interior door, set into dining room wall to my right. The door itself was padded and silk-covered in pale yellow, with a hand-painted scene of a Japanese Geisha standing outside what I guessed was a Japanese tea house. Through this door I found myself in an elaborate library-cum-office. Apart from the floor-to ceiling book cases, containing magnificently bound volumes of every size and subject, there was also a couple of black leather padded chairs, a round, oak, coffee table, upon which were a couple of magazines, a kidney-shaped antique desk-table with a large, red, leather-edged blotter, plus a cream coloured telephone. Behind it, was a red-leather thickly upholstered swivel office chair, and, under the window, a matching bow-fronted set of drawers which I found contained writing paper with the address embossed, together with the Earls family crest.

Fixed to the wall to my left, was a large glass case containing a magnificent model of a Victorian- era packet ship. Apart from the door through which I had come, there was another which led out into the parquet floored, rug covered hall, at the far end of which I found a small elevator to take me to the lower level, as well as a broad, light oak staircase that did the same thing.

On the lower of the two floors, was another wide hallway, thickly carpeted in dark blue. There were three doors on my left and two on the right. The first, on the left, led into a large, well-appointed kitchen, at the end of which was another room that I discovered was a pantry The second door off the hall turned out to be a large walk-in cupboard, containing brooms an ironing board, and other household equipment. The third door led into a smallish bedroom, although large enough to contain a double bed, with eggshell blue satin sheets and pillowcases. It also had its own private bathroom, decorated in exactly the same colour blue as the satin sheets.

Across the hall was the main bedroom, with its own dressing room and bathroom. It was of a level of opulence that I have never seen equalled. I will tell you a little bit about this room later. Suffice it to say that in the course of my life I must have been in more than a hundred so-called luxury bedrooms. I have slept with multi-millionairesses in their beautifully appointed homes, and I've fucked film actresses in their expensive hotel suites, but I have never before, or since, seen a bedroom and bathroom quite so opulent as this.

The remaining room was yet another bedroom with its own private bathroom. I spared a thought for those poor lads living in that miserable, draughty, smelly student's hostel up there in Newcastle, of whom, until a few hours ago, one was me. As I made my way back upstairs, I could not resist whistling a chorus of 'What a Difference a Day Makes'.

Once back in the main hall, I opened the door opposite the dining room to find myself in a long, luxuriously furnished drawing room. There was a long dark-brown leather chesterfield at one end, and a newish Bluthner baby grand at the other. Next to the piano stool was a standing lamp with a Tiffany lamp shade, also lit. The main body of the room consisted of three coffee tables with lit table lamps, two glowing green, and the other, yellow. Facing the low, wide fireplace, with its glowing log fire, was a dark green velvet sofa. On either side of the fireplace were two large alcoves. On the piano side, the alcove contained a long, dark walnut liquor cabinet, whilst on the chesterfield side there was a huge HMV radiogram and television combined into a cabinet exactly matching the liquor cabinet, which I found to be crammed with drinks and glasses of every kind.

In fact, after the second and far more elaborate exploration which I carried out later that night, I found it so well appointed that it left me with the feeling that the owner had just popped out to buy something, soon to return, rather than an apartment which the owner had vacated for a couple of years. There were still a couple of dozen suits hanging in the large dressing room. I also found a pile of shirts in one of the ten or so dressing room drawers that occupied an entire wall of the oak panelled dressing room, adjoining the main bathroom. I also found other personal effects, such as gold cufflinks, a dozen handkerchiefs, several ties, an address book, and many other things that you would have thought the noble Earl would have packed away, or indeed, taken with him on his world cruise. Probably because of my young age, it never occurred to me that he must have been in a very big hurry to leave his apartment in this way.

After returning to the Japanese-style dining room to partake of the delicious repast and downing half of the bottle of wine that someone or other had left out for me, I returned to the drawing room, put on the radio, and sat on the dark-green, velvet sofa, surveying the vast abundance of luxury I had been handed on a plate, so to speak. It was all too much for me and I got to wondering who to invite over to sample the delights of this fantastic apartment. Then it hit me: of course, Miss cock-grabber herself, Candy Elman.

I went back to the front door, where I had dumped my bags, carried them to the lift and thence down to the huge wonderland of my bedroom, where I set them down on to the deep, lush carpet.

It is neither my wish nor my style to spend a half-dozen pages describing the magnificence of this bedroom suite. But I think you do deserve just a little taster so to speak.. Firstly the bed: it was a huge four poster, about ten feet square, with dark red satin sheets and pillowcases. Acting as the bedspread was a giant fur overlay. I didn't know one fur from another, but under the sweetest of circumstances, I discovered that it was mink. The four posts supporting the dark red velvet canopy over the bed were of a oak, engraved from bottom to top, with every kind of sexual coupling imaginable. On the wall behind the bed was an oil painting, about eight feet wide and four foot high. It was illuminated by four small pin-spotlights set in the wall above it, and was a back view of two Arabs sitting on the desert sands looking at, and presumably trying to decide who was the most desirable of four naked, nubile women provocatively posed before them. What was most exciting for me in those far off and sexually repressed days was that the artist had painted in the pubic triangles, unlike any nude I had ever seen previously. And what with all the concealed lighting controlled by a little console at the side of the bed, it was far too sexy to sleep in by yourself.

I rummaged through my attaché case until I found my address and telephone number book. Then I kicked off my shoes and flung myself full length diagonally across the fur bedspread, reached for the nearest of the two telephones which were on identical tables set on either side of the bed, and dialled Candy's private number.

"Hello."

"It's me, Jake. If there is anyone in your room with you pretend it isn't me. Okay?"

"Er...yes" Then, after a short pause, she tipped me off as to what the situation was, by saying "No mother, leave them where they are." Then again to me in a very matter-of-fact voice:

"I'm sorry, what was it you were saying?"

"Listen Candy, I'm in London now. Only no-one must know. It is a dead secret for the time being."

"Of course. I think I can do something about that," she said matter-of-factly, obviously to put her old boiler of a mother off the scent.

"I've got myself a place in Knightsbridge." I told her. I deliberately underplayed it for the surprise value it would have when she sees it.

"I want to see you" I said in a pleading voice. "Just say yes or no. Can you come over tomorrow?"

"Er, 'fraid not." She was speaking in such a convincingly formal way, that I was starting to believe it myself.

"What about the next day then?"

"I think that would be fine."

"Can you write down this address?"

There was a short pause, after which she said "Er, not at the moment."

"Okay," I said trying to hide the disappointment I was feeling. "I get the picture. Ring me the moment you are alone. The number is Knightsbridge 7744. Can you remember that?"

"I'll write it down so that I can tell her to contact you when she has a chance. I'll try to get hold of her tonight..."

I clearly heard a door shut on the other end of the line. Then Candy said urgently "Wait."

After a little while, she came back on the phone. This time she was speaking normally.

"Okay, the old bat has gone." Then she said quietly. "Jake what are you doing in London and why are you not staying with your Aunt Sarah?"

"Listen. I've chucked university and taken a job playing piano in a brand new little club. The family mustn't know a damned thing about it until I am properly settled in. I'm bloody sure that if they knew right now, they would go their ends to try to fuck up, er, sorry, to screw up the entire thing and ship me back to Newcastle."

She gave a throaty little laugh: "Jack you don't have to apologise for saying 'fuck' to me' It's one of my favourite words."

Just the way she said it gave me an instant hard-on. Then she said softly "Jack?"

"Yes."

"Am I the first person you've told?"

"You're the only person I've told" I said quietly.

Her voice became silkily conspiratorial: "That's really sweet of you Jake. To tell me before anyone else"

She clearly thought that I was putting her above everything. She was wrong. I was putting fucking her above everything.

"Listen Candy, can't you come over tomorrow? It's really important to me."

"Well," she said doubtfully. I kept silent to give her time to think.

"I am supposed to have lunch with a friend and then go on to my hair-dresser at half past three."

Couldn't you cancel your lunch date and have it with me instead?" Then I added as meaningfully as I could, "I just can't wait to see you."

Then, in a voice pregnant with sexual innuendo: "Well, if you can't wait Jake, okay. I'll come over at about half past twelve. But I must be gone by a quarter past three at the very latest."

"I guarantee it," I said, with phoney sincerity.

"What kind of a room have you got? Is it as nice as the one you had in Newcastle?"

After killing off the urge to laugh, I replied I hoped in a serious voice; "I think, taking all things into consideration, that it's actually a bit better than my room was in Newcastle. Anyway, it is big enough for the two if us, if we stay... really close together." I was trying to be artfully sexy.

"Ooh" she said with kittenish glee. "I can't wait to see it." Then she added "And I can't wait to see your room either. Now give me a big kiss and I'll see you at your hidey-hole at half past twelve tomorrow."

I gave her the biggest kiss I could over the phone. I heard her door open followed by the coarse, hoarse voice of her mother. I didn't hear what she was saying because Candy put the phone straight down. I got up off the bed, still amused at Candy describing this paradise of an apartment, as a 'hidey-hole'.

"It's not this hidey-hole, but your hidey-hole that I am after," I said out loud, as I bounded up the wide oaken staircase and back to the drawing room.

The fire had died a little, as I went over to the magnificent carriage clock that sat on the mantelpiece to find and retrieve the folded piece of paper that was located behind rather than underneath the clock, as the porter had so secretively imparted to me.

I poured myself a large whiskey which I took from the cocktail cabinet. Then I lit a cigarette, picked up an ash tray, and with cigarette in mouth, drink and note in one hand, ash tray in the other. I strolled across to the piano stool, where I sat down and read it. It started off by giving the safe's location, which was in the library. This was followed by the combination itself, and then the rather mysterious instruction 'For access, remove 'Great Expectations'. I went back to the library to begin my search. It took me a full ten minutes to locate the gold embossed, leather volume. It was at the end of one of the shelves nearest the glass encased model of the packet steamer.

As I pulled the volume from its place, I heard a small click from the direction of the glass showcase. I turned to find that it had swung outwards to reveal a small, round safe in the wall behind. I immediately fantasised that I was some latter day Raffles as I carefully spun the combination wheel on the safe this way and that as directed, and after giving the door a gentle tug, hey presto, it swung open. I peered into the blackness of it, but could see nothing. However, when I reached in with my hand, I found at the very back, an envelope which I brought out. It was unaddressed, but stuck down, and I felt a pang of conscience about opening it, but my inquisitiveness got the better of me especially as I noticed that the envelope was a standard plain white one. 'So nu' I reasoned, 'I'll open it now, and tomorrow I'll buy another envelope exactly the same, put it back into the safe, and nobody will be any the wiser'.

I tore open the envelope. 'Holy Jesus' I said softly as I looked at the contents.

Inside, were two photographs. The first was of a tall, beefy man of around forty years of age. I noticed that he had his hair parted in the middle, like Oscar Wilde. He was sitting on a high backed chair and smiling at the camera. His legs were parted, and on one knee sat a smiling young boy of not more than twelve or thirteen. Both were naked and both had erections. The other photo was far worse. As near as I could tell, it was the same man, naked as before, but this time he had a naked boy standing on his parted thighs, his cock half way into the man's mouth. At the same time there was another lad crouching down between the man's thighs with his mouth over the man's cock.

I suppose in these over-enlightened days, such photographs would create little more than mild amusement to an eighteen year old. It certainly would not cause the great sense of shock, which I felt, back in the comparatively sweet and innocent year of 1948. In addition to that, I was more innocent of matters sexual than most boys of my age. Barring my one little run-in with Janine Gregson, and the odd tit-bits of information I had gleaned from Harold

Landing, I was sexually as innocent as a new born babe. I had never even seen pornographic book let alone read one. It was to be another two years before that would happen and even then, it made no mention of paedophilic homosexuality.

I was not only shocked; I was also puzzled. Why would anyone want to get a boy to do something like that, when you can get a beautiful big-bosomed chick to do it for you?

I put the photos back into the safe, replaced the book, swung the glass encased packet steamer back against the wall and went back to the drawing room, still shocked and confused. After a couple of hours of playing the piano (which was a little out of tune, but otherwise in very good condition), I had another scotch, one more cigarette and went to bed.

The bed was the absolute, diametric opposite of that lumpy, rattling misery, that I had been forced to endure in Newcastle. Little wonder that I fell into a deep, satisfying and dreamless sleep.

For no particular reason, I awoke suddenly. At first, I could not remember where I was. I looked at my watch; it was nine-thirty. Still more asleep than awake, I automatically went into the same daily routine as I did in Newcastle: put the kettle on first, and while it is coming to a boil, take a pee.

I wandered naked and numb with sleep, into the kitchen to fill the kettle. I also had half a hard-on, a condition not too unknown in boys of eighteen, especially before taking that first pee of the day. No sooner had taken my first step into the kitchen, than my semi-somnambulistic dwaal was shattered by an ear-piercing scream. "Ay, Madre Mia."

I had completely forgotten that Jack had said the apartment came with a daily servant. She had apparently been sitting at the kitchen table having her morning coffee, when I waltzed in, cock first. On reflection, I guess I must have looked like some unkempt Satyr.

Not only did she scream; she also threw her coffee cup in the air in her haste to have both hands free to cover her eyes as she slid under the table and crouched there, surrounded by pieces of broken china, and little puddles of coffee.

I had nearly jumped out of my skin at the shock of it all. At first, I just stood there and tried to mumble out some form of explanation and apology. Then I suddenly remembered that I was stark naked and turned to rush for the bedroom. I did not stop running until I was in the lavatory, with the door securely locked behind me. I was smothered in embarrassment. To start with, not since I was a little lad had I appeared completely naked in front of a female, and then it had been my Mother. But as I put on a thick, soft, black and white chequered bath robe I had found in one of the many bathroom cupboards, I started to see things in better perspective. There was no point in acting embarrassed or contrite. It had been an honest mistake, and after explaining why it had happened, I had to trust that I would be forgiven.

Now respectably covered with the bath gown, I returned to the kitchen. Apart from wishing to make my peace with this girl, I was also desperate for a hot cup of tea or coffee. I found her where I had left her, still crouched under the table; knees were drawn up to her chest and her hands still over her eyes.

"Look," I said, in as friendly a fashion as I knew how; "I'm really sorry. I was half asleep and forgot that you would be here." I bent over and put a hand out towards her, "Please come out. I had a shock too y'know."

She parted the fingers over one of her eyes and peered at me from between them. Then ignoring the hand I had held out to help her, she slowly came out from under the table. I gave her time to stand up and flick some blobs of coffee from her sleeve, before going towards her to shake her hand. But she immediately backed away from me, never once looking me in the face. I saw that she was short and dumpy, and that her face was round and sallow with Peruvian Indian type features. Her forefinger and thumb were clinging hard to the large silver crucifix which hung around her neck.

I took another step towards her, but again she jumped backwards, crossing herself and muttering some imprecation or other, either in Latin, or her own mother tongue

Noticing the coffee percolator still standing on the kitchen table, I said in a warm and informal way; "I only want a cup of coffee, that's all."

Shying her face away from me, she managed to take a coffee cup out of one of the cupboards, reach for the percolator, fill my cup and hand it to me, without ever looking at me, her gaze concentrated to one side and downwards.

I decided on a cheery, airily informal approach. As I reached for the sugar, I said "My name is Jake. Jake Silver. But you can call me Jake. What's your name?" I hoped that the tone of my voice would convey to her just what a warm and friendly fellow I really was.

At first she said nothing as she busied herself with clearing the wreckage brought about by her under-the-table dive. I stood and watched her clean, while sipping my coffee (which was very strong, but not hot enough: in other words, typically Latin-American.).

"America," she said sheepishly, still looking away from me.

"America," I repeated, genuine surprise in my voice. "I've never heard of that name before. But it's a lovely name."

"The other master, he call me Meri."

"Is that what you want me to call you? Or, do you prefer America?"

"Wharever you weesh, master."

I dug being called 'Master'. It made me feel like a jazz version of Heathcliffe.

"I think I'll also call you Meri," I said.

I was about to take the now empty coffee cup to the sink, but she took it from me and put it there herself.

"Thank you Meri," I said, because I wanted her to know what an appreciative 'Master' I really was. But I also said it because I fancied saying her name, which I found pretty cute. Then I remembered.

"Meri, I am expecting a lady friend for lunch."

Do you think you could make us up a little something? After that beautiful meal you left for me last night (I noticed the first sign of warmth in her expression as I said that), I am sure you could think of some little snack for us."

The way I saw it, there was no profit to be made out of taking Candy to a restaurant, because she would probably head off to her goddamned hairdresser straight after. But if we ate here, there is a bedroom. And where there is a bedroom, well, who knows?

Now at last, she turned her gaze from the floor to look at me. "There is no food master. You must go to the shops and buy some food. I cook eet for you" She spoke with the up and down tonality of a Latin American. I persuaded her to do the shopping instead of me. I gave her five pounds, which was a huge amount in those days for one meal. I asked if she ever had to buy in food for the Earl. She said that she did sometimes. I told her to buy whatever she would have bought for him.

After she had gone off to the shops, I got myself a bath. As I lay there in the bizarre luxury of the huge, square, black marble, bath, steeped up to my shoulders in piping hot water, my thoughts turned to the Earl who owns this wild, wonderful, pad. I could not get over my sheer good luck, not only for landing a place like this, but for getting it equipped with everything, including booze, towels, sheets, all of the very finest. At that moment, as I lay there in steaming, almost magical luxury, I thought; 'Fuck Earl Hines. Give me Earl Brackenberry every time'.

I decided to put on my best suit. Then, with a handful of jazz records removed from my still unpacked suitcase, I headed for the drawing room. I made my way to the radiogram (as they were called in those days), which was the best I had ever seen or heard, with a pentagonal speaker section containing five separate speakers. I put three carefully chosen discs on the chromium-plated record changer, lit my first cigarette of the day, sat in one of the soft, pale green, armchairs, and to the accompaniment of Joe Sullivan's 'Gin Mill Blues,' I planned my seduction of Candy.

I reckoned that the best and most subtle way of making it with her would be; after a couple of glasses of wine I'll offer to show her around the apartment. Then, when we get to the bedroom, I'll casually suggest that she tries sitting on the bed, merely to sample its luxurious comfort. 'That is when I will make my move' And even if I screw up' I rationalised, 'the worst that can happen is that I never see her again. So nu, big deal. I don't even fancy her'.

I stubbed out my cigarette, switched off the record player and went over to the piano to do a little work. I was trying to work out a new way of playing 'The Peanut Vendor, or, to give it its original title (because out here in Cuba, it is a second national anthem), 'El Manisero'. In its original Afro-Caribbean form it has just three chords. I was dreaming up a version that would broaden this harmonic base considerably.

My concentration was broken by a small noise behind me. I stopped and turned to find Meri standing there listening, clutching a large carrier bag of food in each hand, a Harpo Marx look of wonderment on her face.

"Aye, I am sorry master."

She spoke sheepishly, staring down at her feet guiltily, as if I had caught her stealing.

"It's okay Meri" I said as gently as I could. "I only hope you liked it."

"Oh si" she said sincerely, and in a far more relaxed and natural voice, than hitherto.

"El Manisero, thees we all seeng in my contry."

"Which country is that?" I asked as she started to head for the door, presumably heading for the kitchen. She turned and smiling at me for the first time, said.

"Cuba master. In Oriente where I leev, we sing dat song from when I was a leedle baby. But I never heard it played thees way."

"No, it's a special version I'm working on."

"Oh si. Ees very nice Master." She went out of the room only to return a minute later.

"Master, I buy feesh. Is da' okay?"

"Fine, wonderful, perfect," I said, echoing Fats Waller's famous saying.

"What time you wanna eat Master?"

I had to think quickly. Do I want to eat first, or fuck first? I decided that FF is preferable to EF.

"I would like the food to be served in the dining room at about two o'clock, if that is alright with you Meri. And Meri" I shouted after her, bringing her back into the room; "Will you tidy my bedroom please. And when the lady arrives, I'd like you to open the door to her and bring her in here. After that could you bring us a couple of glasses of wine?"

"Si—I mean yes Master. We have champagne in the frigo if you prefer. Master John, he always have champagne before lunch."

"Definitely yes. Thank you. We would much prefer champagne."

She went out of the room and I started to play 'Hallujah' or something equally up tempo, to express my feelings of excitement and exhilaration.

Time suddenly become leaden. Minutes took hours to pass. 'Where the hell is she?' I kept saying over and over, as I watched my hands playing tune after tune.

And then, in the middle of 'More Than You Know' I heard the gentle front door chimes. I quickly looked at my watch, feeling that it must already be after one o'clock, which would leave me with no time to carry out my plan, but was relieved to see at it was only ten minutes after twelve. I hurried across the room to put on the Nat 'King' Cole recording of 'Sweet Lorainne'. Then I ran back again to the pale green sofa and sat there, trying to look casual, as I waited for her to come in.

Meri opened the lounge door to let Candy come bounding past her into the room. I stood up as she ran to me, arms opened wide, "Ja-a-ake" she said until she was in my arms. Once there, she held her face up to me to be kissed, which I duly did, whilst noting Meri's stone-face glare of disapproval as she backed out of the room, quietly closing the door behind her.

"Oh, it's lovely to see you again Jake," she said softly, her head resting against my chest. Then she suddenly pushed me away from her until she was holding me at arms length, and with eyes dancing with pleasure, she said "Let me look at you." As she gave me the once-over from head to toe, I took the opportunity of doing the same to her. She looked quite attractive, considering that her basic supply of God-given attributes did not add up to very much. She was wearing black, patent leather high-heeled shoes, giving her short legs a longer, thinner look, black silk (or Nylon, who knows?) stockings, a knee-length dark grey skirt with a lighter grey, vee-necked sweater, underneath which was a white blouse with a blue silk scarf tucked into it. Her face had been considerably improved by her hair style which was now softer and straighter and shoulder-length. No more the fuzzy-wuzzy locks she had sprouting from her head the last time I saw her. She was also sporting shiny, orange-coloured lipstick over her none too generous lips.

"You look wonderful Jake" she said as she reached up with a handkerchief to wipe off the lipstick from my face and mouth. Then she added; "I think you've grown since I last saw you."

Before I could answer she said, with arms flung open wide; "And what about this fantastic apartment! How did you find it? Jesus Jake, you really are a smooth operator, d'you know that? You've only been in London five minutes and you've already got yourself this great place."

I nodded knowingly, choosing not to change her opinion of me.

Before I could say or do anything more, she grabbed my arm, and with all that manic energy that bounds out of her, pulled me towards the door, saying as she did so:

"I want to see the entire joint now."

"But don't you want to have a dr..."

"NOW, please Jake" By this time we were in the hall. She walked ahead of me looking and touching everything as we walked. Every so often she would murmur in genuine appreciation, 'wonderful', or 'this is really something.' Somehow, with all that pzazz buzzing out of her, and with me dragging along behind, it was as if she showing me around, instead of vice versa.

She let out a 'Wow' as we entered the quasi Japanese dining room, staring in almost childish awe as she looked about her, taking in the Oriental wonders of it. She either ignored, or was unaware of Meri, who had already set two large, shiny, black, cane table-mats at either end of the shiny, black-lacquered dining table with all the hand-painted figures so exquisitely set into it. Meri had also put out some wonderful heavily ornamented ivory handled fish knives and forks, and was now in the process of gently polishing two elegant, long-stemmed wine glasses. After she had carefully looked at every bit of furniture, not to mention Meri, whom she rewarded with a vague, distant smile, I followed her into the library cum study.

I stood by the door and watched her as she slowly walked around the room, touching everything, her forefinger running lightly along the rows of gilt embossed leather bound volumes, her mouth half open with wonderment.

"God, Jack and Phoebe would love this room," she said abstractedly.

"And who is Jack and Phoebe?" I asked.

"Friends" she said absent- mindedly, while wandering over to gently spin the yellowed antique globe that sat on a low mahogany table against the wall to the left of the door we had come through.

"Let me show you something," I said.

She turned to watch me remove the Dickens book and gasped as the glass encased packet ship swung away from the wall to reveal the safe.

"God," she said, her eyes wide with amazement. "Have you tried to open it yet?"

"Yes, I did open it, but there was nothing in it." I lied, being too embarrassed to tell her about the pictures inside.

"Please open it for me darling."

"Well, you see..."

"Oh please, please," she grabbed me around the waist and looked up at me so pleadingly, that I was powerless to refuse.

"Okay, I have to go back to the drawing room to get the combination. I'll only be two minutes."

By the time I came back with the folded piece of paper containing the combination, I had decided that if she finds the photos, I was going to pretend to know nothing about them, and was also seeing them for the first time. She insisted on opening the safe herself. "Ever since I saw my first Boston Blackie film, I've wanted to do this."

"Doesn't your father have a safe?"

"Yes," she said as she bent over in front of the safe door, holding the combination in her left hand.

"But if you fiddle with it too much, you set off the burglar alarm, and that gets you into a whole load of trouble."

I watched her as she slowly and carefully followed the written safe-opening instructions.

"Yes," she shouted jubilantly as the safe handle clicked down and the door opened.

I need not have bothered to have worked out a whole film script about how I would play the discovery of the photos scene. I should have remembered that they were invisible to the naked eye, and that I had to reach in and feel about in order to discover them.

I moved forward to shut the safe door;

"Just a minute" she said. She took a small note-pad from the little leather handbag she was carrying, removed the tiny pencil that was slotted in the back of it, and wrote something.. She showed me what she had written before tearing it out of the note-pad and putting it into the safe.

It said, 'Too late. I took the lot'. It was signed, 'Boston Blackie'. (Who was the eponymous hero of a dozen or more Hollywood movies about this adventurer cum safe-cracker.)

I faked a bigger laugh than the prank deserved, because I wanted her to think that she had succeeded in impressing me with her zany humour, which was all part of the build-up necessary for me to 'get lucky' before lunch. Incidentally if any young stud happens to be reading this, then take this piece of advice: always laugh aloud at your girl's jokes, whether you find them funny or not. It makes them feel great and is a very hip move in helping you to get them into the sack.

"Hey," I said, as if struck by a sudden inspired thought. "I haven't shown you my super-duper bedroom. (I deliberately used that silly expression because I felt it was the kind of thing she might say, and I wanted her to see me as someone on her wavelength.)

"Oh yes, I must see that." She seemed excited at the thought. And so was I. As we got into the lift that was to take us down the stairs, and which I suppose, was actually installed to help the servants bring the food from the kitchen, up to the dining room, she said to me:

"Shit Jake, I think you've hit the jackpot. This place has everything." Then, after a pause; "Except one thing."

"What's that?"

"Me" she said as we got out of the lift.

"Yeah," I said. Small talk was over now. We were approaching the moment which, if I play my cards carefully, might become a very magic moment indeed for me.

I opened the bedroom door to allow her to enter first.

After staring around her speechlessly, at the sheer magnificence of it all, she said quietly and in an awestruck voice: "This is ridiculous Jake." Christ, this is for Joan Crawford or somebody."

"Try the bed" I said. "They're real satin sheets."

I noticed thankfully, that Meri had made it and also tidied away my clothes.

She either ignored or did not hear me. "Is that the bathroom through there?" She was heading towards it as she spoke. I said nothing, preferring to follow her and dig the reaction when she saw it.

She must have said 'Oh my God' at least half a dozen times. She said it as she kicked off her shoes before stepping down into the magnificent black, sunken bath. She said it as she slid open the large, deep drawers and stared into cupboards. She said it with even greater intensity when she found the cupboard containing the bath wraps, which hung on a rail that automatically slid in and out at the press of a recessed button just inside the cupboard door. I said it too because until that time I knew nothing of it either.

And so her 'Oh my God-ding' went on over everything from the soft, deep fluffiness of the huge bath towels, etc. and the huge stained glass window at one end of the bathroom, to the fittings in the dressing room beyond.

As we were re-entering the bedroom with me walking silently behind her, racking my brains as to how to get her to just sit on the goddamned bed, she said quietly, casually and seemingly absent mindedly: "Jake, be a good boy and shut that bedroom door for me."

I had no idea why she asked. Even as I was in the act of closing the large door, I was trying to work out why she wanted it closed. The thought flashed through my mind that maybe she wants to tell me something secret and didn't want Meri to overhear.

So I closed the door as noiselessly as I could. I turned around to ask why the door had to be shut. to find Candy in the act of taking off her sweater and blouse in one action. I stood watching her, utterly confused by the speed of events, as she reached behind her to unclasp her red brassiere and let it drop to the floor on top of her blouse and sweater. She seemed not to notice me as she busily wriggled out of her skirt.

"C'mon Jake darling, get your clothes off." She said as matter-of -factly, as if she were saying to a hotel page, 'put the cases over there'.

I stood unbelievingly, watching her, now only clad in lacy, black cami-knickers and black stockings held up by inch-wide, red, garters. She was busily smoothing down her hair and appeared to be oblivious of me. I noticed that she had small, but shapely tits, with tiny, pink nipples. She suddenly looked over to where I was standing and gawking.

"For Chrissakes Jake, get your bloody clothes off."

By the time I had my jacket off and my shirt unbuttoned, she was naked.

Flinging back the bedclothes she leapt on to the satin sheets and lay on her back, her fingers interlocked behind her head, in much the same pose as Goya's naked Maja, except that Candy's tits were far smaller, her legs much shorter, and her thick black, triangle of hair, much larger and far more prominent than Goya's Maja.

She lay there watching me intently as I kicked off my shoes, dropped my pants to the floor and stepped out of them. I took off my socks a bit slower than I could have, because, to tell the truth everything was happening too quickly. I had expected to be in charge of this seduction scene and was a bit discombobulated by this role reversal. I needed a bit of time to come to terms with the fact that it was I who was getting laid, rather than doing the laying.

Then she said in a husky but teasing voice; "C'mon shy boy, let's see that big knob of yours. As I slipped out of my underpants, my cock only half erect, she opened her arms to me, saying as she did so; "Come to mammy's lovin' arms."

I lay on top of her, kissing her, my mouth shaping the unspoken 'aah' as instructed by Janine, Candy's tongue fluttered in and out of my mouth in a far more exciting manner than Janine's had done. Our naked thighs were intertwined and as we kissed and moved our bodies against one another, I was conscious of the roughness of her thick, pubic mound as it ground against my thigh. We stayed kissing passionately for a while, her finger-nails running up and down my back, sometimes gently and then suddenly savagely, as if she wanted to tear me to pieces.

I moved down to kiss and caress her nipples with my tongue. As I did so she took my head between her hands. After allowing me the shortest time to enjoy the heady sensation of her hard nipples on my lips and tongue, she started to push me downwards. My cock was now violently rigid and desperately needing some kind of satisfaction, but she clearly had other ideas. And so, as she gently but firmly pushed me down her body, with me kissing everything my mouth came into contact with, on its enforced journey southwards, my cock had to content itself with the pleasures of being rubbed against the sensuous softness of the satin sheet beneath me.

Then she moved her hands from my face to my shoulders, to push me just a little more urgently down over her navel, past her soft satin-smooth little belly, and on, through her rich, deep, triangular thicket of black, curling hair.

All I knew at that time about 'going down' on a woman was what I had gleaned from Harold Landing, when he had deigned to let Meyer and me into some of his sexual experiences. I had never even heard of the word 'cunnilingtus'. So, having arrived at my destination, I had only the vaguest idea of what to do.

But I had no need to worry. I am pretty sure that like me, you must have seen at least one movie in which some fifteen year-old lad finds himself in an aeroplane in which the pilot (often his dad), suffers a heart attack or something, and with no experience whatever, the lad is forced to take over the controls. Fortunately for him, there is a veteran flyer (who was an air ace when younger), now working in the control tower, who calmly talks the kid down into making a bumpy, but totally successful landing. In this bedroom version, I was playing the kid, and she, the very experienced pilot.

"Go a little higher... no, a little lower now... that's it. Do it gentler. Mmm... Now go up and down it...Go a bit quicker... QUICKER." Her voice took on a strange urgency. "Don't stop. Don't...ooh, yes." She sensed that my tongue was getting tired, which in fact, it was. "Oh for Chrissakes, keep going." Now she began to buck and rear, and it became more and more difficult to keep my tongue on the same spot, but I gamefully hung on in there.

We had reached the stage metaphorically speaking, where I had succeeded in lowering the undercarriage, and now had the runway directly in front of me.

"That's it. Keep going, for God's sakes...more...more...M-O-R-E-AHH. And then she orgasmed, her arse off the bed and high in the air. I still kept going, my mouth salty with her. Her body shook as spasm after spasm racked her body. Slowly it subsided until she finally lay still.

I felt wonderful. What that kid in the movie felt after getting the plane onto the tarmac, was nothing compared to the sense of elation and satisfaction I was feeling at that moment.

I was about to take my head away, but at the first sign of movement, her thighs locked tight around my ears. I could just about look up to see her gently fingering her nipples. But my face was being held hard against her cunt. So, having nowhere to go, I started again, but she opened her legs and putting a foot on my shoulder, gently pushed me away, saying; "Not yet darling. Give it a minute."

I contented myself with kissing the insides of her thighs and running my lips up and all the way down to her knees and back again. But I did not put my tongue back inside her until she half said, half moaned, "Now. Do it again."

And so we did a second take of the 'young-man-lands-aeroplane' sequence, but with a few technical differences. This time it was, "Press harder... harder... go in deeper... now come out again...oh yes...now faster...faster...oh...oh...OOOHHH. And then she came, more quietly, but for just as long as she did in the first take.

Then an unfortunate thing happened. I was just about to go into a third re-take, when little Meri, decided to bring in the Champagne that I had ordered, but forgotten about completely in the heat of the action. Needing both hands to carry the tray with the ice-bucket containing the Champers, plus two flute glasses, she managed to push down the handle of the bedroom door with her elbow, after which, she used her ample bottom to shove open the door, entering backwards and not turning around until she was inside the room, to find the same young man who had earlier invaded her kitchen at half cock, now at full cock and with his face buried in madam's cunt!

What with Candy's thighs being pressed hard against my ears, plus all my concentration being taken up with, shall we say, trying to land the plane for a third time, the first I knew of Meri's presence was when I heard a shriek, 'Virgin Maria Santisima', followed by the thud, crash and clink of the tray hitting the carpet.

By the time I had extricated my tongue from Candy's candy cunt, all I got was a glimpse of Meri's rear end as she ran out of the door, slamming it shut behind her.

Candy's reaction was astonishing. She just grabbed a handful of my hair and shoved my face back to where she had clearly decided it belonged. "Go as fast as you can my baby. As fast as you can." It was as if Meri's entrance, her shrieking discovery of us, not to mention the dropping of the tray, had never happened. "Oh y-e-e-s-s," was all she said as we at last made the perfect three-point landing that I had tried so hard to do in the two previous takes.

Now manfully fighting severe tongue fatigue and jaw-ache, I was finally allowed to crawl up over her body and put my now aching cock into the place it was made for. But just as I was moving in and out of her nice and slowly in order to savour the moment, she suddenly wrapped her legs around the small of my back and holding me tight inside her, rolled me on to my back to sit astride me. Once again it was she who set the pace and style she liked best. She started with long, languorous ups and downs, gradually changing to quicker, shorter and fiercer movements, until she was moving up and down only an inch or two, but very quickly and intensely. Then she had what I can only describe at 'The Last of the Red-Hot Orgasms', replete with loud ecstatic shrieks intermixed with deep gasps.

"Keep going," I said frantically, which she thankfully did, and couple of minutes later, I forgot about my aching jaw not to mention my sore cock from the intense rubbing she had given it, as I too joined her in the golden world of Orgasm. Then, she collapsed on top of me, her hair tickling my chin.

After a minute or two, she rolled off me, to lie beside me, her eyes closed.

"You are some man Jake Silver," she said in a slow, dreamy voice. "How did you manage to keep fucking me for so long? I always thought that teen-age boys come in two minutes."

"If you really want to know," I said, "I took the advice of a friend of mine in Newcastle, who told me that the best way of keeping it up was to think of something else."

"So what were you thinking about?"

"I transposed 'All The Things You Are' into the key of E major actually.

After a long pause, she said dreamily, "What does that mean; transposing something?"

"It is written in A flat Major. If you hadn't come when you did, I was about top start doing the same with 'The Song Is You'.

After another long pause she said in a soft, sleepy, satisfied purr of a voice; "Next time, what about trying to transpose Beethoven's Fifth Symphony? Gee, that might take you all night," she said playfully. Then she rolled on to her side, put her arm over me and gently bit the lobe of my ear, whispering "But you were great."

I lay there thinking about what to say to Meri, in order to make my peace with her, when Candy interrupted my thoughts.

"Jake, am I the first woman you've ever had?"

"You too?" Is every woman I go to bed with going to ask me the same question? I mean what's it to you if I answered yes or no to that question?"

"I'm sorry honey. I didn't mean to..."

"You're the second" I said.

She took her arm from over me and turned to lie on her belly, with her chin resting on both hands. Then she said "Tell me about her. The first one I mean."

"Do you really want to know?"

"Please tell me."

So I told her all about Janine, including her penchant for virgin boys and girls as well as her lesbian activities with Mathilde.

After a long thoughtful pause, she said "I tried it with another girl when I was thirteen. She was fifteen. We'd sleep over at each other's house, on alternate week-ends and go at it all night. But then I met a boy of nineteen, who worked as a messenger for my father, and I fell head over heels for him. That was when I lost my virginity, when I was fourteen. After that, I lost all interest in girls. This is what I love now" and she gave my hardening cock a squeeze.

"So I suppose you've had lots of men since then" I said. I had no feelings of jealousy whatsoever. I guess the reason was that I did not really fancy her. She was just too far removed from my idea of beauty. I was also too utterly green to know that this is one question a male should never ask a female. And that still goes, even if he is married to her.

"Only a couple Jake. I'm being completely honest. 'Course I've had heavy petting sessions with heaven knows how many, but I have actually done it with only two others. You're the third." She gave me a quick peck on my shoulder before adding, "and the best."

Then after another long pause, during which I was trying to decide whether to cut the chat and get dressed in order to find and straighten out Meri, or fuck Candy for a second time, when she said, softly and seriously: "What do you think of me?"

"What do you mean?" I answered.

"I mean... do you think I'm nice?"

('You're not terrible' I thought). "Sure, I think you're great," I said.

"Because lots of boys have told me that I'm selfish, and want everything my own way."

('If today is anything to go by, they were absolutely right.) "They were completely wrong Candy," I said.

"They say that I'm always taking over and that I'm inconsiderate Jake. Listen, if I ever do anything like that, you'll tell me won't you?"

('Oh for Chrissakes, who cares? We're talking fucking here, not behavioural eccentricities'.) "Listen babe, those boys were wrong. Completely wrong. But if you do ever try to take over I will tell you, although I can't imagine that you would ever do anything like that."

She smiled at me contentedly but mischievously as she reached over to gently fondle my half hard cock. No sooner had she worked it up to full fighting fitness, than the bedside phone rang. I reluctantly rolled away from Candy's expert handlings, to answer it.

"Hello,"

It was Meri's voice on the other end. "Master, there are two men here to see you."

Her voice was cold and very matter-of-fact.

"Did you get his name?"

"No master. He ees from the police."

"The police!? Christ, ask him to wait. I'll be right up."

I leapt off the bed and started to dress as quickly as I could. I just could not imagine what they could want. I knew that I had done nothing. Then the thought occurred to me that something terrible had happened to my Uncle or Aunt, or, maybe Ivan, and that they had come to tell me about it.

"Do you know what they want?" Candy asked, as she took my cue and was also busily dressing.

"I only hope and pray that they are not here to give me some bad news or anything," I said as I knotted my tie.

"You go ahead when you're ready, and leave me here to straighten the bed and everything."

I didn't answer. My mind was firmly fixed on the proposition that the police were here to give me some bad news. Instantly, the ever-lurking memories of standing in that smoke-filled Brixton Road, watching that big old copper leaning over to talk with his mates in the police car, flooded into my mind. All the emotions and feelings of that unthinkable night were back as if they had never been away.

As I made my way to the stairs I passed the kitchen to find Meri sitting at the kitchen table, drinking a cup of coffee.

"Where did you put them?" I asked her, having completely forgotten about her finding me in flagrante delicto.

"They are in the beeg room," she said without turning round to look at me. Her voice sounded tired, hurt and careworn.

I found them both standing with their backs to the fire. The younger one was tall, thin and had pale skin with hair to match. The other was on the stout side and a good three inches shorter. He looked utterly sad. His eyes slanted sadly downwards at the corners. His moustache sloped down sadly past the edges of his mouth and his shoulders drooped in sorrow. They were both wearing ill-fitting and badly creased beige coloured raincoats. And both were wearing heavy, black leather shoes.

"How do you do" I said on entering the drawing room, my hand outstretched as I came toward them in what I hoped was a real grown-up gesture. I shook hands with both of them.

"And who might you be sir?" The older one asked during our hand-shaking ceremony.

"My name is Jake Silver. I'm renting this place whilst Earl Brackington is away."

"Oh I see sir," said the sad one. "Only, when the maid said that the master is downstairs, we quite naturally assumed that it was the Earl she was talking about" Then he added in the most off hand way, "You wouldn't happen to know where we could find the Earl would you?"

"No, I'm afraid not. I understand that he's aboard a yacht with some friends. He is on a world cruise, but I have no idea which part of the world he is actually cruising in at the moment."

I wondered if my voice revealed the relief I feeling at the realisation their visit did not involve my family.

"You see sir; he was supposed to pop into the station for a chat, to help us with some enquiries we are making. He said he was coming in on November the second, but he never turned up. This is the second time we've been here, and we seem to have been unlucky again."

"I'm sorry but I can't be of any help to you. I've never even laid eyes on the Earl. And there are no pictures of him anywhere in the flat." On the spur of the moment, I had decided to say nothing about the photos in the safe.

"May I ask how you came to rent this place, and who from?"

I told them about my new job and how Jack Montgomery, who was a friend of the Earl, had organised the whole thing.

"Well, it is most important that we see the noble Earl. Er... I wonder if you would have any objection to us looking around the place, to see if we can find something that might give us an idea of his whereabouts."

"No objection at all," I said. "But do you mind starting up on this floor? You see, there is a lady who is er ..." I was struggling to find a way of putting it. To my surprise, the sad looking copper seemed to dig my embarrassment; "You mean you have a lady friend down stairs sir. We quite understand. Well be a good ten minutes up here. That should give her time to make herself decent, if you'll excuse the expression sir." He smiled at me knowingly – although still maintaining his sadness.

"Fine" I said, surprised and grateful for his perspicacity.

I watched them go out into the hall to commence their search, the tall pale one first followed by the sad one. I could not help noticing that he even walked sadly. He was the only guy I have ever known with sad ankles.

I hurried down the stairs, stopping at the kitchen to tell Meri that the police were wandering about looking for clues as to the whereabouts of the Earl. She was polishing a whole pile of silver cutlery when I came in. She continued to polish, not once looking up while I was speaking. As I was leaving, on my way back to the bedroom, she said to my back, "I leave master. I no like staying here. I go."

I turned back to look at her. She was looking down at her feet, but I could still see that her face was a picture of misery. I was genuinely upset for her. I went over to her and almost involuntarily put my arms around her, saying as I did so, "You can't do that to me Meri. Look, I did not know what happened was going to happen. I give you my solemn word of honour that it will never happen again."

Her head was on my chest when she said "The madam, she will not want me here."

"The madame? Oh, you mean Candy. Don't you worry about her." Then I whispered in her ear, "You're much more important to me than Candy. Please stay."

The idea that she was more important to me than Candy, seemed to change her mood immediately. She looked up at me wet-eyed, but now smiling: "You men. You all bery bad. With Master John eet was always boys. And now eet will be girls I suppose."

I played my luck. "But whoever I bring in, you will always be more important." Her smile became just a little coquettish. "Why you like me so much Master?"

I realised I had pushed it too far. I had to say something that was nice but that did not imply I fancied her in the slightest.

"Because you are nice and sweet, and you are a great cook, and (another breathtaking example of the smart mouth of Jake Silver), because it makes me happy just to look at you."

She was now all smiles. "I like you too, Master. I stay."

I gave her a peck on the forehead and started to go out of the room, but came back to whisper to her, "Meri, do not say anything about Master John and his little boys to the police. Not today anyhow." She nodded.

The reason I said that was because in the short time it had taken me to run down the stairs to the kitchen, the realisations had hit me that if they issue a warrant for the Earl's arrest, they will in all probability find him and then bring him back to England to stand trial. In that case, in the interval before he goes to jail, he'll want his home back, and that was just about the last thing I wanted him to want.

I went back into the bedroom to see how Candy was doing.

I found her once more naked on the bed. "I decided to give lunch a miss," she said. Then opening her legs, she added "I thought you might want to take your lunch down here."

I ignored my stiffening cock. "Listen, the cops are on their way down. They are looking for clues as to the whereabouts of the bloody Earl. You had better get dressed."

As she got off the bed and started to gather her clothes, she said, "What do you think they want him for?"

"I believe it's about his liking for little boys."

"Dirty bastard," she spat out viciously as she stepped into her panties.

I went over and kissed her, stroking her cunt at the same time; while still holding her, I said "If he'd met you, he would have given up little boys, I'm damned sure."

"She took a grip of my semi-hard cock, saying as she did so "And anyway, who wants little boys when there are nice big boys like you around."

I released her to let her get dressed.

"I've got something to tell you Jake," she said as she wriggled into her skirt.

"Tomorrow I have to go with Daddy down to Cannes. He wants to change some of the furniture on the yacht, and arrange to have some repairs done. We'll be gone for a couple of weeks at least. Daddy'll be staying in Cannes the whole time, but I'll be staying in Paris with an old school chum for the second week. So if you want to come with us, either for the whole two weeks or just do the week in Paris, I think I could arrange it."

I shook my head. "It's not possible darling. I have already signed a contract. I can't back out of it."

"You don't have to worry about that. I bet Daddy could fix it with your boss. He's great at fixing things." Then turning to look at me, her face an even mix of churlishness and randy sexuality, she said "Or maybe, you just don't want to be with me."

"You know that isn't why" I said. "I've already signed the contract. And anyway, I like the idea of earning my own living. I've lived off my Uncle and Aunt long enough."

"How bloody noble of you" she said, now clearly a bit miffed.

There was light knock on the door. As Candy was now fully dressed and doing nothing more revealing than patting her hair into place in front of the full length mirror, I opened the door.

"'Afternoon miss," Sad Ankles said as he came into the room followed by Paleface, his partner.

"Oh hello" Candy replied. "I'm afraid there's nothing down here 'cept us chickens," she said, quoting, I believe the title of some terrible British pop song.

"You are probably right miss. But we have to take a look nevertheless" The copper seemed to be getting even sadder as he spoke.

We left them to it, while we went back upstairs to the drawing room. I went straight to the piano. "Do you know what I am playing?" I asked her. Even before she could hazard a guess, I told her. "It's 'All The Things You Are' in the key of E major. You know something else? I'm going to get a hard-on every time I play it in that key. She came over and stuck her tongue in my ear, before whispering into it, "Well, don't play it in that bloody key, unless I am here to suck it for you while you do."

Any further developments were halted by Meri wheeling in a trolley bearing a jug of coffee and a plate of biscuits. I noticed that this time, she knocked loudly before coming in.

As we sat, side by side on the sofa drinking our coffee, and smoking our cigarettes, she said to me in all seriousness "Jake, when you get a stiffy, will you think of me?"

"What do you think," I replied, and kissed her on her cheek.

She looked at her watch. "Christ I have to go," she blurted out, banging down her coffee cup and stubbing out her cigarette before leaping to her feet.

After a few more kisses, a last fondle of my cock, which she now referred to as 'Mister Big', and a solemn promise to phone me before leaving for Europe, she left. I went back to finish my coffee and cigarette, for some reason relieved to be on my own again.

The two policemen reappeared to ask me if I knew the name of the yacht the Earl was supposed to be cruising on, and also if I know the identities of his sailor buddies. When I told them I did not, Sad Ankles gave me his card, and asked me to phone him if I hear anything that might be of interest to him. I promised I would, and they left.

Then Meri came in to ask me if she could have the afternoon off, to 'veesit my seek seester.' I told her she could. She also asked me what she should do with the food that she had laid out in the dining room. I told her to leave it, in case I get hungry.

I went back to the bedroom to get some music from my still unpacked attaché case, with the object of spending the rest of the afternoon and evening practising the piano. Just beside the cupboard where Meri had stowed away my cases, I found the unbroken bottle of champagne and, not far from it, one of the flute glasses, also unbroken. I guess the depth and softness of the carpet had broken their fall. On searching around the room, I found the other glass and the tray under the bed. I took the lot back to the kitchen intending to leave them there for Meri to deal with upon her return in the morning. But the temptation was too much for me. Using my handkerchief as a napkin, I opened the bottle of Veuve Cliquot with a loud pop and poured myself a glass of the brilliant, fizzy bubbly.

I drank the first glass straight down, almost at a gulp. I poured another, but suddenly felt a little woozy and very hungry indeed. So taking the bottle and glass with me, I burped and hiccupped my way upstairs to the dining room where I polished off the two plates of poached fish which Meri had set out at either end of the table. I also wolfed down the bowl of boiled, but now cold potatoes and the excellently prepared salad that was sitting on the black lacquered trolley beside the table. I managed to polish off not only all the grub but the rest of the champers as well.

Then I went back to the drawing room, put four or five records on the record changer, and sat down on one of the deep, comfortable armchairs, to listen, eyes closed. The next thing I remember was being torn out of a deep sleep by an insistent telephone bell. I looked at my watch whilst trying to get my head together, prior to picking up the receiver. It was ten minutes before midnight, which meant that I had been zonked out for around seven hours.

"Hello."

"It's me." It was a woman's voice.

"Is that you Meri," I stumbled out. Why I thought it was Meri I cannot explain. I was obviously not yet firing on all cylinders.

"No, it fucking well isn't Meri. It's me; that person you were in bed with this afternoon."

"Oh Christ Candy" I said, now fully awake. "I ate all the fish that Meri had left out for us both, as well as a pile of potatoes and other stuff. And I also drank the entire bottle of champagne. I must have fallen asleep. You just woke me up. I'm only becoming compos mentis now."

"So you haven't missed me at all. After this afternoon I would have thought you might have given me one thought" Her voice was small and soaked in disappointment.

"Don't worry Candy darling" I said reassuringly... "I've already had my night's sleep. So, when I do go to bed, I'll lie awake and think of nothing but you. Count on it."

I was busking like mad, but it worked. She reverted to her normal sexy self.

"And what if thinking of me gives you a stiffy. What will you do then?"

"Why do you want to know?"

"Well," she said huskily, "I'm going to bed now, and I want to lie there and think about what you are doing inside those satin sheets."

"Well, if I do get a stiffy" I said, deliberately using her silly descriptive noun, "I'll transpose 'Cherokee' into F sharp major. That should fix any stiffy."

There was a long pause. This was clearly not the picture she wanted to conjure up as she lay in her bed. So she tried again.

"And what if you still have a stiffy after you have transposed whatever it was you said?"

"I'll just take myself in hand" I said quietly, knowing that this was what she wanted me to say.

"God, you are so rude Jake," she said kittenishly, but also happily. "But it's my property now, so be bloody careful how you handle it."

This typically adolescent banter went on for another fifteen minutes or so. Before I put the phone down, I had to promise that if I did 'take myself in hand', I would phone and tell her, no matter what time of the night it was.

I went downstairs to the kitchen and cooked up some scrambled eggs, made some tea and finally hit the sack about one o'clock in the morning.

I slept until eight-thirty in the morning. Carefully covering myself in a bath gown, I went into the kitchen, where I found Meri busily washing up the remains of the fish meal and my late supper.

"Good morning master" she said. She actually seemed pleased to see me.

I was in no mood for small talk. I never am at that time of the morning. But I did ask about her sister.

"Oh, she ees moch better, thank you master."

"Could I have a hot cup of anything?" I asked.

"Si. But what about your breakfast?"

"No, nothing just yet thank you Meri. I'll eat something after I am dressed."

"Okay, I make you a fresh pot of hot coffee."

"Good," I said. "And while you do that, I'll pop upstairs and find my cigarettes"

I had only just found them (under one of the armchairs), and stuffed them into my, or rather, the Earl's bath gown pocket, when the front door bell chimed. Being upstairs and knowing that Meri was busy making my much needed coffee, I answered the door myself. "I'll get it Meri," I yelled, as I went into the hall and up to the front door.

"Hello lover boy" Candy said, pushing past me down the short flight of stairs into the hall and on into the drawing room. As soon as I had followed her in and shut the door behind me, she opened her arms to me, eyes closed, face tilted upwards, lips shaped into a moue, waiting for me to take her in my arms and kiss her, which I duly did. Having done so and while she stayed nestled in my arms, I said "I didn't expect to see you again until after your Mediterranean jaunt."

"We don't leave until this afternoon" she said, looking up at me. "Aren't you glad I came?"

"Of course. But it is such a surprise."

With my arms still around her, she buried her head in my chest saying at the same time something which I didn't quite hear. It sounded lot like 'the manhole needs fixing again'.

As I reckoned that this was not the time nor the place to discuss London's sewerage system I reckoned I must have misheard what she actually said and thought it best to say nothing. Instead, I kissed her on top of her head, prior to asking her if she would like to join me for breakfast. But before I could get a word out she said it again, and this time I was sure of it. But probably due to my usual pre-coffee mental dwaal, I still didn't get it.

"What do you mean, the manhole needs fixing again?"

She put her arms around my neck and looking at me hotly, said "I mean that the manhole needs fixing again."

I still had no idea what the hell she was talking about.

"What manhole?"

"This manhole idiot." And she rucked up her skirt high enough to reveal that she was wearing nothing underneath. Then she slowly pulled the cord on my bath wrap, until it fell open. She pushed it over my shoulders, until it fell to he ground, leaving me naked. Taking my flaccid cock, in her hand, she backed me over to the settee. Then with skirt still rucked up, she lay down on it, one foot resting on top of the back of it, the other, obscenely dangling over the side.

"I've only got a half hour to get my manhole fixed" she said quietly but intensely. Then pointing to her cunt with her forefinger, she added, "So, Mister Big the plumber, get to work and fix it for me."

As I lay on top of her, she murmured breathlessly, "Oh God, I've been thinking and dying for you all night."

She took my hips between her hands so that she could control the speed and depth of our fucking.. Then, she suddenly wound her legs around me, holding me tightly. After a few minutes she started to gasp and moan.

"Oh keep it just like that, you sweet man. Oh yes don't stop. Oh yesss."

It was somewhere around this point in Candy's orgasmic cycle (I was frantically transposing 'Stella By Starlight' into F sharp major), that Meri, would you believe, decided to arrive carrying a tray with coffee pot, sugar, milk and two cups and saucers. Once again she had to back into the room. Once again she turned to find me stark naked, going at it hammer and tongs with Candy. And once again she shrieked, this time, thankfully, a lot less shrilly. But this time she was familiar enough with the routine to put the tray down on the coffee table before rushing out of the room.

As I turned my head round to see what Meri was up to, Candy gasped, "Just keep going. Don't stop. Oh, just keep...oooh. And she came, loudly and long. I followed her less than a minute later.

She immediately pushed me off her. "I must go" she said, getting up from the sofa and smoothing down her concertina of a skirt.

"Pour the coffee and light two ciggies," she said matter-of-factly. "I have to go to the little girls room."

"It's next to the front door," I called out after her as she disappeared out of the room.

I got up off the sofa, recovered my bath gown and put it on. Then, as I sat, drinking my desperately needed cup of coffee and dragging in deep lungfuls of cigarette smoke, I realised that I was just a wee bit annoyed by Candy. She always appeared to be in a hurry and was always annoyingly pushing me into doing what she wanted, regardless of my feelings. It was like being in a fast car, with her always at the wheel and always deciding what route to take. I was being subjugated by her selfishness. I knew she was going away for a couple of weeks, so I decided, there is not much point having it out with her now. I thought it best to wait until she gets back to London, when I will probably be calling the whole thing off anyway.

Having now made that decision, I was more at ease when she came bustling back into the room. She snatched up her coffee cup and cigarette and drank and smoked standing up.

"I'm getting bloody sick and tired of that Latin-American maid of yours" she said. "She's always there when you don't want her to be." As she bent down to put her now empty coffee cup onto the saucer, she added "And another reason I hate her is because she's seen more of your arse than I have."

"She has seen more of my arse than I have" I said as I stubbed out my cigarette, and stood up to escort Candy off the premises.

As I led her towards the drawing room door, I asked her, "How's the manhole?"

"Completely fixed. You know you give a wonderful plumbing service. God, I wish I could cut that mister big of yours off and take it with me to Cannes." Then at the front door, she said, "Promise me that while I am away and you do it to yourself, you'll think of me. Because when I do it, I'm definitely going to think of you—and that wonderful big thing of yours." Then getting up on her toes, she put her arms around me, and we kissed passionately and long. She suddenly broke off the kiss, turned and ran for the front door, still in a hurry for heaven knows what.

I tip-toed past the dining room, where I could hear Meri cleaning. I ran down to my bedroom, showered and dressed as quickly as I could and sneaked out of the apartment. After what had happened so soon after I had assured her it wouldn't, I did not know how to face her.

I walked as quickly as I was capable the quarter of a mile or so to Harrods, where I bought a large bunch of flowers for a pound, pinned a little note to it saying 'I am very sorry Meri. It will never happen again and I really mean it. Forgive me. Jake'. I put the card into the little envelope provided, and also folded in a pound note before sticking it down. Then I hurried back to the apartment block and gave the cellophaned bunch of flowers to the hall porter, asking him in my very best Noel Coward accent if he would be a good chap and bring them up to my apartment in about ten minutes. I bunged him a ten shilling note at the same time.

"My pleasure sir" he said as he took the money.

In the lift on the way up, I became aware of how hungry I was, But I decided to wait until after Meri had received her flowers, before venturing down to the kitchen to ask her to make me some grub. Hearing her vacuuming one of the downstairs carpets, I kept out of her way, by staying in the study, trying to work out the best way to write the letter I know I have got to write to my Aunt and Uncle.

A few minutes later, I heard the front door chime. I inched open the door that leads from the study into the hall, in order to listen and watch. I heard Meri answer the door, and after a very few words with the porter, I watched her go past me on her way down stairs, holding the flowers. I waited another full five minutes before going to the kitchen to ask for some breakfast.

As I came in, she said, with not a trace of a smile, "Yes master?"

"Hello Meri" I said. Neither of us said any more as I watched her busy little hands clean and dry the two coffee cups as well as the black, glass, ash tray into which Candy and I had stubbed out our cigarettes. Her face was expressionless and cold. I noticed that the flowers were lying on the kitchen table, unopened and untouched.

"Look" I said, "I really am sorry for what happened. It certainly won't happen again. I was hoping that the flowers..."

"Yes, the flowers," she said, cutting me off. She indicated them with her head as she continued with her washing and drying.

"Do you weesh me to send them to her, or ees she coming here to collect them?"

I picked the flowers off the table and holding them out to her, I said "No Meri, they are for you. It was the only way I could think of to show how sorry I am for what hap..."

"For me?" she said, turning around to look at me, her fat, soapy little fingers spread against her chest, her eyes wide with surprise.

"For you. See, your name is on the envelope here," I said pointing to the little pinned-on envelope.

"I not know how to read master." She said, taking the flowers from me and after lying them gently back down on the table, standing for a time gazing at them in awe, as if they were the crown jewels.

"They are for me master?" she asked again in half disbelief.

"Yes Meri. They are for you."

I watched her as she unpinned the envelope with great care, gently opening it and taking out the card and the money. And with card in one hand and money in the other, she switched on her Harpo Marx expression as she looked in wonderment, from the card in one hand to the money in the other and the cellophaned flowers resting on the table.

"The card just says how sorry I am. And I am sorry Meri. It really won't happen again, and I mean it."

Now, to my utter surprise, her attitude changed to flirtatious. "You are very naughty master. But very nice" She gave me a meaningful little smile, fluttering her eyelashes at me at the same time, like some silent movie vamp.

'Oh, shit' I thought. 'I've overplayed it again'.

"I'm a bit hungry" I said, not only because I was, but also in the hope that by saying something so mundane, it would bring her out of her love-daze and back into the real world. She acted as if she hadn't heard me as she gently gathered up the flowers and laid them down lovingly at the far end of the room.

"It hasn't got to be special" I said. "I'll eat anything you've got handy."

Then, still stroking the cellophane wrapping she turned to face me. "Would you like me to go out and buy some sausages and bacon and theengs like tha'?"

Her face still carried a knowing, secretive little smile, and her eyes were still shining, whilst her eyelids continued to flutter Theda Bara style.

"No, no. Just some tea and toast and, if you have any, some marmalade or jam. After that, I will work out with you, a shopping list which you can then go out and buy." I was trying to sound and act as business-like as I knew how.

As she poured the cold tap-water into the kettle, she said "The yong lady, she mos' love you bery much. Eet ees because master ees a very nice yong man" Then she turned to me, presumably, to check on the effect of her compliment. I made the mistake of smiling back at her, because she immediately went back into her silent movie-queen routine. It was clearly time for me to get out of the kitchen.

"Well, I have some work to do in the study" I said in what I hoped was a cheerily and off-hand manner. "If you don't mind Meri, serve the breakfast in the drawing room and then call me."

"Whatever you weesh master," she answered, still somewhat flirtatiously.

I went up the stairs to the study, where I retrieved the three or four attempts I had already made at writing to my folks. I extracted sentences or ideas from each, finally coming up with a pretty good stop-gap of a letter. Before writing it, I carefully cropped the top couple of inches off the writing paper, because it was necessary to lose the Earls family crest. The final draft went like this:

My dearest Auntie, Uncle and Ivan,

I write to tell you that I have some great news for you. However, at this time I am too busy to be able to explain fully what it is. But, over the next few days I will be in touch with you about us all getting together, when I will tell you everything. But please be assured that I am in good health and high spirits. You can definitely expect a call from me early next week. Do not worry in the meantime. I hope you are all well.

Love,

Jake.

I folded it carefully into an envelope and after sealing it put into my inside jacket pocket.. Then I counted my money to see how much I had left. It came to seventy-two pounds. I took out ten pounds for Meri to buy food with, plus another fifteen pounds, to cover her two weeks salary, which would take me up to the end of the month. After that, I will be earning money, so paying her thereafter, should represent no problem.. The remaining forty-seven pounds, I stuffed back into my side trouser pocket. I reckoned that this was ample to last me for three weeks before I get my first pay-check. Meri, with hands held provocatively on hips, came in to inform me that my breakfast was on the table in the drawing room.

I pretended not to notice her attempt at sultry sexuality. "Meri, here is some money to buy us some food, and here is your salary up to the end of the month" I spoke in as formal a way as I could. She took the money from me in a manner that suggested it was for her sexual services, rather than a straightforward arrangement.

"Oh master, thank you. I hope you like me master." And then into the Theda Bara bit again as she said "Because I like master *bery* much."

"That is very kind of you" I said, unable to think of anything more apposite.

"Now, I must eat because I am very hungry." I used this as cover for hurrying out from under her loving gaze, making my way briskly into the drawing room, to find not only a superbly made omelette to accompany my tea and toast, but she had also taken one of the roses from the spray I had bought her, and laid it alongside the meal. I picked up the rose and as I put it on the piano, to keep it out of harms way, I said to myself, 'Shmuck, what have you got yourself into'.

After breakfast I went back to the florist in Harrods, where I again bought a large spray of flowers, this time for Aunt Sarah. I pinned my letter to the cellophane, and paid the extra five shillings the shop charged for it to be delivered that very day.

After that, I took a stroll around Knightsbridge, digging its smart sophistication, and congratulating myself on my wonderful life style. Here I was, with over forty-five pounds in my pocket, a great job, doing what I like to do more than anything in the world, as well as a fabulous apartment in the most fashionable part of London.

Being at a loose end, I decided to see how the 'Four in Hand' was coming along. I knew it was in a street called Montrose Place, near Belgrave Square, because Jack had already told me that much. But finding it was another matter. It wasn't until I had walked all the way down to Hyde Park Corner that I found a newspaper seller who knew where Montrose Place was. Prior to that, I had asked at least a half dozen people, none of whom had ever heard of it, even though I discovered that they were professing their ignorance of a street that was not more than a couple of hundred yards from where they were standing at the time. Since then, the same thing has happened to me in New York City, Chicago, Washington, Johannesburg, and indeed every large town I have ever visited; local people often know less about their own cities than the visitors and tourists.

The 'Four in Hand' was still a complete mess. Men were hurrying in every direction carrying long planks of wood, large rolls of carpet, lengths of wiring and piping. A large paint-stained sheet lay in one corner of the large room, on which stood a table laden with tins of paint, drills, and some other equipment, which, not being a builder, I could not identify. Also the noise of hammering and drilling was deafening. I looked about but could find no-one there that I knew. I did finally manage to find the architect overseeing the work who told me that Jack Montgomery was away in France, and that the piano would not be arriving for at least another two days. So, it being a cloudless, crispy cold, but invigorating day, I opted for a stroll around Belgravia to take in the magnificent mansions around Belgrave Square.

For those of you who don't know London, Belgrave Square is just a short walk from Buckingham Palace, which, according to my Modern History tutor, was why the aristocracy chose to put their grand houses there. In fact, the histories of these uppest of our upper classes would make Al Capone appear small time. The vast fortunes amassed by these titled and deeply respected families was mostly founded in murder, robbery, slavery and crookery on a scale that Scarface Al never even dreamed of. And that was only for starters.

But those kind of thoughts were far from my mind as I strolled around the tree-lined square that late, early winter morning. After all, without houses of this grandeur there would not be a club called 'The Four in Hand' opening its doors shortly, because it was set in the basement of one of them, even though in this particular case, the rest of the building served as the European Head office of an American-Arab oil corporation. And without the aforesaid club opening, Jake Silver would still be occupying a draughty, freezing cold, ferschtunkene little room, schlepping to and from Newcastle University, instead of being the young man about town I now saw myself as.

Quite suddenly, I was struck by a mad desire to start practising the piano again. I all but ran back to the apartment, where I flung myself at the piano and happily did three straight hours of finger exercises.

Meri came in to see me, apparently after she had done the shopping, because she was carrying four carrier bags, full of food.

I got her to make me what was then my favourite meal; a large rump steak, with fried onions and a couple of fried eggs over, together with a pile of French fries. I went on practising while she cooked it and after I had polished it off, did yet another couple of hours.

Thereafter, I practised the piano for five hours or so every day. Meri, still eying me coquettishly, told me that she was worried 'because master work too hard'.

I told her not to worry, and that I do not work as hard as she does and also that I am bigger and stronger than her. Occasionally, she would shyly ask me to play some Cuban music, and I would always oblige, even though I always played the same two or three pieces because I did not know any other Cuban songs.

Chapter 20

The very fact that I had promised to phone Aunt Sarah but had not yet done so, weighed upon me more with every passing day until finally, it got too heavy and I decided to go for it, regardless of whether or not it meant a big wrangling argument.

"Hello, who's there?" There was no mistaking her voice, nor the sentry-box technique she always employed when answering the phone.

"It's me Auntie. Jake." There was a long silence before she spoke: "Oh, so you finally decided to telephone your old Aunt and Uncle, Mister Big-shot-who-is-too-busy-to-tell-his-Auntie-what-he-is-doing."

"I know I should have phoned you earlier Auntie, but I've had so much to do setting up my new life."

"YOUR new life! YOUR new life! What about MY old life? Don't worry about that. Don't worry about the fact that I've been worried sick about you. Just concentrate on your new life and the hell with all those who love you."

"I'm sorry Auntie. But you did get my flowers didn't you? That should have made you stop worrying about me."

"Made me stop? Made me stop?" She was really swinging now. She even invoked over the phone the invisible friend she always brought into her arguments. "He walks out of university without a word to anybody," she told it. "He then sends us some meshugenah letter without any explanation as to what has got himself into. And then I'm supposed to stop myself worrying."

There was a long angry silence after that because firstly, I didn't respond and secondly because she had got off her chest everything she wanted to say. So, when she did speak again it was in a far more conciliatory tone of voice.

"Anyway, thank God you are safe. So where are you staying? Was my house not grand enough for you Mister Big-shot? And then in a voice hard-edged with suspicion; "Or are you shacking up with that shiksa? Oy, you and Ivan, you're a right pair, you two.

"Auntie, listen to me" I said patiently. "The reason I am not staying with you is because it is too far from where I work. And the affair with the Janine, or the shiksa, as you choose to call her, is over, if it ever really began."

"Does that mean that I am expected to believe that you are living all on your own and doing your own laundry and cooking your own meals? Do you think I was born yesterday?" Then, suddenly in a horror-struck voice, "Oh my God you haven't got married?!"

"No, I have not got married and..."

"Gott se danken..."

"...I have a maid who comes in every day to look after me. I really phoned (even though I had only just thought of it), to ask you, Uncle Harry and Ivan to come and have some tea with me here at my place. Then you can see how and where I am living. At the same time I'll tell you what I am up to. Oh, yes, and tell Ivan he can bring his fiancée, whose name I have forgotten, with him."

"Over my dead body will he bring that scheming little shiksa along" she said venomously.

"Shiksa? What are you talking about? Ivan is marrying one of the most typically Jewish girls I have ever met. Aren't they eng...?"

"You see, you've been out of touch for so long that you don't know."

"I don't know what?"

After a pause, she said "You don't know that Ivan, my beautiful Ivan, who NOTHING has been too good for, who we have treated like a PRINCE, has repaid all our loving care and devotion by giving up his wonderful, sweet natured, decent, Jewish girl-friend, to fall into the clutches of some shiksa from Leeds." She was crying now as she said, "And he doesn't even care that he's breaking his mother's heart."

I have never been able to stand idly by when a woman cries. And when that woman is someone I love, it becomes doubly so.

"Look, I don't even know what this is about but please stop crying Auntie. Come over tomorrow afternoon at around four and I'll talk to Ivan. Maybe I can change his mind. I can make Ivan listen to me, I'm sure of it. Don't you worry Auntie. Come over tomorrow and let me see what I can do."

Of course I had no intention of even bothering to try. As far as I was concerned any chick would be better than that rich, no account little goody-goody he had been engaged to. But it was the only thing I could think of saying to make her stop crying.

"You're a good boy Jake darling." She managed to tumble out through her sobs. "We'll come to you tomorrow for tea, please God." I noticed her crying was lessening; "And don't worry about food. We'll bring it with us."

"Bring nothing but yourselves" I said firmly. "The food has already been bought."

The sobbing had by now almost stopped. "Okay, Mister Big-Shot, Big Spender. We'll come to you tomorrow. And Jake darling, promise that you will do your best to talk Ivan out of this terrible mistake he is making."

"I promise I'll try."

She brightened considerably. "I know you will. And who knows? He may listen to you, please God. He won't listen to his father or mother."

I gave her my address which she wrote down and read back to me, adding "It sounds very fency-shmency Jake" she said before ringing off.

Looking back on it now, it seems incredible to me that someone as utterly practical and down to earth as Aunt Sarah, could entertain for a single minute, that I, a lad of eighteen years, would be capable of persuading an adult man to give up the girl he was quite clearly so much in love with that he was prepared to defy his parents over. And for Ivan to actually go against the wishes of his mother and father was something that had never before happened. 'So, what did she expect of me? That I knew the magic word that would break the witches spell and turn Ivan the Frog-Shiksa lover, back into Ivan the Prince-nice-Jewish-girl lover'? How someone as hard-headed as my Aunt could have seen Ivan's future through the stuff of fairy tales should have seemed ridiculous to me even then, when I was in reality just a kid. It for sure seems crazy to me now.

What did occur to me shortly after I had put the phone down was that her troubles with Ivan might prove to be a Godsend for me. Without that distraction, I was sure that I would have had trouble about giving up my studies. But with Ivan front and centre in her mind, my career move might appear to her to be just a minor indiscretion. Especially as I am still seeing Candy.

I went downstairs to find Meri ironing my shirts, handkerchiefs and underpants. I could not help but notice that she was wearing one of the flowers I had given her in her hair. I felt it was incumbent upon me to mention it.

"The rose looks nice in your hair Meri" I said.

I think she blushed at this compliment. With her pale complexion it was difficult to be sure.

She smiled demurely, and looking off to the side of me, while flashing her eyes across at me, she said "I wear eet to theenk of you master."

'Oh shit' I thought. "That is very nice of you," I said. Then, in order to break up her embarrassing attempt at being romantic, I went into my business-like thing.

"Listen Meri, my Aunt and Uncle are coming to see me tomorrow for tea. I want you to go out in the morning and buy some lovely cakes and currant buns and anything else you can think of. Then I want you to buy yourself a new pinafore so that you look lovely and smart when they arrive."

"Does the Master theenk I am lovely then?"

('Oh Christ, why did I use that word'.) "Well I think you are a very nice girl, and you are lovely to me" I had to hope I had got myself out of it. Judging by the look on her face I had not.

I gave her another five pounds to buy the food and pinafore, saying, "If this is not enough tell me."

"Eet ees plenty master."

I was just leaving to go back upstairs when Meri called me back. "Master."

I turned round to her. She was still ironing as she asked "I no see your lady frien' no more. Have you finished weeth her master?"

"No Meri. She has had to go somewhere with her father. She'll be back in a couple of weeks."

Her face fell. "I'm not sure for how long though" I added confidentially, although I'm buggered if I can remember why I did so. Upon reflection I suppose it was to cheer her up. It certainly succeeded.

"That ees very good master" she said smiling broadly. Then she added, "Ees tha' because master has found a new lady frien'?" Her gaze was heavily concentrated on the pair of my underpants she had on the ironing board before her.

"No Meri, I have not found myself a new lady friend yet." And I got out of there before the conversation led into something I instinctively knew I would not be able to handle.

Around half past noon the next day, just as I had completed my three hours of piano exercises, Meri brought in my coffee. She was wearing her new outfit, which was very nice although a trifle wrong for her. She had bought herself a French maids' outfit, with the black satin dress and the frilly little white apron over, as well as the white, starched cotton coronet in her hair. On Lana Turner it would have been a gas. On podgy little Cuban Meri it looked all wrong. But it was crisp and clean and I was far too immature anyway to tell her to take it back and get something plainer,

"You look very nice Meri" I said, and before she could go into her silent movie-vamp number, I changed the subject abruptly by asking in a very matter-of-fact way, "Now what have you decided to make for our tea."

"I buy brown brea', som caviar and som smoke salmon, som chocolate éclairs, som plain cake an' som biscuits master. I also bring out the Seelver tea set and I also have som champagne in the freedge."

"Wow," I said.

"Eet ees what master John buys when he has the yong boys to tea. I buy the same."

"But he orders it for another reason"

"Pardon master?"

"Nothing. What did it all cost?"

"I have the beels downstairs master. It cost nine pounds, five pounds for the food and two pounds for my new clothes.

I gave her the extra four pounds. But what with having to keep back another twenty-five pounds for my new dress suit and with still almost three weeks to go before getting paid, I was starting to worry about my rapidly shrinking stash of money.

As she took the four pounds she gave me that sly smile and glittery-eyed look some girls assume after you have paid them for some sexual service or other. I found myself thinking, after she had gone out of the room, and while I was drinking my coffee, why it was that now that I actually have two chicks who fancy me, both have to be physically the opposite of everything I like in a female. 'Maybe I'll get lucky once I am playing at the new club. Maybe some dish of a doll will ditch her boyfriend and come home with me.' I thought.

The visit of Aunt Sarah, Uncle Harry and Ivan turned out to be much as I had expected... Aunt Sarah was quiet and watchful, sitting primly on the drawing room sofa, like someone on her best behaviour. She was clearly intimidated by the opulence plus the unfamiliarity of the place. The only time she came to life was when Meri came in with the champagne. Then she switched on her x-ray vision to study Meri's brain wave patterns, quite astutely as it happened. The moment Meri had left the room, my Aunt said to me, "She's a nice girl that one. But don't let her get too close. I know these peasant types. If you get too friendly, she'll think you're in love with her, and then you'll have to throw her out."

Meanwhile, Uncle Harry and Ivan were wandering about the room, examining and valuing every item. 'Fency-shmency' the family word invariably used to describe anything classy, was being thrown around like confetti at a wedding. When we went into the Japanese-style dining room, it was as if they were unused to luxury, which I of course knew to be untrue. Uncle

Harry and Ivan were ooh-ing and aah-ing everything from the tall, pale green vase with its single yellow orchid, also made out of glass, gracing the centre of the table, to the hand painted silken panel that covered the entire door leading into the study.

Their biggest accolade was reserved for the ornate Georgian teapot and milk jug which Meri wheeled in on the ornate black lacquered food trolley.

"This tea set must be worth a thousand pounds" my uncle authoritatively informed us. After our tea, which he remarked must have cost me a fortune (which it had), I showed them the study-cum-office. Aunt Sarah was almost silent throughout the inspection tour. "Very nice," or, "Very nice indeed" was about the most that left her lips.

Uncle Harry and Ivan on the other hand were fulsome in their praises. Every book was looked over. The desk and the other furnishings were all minutely examined and valued.

Even my Aunt gasped when I showed them the trick that by which you gain access to the safe (although I lied by saying that I did not know the safe combination. The reason I did so, was because if my Aunt knew about the photographs that lurked inside, it would have been the end of my staying here). When we once more returned to the drawing room, she asked me "So where do you sleep?"

"Downstairs, in the main bedroom. Would you like me to show you?"

"Couldn't you get the maid to show Harry and me? I'm sure that Ivan wouldn't be interested."

"But I would be interested" he said in a protesting voice.

"I want you to stay here Ivan and talk to your cousin" Aunt Sarah said. "Maybe he can talk some sense into that fool head of yours."

The atmosphere changed from sunny to overcast in an instant.

"I don't want or need to get advice from anyone about my Janet" he answered, surprisingly belligerently for someone as even-tempered as Ivan. Before things got out of hand, which I knew only too well could be any minute, unless immediate action was taken, I jumped in with; "anyway, I want to talk to Ivan about Candy. So I'll take you two to the lift that will take you down to the lower level and Meri will show you around. And when you come back, you'll have some more tea while I show Ivan around" As I got up to go over to the special telephone that automatically connects with the kitchen, Uncle Harry said, "You are saying when you want to go to bed, you have to go back out into the hall and wait for the lift to take you down a floor?"

"No, no" I said laughing. "Of course not. This apartment has its own private, internal lift. It's at the end of the hall. I'll show you" I walked the two of them to the small lift at the end of the hallway. As they got into it, Uncle Harry said to me; "I must offer you my congratulations Jake my boy. You have found yourself an apartment in a million. You're living like a king. But try to remember that this won't last for ever son. Enjoy it while you've got it, but prepare yourself for when you have to move out of here and back to reality."

Aunt Sarah, who was already standing in the lift all the while Uncle Harry was unloading his words of wisdom, now cut in; "Leave the boy alone Harry. Let him go back and see if he can talk some sense into our idiot son."

As my Uncle stepped into the lift, he turned to me and said out of the corner of his mouth, "You can see, I've got big troubles here." I was conscious of the change in attitude of Aunt Sarah and Uncle Harry towards me. No longer was I the orphan baby of the family. Suddenly, I was being talked to and treated like I was their eldest. Probably, because I was no longer living with them, I had gained in stature in some way. Whatever the reason it made me feel adult and important.

When I came back into the study, Ivan was looking out of the French windows at the far end of the room. As he heard me come in, he said.

"Do you know that you can see almost as far as Hyde Park corner from here?"

"Yes," I said. "The view is wonderful from those French windows."

"Christ Jake, this is the best flat I have ever seen—and I've seen a few, believe me. In fact," he moved across the room to sit down in one of the two large armchairs that faced the merrily blazing fireplace, "I was wondering if Janet and I could stay here for a couple of nights, before we head off to America on our honeymoon?"

"You know you can" I said as I sat on one armchair while he took the other and turned it to face me. "But fill me in. When I last saw you, you were engaged to be married to what's-her-name. And then I remembered: "Irene I think her name was." Ivan nodded. "So what happened?"

"Ach, it's a long story Jake. I'll try to cut it short. Irene was and is a nice girl. She is really sweet. But too much sweetness can make you sick. Of course I didn't know it at the time. I thought that my life was now mapped out. I'll marry Irene and go into the movie making business with her father. But you once told me that business is not all that there is to life. And you were right Jake lad." He took out a leather cigar-case, took out a small Romeo and Juliet and offered me one. I opted for a cigarette instead. After we had both lit up I asked; "So nu, how did you meet this Janet and who is she?"

"Okay, I'll make it as brief as I can. Every week I go to a different provincial town and look around all the jewellery shops to see if they've got anything that might interest me. I do that because prices outside London are normally fifteen to twenty per cent lower and I sometimes find myself a real bargain. Well, this particular week, I chose Leeds to visit. When I told Irene she asked me to say hello to her cousin, Hilary Phillipson, who is around the same age as her, and who goes to Leeds University. So, having tired myself out schlepping around the town looking for bargains, I stopped to have a cup of coffee, and I thought that this is a good a time as any to phone this cousin of Irene and invite her to lunch. I was also thinking that even if she couldn't come, she might at least tell me the name of a good restaurant, because I hadn't been to Leeds since I was nine or ten years old, and I didn't know my way around. Anyway, Hilary Phillipson tells me that she would love to have lunch with me and can she bring along a friend who also goes to the University and whom she was supposed to be lunching with. I say sure. I take her advice as to where we should eat, and I arrange to meet her there at one o'clock. As I had never seen her or she me, I described myself to her as she does to me. I remember her saying, 'Look, there is nothing special enough about me to guarantee that I'll stand out enough for you to make an identification. But I will be with a girl who is tall and blonde, so if you see a short brunette with a tall blonde that'll be us. Oh yes, and she'll have a red ribbon in her hair.'

So, I went to this restaurant and I waited for them. It was a little place and I was glad I got there early, because I hadn't been in there fifteen minutes, and there was already a queue for tables that stretched out of the door. Suddenly, I was aware of this tall girl arguing with the head waiter. He was telling her that she had to take her place in the queue like everyone else and she was saying that she and her friend were meeting someone and wanted to see if he was in the restaurant.

Then I saw this little schnipke of a brunette standing next to her, clearly embarrassed by the argument. It didn't take me a minute to realise that the schnipke was Irene's cousin. They were so alike, and just like Irene she was clearly embarrassed by anyone making a fuss.

Anyway, having guessed who they were, I went over to them, identified myself, sorted the whole thing out with the head waiter and brought them over to my table, where we introduced ourselves. In fact, she didn't wait for Hilary to do the introductions. No sooner had I shaken hands and said hello to Hilary, than she put out her hand straight out to me and said, 'And my name is Janet Knowles-Robinson, how do you do'. And she looks me straight at me as she does so. I mention that because I was so surprised by it. I suppose it was because I had got so used to Irene, who most of the time, looks away as if she does not want her face to be seen. So as we shake hands and I am looking at her, Right away I am aware that she is very beautiful, with startling blue eyes, a perfect complexion; but best of all for me Jake, I knew right off that she was not complicated or complexed in any way. With Janet what you see is what you get. Anyway, over a plate of tomato soup, some chicken Kiev and a wedge of apple pie, I fell in love for the first time in my life. To start with, Cousin Hilary was so like Irene in attitude and temperament, that it was easy for me to make comparisons between Janet and her. Hilary withdrawn, shy mono-syllabic and secretive; Janet, open-faced, out-going, honest and with lots to say. And a stunner to look at."

"She sounds great" I had to admit.

"You haven't the heard half of it" He was clearly relieved at having someone who was sympathetic he could talk to about his great, all-consuming love. "When she got up to go to the loo as she calls it, I made it my business to take a long look at her from head to toe."

"And?" I asked

"And" he repeated, I see that she has a great body, about two or three inches taller than me, with long legs, and an athletic figure rather than a show-girl's shape." His face had assumed an expression of pure joy as he went on kvelling about her. "But it wasn't just her face and figure Jake; it was the way she looked at you when she spoke to you, her mannerisms as she turned her head or something, the way she sits..."

While he went on eulogising, his eyes alight with rapture, I could not help thinking that there was more chance of being struck by lightning on a cloudless summer day, than there was of talking this guy out of miss Janet Knowles-Robinson.

..."Anyway," Ivan was saying when I re-tuned in "She was going on about the fact that she was in her final year before becoming a doctor. Meanwhile, all the time she is talking" he went on, "I'm falling more and more for her. So now we've finished lunch, I've paid the bill and we are getting up to leave the restaurant and go our separate ways. Honestly Jake, I could not stand the thought of that. I had to see her again. Quick as a flash, I came up with the idea that I am throwing a party on the Saturday night in London and would they both like to come. Hilary said she would love to. Janet says she would like to come as well but can she bring her fiancée along. When she said that, my heart fell though the soles of my shoes. But I said it would be okay. At the same time I got her home phone number, on the pretext that should anything go wrong I would like to phone and postpone it. Well kid, I wandered around Leeds supposedly doing business, but unable to think about anything but this Janet Knowles-Robinson. And the more I thought about her, so the more I realised that not only did I not want to go back to Irene; I knew I would not be able to face the whole sham of trying to pretend to her that nothing had changed between us. I was sitting in the taxi that was taking me back to the train station, when I decided; I would stay overnight in Leeds, and try to see her once more before I leave. The moment I got into my hotel room, I phoned her. I swear my heart bounced when I heard her voice say 'hallo'. I had no idea what to say, so I began stumbling out the first thing in my mind. "Why weren't you wearing the red ribbon in your hair?" I asked her.

'How do you know I wear a red ribbon in my hair and what difference does it make?' she said.

'If you had worn your red ribbon, I would have known it was you. Then I could have saved you an argument with the head waiter'.

'I only wear it when I am cycling' she said. 'It's to keep the hair out of my eyes. Hilary gave me a lift in her little car, so I left the bicycle back at college". But then, being Janet, she then goes on to say; "But that is the flimsiest reason I have ever heard for anyone phoning anybody. So would you have the good grace to tell me what this phone call is really about?"

"Guess what I said Jake?"

I hoped the raised-eyebrows expression on my face indicated that I had no idea.

I said, 'The real reason for this call is to tell you that I think I have fallen in love with you'. Before she could say anything, I said 'I am staying in a hotel here in Leeds instead of returning to London, because now that I have met you, I can't face going back to my fiancée. Look Janet' I said, 'I must see you just once more before I go back to London'. Jake, I couldn't believe that it was me saying these things."

"So what did she say to that?" I was actually intrigued with this hitherto unknown romanticism lurking in the heart of my cousin.

"Well" he said," It began with a long, long pause. It was so long that I was just about to put down the phone. Then she said quietly 'That was a wonderful thing to say to me and I am wildly flattered. I have a lot of studying to do tonight. But, if you wish I could meet you for a pre-dinner cocktail, at about six-thirty'.

'Where?' I asked:

'Where are you staying?' she said.

'I am at the Station Hotel.'

'I'll see you in the bar in half an hour', and she put down the phone.

"Well, she arrived smack on time and we talked for a solid hour. She told me her fiancée was also at the University, taking a law degree. She said she assumed I was Jewish because Hilary had told her as much. She wanted to know if my family would object to me dating a non-Jewish girl, let alone marrying one. I told her that I had my own business, and that I did not know how my family would react to me giving up a Jewish girl in favour of a non-Jewish one, but that I did not care how they felt. I told her that I would like to come to Leeds at least once a week to see her. I also said that if after say six weeks or so, I was still as crazy about her as I am at that very moment, and if she could find it in her heart to learn to love me, then I would consider it an honour if she would consent to marry me. That was two months ago. Ten days ago, I met her parents to ask for their daughter' hand and they agreed.

"Two questions" I said.

"Well?"

"The first question is; what happened to the fiancée she already had when you first met her? And the second is; what happened when you told Irene?"

"As to the first question it was a case of lucky timing. To start with they were not actually engaged to be married. It turned out that it was one of those things where they had known one another since they were kids. And the two families were close. Janet's father served in the Navy as a naval surgeon and the boy friend's father was a naval officer also. Apparently, they both joined up the same day. You know, it was the usual crap when families are that close. Both families assumed that the marriage of the oldest daughter and the eldest son was a guaranteed certainty. But it turned out that the boy friend is stuck on joining the Royal Air Force once he gets his degree in engineering, which apparently means that he must be available for an overseas posting. And Janet, after she becomes a doctor, wants to do research into tropical diseases at the Hospital for Tropical Diseases here in London and so has no intention of going overseas to live. He refused to change his career plans and so did she. So there was an impasse. And that is when I came along."

"She sounds just a bit obstinate to me," I ventured to suggest.

"No, it's not that. Rather it is that she knows what she wants, and, in any case, I don't think she was in love with the guy."

"And she's in love with you?"

"Well, she is going to marry me. Isn't that sufficient proof for you?"

"And what about Irene?" I asked.

After a thought-filled drag on his cigar, he said.

"Well that was a different matter entirely. Of course there were floods of tears. But after she had cried herself out, she grudgingly accepted that I had a right to change my mind, and that it was better to do it now before the engagement party, rather than after it. Unfortunately, Irene's mother phoned to give my mother the news before I could tell her myself. And you know your Aunt Sarah: she believes that if it's a family matter, she must be the first to hear it. So I was confronted with big, big trouble on two fronts. Not discussing it with her before I told Irene, and daring to fall in love with a non-Jewish girl..."

..."And thwarting the plans she had made for you," I added.

He nodded. Then he said with sheer misery writ large on his face, "Jake, from that day to this, it has been a nightmare for me. It's driving me mad. The only time I am happy is when I am with Janet. Living at home is now pure torture" Then, his hurt expression now tinged with hope he asked; "Actually, I was wondering if you can help me by talking to Mom. I think she has got a bit of respect for you. I mean you have found your own feet. And you have got a Jewish girlfriend in Candy..."

"Not for long," I said.

"What does that mean?"

"It means Ivan, that even though I like her, she's way too selfish for me. She only thinks of herself. What pleases her seems to be the only thing that matters.. She doesn't need a husband; she needs a guy with a slave complex. And I am not that person. So when she returns from Cannes, its heave-ho time for her, I'm afraid."

"Is that absolutely definite?"

"Absolutely" I replied.

"Well...in that case I'll tell you something you were not supposed to know"

"What is it?"

"After she's been with her father in Cannes for a week, she's off to Paris with a close girl friend of hers...

"She told me was going..."

"To get an abortion."

"How could you possibly know that?" I asked. For no reason I could fathom, I felt hurt, jealous and angry all at the same time.

"It so happens that the girl friend she went with is also a close friend of Irene's."

"Does her old bat of a mother know?"

"I don't know, but I doubt it."

After a pause in the conversation, because there was nothing more I could think of to say, Ivan continued, "What I was going to ask you, before the subject of Candy came up, was to talk to my mother to try to get her to change her mind about Janet."

"Well, here's something you didn't know" I said. "Aunt Sarah asked me if, while they are out of the room, I could talk you into changing your mind about Janet."

I waited while Ivan took a couple of drags on his now dwindling cigar. Then he said quietly without looking in my direction: "So how well did you think you did—in talking me out of her, I mean?"

"About zero out of a hundred" I said.

He nodded happily, "That's about right." Then a thought seem to strike him. "One more thing Jake: for Chrissakes, don't tell Mom anything about Candy. Don't mention that you two are breaking up. She's suffering enough with me giving up Irene..."

..."To marry a scheming shiksa," I joked.

"That's not funny, even as a joke. But if you were to add to it by telling her about you and Candy, it might prove too much for her."

"Don't worry about that Ivan." I said. "If the opportunity arrives naturally, I'll do my best to try and get her to at least meet Janet."

"And her parents. That is just as important." Ivan added.

"Okay. Janet and her parents"

Thanks Jake" he said earnestly, reaching over to grab and then squeeze my forearm. It was clear that he really appreciated my being in his corner.

"And if the opportunity does arise, mention this..."

But I never found out what 'this' was, because at that moment, Aunt Sarah and Uncle Harry came back into the room. Uncle Harry was as near to excited as I have ever seen him.

"It's wonderful. You've got a wonderful place here Jake my boy. Try to hang on to it as long as possible"

"It's very nice. Very nice indeed" said Aunt Sarah. But I could hear and feel the reservations in her voice.

"But?" I asked her.

She did not respond. I tried again.

"Auntie," I said. "You said it was very nice, except you left a big 'but' hanging in the air."

"Well, I was talking to Meri" she said, "And she is a very nice girl. A bloody sight more efficient than my Olga. But she is also an innocent little girl, and from what she gave away to me about this Earl of somewhere or other, who owns this place, well I don't want to be too graphic, but I think this apartment was a hotbed of corruption and I don't want you having to mix with those kinds of people, even if it means moving out of this place."

Uncle Harry jumped in to tell her that she is talking nonsense, saying that I am living like a king, and she should be happy for me, not raising silly obstacles.

"Auntie," I said, switching into my confident smile routine in the hope that it would make her feel less worried; "The Earl is way for at least two years. None of us really know what he got up to while he was here and I personally don't really give a damn. After all he's not staying here is he?" Even while I was speaking, I was aware of my admiration for her Sherlock Holmes powers of perception and deduction.

After another hour or so of small talk, the three of them rose to their feet simultaneously, like herons rising from a lake, in order to take their leave. Uncle Harry came over to me and put his arm around my shoulder to turn me away from where Aunt Sarah and Ivan were standing, presumably so that they should not know what he is saying, asked me in a low, confidential voice, if I needed any money. I told him I had plenty left over from what he has been sending me in Newcastle. But at the same time I made a mental note to phone the University in Newcastle and ask them to forward my mail, among which should be two further week's wages from Uncle Harry, which would be more than enough to see me through until my first payday.

As they filed out of the front door, Aunt Sarah hung back in order to ask me about my conversation with Ivan.

"I'm worried about Ivan" I told her. "He is driving himself mad trying to bridge what he sees as an unbridgeable chasm. On the one side is the girl he is crazy about—and I do mean heavily in love with. On the other side he is torn with guilt and worry about you. If this goes on much longer Auntie," I said with all the phoney sincerity that I could summon up, "I think he could have a complete nervous breakdown. Only you can stop it from happening."

"So I must put my head in a gas oven in order that my son to be happy. Is that what you are saying?"

"No it isn't Auntie, and you know it isn't." I said. Uncle Harry was now calling her to say that the lift was waiting. She appeared to take no notice.

"You have given most of your life to making Ivan and me happy" I said. I placed my hands on her sturdy shoulders; "Make one more big sacrifice Auntie. Agree to meet Janet and her parents. That would make Ivan happier than you can possibly imagine. It might also save his reason."

She stared hard into my face, saying nothing. But I thought I detected at the back of her eyes, a glimmer of recognition of the immutability of the facts as they now were. Without another word to me, and clearly deep in thought, she turned and walked down the corridor to join my Uncle and Ivan who were wrestling with the lift door to keep it open for her.

I knew I had exaggerated Ivan's position, but as I think back on it now, I realise that I was doing to her what she had been was so expert at doing in her dealings with Ivan and me: lading us with guilt. As she walked away from me, I had the feeling that it might have just worked.

Chapter 21

Around lunch time on the day before the opening, I went again to the 'Four In Hand' to see how things were progressing, and it was a helluva lot different to when I last saw it. Now, the club itself was completely finished, even though there was still some banging and sawing coming from somewhere out of my sight. Jack, who was busily checking and signing a pile of invoices, greeted me with a smiling "Ah, Jake my lad, good to see you." He asked me to give him another ten minutes or so to finish up his paperwork after which he suggested we lunch together. So I passed the time by trying out the new Steinway baby grand which was already set upon its six-inch high dais in the corner of the room. It was, like nearly all the Steinways built in Hamburg, a superb instrument. There was a spotlight built into the ceiling, which someone switched on while I was playing, and which bathed me in a pool of light. The piano lid had been removed and Jack had got someone to build a foot wide, felt-lined shelf, about six inches higher than the piano but which followed around the piano's shape. There were already three or four high stools in place around the piano. This was where the music lovers and lone drinkers could sit and get to know me or each other. As I sat there, fooling around with 'Smoke Gets In Your Eyes' (which I remembered from when I played at Jack's other club, was his favourite tune), I fantasised myself playing, whilst beautiful, deep bosomed, sexy women sat on their high stools, watching me play, love and desire for me pouring out of their eye-linered eyes. Some hope! But it did make me look forward to tomorrow's opening even more excitedly than before. Across the room I could now see Jack standing up and waving me over for lunch.

We ordered fillet steaks, which were very good indeed, and while we ate, I listened to Jack telling me about the club's lineage.

I learned that the entrance to the club was originally the tradesmen's entrance for the mansion, although no-one would ever think so now. Jack had put in a new, highly polished, black lacquered door, dressed with elegant brass fitments. (From the outside, the name of the club was nowhere to be seen. The only indication of where you were, was a small Victorian plaque, set just below the glistening curved door knocker, bearing a picture of a carriage, upon which sat a red-coated fellow, driving four high-stepping horses). I had already seen that the club was designed on the same lines as Jack's other club, in the Strand. There was a small vestibule, with a hat check cubicle, plus a George-the-something card table, with a large crocodile-bound signing-in book, for the members and their guests. From there, one went through heavy, dark red, floor-to-ceiling drapes, straight into the club itself.

Jack went on to tell me how the 'Four in Hand' was originally two large kitchens with an arched opening dividing them, to enable the kitchen staff to move easily from one kitchen to the other with their hands full. The larger of the two rooms had been for cooking the main courses, and contained a huge log fire with a large, copper turnspit. The smaller room was for baking cakes, savouries and pies etc. There was another room behind the baking room in which His Lordship's wines and spirits were stored.

Jack explained how he had widened the arch between the two rooms, so that it was now actually one very large room. The area that was originally the smaller kitchen together with part of the wine cellar behind it, was now a bar, with high stools running along it, plus a carpeted space, where members could stand and chat while they downed their booze. The remaining part of the wine cellar had been converted into Jack's private office.

He had retained the long, large, fireplace, in what had been the larger of the two rooms, and the turnspit had been polished up and retained for decoration. This main section of the club was designed so that about half of it consisted of armchairs and sofas, with small glass-topped tables close at hand, in order that there was always somewhere to rest your drinks etc. The other half was for those who wish to eat. There were about nine or ten smallish, round tables, all with tiny wheels attached to the table legs, so that your table can be wheeled over to you, should you wish to partake of the cuisine in some other part of the club.

I told Jack how crazy I was about my apartment.

"Oh, I'm so glad" he said. "D'you know, I've never been there. I have been told quite recently that the only reason he asked me to find someone to look after it, rather than a really close friend, or even an estate agent, was because he wanted to get away in rather a hurry, and I understand that he had good reason for not wanting any of his close friends to know anything about it. At least, not until he was a long way away."

I asked him what the Earl looked like.

"Johnny Brackington? Oh, I would say he's about your height, but much heavier than you of course. About forty years old I would reckon."

"Does he wear his hair parted in the middle, a bit like Oscar Wilde?" I asked.

"Now that you actually mention it, he does. But how do you know that? And why do you ask?"

I told him of the photos in the safe, and how the man in the pictures would appear to be the Earl, judging by Jack's description of him. Then I told him how the police had been to the apartment, enquiring about him. I also mentioned that they asked me to contact them if I hear anything of his whereabouts.

Jack looked up from his food, a strange, wry smile on his face. "You know lad, we all have our little secrets that we'd rather the world never heard about" Then he added, a little more pointedly; "I've always found it the best policy to keep quiet about any of these little secrets, whenever they came my way."

I nodded understandingly, a look of sagacity (I hope), on my face.

Opening night: I arrived early, about two hours before I was due to start playing. The club was now dressed in its finest finery. A red and gold canopy had been erected that reached from the front door to the pavement edge, under which stood a top-hatted, liveried doorman. Inside, there was now a young lady at the hat and coat cubicle. But unlike many of the places I later worked in, when I was in the USA, she was not scantily dressed. She was smartly, but primly attired in a black dress adorned with a string of pearls. I did not check my overcoat with her, preferring to leave it in Jacks office. Jack told me that the club already had over a hundred fully paid up members. And at fifty pounds a year per member, it meant that he was already five thousand pounds to the good. But, he added that he had already spent more than ten times that much preparing for the clubs opening.

"So Jake, don't expect a pay rise, for quite a long time."

I assured him that I didn't.

The main room of the place looked beautiful. The bar, with its two barmen polishing the champagne glasses; the soft, concealed lighting making it look the most inviting place to be. The fire was now lit and glowing red, the round dining tables were covered with white table cloths, upon which the silver cutlery and the empty wine glasses glistened as they reflected the lights from the candle-shaped electric table lamps that adorned each table. A couple of red jacketed waiters stood in one corner talking animatedly.

Jack and I had dinner together, although I barely ate, being far too excited to bother myself with anything as mundane as food. After we had eaten, Jack did a rather nice thing. He assembled the entire staff, including the doorman for a champagne toast to the new club.

The first customers started to dribble in at around eight-thirty. They were mostly friends of Jack, and by nine o'clock, when I started to play, the place was already half full.

Nothing much happened during the early part of the evening. Nobody took more than a moment's notice of me, which was, in a way, how I liked it. It allowed me to get used to the piano as well as the overall ambience of the room. It also allowed me to be musically more adventurous than I would have been if I were being listened to. Also, not getting any request tunes to play meant that I could give out with a selection of songs of my own choosing. Sadly for me, no beautiful women had been drawn by my magnetic personality to sit around the piano. In fact, not one single arse had yet come into contact with the red velvet stools set around the piano.

By ten o'clock, the club was full, mainly of business men, many of whom were American, and many of whom were already red-faced with drink. Some spoke very loudly in what I presumed was a Texan drawl, since they sounded to me like John Wayne (and some of them were every bit as big and beefy), and were not averse to shouting to one another across the room. I guessed they were probably executives from the oil company that occupied the rest of the building above us.

At about half past ten, by which time I had got quite used to my anonymity, a waiter came over to me bearing a glass of champagne and a five pound note on his tray. He put both down on the little table next to me which I had put there for my own drinks etc., and whispered in my ear as I went on playing; "It's from that big, tall American standing over there by the fireplace. He would like you to play 'Run Rabbit Run'." This was the very first tune requested by a customer and I hated it because it was so boringly 'British' in the worst sense of the word. But a five pound note is powerful inducement indeed. So, I stopped playing 'Mad About the Boy' and went into a couple of choruses of 'Run Rabbit Run'.

I was just coming to the end, when this six feet four inch, beefily built mountain of a man came over to me, and putting down another five pound note on the piano music rest, said in a deep, resonant, but powerful voice; Play it again for me will ya? Hey what's your name son?"

He looked to me to be about forty years old with a thick head of auburn-coloured hair on top of his thick, tough-looking florid face. He was smartly dressed in a single-breasted blue pin-stripe suit.

"Jake" I said as I slid the second five pound note into my inside jacket pocket.

"Stop playin' for a minute Jake willya?"

When a guy as big and as drunk as he was, says 'stop playing', the hippest thing to do is stop playing.

I stopped playing.

He turned to face the crowd, clapping his T-bone-steak hands together, as he boomed out in his Texas drawl, "Okay, okay. Now I wanna bitta silence here." He said it so loudly and stared so belligerently, that he got a kind of stunned acquiescence. Then he boomed out to the array of enquiring and somewhat fearful faces that peered back at him out of the dimly lit room: "Ladies and gen'elman" He held his hand out towards me. "This here is Jake. And because Jake is a good ol' buddy o' mine, he is gonna play mah lucky toon again. An' Ah want you all to stand an' raise your glasses and sing it along with me an' mah goodbuddy Jake. His aura of sheer physical strength and violence was so strong that not a dissenting voice was to be heard. So, with me banging out the tune, he went into a loud and horribly out of tune rendering of 'Run Rabbit Run' while at the same time energetically and forcefully conducting the rest of the audience, even going over to various tables where the recalcitrant occupants were not joining in. I noticed how, the moment they saw him approaching their table, they immediately got to their feet and started singing their hearts out.

When it was finally and thankfully all over, he beamed drunkenly around the room saying, "Thanks y'all." Then he turned to me saying "Thanks good ol' buddy YEW" and he strolled back to his noisily laughing and clapping 'good ol' buddies' who were standing by the fireplace.

The rather frozen-faced and shocked audience once more sat back down on their respective armchairs and slowly the atmosphere found its warmth again.

I went back to playing good tunes again, but a couple of minutes into 'Embraceable You', Jack came over to me and leaning over the piano, said to me, "If he tries to do that again, tell him that singing is not allowed in the club."

"Did you see the size of him?" I said. "Why don't you tell him?. You've lived your life, I'm just starting out." Jack chuckled and went away.

As I got up from the piano to take a ten minute break, big Tex waved me over. After the introductions to his two pals had been got over, I asked him in what way 'Run Rabbit Run' had been lucky to him.

"Well, I'll tell yer" he drawled, lighting a fresh Camel cigarette. "Even though mah first name is Rory, all mah buddies call me Lucky. It began when I flew B29's in the war. Do you know goodbuddy Jake, how many aircrews came through a tour of twenty-four daylight missions over Germany? Well, I'll tell yer. Not much more'n ten percent. Well ol' buddy, I made thirty-seven daylight runs without a scratch to mahself or mah crew."

"That's fantastic," I said. "No wonder they call you lucky. But I still can't see how that has to do with 'Run Rabbit Run'."

Before answering, he boomed at a waiter who was busily serving a middle-aged couple resplendent in evening dress, and who were sitting quietly on one of the many sofas that adorned the room, "Hey wader, get your ass over here. We're thirsty, aint we boys?" We all nodded affirmatively, as if our lives depended on it. Having seen the 'wader' raise his finger to him to indicate that he had heard and understood, he turned his bloodshot eyes back in my direction.

"We had this Canadian pilot serving with us. He had a record o' that tune which he would play over and over. Well goodbuddy, on the morning of the day o' my first daylight raid over northern France, to bomb some heavily fortified German positions, I guess I was just a little too tensed up to listen to anymore o' that goonball Canadian's record. So, after he'd played it for the tenth time, I just got outta mah chair and ah picked up his Goddamned phonograph while the record was still playin' and I dumped it on the floor an' then ah put mah foot through the whole damn contraption." Chuckling, he added: "This Canadian guy was of course just a little upset at my intemperate action. But possibly because he was about five foot six, an' I'm six feet four and a University heavyweight champion, he wisely thought better of making something physical out of it. But strangely enough, I could not get that goddamned toon outta mah head"

The waiter nervously interrupted his flow. "Bring us three Texas-style bourbons," he said, booming out the word 'Texas' twice as loudly as the rest of the sentence. "That means you fill the glasses right up" he said belligerently glaring at the waiter. "None of your quaint British pissant quarter inch at the bottom o' the glass."

Then turning to me, he asked; "and what are you drinkin' goodbuddy Jake?"

"I'll have a scotch, if you don't mind"

"An' bring Jake here a scotch, Texas-style also." His voice had such depth and timbre, that it carried right across the room, even when he was trying to speak quietly. He watched the waiter hurry off towards the bar. Then he turned to me and glared at me for a while through heavy-lidded, blood-shot eyes. Suddenly, for no reason at all, his blank-faced expression giving off no signal to me at all, he said "Yer alright kid." And he rested his huge paw on my shoulder.

"You were telling us about 'Run Rabbit Run' I reminded him, not a little relieved that this big, ugly bear was on my side.

"Oh yeah." He said heavily. "Well, I'll cut this story down to manageable proportions. I found mahself singin' that screwy toon all through that first bombin' raid.. Twenty-five B29's took part in that raid and only ten returned. I was the only one who got back without a scratch to crew or plane.

As I was gettin' outta the aircraft, countin' my blessin's I decided that I was gonna buy Canada—that's what we called him—a noo record of the toon and a noo phonograph to play it on. I was also gonna make an apology for mah bad behaviour. But the poor sonovobitch never returned. Well sir, from that day on, I an' mah crew would always gather under the port wing, an' sing that ol' toon to Canada, where-ever he was, before goin' on our missions. Y'see I had this feelin' in mah bones that in return for singin' him his song, ol' Canada whichever cloud he was sittin' on would keep me and mah crew safe all through them daylight runs. "Yessir" he said as the waiter appeared with our giant 'Texas' style drinks, "That is mah lucky toon alright."

"It wasn't exactly unlucky for Flanagan and Allen either," I said, leaving them all looking very puzzled as I made my way back to the piano, clutching my sextuple scotch. (In case you also don't know, they wrote the song and collected thousands of pounds in royalties.)

Of course, not everyone sent up a five pound note, if they wanted me to play a request. Lots of people thought that a ten shilling note (or less), was ample payment for me to play their requested song. But I made it a habit to send back anything less than ten shillings.

Over the first week, I got to realise that those who came into the club after midnight were completely different from the frozen-faced, cornball businessmen and their eager little secretaries, who arrived shortly after work, to leave again well before the bewitching hour. These people, if they noticed me at all, would mostly request Ivor Novello or Jessie Mathews songs, associated with current British stage and movie shows.

"I say, Band" was how some stuffed-shirted schmuck addressed me in his la-di-da Brrritish eccent, early one night. "Do you know 'The Flies Crawled up the Window?'

This was one of those excruciating examples of British musical excrement, sung by Jack Hulbert, a particular darling of the British upper classes. The twit just stood there, staring at me, his hands deep in his jacket pockets, his thumbs sticking out, whilst I played his silly, jolly English song. He was tall and fat, with a big arse, made to look fatter, by the way he pressed his hands down into his jacket pockets. He was smoking a cigarette through a six-inch long cigarette holder. The moment I had finished it, he just turned blank-faced, and made his way back to his friends who were standing at the bar. There was no thank you, or even an offer of a drink, let alone any money. I was nothing more to him than some lowly tradesman, who, having made his delivery, ceased to hold any further interest for him. Fortunately for me, these class-ridden 'tirribly Brrritish' types would usually be gone before midnight.

After midnight, the people who would come to the club were often great fun, and on some nights it could really be a hip place.

I remember an American couple who arrived at around 1.30 am. They wasted no time, coming straight over to the piano to occupy two of the high stools on either side of me. They were in their mid-fifties I would say, he smallish and fattish, with a big cigar held firmly in his Edward G. Robinson-like mouth. She, as well preserved as a medical specimen, her carefully dyed blonde hair, perfectly upswept to allow a sight of her long, jade earrings, which in turn helped to accentuate her elegant, classical, high cheek-boned face.

I'd just finished playing 'Stella By Starlight', when he said "You play good kid. What's your name?" He unclamped his cigar and ignoring the ash tray not more than a foot away from where he sat, tapped an inch of cigar-ash on to the carpet.

"Jake. Jake Silver."

"My name is Ben and this here is Lindy" he said pointing with his cigar to his companion. "Tell me Jake, do you play any Gershwin tunes?"

"Sure" I said. "Which particular one do you want me to play?"

"Any" he said. "I know every Gershwin tune, don't I honey?" He looked across to his wife (or mistress) for confirmation, who duly nodded in agreement.

You should know dear reader that probably no musician in the entire world (with the possible exception of a wonderful and brilliant New York piano man called Dick Hyman), knows the entire Gershwin catalogue.

So, as I swung into 'Irving Berlin's classic 'Cheek to Cheek', I said, "I very much doubt that."

"When I had finished playing it, and Ben and Lindy had honoured me by applauding, he said to me; "So you doubt me ha? I'll tell you what." He reached into his jacket and withdrew a black snakeskin wallet. He took twenty-five pounds out of it and laid the five fivers in front of him.

"Okay kid" he said. "If you can play a Gershwin tune that I can't identify, you win the money"

"Are you serious?" I asked him.

"Sure I am. But you can't win you know, 'cos I know them all."

I played 'These Charming People'. He didn't know it. (Not many do.) I went home that night with an extra twenty-five pounds in my pocket.

Over that first week, I made an additional fifty-five pounds in tips, which, together with my salary, left Jake standing Pat, if you'll excuse this muddled attempt at being clever. Unfortunately, I never again made anywhere near that much in a single week during my stay at the club.

On the first Sunday after I started work, it being my day off, I looked forward to a long lie-in, followed by a relaxing afternoon and in the evening, taking in a movie.

I crawled into bed at about 3.30 am, and tired though I was, I lay awake for another half hour or so, reviewing my first week's work. On the whole, I decided I loved it, although I was a bit disappointed by the large number of lousy tunes that I had to play on request. I also found myself reflecting on the fact that those people who requested terrible tunes invariably gave terrible tips, whereas a request to play say, a Cole Porter song, would usually result in either a pound note or at least a glass of champagne being sent over to me.

The other disappointment was that so far, no beautiful, sexy chick had come near or by me. In fact, not that many beautiful chicks had been in the club at all! The clientele was generally about the same that chose to sit around the piano: serious businessmen in serious suits, or middle-aged married couples, plus a few faggots. The only pretty girls I had seen were too busy cuddling up to the men (usually twice their age), who brought them in, to pay any attention to the piano player. I drifted off to sleep fantasising about Lana Turner sitting next to me while I played.

I was shocked out of my deep sleep by the piercing intrusion of the bedside telephone. I checked my watch; it was nine o'clock in the morning. I lay there for a while wondering who could be phoning me so damned early in the morning. I rolled across the bed and grabbed the receiver.

"Hello."

"Monsieur Jacques Silvair, si vous plait."

"Oui—er, I mean yes, this is Jake Silver."

"Un moment."

After a minute or so, during which I all but fell back to sleep, she came on the line, her voice warm and sexy: "Jake. It's me."

"Who's me?" I said, still too half asleep to come to the obvious conclusion.

"Oh for Chrissakes. Who else is gonna phone you from France, first thing in the morning?"

The penny dropped. I sat up as I said "Candy. So, how's it all going?"

"I'm missing you Jakey" she said petulantly and kittenishly.

I hate being called Jakey, but I let it pass. I was fully awake now, and very conscious of what Ivan had told me. I decided to pretend to know nothing about her pregnancy and to carry on the charade of her being in Cannes or somewhere in Paris with her girlfriend.

"Are you in Paris yet or are you still with your father in Cannes?"

There was a long pause.

"Jake," her voice sounded very serious. "Are you sure you want to marry me?"

The words may have come out of the ear-piece, but they hit me bang in the middle of my head! Good as I thought I was at talking my way out of dicey situations, this time my brain just froze up on me. I knew I had to say something, but I could not find any words.

"Well, hey Candy, er I mean, well..."

"I'm not in the south of France" she interrupted my stumblings to say. "I'm in Paris."

I still went on with the charade: "How tres jolie. Have you been up the Eiffel Tower yet?"

Another long pause. Then, "Jake, while you were up at that bloody University, I met a man. He was an American. Very nice and very sweet." Her voice suddenly took on a defensive air."Well, I was lonely Jake, and in any case I did not know yet how great it was gonna to be with you. Anyway....a couple of weeks ago, the day before you came back to London, and after he had returned to the States, I found that I was pregnant."

She left a pause, presumably for me to say something. I said nothing.

"Are you still there?"

"Yes Candy, I'm still here and I'm listening to what you have to say."

"Well, I'm over here in Paris to have an abortion. A close friend of mine, Millie Jacobson knows this doctor here. I'm due to have it done at three this afternoon. Last night I phoned Zack—that's the name of the baby's father—Zack Landsdorf, to tell him. He has just phoned me back to say that I should not have the abortion and that he will come over to Europe and marry me."

There was another pause, but again I refused to fill it.

"Jake, Zack is a very nice man. He's very rich. My father does a lot of business with his father's company. But he's not half as handsome as you. He's only about three inches taller than I am. And he's fattish and about thirty-five years old and already starting to lose his hair. He's also been married before and has two children from his previous marriage. I know you're the guy for me, not him. That is why I need to know that you love me. If you do, I'll go through with this bloody abortion, and we can start afresh. But darlin' if you don't, you must tell me now, in which case, I'll keep the baby, marry the father and live unhappily ever after in Boston—if you can call it 'living'." I had never heard her speaking so seriously before.

I did not know what to say, because my own feelings were too mixed to express them. Also, I was being asked to make a decision that was far too grown up for me to handle. All I can now remember about that phone call is having the same feelings of anger mixed with jealousy that I felt when Ivan first told me. But I also recall the wonderful relief of knowing that I now had an easy way out of the affair.

"I'm waiting Jake. This is put up or shut up time." Her voice now small and sad. Probably, for the first time in her life, Candy, who had lived such a carefree, selfish, and privileged life, was confronted with the first serious problem her daddy couldn't buy her out of, and she clearly hated it.

I was now very wide awake indeed. I decided to level with her.

"Look Candy" I said. I'm not yet nineteen years old. I've just started my first job. I don't honestly think that I could contemplate anything as..." I searched for the right word ..."rigid as marriage." I knew I was hurting her and was desperate not to. But I stumbled on; "I mean, If I were say, twenty-six or so and making plenty of money and could give you all the things you are used to getting, well that would be a very different story. But..."

"I can't give you anything but love" she sang over me. "I know that tune too. And I also know when somebody is shooting me a line." Then she said quietly and slightly pleadingly; "But what if love is all that the lady needs? What then Jake?"

That was a tough question. I was in a corner. I did not want to hurt her by just coming out and saying baldly; 'Look Candy you are a nice girl but I am not in love with you, nor is there slightest chance that I ever will be'. I did not have the heart (or the guts), to say that, even though it was the truth. I racked my brain for an angle that would coat the bitter pill with something sweet.

"Candy baby" I said as gently as I could, "how can I commit myself to something that is at least six, and maybe even ten years away? I mean, you are only eighteen years old, like me. You can't guarantee that you will want to marry me that far ahead in time, and it would be quite wrong of me to expect you to do so. And now you are asking me to decide for you whether or not to have an abortion this afternoon. Okay, so what if I say, get rid of the baby, and then..."

"Okay, okay, OKAY," she said, cutting across me. "You don't have to make drawings for me Jake darling. I get the picture. So, if it's not going to be Candy Silver, then it might as well be Candy Landsdorf."

The silence that followed was I suppose, intended to give me one last chance to change my mind. But I said nothing.

"Bye Jake" she said tonelessly. "If ever you're in Boston, come and look us up."

She put the phone down before I could say another word.

I got up and went into the kitchen and this being Meri's day off, made myself a pot of tea and sat at the kitchen table drinking and smoking my last four cigarettes, while I tried to work out why I felt so upset and frustrated, when what had transpired was what I hoped would happen. If I didn't love her, which I knew to be the case, why did I suddenly feel so drawn to her? I went back to bed feeling terrible.

I must have dropped off to sleep again, because the sudden ringing of the phone shot me bolt upright, heart banging and nerve-ends jagged.

"Did I wake you up, or were you already awake?" I recognised the voice immediately.

"Oh, hello Auntie. I was only dozing" A glance at my watch told me that only fifteen minutes had passed since I had crawled back into bed.

"I phoned because I thought you would like to know that I have agreed to let Ivan bring the shiksa to London next week to meet me."

"That is great. But, you shouldn't call her a shiksa Auntie. Firstly, she is going to be a doctor, and secondly, she is probably going to be Ivan's wife."

"Well" she said arcanely, "We'll cross that bridge when we come to it" Then, changing to a matter-of-fact delivery; "Meanwhile, I want you to have dinner with us tonight."

I accepted, not only because I knew that I would be in no mood to sit by myself in a cinema, half watching while still trying to come to terms with myself about Candy. So having accepted, I was just about to ring off, when she said.

"One other thing. Who was on the phone before me? I tried to call you earlier, but you were engaged. So who was phoning you so early?

Before I could tell the lie I should have told, the truth slipped out.

"It was Candy phoning me from France."

"Now that is nice" she said, glowing with self justification. "I told you she was a nice girl. Imagine, phoning you all the way from Cannes just to make sure you are alright. Do you think Ivan's shiksa would do a thing like that? She doesn't even phone him from Leeds, let alone the south of France." Maybe it was because of the mixed up frustration and anger I was feeling about Candy I don't know, but, her constant use of the word 'shiksa' suddenly pissed me off.

"It wasn't the south of France, it was from Paris. And it wasn't to ask about my health. It was about something else entirely." I knew as I was saying it I was making a mistake.

"So, what did she phone you for?"

"Ivan knows all about it. You can ask him;"

"I don't want to ask him. And in any case he is in Leeds with the shicks...with his girlfriend. So now tell me what she wanted" Her voice took on a kvetchy edge; "And don't lie to me. I know you too well. I'll know if you are lying."

"She...was...asking me to help her make a decision" I was now sorry I had got myself into this and I tried to extricate myself by keeping my voice sounding even and normal. But she didn't just have x-ray vision; she had the x-ray hearing to match.

"Well that is very nice" she said disarmingly pleasantly. "It's correct for a young lady to ask her future intended husband's advice" Then, with a slight added edge to her voice, "I mean that is what you aren't you? Nothing has changed between you two, has it?"

'Fuck it' I thought. 'I might as well tell her now. She'll learn about it anyway'.

"Look Auntie. Candy is in Paris with her friend, Millie Jacobson..."

"Millie Jacobson eh? She said, interrupting me. "Lovely girl, Millie. That's the kind of girl Ivan should marry."

"Millie Jacobson is there with Candy, because your lovely Millie knows an abortionist who lives in Paris."

"Oh, my God!." The shocked voice now took on an edge of hard practicality. "Now you listen to me," she said. "Phone Candy back right away and say that she must keep the baby. You will of course marry her right away."

"Why should I? I'm not the father."

After a long, shocked silence, she said in a quiet measured tone of voice:" Well, if it's not you, who's the father?"

"She says it a divorced American, who comes from Boston. She says he already has two children."

"So, why did she want your advice, if you're not the father?" she asked suspiciously.

"Search me" I lied. "Anyway, she is going to marry this Zack someone-or-other and live in Boston with him and his two other kids." Then I added for reasons of adolescent pride, and not wanting my Aunt to think that she preferred this other man to me; "Even though she swore to me that she didn't love him."

"We'll talk tonight about it," she said in a distracted manner, and put the phone down, clearly wanting to devote all her thoughts to this thunderbolt-like piece of information.

As I shuffled across the deep pile of the soft, silken, bedroom carpet, on my way to the bathroom, I said to myself; 'What a great day off this is turning out to be!' And, as I slowly lowered myself into the steaming hot bath water, I found myself thinking; 'I wonder how many young men's first fuck, turned out to be a pregnant woman?'

Chapter 22

The next morning, I was awakened by a gentle but insistent knocking on the bedroom door. It was Meri, carrying a huge tray, containing a tall glass of freshly squeezed orange juice, a plate of bacon, sausages, baked beans, a couple of fried eggs and three slices of thickly buttered rye-toast.

"Wow Meri," I said as she proudly bore the tray over to the bed. "That looks just wonderful." I watched her, as she flipped down the six-inch high legs that were fitted at either end of the tray, to allow it to be set across me, without it having to rest upon my thighs.

Having set the tray down with great care, not to mention a flirtatious smile, I watched her go over to the cream and gold floor to ceiling sliding doors that extended along almost one entire wall of the bedroom, and which, when slid back, revealed a huge, cavernous wardrobe and an equally large bank of cupboards and drawers. Meri opened one of these drawers and took out a large, deep, green satin pillow, which she carried over to the bed and pushed down behind my naked back for additional support whilst I ate.

"Madame, she always like me to do thees, when I bring her breakfast."

"What madame is this Meri?" I asked as I unrolled my napkin to release the silver cutlery.

"The other master's wife. She always have breakfast in bed."

"I never knew that the Earl was married."

"Madame went away after very, very bad argument" A serious expression flitted across her face like a scudding cloud hurrying across the face of the sun. Then it was gone as suddenly as it had appeared, and she was back to her normal smiling self; "but while Madame ees here, she always like thees." She held out her pudgy little upturned hands towards me, "Always the beeg breakfast, always the pillow behind." She started to make her bouncy little way out of the bedroom, but stopped, turned, and with hands on hips and eyes alight with promise, said "Eef master wants anything else from me, he peek up the telephone and dial the number one and the phone een the keetchen, it ring."

Watching her go out of the door, I thought as I sipped my orange juice, 'I'll tell you what I want from you Meri, my Cuban cookie; I want you to look more like Lana Turner."

Unlike the vast majority of jazz musicians, I cannot fuck just any woman who puts out. I actually have to fancy at least something about her. This is very unusual among jazz musicians. Wherever I have travelled in this world, it has always been the same: among the over-thirty year-old female jazz-loving population, there seems to be an unspoken rule that all jazz musicians are available for one-night stands. One of the reasons for this I guess is the transience of the musician. She gets laid, he leaves town and no-one is the wiser. In small towns where gossip is the only thing anyone is any good at, provided you can keep the whole thing quiet, there is a ninety percent chance that you will find some seventeen year-old girl or an over- thirty something divorcee woman who is ready and willing. Another reason why these slightly older chicks go for jazzmen is because the lady invariably presumes that because of your lifestyle plus your chosen profession, you have had lots of women already and are therefore going to be good in the sack. There is a third reason also. There is something about the basic primitivism of the swinging jazz beat that causes these women to identify jazz with sex. Just listening to a few sets of jazz, can get these ladies seriously turned on. In Leeds in England, New Orleans in the States, and in Cape Town South Africa, there were a few women, quite famous to the jazz fraternity, who would come into the bandroom after the gig was over, and offer to give head to the entire band. But thank heaven; they were quite nice looking chicks. If they were ugly, I would have to duck out because quite frankly, I cannot get it up for an ugly chick. But my attitude is very much at variance with that of most jazzmen.

I remember, on one of my free Sundays, playing an out of town gig with a jazz group, comprising some of the best jazz musicians in Britain at that time. The only hotel in the shitty little town where we were playing being full, we were forced to stay over-night in a bed and breakfast boarding house.

This damp, murky, smelly establishment was owned and run by a concave-thin, bony, round-shouldered old lady of at least sixty years of age. She clearly hadn't dyed her frizzy, short hair recently, because it was red at the top but with a good two inches of gray at the roots. She was grubbily dressed and had a moustache which, with a bit of encouragement, could have rivalled Clark Gable's. She did have nice teeth though—all four of them! The price for staying in this palace was five shillings per night, per person, two in a room. (In case you are too young to remember kiddies, five shillings was a quarter of one British pound.)

The following morning, as we all assembled in the dining room for our breakfast, the trumpet player said to the tenor sax man, who was supposedly his room-mate, "Hey, where did you get to last night man? You went out of the room, you said, to take a crap and never came back 'til this morning." At that moment, Mrs Clark Gable came in with our breakfasts, so all we got from him in reply was a mumbled "Later man. Later."

It wasn't until we were all on the hired bus, and well on the way back to London that I yet again broke the 'Rule of Cool' by asking the tenor sax player (if I hadn't, I'm damned sure no-one else would have), "So where did you get to last night?"

"I got lucky" he said, smiling broadly. Incidentally, he was a tall, good looking kid of about twenty-five years of age.

"Who was the chick?" His erstwhile room-mate, the trumpet player asked. To the best of our knowledge, there were no females staying in the joint. As far as we could tell, the only room not occupied by the band, was occupied by two slightly faggy commercial traveller-type men.

"It was the old lady" he said triumphantly.

"The old bag that ran the joint?" I asked incredulously. "Jesus, how could you fuck that, man?"

He looked at me, puzzlement all over his face. "What do you mean?" he said. "She was the only available fuck. You know that? And anyway," he said with a triumphant smile, "I didn't have to pay a thing for the room. And she said that I could come back any time I like."

Being at that time utterly inexperienced in the world of jazz, I found this too bizarre to let pass.

"Are you saying that you put your twenty-five year-old dick into that fercuckte old bag just to save five shillings?"

He reacted defensively: "Look man, I met her in the hallway and she was clearly putting out, y'know what I mean? And in any case, a fuck's a fuck. Right?" He looked around at us all, and apart from me who was aghast at the whole idea, the rest of the band nodded knowingly and understandingly.

"Was she any good?" asked the drummer after a longish silence.

The tenor player thought about it for a while, before answering off-handedly "She'd done it before."

And that was the end of it. The subject was never mentioned again.

Now, before all the feminists start jumping up and down about the callous and uncaring way that men treat women, they should know that later on, I am going to tell of elegant, wealthy, women who were every bit as sexually voracious as any man I have ever met, and then some. They will realise then that the credo, 'A fuck's a fuck' is as common among women as it is among men.

Around about eleven o'clock one night, when I was only half way through my second set, Eliot came into the club. He had returned only that morning, from New York City. But, having sailed over on the Queen Elizabeth, or some other grand trans-Atlantic liner, he was not subject to any of the jet lag that trans-oceanic travellers have to learn to live with these days. He was fresh as a daisy, as were his male and female companions. The guy was shortish, and sharp in every way. He had a sharp, pointed nose, sharp piercing brown eyes, a tight line of a mouth and a sharp, small pointed chin. He was wearing a black, silk tuxedo that shone almost as much as his black, receding hair.

But it was Eliot's female companion who interested me far more. She had been a Hollywood super-star. Admittedly, this was a few years ago, but she was still a household name.

And I am not going to tell you who she was.

I may be just an old drunk these days, but dammit, I am an honourable old drunk. And honourable people, drunk or sober, do not reveal confidences about ladies, without their express permission. I don't even know whether she is still alive, because out here in Cuba, Hollywood and all that glitzy jazz, is a very, very long way away. So, I am going to give her a false name. And I am going to do the same for her male companion, who turned out to be her agent. This is just in case some super-hip, movie-wise reader could deduce from it, the film actress's name.

Maybe it was due to the dim lighting in the club, but as Eliot ushered them both over to the piano she still looked wonderful to me.

"Hey Jake" Eliot said, as I stopped playing and stood up to greet them.

"Well, where have you been?" I asked as they came straight over to the piano.

"We only got back from the States a few hours, and here I am with my two new but good friends to say hello" Then putting his arm around my shoulders he said, "Lola, this is Jake Silver."

"And you are the wonderful Lola Stevens" I said shaking her hand without waiting for Eliot to complete his introduction.

This was the first, really big-time film star I had met. And whilst she had aged and coarsened a little, as the years (and as I later found out, the booze), had taken their toll, she still possessed the same magnetic, sexual presence, she had on the screen, no matter what kind of part she played. Her hair was as ebony black and luxurious as ever, as it softly draped over her bare shoulders. Her emerald green full-length evening gown hugged a figure that may have thickened somewhat around the waist and bottom, but her eyes, which seemed to be the exact same colour as her dress, although they were far more incandescent, and her long, long legs just visible through her evening gown, were as they had always been.

"And this is Herschel Weinstein, Lola's agent and personal manager" Eliot said.

"As we shook hands, he said in a clipped, street-wise 'N'Yawk' accent, Eliot thinks that you're one helluva piano player."

"Thank you" And because I was being paid to play the piano and not socialise, I added; "Is there any particular song that either you or the enchanting Miss Stevens would like to hear?"

"She spoke in the kind of soft, husky voice that one immediately and instinctively associates with sexual excess: "D'you hear that Herschel? Jake thinks that I'm enchanting." Then turning those maddeningly green eyes on to me, she said "You haven't yet played one fucking note baby, but I already think you are a great kid."

Herschel turning to Eliot said, "Or a great kidder."

"Lola, ignoring this crack, took the high stool nearest me and with her Kryptonite eyes all but burning a hole right through me, said "Do you know a song written by my friend, Kurt Weill, called 'Speak Low'?"

I trust you have already worked it out for yourself dear reader; I was heavily influenced by everything that came out of Hollywood. Even the manner in which I would walk home after seeing a movie would be influenced by which film star I had just seen. If it had been a Bogart or Cagney gangster drama, then I would come out of the movie house a helluva lot tougher and meaner than when I went in. Likewise, I would be more dapper and debonair after watching a Fred Astaire or Gene Kelly musical, or I would stroll along feeling utterly suave and sophisticated after watching Otto Kruger or William Powell for a couple of hours. In truth, damn near everything I did back in those days was influenced in some way or other by the Hollywood movie (including how to kiss, until Janine Gregson taught me just how little the Hayes office knew about kissing). Certainly all my phantasies and dreams were hopelessly intertwined with Hollywood; and I was a pretty imaginative kid.

So, as I started into my introduction to 'Speak Low' with the fabulous super-star Lola Stevens sitting there in the flesh, staring at me, I suddenly found myself fantasising that this was actually a movie starring Lola Stevens playing the older woman-scientist who has fallen hopelessly in love with the handsome young night club entertainer played by Hollywood's hottest new discovery, Jake Silver. And here we are in the pivotal scene in the movie when she realises that she just cannot continue her important scientific work without the love of this suave, sophisticated, young performer.

In order to extract the maximum Hollywood-style drama from this tense yet tender scene, I found myself playing 'Speak Low' like it was a cross between the 'Warsaw Concerto' and Rachmaninov's second piano concerto. After all, this is the scene that earns Jake Silver an Oscar for this, his first movie appearance.

I gave it everything I had. I gushed and sloshed all over the keyboard. I cannot remember anymore exactly how I played it, but I'll give you odds of fifty to one that it was an exhibition of the most vulgar kind of sentimentality; in other words, exactly the type of music that would actually have been playing on the sound track if it really had been a Hollywood film drama.

Just before bringing the tune to its shattering climax, I looked up at Lola. (I could almost hear the director shouting; 'Look up Jake, look up at her for Chrissakes." Then, turning to the cameraman he says; 'Gimme a close-up of Jake looking at Lola with wild passion in his eyes, as he discovers that he, for the first time in his young, reckless life is in love with her also'.

As I looked up at Lola I found her looking back at me through half-closed eye-lids; her mouth half open, her still full lips moist and lubricious. One of her elegantly manicured and bejewelled hands was resting half way across the piano as if she was reaching out to me. Her breasts seemed to have actually swelled inside the deep, décolletage of her emerald green evening gown.

All it needed was Claude Rains, playing the wealthy but dangerously jealous husband, and we would have had a box-office smash on our hands.

When I finished, she sat for a moment before getting up off her stool, and taking my face in both of her hands, she kissed me wetly and softly on the cheek. Then, with her lips not more than an inch from mine, she said to me very softly, "You know you are a very passionate young man."

All it now needed was for a director to shout 'cut; it's a wrap'.

"Hey, how about a little jazz, Jake?" Eliot's voice dragged me back into the world of reality.

I went into an up-tempo version of 'What Is This Thing Called Love' in the first chorus of which, I play the tune with my right hand while playing Diz and Bird's 'Hot House' with my left. I was gratified to hear Herschel say to

Eliot, "Say, he's putting down 'Hot House' at the same time. Cute." Lola was still staring at me as she went through the motions of snapping her fingers although the veiled-eyed, half-open-mouth expression never changed. She was all dark mystery and sex personified.

Then Jack appeared seemingly from nowhere, and they all moved away from the piano while Eliot did the introductions. Jack led them over to two sofas facing one another, where they sat chatting, laughing and drinking champagne.

They left an hour or so later, but not before Lola came over to me to again to say how nice it was to meet me and that she hoped we would meet again soon. Herschel, who had brought her over to say her goodbyes, shook my hand limply, while saying; "It was great man. You made me feel like I was back at the Three Deuces in N'Yawk." As I watched them go I found myself wondering what the story was behind the name, "Three Deuces".

The following afternoon, Jack phoned me to say that he wished to speak to me about something and would like me to meet him at the club in an hour.

When I got there, Jack was behind the bar, scotch and soda in hand, poring over the racing page of the 'Evening News'

"Oh, thanks for coming in Jake" he said almost absent-mindedly, while still concentrating mainly on the little ticks he was putting against the names of various horses. "Get yourself a drink and go and sit at one of the tables. I'll join you in a trice old chap"

I was a bit worried about why Jack needed to see me so urgently that it could not wait until I got to the club at the normal time. One of the waiters had already told me of the rumour that Jack was losing a bundle of money on horses, and as I was happier now than I had ever been, I did not need to hear any news that might change anything in any way, but I could think of no other reason for this sudden emergency meeting other than something bad involving me, and my stomach did a few back-flips as I saw Jack making his way towards me.

Thankfully, it turned out to be a needless worry. It seemed Jack had received a telephone call from Lola Stevens a couple of hours ago. She was giving a small party in her hotel suite, and she asked if I could be released from club duty to play at it.

"I suppose you explained to her that I am contracted to start work here at nine o'clock?"

"Well, I tried to Jake, but she was adamant. She even agreed to pay me two hundred quid for your services."

"Shit," was all I could think of saying.

"Technically Jake, as you work for me, all I have to do, is to tell you that tonight you will be playing somewhere else, but that your salary will be paid as normal, while I hang on to the two hundred quid. But as you know, I am not a money grabber. Also," Jack went on; "if I did allow you to play at Lola Stevens' little soiree, I will have to find someone else to take your place here at the club, and that takes time, not to mention a fee for your replacement. So, I suggest that we split the money right down the middle. You take a hundred quid for the night, even though you forfeit one sixth of your salary, which is roughly six pounds. So you will earn ninety-four pounds extra this week, while I will take the other hundred to cover my costs and my time. How do you feel about that?"

"Is that it? Is that why you wanted to see me?" He nodded.

"Jesus Jack, you could've told me that over the phone. Of course I'll do it. Where do I have to be?"

"Oh that's good Jake. I'll phone and tell her. She is staying at the Dorch (which is up-market slang for the Dorchester Hotel). He wrote down the number of her suite and handed it to me. "One more thing," he said. "She will be paying me the money. I will add it on to your salary at the end of the week.."

"Fine, anything you say."

I checked my watch as I got out of the elevator and walked along the carpeted hallway leading to the double doors of Lola Steven's hotel suite. It was eight-fifty. Perfect. This gave me ten minutes to say my hellos to Lola and Herschel, check in my new overcoat, dig the kind of people Lola had invited (so that I could decide on what kind of music to play), and take a pee before starting the actual gig.

I rapped gently on the door. It was almost immediately opened by the Prince (or maybe I should I say Princess), of Faggotry. This Queen of the May was tall, about my height, and very thin. The first thing I noticed was his hair. It had to be dyed, because it was of such an outrageous orange colour, that I was sure that God, not even in one of His more capricious moments would play such a cruel practical joke on any of His creatures. It had also been permed so that the sides were upswept, rising to a high pile of tight curls on the top. Maybe he thought he was Lucille Ball. If he did, then baby, did he have the wrong number!

He was dressed in a black, shiny, evening suit, with the sleeves pushed back, half way up to his elbows, gold bangles and bracelets adorning his thin, bony wrists. Under the suit, he had on a black, cotton, crew neck vest, with a canary yellow scarf around his neck, knotted to one side, the ends being thrown back over his shoulder. He wore no socks. Inside his black, wedge-heeled open-toed leather sandals, his feet were bare, revealing his toes and toenails, each of which had been lacquered a different colour. In his right hand, was a foot-long, ebony cigarette holder, adorned with an unlit pink, gold tipped cigarette.

Before I could announce myself, he said in a high faggy American voice:

"Are you Jake Thilver?"

"That's me."

"Oh well, come in then. Mith Thtevens ith ekthpecting you."

He opened the door wider to allow me past him and into the vestibule of the suite.

"Let me take your coat," he said, as he shut the door behind me.

I let him take my coat.

With my overcoat over his arm he ogled me up and down: "My, what big thtrong shoulders you have."

I ignored that remark. Pointing to a closed door off to the left of the vestibule, I asked "Is it in there?"

"Yeth" he said, as he carefully put my coat on a hanger.

I went in to find myself in a large, dimly lit room, with wide, tall windows overlooking Park Lane and Hyde Park.

At the far end of the room, a white screen, about six feet wide by four feet tall had been erected. Directly in front of me, not more than three feet from where I was standing, a film projector stood silently and sightlessly on its tripod. A couple of feet in front of that, facing the screen, was a chaise longue. Two small, round tables had been set at either end of it, each bearing a large round glass ashtray. The rest of the room was sparsely furnished, with a couple of armchairs, and a long glass-topped table, which ran along the wall to my right, upon which were several bottles of booze, with glasses of every type, lined up in front of them. In each corner of the room were standing lamps, creating pools of light about themselves, but leaving the entire centre of the room eerily dim. Why the large, ornate chandelier that hung from the centre of the ceiling had not been switched on, I could not fathom. Apart from these items, there was nothing else in this large, high-ceilinged room, barring the beautiful silk, Persian carpet, which was almost wall to wall.

Also, I was alone. Where were the people, and weirder still, where was the piano?

As I wandered over to the window to idly watch the bright headlights of Park Lane's busy traffic hurry past below me, I rationalised, 'Maybe the party hasn't started yet, or maybe it is in some other room, although I could hear no sound of voices.

And then the strange uncanny silence was broken by a door opening. I turned to see yet another gift to the world of Faggotry wafting in.

"Hello" he said as he minced across the room, his limp-wristed hand was already hanging out in front of him, ready for me to shake. "I'm Georgio, Miss Stevens' dresser. She asked me to tell you that she won't be long and to fix you a drink while you are waiting."

"Okay" I said. I'll have a Chivas with a dash of soda water, if you don't mind."

"You British" he said, in a chiding voice, as he minced across the room towards the bar. "You mean seltzer water, don't you?"

"I mean water with little bubbles in it. You can call it what the fuck you like."

I do not know why, but all my life, up to this very day, if I am in the company of an effeminate man, I automatically adopt an excessively macho pose, as if by doing so, it will somehow even up the masculine imbalance between us. Or, maybe it is to ensure that he doesn't make a pass. He said nothing, until he came back with my scotch. "Here you are" he said: adding as I took it from him, a Mona Lisa enigmatic smile playing coquettishly on his lips, "Macho Man".

Just so you get the picture, Georgio, who spoke with a nasal New York City twang, was slim, muscular, and about five feet six inches tall. This simpering, scented apology for manhood, had a thin face, topped by thick wavy hair with two inch-long side burns. He sported a full moustache above his thin, feminine lips, a high forehead, a straight nose and a firm chin. He too was dressed all in black; black, tight cut pants, a black satin shirt, with the top two buttons open, and a thin gold chain around his neck, carrying a small, gold crucifix. On his feet were black, patent leather dance pumps. Worst of all, he was smothered in some heavy, pervasive perfume. All in all, he looked (and smelled) like an inmate of an Argentine bordello.

After giving me my drink, he backed away from me, still giving me the flirtatious half-smile, before turning and disappearing behind the film screen. I heard the opening and shutting of a door I hadn't known was there, because the screen was shielding it from my view. Standing there in the half light sipping my drink, I thought to myself, 'Nu, it could have been worse. It could have been a Star of David he had hanging off his neck-chain'.

Faggot the first, then came in. "Oh, I thee that you've got a drink already. I'm going to order food. Ith there anything you particularly fanthy?"

"No thanks. I already ate at the club."

"But you *mutht* let me order you *thumthing*" he insisted. "I've got to order for Lola—I mean Mith Thteventh, and she doethn't like to eat alone." As he opened the door to return to the vestibule, he turned, and looking at me meaningfully, said, "Anyway, I'm sure a big boy like you can alwayth handle a little more." Having planted his double entendre, he shook his shoulders like some sexy hoochie-koochie dancer, and left the room.

In case you get the idea that I am some sort of a 'queer basher', let me disabuse you of that thought right away. I am a strong believer in Frank Sinatra's dictum, 'whatever gets you through the night'. I really could not care less about anybody's sexual proclivities, but there are some gay men, of which these were two prime examples, who feel it necessary to flirt with every man who crosses their path. I am put out even when women do it, but I am doubly so when queers come on to me in this way.

"Daahling" she exploded, as she swept across the room towards me, smiling and with arms outstretched before her. Lola was wearing a flame coloured negligee which flowed down to her ankles. What she had on beneath it I could not tell. But it was immediately obvious to me what she did not have on underneath. A brassiere. Because her nipples were proudly prominent against the reddish orange material. Her rich, black hair was upswept into a top knot and held in place by a flame coloured ribbon with a diamond clasp at the front. On her feet were mules of exactly the same colour, with heels high enough to enable her nose to reach to my chin.

When she got to me, she put her still outstretched arms around my neck and kissed my lips with her open mouth. Her breath reeked of vodka. As we kissed she positioned herself so that our legs intertwined, her right thigh pressing hard against my cock, whilst at the same time she pressed and rubbed herself against my right thigh. After we de-clinched, I was embarrassed to find her two gay servants standing not five feet away, holding hands and smiling or maybe it was leering. She clearly did not give a damn.

"Stacy" she said, turning to fag the first, "What food did you order for us. I'm fucking famished."

"I ordered thum caviar and lobthter thermidor, followed by chocolat mooth" He followed her across the room as she went to the bar to freshen her vodka and tonic. "And I also ordered the two bottleth of champagne. We already have thum port wine up here, if that ith what you prefer with the chocolat."

She turned vodka in hand, and beaming her fascinating green eyes on me, said in her husky voice; "I thought we would have a little something to eat, and then watch the first movie I ever starred in. That was when I was only twenty-two years old." She came over two me and putting an arm around my shoulders, asked; "And how old are you Jake?"

"I am nearly twenty " I said, trying to make myself as old as I reasonably could. She jumped back. A horrified look on her face.

"Omygaad" she said. "Fuck it. Why I'm old enough to be your..." She rather pointlessly stopped herself from finishing the sentence. Instead, she turned sharply to Georgio and Stacey, who were once again holding hands.

"For Chrissakes, get me some cigarettes. And then freshen Jake's drink."

They both leapt into action. Georgio relieved me of my glass and hurried over to the bar to refill it, while Stacey all but ran into the room behind the screen to return with Lola's gold cigarette case, already clicked open.

"Where is the piano?" I asked in all innocence.. "And what time are the guests arriving?"

For a second there was a look of disbelief in her eyes, but it changed very quickly to one of humorous, playful tolerance.

Taking a long drag from her cigarette, she said into the smoke that was pouring out of her mouth, "Actually, Jake darling, I've called the party off. I thought it would be more fun if it were just the two of us."

"Well, in that case..." I said. But she cut me off.

"Don't worry baby. The three hundred pounds still gets paid. You don't have to play the piano to earn it." And with cigarette in one hand and vodka glass in the other, she put her arms around my neck, and rubbing herself in a circular motion against me, she whispered, "There are other ways."

I could feel my 'Mister Big' as Candy used to call it, starting to live up to it's name, as it reacted to Lola's pelvic urgings.

But at the same time, I was helluva annoyed at Jack seemingly trying to cheat me out of fifty quid. He had clearly told me that this gig was worth only two hundred, not the three hundred on offer.

There was rattle of keys and I heard the suite door being opened.. As she broke off her hold from around my neck, there was a polite knock on the room door. Stacey went over right away and opened it and the procession began.

It could have come straight out of a Hollywood musical, in which someone like Eric Blore plays the maitre. Indeed, all that it lacked was Blore himself plus some bustling Hollywood-type music. Firstly, two dinner-jacketed men pushing a large, round, table, made their way into the room, and under Georgio's and Stacey's fussy supervision, pushed it to an exactly directed position in the centre of the room, under the large but unlit chandelier. Two more similarly suited minions then briskly followed bearing a high-backed dining chair apiece. They too were instructed exactly where to set them.

Then two more made their entrance, one carrying a fold-up serving table, which he set down and opened out directly next to the dining table, whilst the other carried a huge, silver, covered-over salver, which he set down on the serving table. As each pair completed their tasks, they turned to walk briskly across the room and stand side by side, like a line of soldiers, with their backs to the tall windows behind them. Now, in came a trio, two waiters in burgundy-coloured jackets, led by a pretty little maid carrying a white, folded table cloth which she flapped open and draped over the dining table. The second of the trio balanced a small silver tray on his left hand, with two champagne flutes sitting on it, whilst the third clutched two ice-bucket stands, their buckets already in them. He carefully set them down at either side of the table. After the waiter with the tray had set them down on the table-cloth, he meticulously cleaned each glass with a soft cloth he had retrieved from his inside pocket. Then he proceeded to set each glass down at either end of the table, with the care and precision of a jeweller setting a ruby into a bracelet. Now, two more maids entered, one carrying a tall, thin, blue glass vase with one a deep blue orchid-like exotic plant gracing it, which she placed to one side of the table. The other maid was carrying two ornate silver candlesticks, with tall, thin, white candles already in them. She set them down with great care in the exact middle of the table.

By now the long line of servants, standing stiffly to attention began to remind me of the Grenadier Guards awaiting an inspection by some visiting dignitary. Now our personal waiters made their appearance. Each of them was carrying a bottle of Mumms champagne which they first showed me for my approval, before snuggling them down in their respective ice-buckets.

One of the waiters brought out a box of matches with which to light the candles.

"Pleeth, no candleth" Stacey quickly said. "Mith Thtevens findth them too bright. Jutht leave then unlit pleath."

"Would you open the champagne and pour us both a glass" Lola asked, excessively sweetly to the glass-cleaning specialist waiter.

"But-a Madam" the Italian waiter pleaded, "The champagne, she is-a not yet quite a-cold enough."

"Who gives a sh..." Lola said roughly, before checking herself, and returning to her sweet-sounding, nice-guy routine, saying to him "Look, waiter ol' buddy, we both want a glass of champagne, don't we Jake?"

I nodded. And then, with sudden drunken impatience she added loudly; "NOW, if you don't mind."

A young rosy-cheeked lad of about fourteen made his entrance bearing a tray with all the cutlery and the napkins on it. The Italian waiter moved to take the tray from him,

"Leave the Goddamned tray," Lola rasped, dropping once and for all her sweetness-and-light shit. "And pour the friggin' champagne will yer? NOW! Not tomorrow morning when the champagne, she issa cold-a, but NOW God dammit!"

Her mock Italian accent clearly caused her and her two fags great amusement, but all I could come up with was an uncomfortable, embarrassed grin.

The waiter who had been the butt of Lola's 'sense of humour', said something in Italian to the other waiter, who took over the task of table laying, whilst he hurriedly opened one of the bottles of champagne, the rest of the army of servants, still standing to attention in a rigid line, watching expressionlessly.

I watched the waiter fill two glasses with the warm champers, place them on a tray and bring them over to us, after which he, together with his compadre waiter took up their places behind each of the dining chairs.

"Lola took a big slurp of the warm fizz, hiccoughed a couple of times, then turned to Georgio and Stacey and said, loudly enough for everyone in the room to hear: "Give'em some fuckin' money an' get 'em outa here will yer?"

Stacey took a bundle of pound notes out of his pocket and handed it ostentatiously to the Italian waiter, saying loudly at the same time, "Itth for you all" At the same time Lola, who had put down her drink on the table, was clapping her hands and shouting; "Thank you everyone. Now will you all please get your arses outa here? Off you all go. Shoo shoo." I watched them troop out of the room, like a chorus line making its exit off stage.

As Lola and I took our seats opposite each other she turned to the fags. "Okay babies, serve us the lobster, and then you also get the hell out, so that Jake and me can be alone to get to know one another better" She smiled hungrily in my direction as she spoke. Whether it was for me or the food I could not tell. In retrospect, I reckon it was probably for both.

After expertly serving the caviar and fixing two plates of lobster with salad which they left for us on the serving table, they freshened our drinks and silently exited through the door hidden by the white film screen.

Over the meal, I told her how I lost my parents. She listened quietly, and when I was done she said sincerely; "Yeah, life's a bitch Jake baby. Life is a bitch."

Then I learned about her life, about Hollywood, and the highs and lows of being a big star. All the while she was speaking, I was saying to myself, 'Christ, here I am chatting with the great Lola Stevens. Me: Jake Silver from Brixton.' I could barely believe it.

She moved on to talking about Herschel Weinstein, whom she clearly loathed. She told me how that "Fuckin' shyster lawyer, I've got for a manager," talked her into signing up with him.

"He promised me a major motion picture within six months of my signing with him. Well honey; I had to face the fact that the studio had dropped me and I was not getting any new scripts popping through my mailbox any more. On top of that, my husband had run off with some young cunt of a starlet, plus two million bucks of my hard-earned money. So I needed work, not so much for the money, but to regain some confidence in myself. And then Herschel, this shitheel, arrives on my doorstep with promises of me being in a big pic within six months if I sign up to him. Well, he kept his word. I did get offered a part in a major movie. When I read the lousy script, I found that it was in a supporting role, playing Loretta Young's mother for Chrissakes."

Even though she hadn't finished her lobster yet, she nevertheless lit a cigarette, taking a couple of drags before putting it down on an ashtray and letting it smoulder away as she went on eating and talking.

"Firstly Jake sweetheart, I am a star. I am not some fuckin' support player. Jesus, by the time I had made just three lousy pictures, I was a bigger star than that cow Loretta Young will ever be. So, I'm supposed to appear in a movie where she gets top billing over me?"

She emptied her champagne glass and refilled it. As she leaned over the table to freshen mine, she said in a quiet, husky, but pleading voice; "And in any case Jake, and tell me the truth; do I look old enough to be Loretta's mother? C'mon, tell me the truth."

The fact was that I could not tell her the truth, because I did not know what the truth was. I had never seen her in any light other than the dimness of the club, or the semi-darkness of this dining/projection room. Of course, in those distant days of my youth, I was too young and innocent to realise that she was deliberately keeping herself in the dark, so to speak, not so much to hide the truth of her aging from me, but from herself. But like I have said before, I may have been callow and dumb; but I wasn't stupid. So I said what I knew she wanted (and needed) me to say "Firstly, you don't look a day older than Loretta Young, and secondly, if I may say so, you are far more lovely."

She positively glowed at that. In a flash she had become like Snow White's step mother after the magic mirror had assured her that she was still the fairest in the land.

"Why thank you Jake darling" she purred, her beautiful green eyes wide with joy, her mouth forming a moue. She had her two elbows close together on the table, her fingers interlinked, and her head resting against them. Whether it was the dim light, or the booze, I do not know, but as I looked across at her, she did look, well, if not beautiful, then wonderful.

"So what did you say to Herschel Weinstein, when you found it was only a supporting part?"

The moue instantly disappeared and her face hardened as she replied "It's not so much what I said to him as what he said to me."

"So, what did he say?"

She lit another cigarette.

"When I called him in New York to tell him that he had no right to offer me a supporting role, and that anyway I was not old enough to play Loretta's mother, he said to me in his cheap East Side N'Yawk nasal accent; "Listen sweetheart, you had better wake up to a few facts. Firstly, you are lucky to be offered any parts at all. Just to get them to offer you this part, I had to promise that you will give up the sauce for the duration of the shoot, and for at least one week before the opening. And secondly, I have to leave financial guarantees against your punctuality. You screw up just once by coming on the set late, or in no condition to act and they take fifty thou' off your fee'"

I was knocked out at how well she impersonated Herschel's voice and accent. It was, to movie mad me, like watching a great actress, playing a big dramatic scene for my private delectation. I watched her, full of fascination, as she continued "I told him that I had never been talked to like that in my entire life, and I said to him, 'who do you think you are to talk to me in this way?' And do you know what he said to me Jake darling? He said, "And there is something else you aint gonna like Lola, but you might as well know it now as later. They are going to want you to test for the role, because they are worried that you might look too old to play Loretta's mother."

'How dare you', I said to him. 'How dare you, a snot-nosed upstart little Jew-boy from Brooklyn, speak to Lola Stevens in this way'.

"Listen kid" he said. "To me you are just another washed-up, drunken old broad who lives on her memories" Can you believe that he could be so cruel Jake?"

"No," I said. And I meant it.

"But he wasn't finished with me yet," she said. He had the fucking nerve to say to me, "I signed you up out of the goodness of my heart, and, well, because I was in love with you when I was a kid. I was trying to get you another break. But," and these are the exact words he used Jake and I will never forget them, or forgive him for saying them. He said "Look Lola, you are an old lady. If you keep your nose clean, I'll try to re-launch you in old lady character parts. You could become another Lillian Gish, if you're prepared to work at it."

She poured herself the last dregs of the first bottle of champagne.

"Be a darling and open the other bottle will you sweetheart?"

Whilst I was doing so, very inexpertly, she went on.

"Well I did the only thing I could do. I just slammed the goddamned phone down.

I didn't hear from Herschel again for six months. That was until about five weeks ago. He phoned to tell me that some producer in Italy with a name like Spaghetti, or Fettuccine, or some fuckin' Italian grease ball name like that, was gonna make a movie about the Spanish civil war. It's about a young woman at the head of a guerrilla band who leads her men to glory by going to Madrid in a number of disguises and infiltrating Franco's high command and finding out their secrets and shit like that. The good news is that I am playing the starring role. The bad news is that I am always in disguise. The only times when I am not, like during the love scenes, they've got a younger actress to play my part."

"They'll have to go a long way to find someone lovely enough to play you" I said.

As I sit out here in Cuba reliving these scenes, I realise that back then, I could be as phoney as the proverbial three dollar bill, when it paid me to be. The only excuse I can offer, is that I was so immersed in the world of Hollywood movies, that being in a room with a famous film star, I had somehow or other deluded myself into thinking that I was actually in a movie, and so fed her the line that I imagined her co-star would or should have had.

But whatever the psychological causation behind it, she again reacted with glowing joy.

"Y'know Jake baby, I wanted to see you again, because of the lovely word you used to describe me, last night at your club. Do you remember what it was?"

I had not the foggiest idea.

"Oh, that" I said confidently, whilst racking my brains trying to recall what I could have possibly said that turned her on so. But unable to remember, I just had to brazen it out.

"Lola, I want you to know that I meant it, really and truly."

"Thank you baby" she purred. "D'you know, it is such a boost to my morale to find someone as young and handsome as you, who can still find an old broad like me enchanting. That was a beautiful word you found for me."

'So that was the big deal word that turned her on so' I thought. I was about to continue with my male leading role in this sad little movie scene, by throwing in a few more compliments, when she cut it short by saying "Just a minute darling. I've just realised that I'm almost out of ciggies. I must get the boys to go out and get me some. Do you want any?"

"Yes" I said, realising that this is probably going to be a long night. "And could I get a cup of coffee too?"

"Sure you can my baby," her voice all soft and furry. "Leave it all to Lola." She came round the table to where I was sitting and licked the tip of my nose with a flicking tongue before whispering with a strange, hungry smile;" I can look after you baby, like you've never been looked after."

I watched her walk away slightly unsteadily towards and around the screen, disappearing behind it. A few minutes later, faggots one and two minced and flounced their way across the room, followed by Lola. Stacey was carrying a cup of coffee, which he handed to me.

"I've jutht made coffee for mythelf with my own percolator. Would you like a cup?"

"Thanks " I said accepting it gratefully, while Lola was at the bar pouring two large cognacs.

She brought mine over to me, and then raised her own glass in my direction, saying "Here's to the last young man alive who finds me enchanting." I was of course too young to appreciate this sad, nostalgic truism.

After the 'boys' had gone on their fag-finding mission (in this instance, fag means cigarettes), I asked Lola when she is going to run the movie featuring herself at twenty-three.

"I don't think I'm in the mood for that right now" she said. "You know what I want to do? I just want to sit with you on my bedroom balcony and hold hands and talk, just like I used to do with my boyfriend when we were both sixteen"

"Where was this?" I had to wait for her to swallow a large swig of cognac before she answered "We lived on a ranch near Abilene. That's in Texas."

"Only, I am thinking Lola that it might have been a little warmer out on the balcony in Texas than it will be here tonight."

But she insisted, taking my hand, and leading me behind the screen and through the door by which, everyone barring me had been making their entrances and exits.

It led into the fag's bedroom. There was a large double bed, a small table with a coffee percolator on it, a dressing table and three wheel-about full-length mirrors in silver frames. She led me through that room into her own bedroom. This also had a large double bed, two dressing tables, a large chest of drawers, and one wall almost entirely made up of wardrobes with cupboards above. On the opposite wall were lace-curtained French windows through which we passed, on our way to the balcony.

And so, just as she had wanted, we stood, holding hands and looking down on the stream of traffic scurrying by below. It would have been quite romantic were it not for the fact that it was a typically damp-cold, bitingly wind strewn December night.

"I think we had better go in" I said. "In that thin dress you could catch a bad cold out here."

She suddenly turned to me, and putting her arms around my neck, said.

"Kiss me Jake, before we go back inside."

We kissed passionately and long. I felt like I was Tyrone Power or someone. After all, here I was, Jake Silver from Brixton Road, with a famous movie star in my arms. Once again I felt like I was actually starring in a movie. But there was no Otto Kruger or Claude Rains, playing the wronged husband to march in on us. Out there on the cold, windy, hotel balcony there wasn't even a director to shout 'cut'. So it turned out to be the longest kiss I had—up to that time—participated in.

When it was finally over, she said laughingly, while still in my arms, "You know what? My fanny has just turned into two large blobs of ice. Let's get into the warm, but quick!"

I opened the French windows and with her following me, went back into her bedroom. I presumed that I was leading the way back to the main reception room. Silly me!

I had not yet reached the door that led into 'gay heaven', through which we had to pass in order to make our way back, when she called to me softly "Jake."

She was standing on the far side of the room, the lampshade's glow behind causing her to be in silhouette. As I looked at her, she peeled off her negligee, leaving it to fall at her feet. Even though she was standing in deep shade, I could see that she was naked.

She then struck a pose, standing on her toes, with right foot crossed over left, head flung back, her left arm hung out at right angles to her body, her right crooked close to her body with her hand dangling limply.

"Do you still find me enchanting?" she said breathily and alluringly.

Frankly, I did and I didn't. On the plus side, whilst she might not have been as fabulous as she clearly must have been when she was young, she still had enough left over to look pretty damn good to my nineteen year-old eyes. On the down side, I found that when we were kissing, I was repelled by the odour of rancid alcohol that seemed to be coming out of every pore in her body, permeating and corrupting the subtle aroma of some expensive French scent, with which she had so liberally daubed herself.

But the sight of her still shapely body (at least, in the darkened room), the shapely, large and still well preserved breasts, and the full, inviting triangle of darkness adorning her crossed thighs, was enough for me.

So, in reply to her question, I replied, as breathily and as alluringly as I could manage; "Even more enchanting than I had thought before."

I went across to her. We again indulged in some passionate kissing, after which she breathlessly told me to take off my clothes. She helped me undress, saying as she did so, "Take your time baby. Don't go too fast. It is so much sexier if you undress slowly."

When I was completely unclothed, we kissed again, still standing up. By now, I was in a state of semi-erection. Then, she knelt down to kiss (nothing more), and play with it until it was fully erect. She asked me to turn around slowly, "So that I can admire that wonderful thing from all angles."

It was a very exhibitionistic kind of foreplay. It was more like the sort of thing you see in porno movies although I did not know it at the time.

Finally she led me to her bed. After we had been doing just about everything barring actual fucking, for at least half an hour, she suddenly half-whispered, half-moaned, "Jake, I feel terrible about what I am doing. I'm a bad, bad girl Jake. Would you punish me? It would make me feel so much better."

"But you have nothing to feel guilty about darling" I naively said.

"Punish me" she hissed. "Now."

I was at a complete loss. "Okay, okay, But, how do you want me to do to punish you?"

She rolled over and away from me, to open a cupboard next to the side of the bed. When she rolled back again, I could see in the dim light that she was holding a large, round, hair brush.

"Use this" she hissed, handing me the hairbrush.

Then she crawled down to the bottom of the bed, and knelt down on the carpeted floor, her head resting on her folded arms, which lay on the bed, her white, shapely bottom, now fully exposed.

"Come round here darling" she moaned quietly.

I did as she wished although I was a bit embarrassed by my erection bobbing about as I walked.

"Now beat me for being for being so bad," she said, raising her head and turning it around to face me. I was struck by her look of pure lecherous debauchery. Thick lips, now in a half-smile-half leer, eyes half closed and heavy lidded, her thick black hair strewn all over her face. I was now beginning to find this affair a bit too much for me. My other two sexual adventures both possessed at least a veneer of emotional involvement. But this was raw sex pure and simple, and of a type that I found sexually off-putting rather than stimulating.

I tapped her bottom, noticing at the same time, how its whiteness reflected the glow of the lamp stationed in the corner of the room.

"No. Hit me hard" Her voice was rasping and demanding. "Hit me as hard as you can. Make me pay for my badness. Be like my father was when I was naughty at home. Beat me for my badness so that I will never forget it."

So I did. I hit her really hard. I landed three hard thwacks on that glowing white arse of hers.

"More" she hissed. "Do it more. And as hard as you can."

I struck her about six times as hard as I could. But I was now utterly sickened by it.

"That's enough" I said. "I don't like doing this any more."

She stood up. Suddenly, her persona had entirely changed. She had become a meek, chastised, fully compliant, girlish person. With her head down in a pose of pure humility, she said quietly, "You can do with me what you like now darling.. I promise to be obedient to your will."

Then, before I could react to this new, different Lola Stevens, she fell to her knees before me, and with her experienced lips and tongue, brought my now semi-flaccid cock back to its full erection.

"Get back on the bed my master and lie on your back."

She straddled me, directing my cock into her with her hands. As it slid in, she let out an involuntary 'aah'.

But at the same time I heard another groan from somewhere else.

I opened my eyes and looked diagonally across towards the faggot's bedroom, which was from where the other groan had come.

I saw that the inter-leading door had been opened and that one of the full-length mirrors had been angled in such a way as to reflect what Lola and I were up to. I knew this because I could clearly see them in the reflection. I could see their heads and the tops of their naked shoulders. I could also plainly see that they were both face down with Georgio's moustached face above Stacey's in such a way that it became instantly obvious to me that one was lying on top of the other.

"Jesus, they're watching us," I whispered urgently to Lola. "Close the door for Chrissakes."

"Why baby?" she said silkily, as she moved her body up and down on my 'mister big'. "I like them to watch. It gives them such a thrill. Don't you like to know that the sight of your lovely hard cock is giving them such big thrills baby?" As she spoke, she raised her body high so that only the very tip of my cock was inside her, the rest of it being made visible for her faggy attendants.

The idea that at that very moment two gay men were getting their kicks by ogling my penis was too much for me. This was sex through a distorting mirror. I took advantage of her raised position to pull my cock out of her. I sat up suddenly, and pushing her over on to her side, I leapt off the bed and grabbing my clothes and using them to cover my now rapidly receding erection, I ran out of the room, through the gay lovers bedroom, without casting a glance at them even for a second and on into the main reception room beyond, where I threw my clothes on faster than I have ever done before or since.

Then, still feeling sickened, unclean, and for some reason, panicky, I literally ran across the room towards the door leading to the vestibule, flung it open, grabbed my overcoat, threw back the front door of the suite, and ran. I ran down the hallway to the stairs, which I took three at a time, ran across the foyer, much to the worried stare of the night porter, ran through the cold night air all the way up Park Lane, and didn't stop running until I had reached Hyde Park Corner.

By then, I felt far enough away from them to feel safe from their clutches. So, once I had recovered my breath, I strolled the rest of the way home, going over the events of the evening in my head. It did not take me too long to come to the inescapable conclusion that Lola's sole intention in hiring me, was to seduce me into her sick, drunken, sado-masochistic, homosexual world.

The way I had worked it out, when Lola excused herself to go into Georgio and Stacey's room, ostensibly to say she needed them to go out and buy cigarettes, she actually went in to plan out the night's entertainment with them, something she had probably done many times in the past. They did go out, because I saw them do so, but only for long enough for Lola to get me on to her bedroom balcony. Then, with the French windows closed behind us, and the roar of the traffic blocking out most other sounds, they slipped back into their room, keeping dead quiet, until they heard Lola ask me if I still found her 'enchanting'. This I reckoned was their cue to silently open the inter-leading door, which I remembered shutting behind me on our way out to the balcony. Lola must have told them that when she utters this cue line she will have just revealed her naked body to me, which they rightly guessed will grab all of my attention and concentration.

Then there was all that strange exhibitionist foreplay. The getting undressed slowly business, 'because it was sexier' Sexier for whom, I wondered? And then I recalled that while we were involved in all this foreplay, I felt I was starring in some kind of a pornographic cabaret act. Little did I realise that this is exactly what it was! Even the extraneous groan that led me to investigate what was going on, had, in my opinion been planned. Presumably the idea was, that once I was in mid-fuck, I would be so 'sent' that even the knowledge of being observed by two queers would not be enough for me to call it off. If I hadn't done so, I reckoned that the two faggots joining us in our bed could not have been very far away.

Shit, I felt cheated, used and sick to my stomach, as I gratefully opened the front door to my apartment. I went straight to my bedroom, undressed and, after standing under a shower for ten minutes, spent another half hour in the bath, until I was sure that I was completely free of the sour, stale, alcohol-mixed with-scent smell of Lola's body. But I could not wash away the sight of the faggots faces reflected in the mirror.

Before falling asleep, I checked the time. It was three forty-five AM. 'Not much later than I would have got home anyway' I thought, as I drifted off to sleep.

On my way to work that night, I found myself wondering how I am going to bring up with Jack, the little matter of Lola telling me she has agreed to pay not two, but three hundred pounds for my services. Then it struck me that she probably won't pay anything at all. After all, the situation clearly was that she had never intended to be paying me for playing the piano. She did not even have a piano in the suite for me to play! It was obvious to me now that I had been hired to give a sexual service, in exactly the same way a man hires a prostitute. And as I had not given the required satisfaction, plus the fact that by now, she had probably pissed off to Rome to make her movie, there was little to no chance of her coming up with the moolah.

This is going to cause Jack to ask me what went wrong and I will be forced into having to tell him the entire embarrassing story. 'Shit' I said out loud as I walked along the street toward the club. Then the possibility crossed my mind that Jack had been in on the whole deal, but I put it out of my mind as soon as I thought of it. I liked him too much to give credence to anything like that.

By the time I walked into the club, I had almost worked out an entire film script in explanation for Lola's refusal to pay any money. But surprise, surprise, as I came in, a smiling Jack Montgomery came over to me and putting his arm around my shoulder said "You must have performed jolly well old chap. Lola Stevens sent us three hundred quid, instead of the two hundred we had agreed. And she sent you a little parcel. Wait, I'll get it."

As I watched him hurry away to his little office, I was relieved to realise that Jack had not been trying to put one over on me; it was simply a mix-up over the original price. But that was as nothing compared to the pleasure I felt and relief that Lola had paid any money at all!

"Here it is old son" Jack said as he handed over my little parcel to me. I went over to the table in the corner where I had my dinner every night, took out a cigarette, lit it and then proceeded to open the silver paper wrapping.

I found a packet of State Express 555's (which was the brand I was smoking in those far-off days), an expensive looking gold lighter, and a folded-up note with a Dorchester Hotel letterhead. The handwriting was rambling and only just legible. It said.

Darling Jake,

Thank you for last night. We all thought you were great and were very sorry when you left so soon. Here's hoping that after you have given it some thought, you will stay much longer, the next time we get together. Remember darling, if you want to live and love life to the full, you have to experience it to the full. Here are the ciggies you ordered but forgot to collect, as well as something to light them with. Think kindly of us whenever you use it.

Lots of love,

(Signed), Lola, Georgio, Stacey

I put the packet of fags in my pocket and used the slim, gold cigarette lighter to set fire to Lola's note, which I let burn to ashes in the ash tray on the table.

On the Friday night of that week, my weekly salary, which was paid in cash, amounted to one hundred and seventy-nine pounds.

I knew that this was a one-off payment. But together with the money I had saved, mainly from the tips I was getting, I now had about two hundred and fifty pounds in my pocket. And that was after buying myself a new overcoat, an expensive suit as well as a sports jacket, and heaven knows how many records and books.

Chapter 23

For the next four months or so, which is up to the time when the proverbial shit finally hit the fan, life was great, even though it had set itself into a kind of steady routine.

To start with, I had regularised my relationship with Meri. After a couple of weeks, she gave up the eye fluttering, ogling bit, although I did get looks of admiration from her after I played something during my daily practising sessions that she particularly liked. But now that the 'love affair' was over, it allowed me to get to know her better, and liking her more and more.

Apart from the care and consideration she gave me, and the dedication to her job in general, she was also extremely interesting to talk and listen to. She told me of the utter poverty that she and her family were forced to endure in Cuba. I learned that only the children of the wealthy and the gangsters (who were indivisible in action and philosophy), went to school.

I remember watching her face as she impassively told me about her father. He had joined a group calling itself 'Cuba Liberacion'. She told me about the night when she was eleven years old and the police came to take her papa away for 'questioning'. "He was never seen again," she said.

She was making me a cup of morning coffee as she told me about this. As I said, her face remained expressionless as she spoke, but tears rolled down her cheeks when, in response to my question, she described to me what he looked like.

I was also very surprised and impressed to discover how politically aware she was. She knew even then, many years before I came to realise it, that the 'American Way of Life' is good only for those of the greed and grab mentality and that if you do it legally you are a 'business man', and if you do it illegally, you are a 'gangster'. But the raison d'etre is exactly the same. I remember her saying, 'The Yankee government, eet value life only in dollars and cents. The ordinary people, they no count. Ees no good Master'.

It had become my regular morning routine to go out shortly after breakfast, which was around 11 AM, and either stroll around the big stores, which abounded in this high gloss part of town, or take a brisk walk through Hyde Park. Even though I was much too young to fully appreciate it, the carefree feeling of being young, well dressed and with plenty of money in my pocket was endlessly exhilarating. Twice a week I would take in a movie, and every Sunday, I would visit Aunt Sarah and Uncle Harry. Life in their house had returned once more to its normal tense, tea-ridden, over-fed state, now that Aunt Sarah had accepted the inevitability of Ivan's marriage to Janet, which had been set for early in the New Year, still many months away. But even then, she did mange to smuggle me into the kitchen one evening, and whisper to me that she would be in my debt not only for the remainder of her stay in this world, but in the next also, if I could find a nice Jewish girl who could steal Ivan's affections away from 'the Shicksa'. But a single glance at Ivan's face whenever he looked at Janet (who I finally met and was really impressed by), should have been enough to convince any but the blind or insane that there was not the slightest possibility of that happening.

I remember how this routine was broken up somewhat by the arrival in London of Harold Landing with his fiancee yet!

The very idea of Newcastle's 'Shtupper-in Chief', the ultimate 'Cock of the North' settling for just one woman for the rest of his life was almost surreal, yet that is how he introduced her to me when I met them.

They were spending a week in London, staying with the girl's aunt, at a house in Golders Green (which, if you don't know, is a very Jewish suburb of London). It was from there that Harold phoned me 'on the off chance that I would not be too busy to see them'. When we did meet, I could not work out whether it was I who had changed or Harold. Or, maybe, it was the effect that London was having on him, but that warm, intimate and easy friendship which we had enjoyed so much in Newcastle had now, sadly, evaporated. As they did not know their way around London. I arranged to meet them at Piccadilly Circus, and then take them for lunch. Knowing that Harold's taste for women had always inclined towards the type of chic I refer to as 'a storm in a D cup' (with blonde hair, blue eyes and pink nipples), I was surprised to find that his intended bride, whose name by the way, was Rebecca, turned out to be a short, petite and surprisingly unglamorous brunette. Even more surprisingly, considering his past, it turned out that she was a schoolteacher.

I tried my arse off to rekindle the old camaraderie, but after twenty minutes of boring conversation interspersed with those blank silences which sit so heavily between stilted sentences, I knew it was all doomed to failure. Harold, whilst never being what anyone could describe as a ball of fire was now positively monosyllabic, and even worse, against the backdrop of London, he seemed positively provincial. He was still the same good looking guy, a kind of taller version of Artie Shaw, but was clearly intimidated by the rush and bustle of life in the Capital. The only interesting thing that came out our lunch was that Meyer is busy writing his first symphony. Beyond that, zilch baby.

Rebecca, was another of those 'nice' girls. But, unfortunately, 'nice' is not one of the traits I find endearing in a female. Character and personality are what attract me. Being 'nice' too often runs hand in glove with being 'boring' which is one of the worst social crimes anybody can be guilty of; spitting when you speak and having terminal BO being the only two social stigmata that rate above it.

They were not even interested in taking a peek at the club where I worked, let alone visit it while it was open. "Thanks for asking us Jake" Harold said, when I suggested it over a post-lunch coffee; "But Rebecca isn't interested in that sort of thing. And anyway, I promised her that we would spend the day shopping. Then we are going to see a film at one of those fabulous cinemas in Leicester Square, and after that it's back to Becky's aunt's place for supper."

I saw them three times during their week's stay in London. Each meeting was more painfully dull than the previous one. When I finally did wave them goodbye at Kings Cross station, I felt a pang of guilt at the relief I was feeling as I watched them, waving back to me out of their carriage window as the train disappeared northwards. On my way back to my apartment, I found myself wondering what magic this plain looking, dry-as-dust school ma'am could possibly possess that could lure Harold away from all those glamorous chicks he had in such abundance.

I guess he just wanted to 'settle down'. Poor bastard.

Which brings me on to my own sex life at that time. During this four month period of which i write, I did manage to get myself a steady albeit only, albeit only a bi-weekly bed-date.

She was an American theatrical and film agent I had met at the club. The agency for whom she worked represented some pretty big names in both spheres of the entertainment world. She came into the club alone one night, waiting for some actor or other who failed to turn up. Whilst she waited, she took one of the high stools by the piano, requesting a few tunes which I duly played. I in turn requested a few facts about some character actors I was interested in, like Jack Norton_and Sheldon Leonard which she laughingly supplied. She found it really amusing that I should want to know about these small-timers, rather than the big stars like Gable, Astaire or John Wayne etc. It ended up with her inviting me back to her hotel for a drink when I was through playing. We had just one drink in her hotel suite before we hungrily fulfilled each other's needs. Evelyn (that is not her real name, but like I said before, I do not give away a lady's name, unless she specifically allows it), came from Los Angeles. Actually she was born in Chicago but shortly after she married, moved out to LA, where her husband became a big- time but over-worked lawyer.

"Either he is so damned busy that he has no time for sex, or, if he has time for it, I am the last to know."

She told me how it was out of boredom with life on the west coast that she took a job with a major theatrical and film agency. To me, the idea of living so close to Hollywood seemed the very opposite of boredom. So I did not believe her. A few years later, I found out just how boring and bloody awful a place Hollywood is. But at the time, it seemed inconceivable to me.

I did believe her when she told me that she has a bed-mate in New York City, another in New Orleans, yet another in San Francisco, and now me, in London. She explained it this way: "I gotta have my regular meat injections baby, or I work at half cock, if you know what I mean."

She told me she would be visiting London every two weeks or so for the next couple of months. Apparently, Warner Brothers, or somebody, was about to make a big new blockbuster movie about the '39-'45 war, and half of it was to be shot in Britain. She represented two of the movie's main stars, which was why she will be coming to Britain with such regularity.

And that is why and how I got myself a bi-weekly bed-date.

Physically, she was not bad to look at. She was slim, sophisticated, elegantly dressed, and in many ways, intelligent. She was (or admitted to being) thirty-five years of age. Like most middle-aged, wealthy, American ladies, she tried to be like Eve Arden. And she was almost as funny.

Once, as we lay in bed, I asked her if she had any hang-ups about the disparity of our respective ages.

"You may not be mature enough for me laddy," she answered, and then reaching out to take my cock in her hand she added; "But this, sure as hell, is." Naturally, her handling of it made it stiff. As I entered her again, for the second or maybe, it was the third time, she said to me "Have you ever considered joining Erections Anonymous?"

Yes sir; all in all, life was just about as sweet as it could be for me. Then, like I said, just four months after I started my job, almost to the day, things went rapidly down hill.

Actually, the shit started approaching the fan a couple of weeks earlier, although I did not realise it at the time.

It began one evening, while I was eating my supper, prior to commencing work; Jack sat down to join me at my table. After the usual pleasantries were completed, he said suddenly; "Jake old chap, I hate to do this; but do you think you could lend me some money for just a couple of days. I will definitely be able to give it you back within a week. It's a rather nasty gambling debt I have to repay, at short notice."

"How much do you need?" I asked.

"Well, actually, I need about ten thou' to clear the whole thing up. But I am sure that if I could give them just some of it, it might keep them quiet for a bit."

"Christ Jack, I've got nothing like that kind of money. Have you asked Eliot? He may be able to lend you some."

"Eliot says he can let me have five hundred and not a penny more. And I have got to raise at least a thousand to keep them from doing something rather nasty to me."

I liked Jack very much. And I was not unaware that everything I had; my apartment, my wardrobe of clothes, and the money in my pocket was due to him. So I genuinely wanted to help him.

"All the money I have in the world is three hundred pounds Jack."

"You couldn't raise any more I suppose?"

"Not really," I said.

He thought for a while before saying "Look, do you think you could let me have the three hundred? I'll try and get the other two from somewhere else. Then, with Eliot's monkey (racing slang for five hundred pounds), I can give them a thousand, which will shut them up, at least until I have sold my house. After that, I can settle all my debts, including yours."

I was amazed at that piece of news. "You're selling your house?"

"'Fraid so old chap. But don't worry about me. I'll find another place, every bit as nice."

As I always carried my money with me, because the feel of a bundle of money made me feel good, I took it out and handed it to him, saying, "There is exactly three hundred pounds there Jack. Let me have it back when you can."

He took the money and without counting it, stuffed it into his inside pocket.

"I'll just pop into the office and write you out an IOU for it," but I stopped him. "Christ, there's no need for that.. I trust you enough to know that when you have it, you'll let me have it back."

"With profits dear fellow" he said sincerely.

I hadn't left myself entirely without money. I still had two postal orders to the value of sixteen pounds, being the last two payments made by my Uncle to me, when he thought I was still in Newcastle, and which had been sent on to me from there. And, as this was Wednesday, with only two days to go before payday, I didn't feel that I had made a dangerous sacrifice.

Another symptom of the approaching bad news (although I thought nothing of it at the time), was a nightly visit by three middle aged men, in serious suits with matching faces, white shirts and dark ties, who would arrive at about nine-thirty and always sit in the darkest corner of the club. I was not sure, but I thought they were the same men who waylaid Jack on my very visit to the Four Jacks. Whether they were or not, every night they would come into the club to be joined by Jack and the four of them would talk for about half an hour, after which, they would leave.

Judging by the look on Jack's face every night after they had gone, they clearly were not exactly bearers of good tidings.

But that was Jack's business and nothing whatever to do with me. I kept my nose clean. I was never late to work. I played my arse off every night, and as far as I could tell was liked by the regulars. In fact, I now I had my own private circle of admirers, who came to the club, primarily to listen to me. These 'fans' invariably came in after midnight, long after Jack's doom-mongers had left. Their attention to my playing and their applause which often followed, reinforced my feeling of job security.

Friday past without my receiving anything other than my pay check. The following Friday, nine days after I had loaned Jack the money and I found myself wondering, while playing the piano, if tonight he will add the outstanding three hundred to my salary. After all, he had said that the loan was only for a 'couple of days'.

At one o'clock in the morning, as usual, the waiter brought over the white envelope that contained my salary. Because at that hour there are always customers near me, occupying all the high stools around the piano, especially on Fridays and Saturdays, I never open the envelope when I get it. I just slip it into my inside pocket and go on playing. But this time I noticed some writing on the envelope which is not normally there. So I put it on the piano in front of me and went on playing whilst I read it. It said: 'Jake, please make a point of seeing me before you leave. It is most important. Jack'.

For some reason, the seriousness implied by the tone of that note, went unnoticed by me. I was sure it was simply to remind me to collect the repayment of my loan. As I ran through my Porgy and Bess medley, which I could now play in my sleep after having played it so many times, I found myself wondering how much Jack will add to it, because after all, he did say that he will return it 'with profits'. Added to this happy thought was the knowledge that I had made twelve pounds in tips that night.

So it was in high spirits that I went into Jack's little office, after the last of the customers was gone.

"Come in old lad" Jack said, as I popped my head around the door. I was struck by how pale and tired he looked. He was hugging to his body a half-full bottle of Armagnac. His desk was awash with what appeared to be letters, documents and bills. Sitting on top of all this detritus was a large green coloured glass ashtray loaded with cigarette ends.

"Care for a drink Jake?" he said lifelessly.

"Er, no thanks Jack. I've had enough for one night." I sat down on the hard wooden backed chair facing him across the desk.

He took a big swig from his bottle. Then he offered me a cigarette.

"No thanks, I said. I've also smoked enough for one night." I was just beginning to get the first inklings that things were not going to go how I imagined they would, when I first read Jack's note.

He set the bottle down on the right hand corner of the desk, took two cigarettes out of his packet, and placed one in front of me. Then he opened his desk drawer and retrieved a brandy goblet which he placed next to the cigarette.

"You'll probably need them before I am finished." His voice was flat and bitter. I was now sure that I was about to hear something I was not going to like because I had never before heard Jack speak in this tone of voice.

After he had lit his cigarette and blown a cloud of smoke into the already smoke-filled atmosphere of the office, he said.

"What do you know about Rights Issues?"

"Nothing" I said, "except that I think I heard my Uncle mention the words once."

"Jack, my old love" he said as he leaned over to fill my brandy goblet, without my bidding; "What I am going to tell you may sound like a load of bloody nonsense to you. But I feel I owe it to you to tell you exactly what is going on."

I was now starting to feel a heavy pall of foreboding enveloping me. I said nothing. But I did light the cigarette and followed it up with a swig of the booze in front of me.

Jack leaned back in his chair, put his feet against the desk and began: "When the directors of a company decide that they need to raise some additional money, one of the most common ways of raising it is by issuing additional shares to the value of the extra amount they wish to raise. This new tranche of shares is known as a Rights Issue. Understand me so far?" He looked across at me, his face ashen, the whites of his eyes rheumy and red.

"I think so" I said. I was unable to see what all this high finance talk had to do with me, except that it might be a prelude to Jack telling me he couldn't pay back the loan just now.

He took a slurp of his drink and a deep pull on his cigarette before saying; "Good."

He leaned forwards, his hands interlocked on the desk in front of him: "When we set up the 'Four in Hand' Jake, I and my three partners agreed that there should be fifty thou' in the kitty. This was to be made up of fifty thousand one pound shares. I was to hold forty per cent, being at the sharp end of the business as it were. My three partners would hold twenty per cent each. This meant that if there was an argument over policy, so long as any one of the three partners sided with me, my view would always prevail because it would represent a sixty-forty majority in my favour. The only time I could lose would be if all my partners disagreed with me at the same time. This seemed very unlikely so long as we showed a good profit. And we are. But I was wrong Jake. Bloody wrong."

He watched his own hand carefully stubbing out his cigarette. Then, taking another, and tapping it slowly on his desk, he continued: "Now, my forty per cent meant that I had to put in twenty thousand pounds, because, as you know, twenty thou' is forty percent of the fifty thousand pound kitty. Unfortunately, due to a rather nasty run on the race track I no longer had that kind of cash. To tell you the truth," he stopped while he refilled his glass, "I could not have laid my hands on twenty thousand shirt buttons let alone that amount in hard cash."

I nodded, I hope wisely, even though I still could not see how I came into this complicated story of high finance.

"When I told my partners that I could not raise this kind of cash at that time, they said it was no great shakes. They volunteered to put up my twenty thou' for me, provided I put up 'Jacks' in the Strand as collateral."

Before I could ask what that meant, he explained that 'collateral' means that should he fail to come up with the twenty thousand pounds, the company takes over 'Jacks'.

"But" he went on, "my partners assured me that there would be no hurry for me to pay them this money, and they also pointed out that in any case, as it would be the company of which I own forty per cent, doing the take over, I would still own forty percent of the club, even if I fail to bung in a single penny of the twenty thou' I owe. Well, that sounded pretty fair to me."

I drank my glass of Armagnac straight down. Even though Jack had said nothing yet to alarm me, the cold clamminess encircling my gut was tipping me off that the old proverbial shit was hurrying in my direction on its way to the fan.

As Jack refilled my glass, he asked, "Do you follow me so far?"

I nodded.

"But what I did not do my old lad, was read the Articles of Incorporation, which in simple language, means the agreed rules by which the company will operate. One of these Articles states that if any of us four directors feels it absolutely essential to call a meeting at short notice, he can do so provided that he gives his fellow directors a minimum of twenty-four hours notice of it. Also, it says that for any meeting to be legally convened, a majority of shareholders must be present or represented at the meeting. It must also be shown that everything within reason was done to inform all the directors of the impending extraordinary general meeting."

I could now all but smell the shit on its way fanwards.

"Two weeks ago," he went on, the expression on his face grim and bitter; "I and some friends flew to Longchamps in France to attend a race meeting there. We left my place to drive to Poole Airport at about 8.30 am on the Friday morning. We returned on Saturday evening at around 10.30 PM. I know that because I was back here in the club by around half past midnight. You probably didn't even notice I'd been away."

I said, "Well Fridays and Saturdays are so busy here, I hardly notice anything. But I do remember that you paid me on the Saturday instead of Friday as you normally do."

"You are absolutely correct my old lad" he replied. "But what I did not know was, that they must have been having me watched, because at 10.30, on that very Friday morning, just two hours after I had set off with my friends (he held up the forefingers of both hands to emphasise the point), a telegram was delivered to my house, summoning me to an urgent Board Meeting, to take place at noon the following day. Of course, I knew nothing of it. And the barman who collected it, held on to it until I got back the next night. So there was a board meeting held, twenty-five and a half hours after I had been officially informed, and which was attended by the other three directors, representing sixty per cent of the shares. In other words it was a perfectly legal meeting."

Now Jack got up out of his chair to pace about, like he was trying to break free from the chains of inevitability.

"They decided unanimously at that meeting, that the company should commence a massive expansion programme, opening up drinking clubs all around Britain, and in Paris and Rome also. To this end, a Rights Issue of another half million one pound shares must be created."

I watched Jack as he marched grim and bitter-faced, across to his desk and venomously ram his cigarette into the ashtray. It was as if he was trying to force the half smoked fag through it rather than just stubbing it out.

"This meant me having to find a further two hundred thousand pounds if I wished to retain my forty per cent share. If not, then my share of the business fell to just four per cent. They also decided, if that weren't enough, that all and any outstanding bills must be called in at once. The only large bill outstanding to the company," and here he talked through gritted teeth as he stomped up and down his little office, "Was my bloody, fucking, twenty thousand which the company originally lent me." He stopped his marching to turn and face me. Gripping the back of his office chair so tightly that his knuckles glowed white he said bitterly "Well, on the following Monday morning, I was served with a notice giving me seven days to settle or foreclosure proceedings against 'Jacks' in the Strand would begin immediately."

"Are your partners those three men who have been coming in every night, and who you've been sitting talking to?" I asked.

"Yep. And I was talking to them, trying to get them to give me a little more time to raise some money. The way I saw it, even if I could not retain my forty per cent interest, I might be able to raise enough cash to buy a big enough percentage to at least hang on to my seat at the boardroom table. They were very kind" he went on bitterly." They gave me exactly one week to raise some more money, but then said that they would have to charge for this extra time. They told me that unless I can find an earnest of a thousand pounds, just for their bloody time, they would have to proceed immediately. That was why I had to borrow your three hundred quid Jake. It was towards the thousand, which, after a bit of a battle, I did manage to raise. Y'see, what I had decided to do, was use the additional week to borrow as much as I could from the bank, using my house as surety, which, although it was above 'Jacks', was not involved with my twenty thousand pound shortfall on the club. But dammit, when I examined the deeds, I found that Sybil, my ex-wife, who had bought me the house as a wedding present, had bought the bloody thing in the name of Berryland, which was the name of her previous but dead husband. And I never thought to ask her to change the deeds into my name after our marriage. Of course I tried to phone her. It was my intention either to get her to send me a telegram allowing me to borrow against the house, or failing that, to just lend me some bloody money. God knows, she's got enough of it. But with the telephone system being as bad as it is, it took me three days to get a call through to Southern Rhodesia, and when I finally did, I discovered she was on a Caribbean cruise with some man or other. So the whole damned idea fell through I'm afraid."

He took another swig of the Armagnac straight out of the bottle, which he proceeded to carry with him as he resumed his prowling around the room.

"So Jake, it means that I now have only a four per cent interest in this and the other club. And on top of that, I now find that I am not even the owner of the house in which I live, so I can neither sell it, nor raise any money against it"

There was a long, ice-cold pause, the only noise being the creaking of the occasional floorboard as Jack made his way up, down and around the office. Then, he stopped and turning in my direction said "Today, I received this registered letter." As he spoke, he retrieved it from his inside pocket and handed it to me to read. It said.

Dear Jack,

As you know, our company has decided upon a dramatic expansion scheme and we have broadened our share capital in order to bring this about. As our expenses will be heavy at the outset, we are sure you will understand that all outgoings must be carefully monitored and controlled. As we also told you, Tristram Investments, Liechtenstein, have taken up our Rights Issue in its entirety and have given us their proxy vote to represent them at all future Board Meetings, until further notice.

In view of the fact that you now have only a four per cent shareholding in our company, plus the fact that we will be undertaking a fundamental review of management policy, this letter serves to inform you that at our last Board

Meeting, you were voted off the Board. You will be receiving a separate letter from our lawyers confirming this.

Further, we have decided that your services as General Manager of 'Jacks, and 'The Four in Hand' will no longer be required after April 1st. 1950. As part of our careful fiscal control measures, we further decided that need for piano music is unnecessary. Accordingly, we hereby instruct you to give the statutory two weeks notice of termination of employment to both Mr. Reginald de Courcey and Mr. Jake Silver. This notice is to be served no later than Monday March 15 1950.

It then went on to thank Jack for all his hard work and the pleasure that their short association had given them.

I noticed my hand was shaking slightly as, having read the letter, I handed it back to him. As he took it, he said "Of course you've guessed who 'Tristram Investments' is? It is a company set up in Liechtenstein specifically for the purpose of doing what they have now succeeded in doing ; namely, now that both clubs are doing so nicely, grabbing them for themselves.

It was now the early hours of Saturday April 13, which meant that from the end of the month, I was out of a job. I felt numb. It was exactly like when I awoke in my Aunt's house on that fateful morning after both my parents had been killed. My beautiful world, upon which my feet had been planted so solidly and happily, had been wrenched away from under me, leaving me tumbling in a vortex of blind panic and disbelief.

Jack may have said other things to me after that. He may have apologised for taking almost all my money and being unable to pay it back. He may have noted how unfair it all was. He could have said a thousand things; I was unaware of them. The screen had faded to black.

The next scene to impinge itself on my memory was walking slowly home from the club. A fine, gritty, granular snow, whipped up by an unseasonable wind, was stinging my cheeks and covering the shoulders of my overcoat like an extreme case of dandruff. But I was numb to it. My brain was and a tumble of disorder disbelief. And beyond that: nothing.

Once back in the apartment, I went straight to my bedroom, where I kicked off my shoes and lay down on the bed, without even removing my overcoat. And I stayed that way until I got up four fretful and restless hours later. I once read somewhere how Marilyn Monroe usually slept in her brassiere, because it gave her a sense of security. It was probably for the same reason that I did not undress that night. I too had to have something tangible of my own to cling on to, and in essence, all I now had left over from the security of yesterday were the clothes I was wearing.

Sleep was out of the question. I looked at my watch; it was 7.30 in the morning. I got out of bed, undressed, put on my dressing gown and hurried upstairs to the study, where, with the aid of a writing pad, I checked over my financial position. I guess I did it because, in the sea of depression and self pity in which I was so damn near drowning, grabbing on to the straw of something as positive as adding up and subtracting figures, seemed to deflect my sense of hopelessness, thus keeping me afloat, if only temporarily.

The analysis of my financial position revealed that I had my thirty-five pounds in salary as well as two pounds left over from the previous week. Plus that, I still had the two postal orders that my Uncle had sent to me in Newcastle after I had left University. That was a further eighteen pounds. So, all in all I had fifty-five pounds, plus of course, two more weeks salary to come. Against that, I had to pay Meri (at that very moment, I heard her opening the front door to commence her day's work. The sudden realisation that I had to give her two weeks notice, from Monday was just too awful for me to contemplate, so I shut the thought out by forcing myself to concentrate more strongly than ever on the mathematics of my future.

The upshot of all my busy additions and subtractions plus assessments of unknown costs, such as telephone, gas, electricity, and general rates etc., and taking into account the fifty pounds I owed Jack's tailor for the dress suit he was making for me, I should have about twelve pounds left over at the end with which to face the cruel world.

There and then, I made the decision to give up smoking and drinking, that is, unless someone else was doing the buying. I decided to give Meri only half the amount I normally gave her to buy food with, saying that I will be eating lunch out every day. I had to accept that my outdoor lunch will consist of nothing more than a couple of slices of toast from the cheapest café I could find from now on. But it would make me a saving of about ten pounds per week.

I phoned down to Meri to ask her to bring me a cup of tea. Whilst I waited for it, I tried to make a list of all the things I had bought since I had moved into the apartment, because they all had to be packed and stored somewhere. My list showed that I had bought ten shirts, three suits, a dozen pairs of socks, a dozen ties, two silk scarves, and a dozen handkerchiefs. This was apart from at least fifty new records, and a half dozen beautifully bound volumes of the Sonatas of Mozart and Beethoven, as well as separate volumes of Chopin's

Nocturnes, Etudes, Scherzi and Mazurkas. All I lacked were the suitcases to pack them in.

Never having had to face financial troubles before, this new experience lay like a large, heavy, ball of concrete inside me.. It destroyed all my appetites; food, living and loving: even sex seemed to lose its magic for me. I reckon, at that time, if Lana Turner and Rita Hayworth had both walked into the apartment stark naked, I doubt if I could have got it up for them. (Well, maybe I would have made an exception for the exquisite Lana and Rita. But nobody else.)

Over my tea, which Meri brought in, and after assuring her that I was not ill or anything, because she said that I looked unwell, I worked out my immediate future, which I duly wrote down in list form:

Tomorrow (Sunday). Phone Aunt Sarah and make some excuse for not visiting that evening. (Because I knew that no sooner had I walked in through the front door of her house, than her x-ray vision would reveal to her at a glance that something was wrong. And frankly, I was in no condition to handle the inquisition plus the worried faces, plus the 'I-told-you-so's', that would follow my spilling the beans which I would have to do if I wanted to get out of her house in one piece. On top of that, the thought of having to eat all the vast quantities of food, which in better days, I so used to enjoy, was anathema to me. I also could not face that other thing I would have to eat; humble pie.)

Monday. Make a round of all the band leaders' offices and other agencies to see if there is any other work going. I also made a marginal note to tell everyone who comes into the club that I am available for work.

Tuesday. Start looking for somewhere cheap to stay.

Just writing down those words filled me with such a sense of desolation and isolation, that I stopped right there. I went back downstairs and lay soaking in my fabulous, luxurious, bath contemplating how lucky I have been and how fucking miserable everything is now. My promised land of sex, money and fun had been a mirage after all.

Monday turned out to be total shit. It began with a phone call from the mother of the young lady who was due to get married the following Sunday, and at who's reception I had been booked to play, thereby earning myself an additional fifteen pounds. She rang to tell me that the wedding was off. The bridegroom's father has had a heart attack and the groom, as the only son, had to return to Australia to be with his mother. She also told me how upset her daughter the bride, was. 'The hell with how upsetting it is for her' I thought. It was a mortal blow to me, because I had taken the earnings from this gig into my financial figurings and the loss of it meant that I would have almost no money left after my job comes to an end.

The sum total result of my making the rounds of the band agencies, plus the phone calls to every band leader I could think of, resulted in me being offered one job, for eight pounds per week, to play in a hotel bar for six hours per night. I turned it down.

When I got to 'The Four Jacks' that night, I went straight to the bar, to have a whiskey with Jack, only to be told by Henry, the barman that Jack is no longer working there. He handed me an envelope, saying as he did so; "And something else Jake. This bar is now off limits to you. As of tonight, it's strictly for the customers only. I can't serve you anything any more. And also, your nightly dinner is no more. You'll have to get something to eat before you get here each night. Sorry Jake."

As I walked towards the piano, I was as depressed as I have ever been. I even found myself missing my Mum and Dad again.

Before starting to play, I tore open the envelope that Henry had given me and unfolded the letter inside. It said.

Memo to J.Silver.

Please note that as of tonight (April 15th), the following rules will be strictly observed. Failure to due so will result in instant dismissal.

[1] You will always use the tradesmen's entrance when arriving or leaving the club's premises.

[2] A late night snack will be served to you in the kitchen, where it will be eaten with the other members of staff. No other meal will be available to you.

[3] You are not allowed to fraternise with the customers, nor ever join them at their tables. Neither are you allowed to speak with them unless they speak to you first.

[4] Tipping by the customers is to be actively avoided. You are being paid by the club to play what they wish to hear, so obtaining extra money for simply doing your job is, in the opinion of the new management, quite wrong.

[5] Like the rest of our serving staff, you will never address any of our customers by their first name. You will always address them as Sir, Madam, or Miss.

(Signed) Reginald ffoulkes-Lyttleton. Manager

The new manager turned out to be tall, fat, and extremely queer. He was also a drunk.

As a result, during the last two weeks of my residency, the club became evermore a watering hole for wealthy fags, not only to stand at the bar, primping, camping, shrieking with laughter, and consuming immoderate amounts of champagne with Reginald ffoulkes-Lyttleton, but also to show off their latest catamites.

And, playing the piano for a bunch of fags sitting around the piano some of whom would make veiled overtures at me was definitely not my idea of having a good time. And it was not improved by having to address these primping, scented queens as 'Sir'. In any case, it was a serious mis-use of the English language. I remember one thin, pale complexioned darling, after I had so addressed him, looking deeply and meaningfully into my eyes and, making a moue with his mouth, saying to me:

"Oh, for God's sake, call me Tiger. Everyone else does."

I could not stop myself. I just cracked up with laughter, at which he said.

"You can be vey cruel, do you know that?"

I tried to mouth some sort of an apology, but I was laughing too much to make it sound sincere.

The only real pass I had to deal with, was when an oldish man who had told me he was a choreographer by profession, asked if he could sit next to me and watch my 'wonderful fingers.' He drew up a chair and sat very close to my left hand. It was while I was involved with the second chorus of some weak little Ivor Novello tune he had requested, that he put his hand on my thigh and stroking along it, said "Those fingers of yours are driving me quite mad you know."

I stopped playing there and then, and in all seriousness I said to him, "If you ever put a hand on me again I will reconstruct the architecture of your face," which was a line I had picked up from some American B picture. In truth, I had never struck anyone since I was a school kid, mainly because I was always aware of the damage that punching could do to my hands.

But with all the frustrations that had built up within me not only from my inability to get another job, but also at what my final two weeks had turned into, I was deadly serious as to my violent intentions. Fortunately, he got up and went back to the bar without uttering another word.

I had still not been able to fire Meri. Instead, I had decided to do a 'runner' when the time came for me to have to quit the apartment. The way I saw it, instead of paying for the additional month's rent that I had promised

Jack I would do, I could give half the rent money to Meri, pocket the other half, and duck out to my Aunt's house. If Jack traces me there to ask for the outstanding money, I'll goddam well tell him to take it out of the three hundred pounds he owes me.

The way things were stacking up, it was becoming more and more obvious to me with every passing, depressing, fucked-up day that London can get by quite happily without Jake Silver's pianistic prowess. I had to face the fact that having to do something else in order to earn a living, was now a high probability. I was sick with misery. I had reached that stage of depression when I did not know what was the more depressing; thinking about the present, thinking about the future, or thinking about how happy I was until so recently.

Every day became a miserable replica of the previous one. It would start with me getting out of bed to immediately start my daily round of phone calls feeling moderately confident about finding a new job. But, after a dozen or so 'we will keep your name on file in case something comes up' or 'I'm sorry, we already have someone', or 'please write in, giving a full C.V', etc, etc, I would slowly sink back down into what was by now, my familiar slough of despair, despondency and self-doubt. I even had regrets that I had not 'settled down 'with Candy.

And if that wasn't bad enough, Jack phoned me at the apartment to tell me that from the fifteenth of the following month, he is going to have to let my apartment to 'one of my bastard ex-partners'. He said he needed to raise every penny he could, and that he could rinse out of his ex-partner, 'a devil of a lot more money than you are paying, old chap'. He also confided to me that he will be going away very soon to stay with some friends in another part of the world, 'until I can get enough money together to pay off some rather nasty gambling debts. Once I've settled those' he said cheerily, 'I'll come back to good old GB, organise getting the house put into my name, sell it, and with the money, we'll open a new place, and we'll call it 'Jakes' and you can work there until you are sick and tired of it. How does that sound old lad?'

I was already old enough, hip enough and bitter enough to recognise a snow job when I heard one. So I knew that this was Jack trying to duck paying off what he owes me, by trying to pull the old 'bright new dawn a'comin'' schtick.

"At the moment Jack, I would rather you pay me back the three hundred you owe me, because, when the job finishes I'm going to be pretty broke. And if that's not enough," I added, "I now I find out from you that as of April fifteenth, I won't have anywhere to stay."

After a long, heavy, silence, he said quite dispassionately, "Sorry, old son, there's no chance of that at the moment. Keep me in touch with where you are staying or working, and I'll send you the money at the first opportunity, I promise"

'And the moon is made of cream cheese, and all the world is love' I thought.

But, on the night of March 23rd, just one week away from the end of my world as I had known it, Lady Luck decided to smile at me once again.

On that night a man I had never seen before, came into the club and without any further ado, sat himself down on one of the high stools set around the piano. As it was only ten o'clock in the evening, quite early in drinking club terms, he was my only listener. He gave me a little smile and a half nod as he sat down. I watched the waiter bring him over a sandwich, together with a half bottle of Bollingers and a champagne flute. Then he brought out an 'Evening News' from his side jacket pocket, and using the reflection from the spotlight that was on me, he scrutinised the racing page, whilst munching and sipping his sparkling drink. I found myself studying him as I subconsciously ran through my usual standard tunes.

To start with, he was not a faggot. At least, he certainly didn't act like one. He was small, about five and a half feet, with a wrinkled, sallow complexion. His jerky, neurotic movements and skinny physique gave him the appearance of having been strung together on bits of wire. He was, as near as I could see, expensively and conservatively dressed, in a blue, pin-stripe suit, a white, cut away collar shirt, some kind of blue gemstone adorning his cuff-links, to exactly match his conservatively patterned blue tie.

You can call me an egotist or a show-off if you like, but when someone comes over and sits by the piano, I expect him to listen and not be pre-occupied with the racing page of the 'Evening News'. Making requests is fine. Tapping or drumming fingers to the music is understandable, if not a little disconcerting (because the chances are, that unless you are Afro-American, a native African, or Cuban, you will tap out of time and probably on the wrong beat). But reading the paper is definitely out!

So I started to play all the flashiest and most virtuosic pieces in my repertoire there and then, instead of saving them for later when the club had filled up. But he just went on poring over the runners and riders, marking off his favourites for tomorrows races as if I did not exist.

In disgust, and because the job was virtually over in any case, I stopped playing and stood up prior to grabbing a waiter and actually paying him to bring me a drink into the kitchen, the main room being now barred to me. Even though I had promised myself to give up drinking, there are times when your spirits are so low, you've gotta have a little taste to revive them. And the way things seemed to me at that moment, this was one of those times.

Suddenly this guy started to applaud me.

"Hey, thank you very much," I said, genuinely surprised. "To tell the truth, I didn't think you were listening to a note I played."

"Oh, I was listening alright. I was listening with great care." He spoke in an affected way. It was obvious to me that he was lowering the timbre of his voice from tenor to baritone, presumably because he felt that the lower sound carried greater authority. Many years later I was to learn that this silly affectation is almost a way of life among the film colony of Los Angeles. But then again, there are more phonies per square inch in the film business than there are flies in Cairo.

I also suspected that he was trying to disguise his accent, which was cockney at its roots, over laden with a dollop of what he thought was Oxbridge English. It ended up sounding more like Uxbridge English. (Uxbridge is a rather shallow and shabby little extension of outer London.)

"Well," I said patting my pockets to make sure that I had my cigarettes with me (I discovered that I had a whim of iron when it came to giving up the weed), "I'd better get my coffee now, before the room fills up."

"And quite right too," he said, but followed up immediately with "I hear you are leaving this place. Is that true?"

"Yep."

"Well" he said, as folded up his newspaper, "I wonder if I may have something of interest to you—that is of course if you are not already booked to appear somewhere else. I should think a young chap like you would like what I have to offer."

Suddenly, all thoughts of drink, alcoholic or otherwise, vanished. Someone had just handed me the most wonderful luxury in the world. Hope. Even though my heart was bounding with excitement, I managed to sound no more than semi-interested.

"Sounds interesting" I said. "Would you like to tell me what it's all about?"

"Not right now," he said, slipping off the stool "I have to run along I'm afraid. But if it's all right with you..." He reached into his top pocket and produced a card, which he placed on the folded down music rest of the piano...

"...I would like you to come to my office, say around eleven tomorrow morning and we can go into it then."

"Yes that's fine with me," I said, still trying to sound cool and detached, and hoping I was hiding the elation that was bubbling crazily within me.

"Well, 'til tomorrow then" he said, reaching out to shake my hand. As we shook hands he said "I'm afraid I don't actually know your name."

"Jake Silver. But just call me Jake."

"Fine Jake. Fine. Until eleven tomorrow morning then. 'Bye."

I stood there by the piano, watching him, my haven of hope, as he made his uneven, half-sideways neurotic, way out of the club.

Then I picked up his card, which was gilt embossed, bearing the legend:

'Star Cast Entertainments Ltd. William D. Coverdale, President'. Below the name was the address; 9 Windmill Lane, London WC 2. There were also a couple of telephone numbers running along the bottom.

With great care, I placed it in my inside pocket. Then I sat down at the piano again and while it is too long ago to remember what tune I played, you can be sure that it was something wild and fast to express the wild excitement and the gratitude I felt for Mister William D. Coverdale, President yet, of 'Star Cast Entertainments Ltd.

Hope is the darling of the emotions, the Father to the dream, the Mother of the imagination. Those without it are incapable of joy. Indeed, the hope is often far better than the realisation. You look across a room, and pin a beautiful chick who is looking back across the room at you in such a way as to tell you that she digs you. Right away, you get that sunbeam of hope warming the very centre of your being. Now the hope is inspiring the imagination. Now you allow yourself to imagine what she is going to look like without clothes, what she will feel like. What you will do with her, and, best of all, what that beautiful, luscious mouth of hers will do to you. That may well turn out to be the high spot of this romance. Later, you may discover that she has bad breath, bad teeth, or a surly, selfish nature. You can even discover that the beautiful chick, with the legs up to here, and the sexy mouth, turns out to be a guy in drag! It can happen, believe me.

But while you are sequestering in the sunny garden of Hope, to quote one of Steven Sondheim's lyrics; 'Everything's Coming Up Roses'.

As I walked home in the early hours of that cold, keen and crispy very early spring morning, I felt as elated as someone emerging unscathed from a plane crash. I was a born again Jewish jazz pianist.

Chapter 23

At 10.55 AM precisely, as I climbed the creaking bare wooden staircase which the display board at the entrance had assured me was the home of 'Star Cast Entertainments', I was telling myself not to be put off by the seeming squalor of the place. 'It is just a typical part of old London' I told myself. 'All the offices around here will probably look like this' With hope so very firmly clutched to my bosom, one dirty staircase was not going to cause me to throw it away.

I walked past 'Turktravel Tours' on the first floor, then up to the second where the words, 'Glamour-Girl Escort Agency' was painted on the glass panel of the door. On the next floor, on a white painted, but badly chipped door, I found what I was looking for: 'Star Cast Entertainment Ltd'. Underneath, it said, 'Reception', in gold italic print.

'Reception' occupied a twelve foot square room, the decorative standard of which reminded very strongly of my student's quarters in Newcastle upon Tyne. Need I say more? In this delightful cubby-hole was an old desk, on which there were two telephones, a pile of pink and white documents on one end, an overflowing ash tray on the other, and an ancient typewriter in the middle. Sitting behind this desk was a young girl with platinum-blonde hair, but dark brown roots. I guessed she was young although I could not see her face, because she was looking straight down at the book which lay in her lap.

"Ahem. My name is Jake Silver." She did not look up.

"I have an appointment with Mister William D. Coverdale in..." I consulted my wrist watch, ..."Three minutes time."

Still not taking her eyes from the book, she pointed a bright red nail-varnished finger at an old kitchen-type chair, which was against and further along the same wall through which I had just entered.

I went to it and sat down. For the next five minutes, we both sat, like a still-life painting, me staring at the blonde head with the dark brown roots, and she unmoving, except to turn a page of the book that held her in such thrall. Finally, I could take it no more.

"I'm sorry to bother you" I said in as friendly a fashion as I could, "But it is after eleven, and Mister Coverdale did say that he wanted to see me at eleven o'clock sharp."

"Oh, sorry," she said, in a high-pitched cockney voice. She looked up at me as she spoke, showing me her full face. It was a pretty-ish little face, with up-tilted nose, and small lips heavily coated with orange coloured lipstick, some of which had left a thin orange line along her small, but even top teeth.

"I quite forgot," she said, "I'll tell 'im right away." She picked up one of the phones and dialled a single digit. After a minute or so, she said, "Bill I gotta..." she looked at me enquiringly, "Jake Silver" I whispered.

"...Jake Silver. Says 'e'as an appointment" After listening for a minute, she said, "Okay" and putting the phone down, she said to me; "You can go in now."

I looked blankly at her, because there was no other door out of this office other than the one through which I had entered.

She looked back at me in puzzlement for a moment before suddenly realising what the problem was.

"Oh sorry. You aint bin 'ere before 'ave yer? You go ou' of this door, turn left along the 'all and it's the last door on your righ'."

I turned to thank her before going out of the door, but it was clear that she had returned to whatever world existed between the covers of her book.

In response to his shouted 'come in', after I at first tapped and then knocked on the door of the President of Star Cast Entertainment, I opened the door and went in.

I found him sitting jacketless behind a large desk, piled high with ledgers on the one side of it and assorted papers in a wire tray on the other.. The central desk space was clear, except for a writing pad and two telephones. One of the walls of the office, all of which were yellow and stained with age, was further disfigured by an old shelf, lurching down dangerously at one end, and overloaded with grubby looking files. On the wall behind the President, was a small calendar affixed to a large picture of Betty Grable in a swimsuit, under which was the legend; 'If it's beauty you're after, contact – and underneath this legend, in large red letters:

'THE GLAMOUR-GIRL ESCORT AGENCY.'

The floor of the office was bare, except for two small, threadbare rugs.

"Take a pew squire, I'll only be a couple of minutes," he said, pointing to a small well-worn leather armchair. I watched him as he checked and initialled various paragraphs of the document he was carefully reading. He had on an immaculate white shirt, with gold cufflinks and silver armbands. He was also wearing a dark green tie with what appeared to be a hand-painted race-horse adorning almost all of it. Unfortunately, the effect was spoiled somewhat by his cheap, green-coloured braces.

He finally put whatever it was he had been reading into the wire tray, and while he was putting the cap back on his fountain pen, said "Well, let me start off by saying how impressed I was when I heard you play last evening. Very impressed I was. Very Impressed."

"Thank you very much," I said.

"Would you like some tea or anything?"

"Yes please, with milk and two sugars."

He picked up one of his phones and ordered two cups of tea. Then he leaned back in his chair, his elbows on the armrests making a steeple with his fingers: "Can I ask how much you are getting at 'The Four in Hand?"

"I get thirty-five pounds a week, plus tips, which average out to another ten pounds a week on top." I deliberately omitted any mention of the manager's new directive, which forbade tipping.

"Forty-five pounds per week," he said slowly and abstractedly, as he wrote it down on the pad in front of him. Then he started writing some other figures, saying as he did so "Sorry about all this figuring out Jake. I have to translate French francs into British pounds."

I was as intrigued as all hell at the idea that this calculation had something to do with my new job. But I chose to say nothing.

He finally signalled the completion of his financial figuring by planting an ostentatious dot at the end of the last set of figures and, for good measure, a line underneath.

"Well Jake," he said, "the job I would like you to consider will pay you, after we have deducted our agent's fees, exactly eighty-six pounds and seven pence per week, with all food and accommodation included."

If I had been anything but a green kid, blinded by the bright sunshine of hope, not to mention still being young and innocent enough to believe anything the grown-up says, I would have walked out there and then. No musicians, other than the big names, earned anywhere near that kind of money in those far-off days. At the very least I should have been suspicious. Instead, I was dancing with joy inside. This was more money than I had ever dreamed of earning. Eighty-six quid a week and all expenses paid? Christ, I'll be rich beyond my wildest dreams.

"Sorry about the rather strange amount of money" he said with a smile. "It's because of the changing of French francs into pounds, shillings and pence." He took a packet of Players Number three from his desk drawer, and took one for himself before offering another to me. I took it and after he had lit both our cigarettes with his expensive gold lighter, he said "Let me tell you about the job. It should suit a young fellow like you down to the ground. Whether you know it or not, all the big airline companies are opening up services down to South Africa. Of course, Air France, BOAC and many others already have their services to Johannesburg. Now others are following suit. I can tell you that Johannesburg is going to become a very competitive route. One of these new airlines is Hermes-Air. As you have probably guessed, it is Greek- owned, but not especially centred on Athens. What they have done, in order to beat the big airlines at their own game, is set up 'Hermes-Air Guest Houses' at each of their stop-overs, en route to Johannesburg. Now these are really luxurious little hotels Jake. No expense has been spared. Chefs have been hired from all over Europe, so that Hermes-Air passengers will enjoy top class international cuisines during their stop-overs. Now, they have decided that they want top class international- standard music in their bar lounges. And we here at Star Cast, have been contracted to provide that music."

He picked up his telephone. "Wendy, would you please bring in the Hermes-Air route map right away. And also bring us our teas. Mister Silver is feeling very thirsty," he said, winking at me.

While we waited, he explained more about the job. Even though each plane will stop over for one night only, you will stay one week in each guest-house before moving on to the next. And as you move on, so another piano entertainer will move in behind you. In this way, we will build up a chain of pianists permanently working this airline's routes. In the end, we envisage upwards of fifty pianists working on one or other of the Hermes-Air routes. As the airline grows and our operation expands with it, we will need someone experienced to oversee the entire operation. In a couple of year's time, that person could well be you Jake, although of course, I can't promise it. But this I can say; after you have completed each circuit, you will work here in the office for a month before heading off on your next tour of duty, so to speak. The periods you will spend with us here, incidentally, at exactly the same salary, will be devoted to training you for higher executive posts. If you live up to our expectations, then in say, two or three years you could well be our Director responsible for all our musical dealings with Hermes-Air. That would of course attract a far higher salary.

This whole thing was becoming far grander and more exciting than anything I could have imagined.

At this point Wendy (who turned out to be the blonde-haired-with-dark-brown-roots book-reading receptionist), arrived, pushing a trolley bearing tea and cake on the top shelf, rolls of maps filling the lower one.

"Ah, good," said President Coverdale. We'll drink the tea directly off the trolley Wendy, so just leave it there. But be a dear and pass me the maps, would you please?"

He carefully selected one, which he unrolled on his desk, using both telephones and an ash tray to hold down three of the corners, the fourth being held down by his forefinger and thumb.

"Now, come and look over my shoulder Jake" he said.

This is the route of the Hermes-Air flight from Brussels to Jo'burg. The places on the map with the red ink circles around them are where they have their guest houses and where you will be playing. As you can see, you will start your journey from Brussels, having flown out from London the night before."

Each port of call was then carefully pointed out by Coverdale's carefully manicured forefinger.

"From Brussels, you fly to Tripoli, where you play your first week. Then on to Kano in Nigeria for your second. After that, your third is spent in Leopoldville, which is right in the Heart of Africa. Then a shortish hop to Elizabethville for week four. Then on to Salisbury in Northern Rhodesia and even more south to Bulawayo in Southern Rhodesia and after six weeks you finally reach Johannesburg. Once you get there, you will have a week's holiday, going and doing whatever you please, and with six weeks pay in your pocket with which to do it. Then you do the whole journey again, but in reverse, arriving back in London thirteen weeks after you left.

He turned to face me, a big smile on his face. "There it is my boy. Now let us have our tea while you ask me the thousand and one questions I know you are just dying to ask." He stood behind the trolley with his tea and cake, while I consumed my mid-morning repast back in the armchair.

"When would you like me to start?"

"I would like you to leave London for Brussels on Sunday the thirtieth of this month. Then you will fly through the night to arrive at Tripoli on the morning of the April the first, to commence work that night."

I thought fast. That would mean, leaving the day after I finish my stay at 'The Four in Hand'. Perfect.

"And when and how do I get paid?"

"I am so glad you asked me that Jake," he said, a pleased look flooding his face. "So many musicians either forget, or are just too damned embarrassed to talk about money. But it's the stuff that makes the world go round. And I must say how glad I am that you went straight to the point. No messing around with you eh? Do you know, I really am starting to think you have the makings of a damn good executive."

Wow! I was knocked out at the impression I was clearly making. As far as I was concerned, this man Coverdale was clearly a really great guy.

I was also wildly excited. Simply flying for the first time in my life was thrilling enough. Flying to a foreign country for the first time, trebled that sense of excitement: and the foreign country, or rather continent was Africa, the land of gorillas, lions, elephants, and Johnny Weissmuller. It was just too much. My cup was running over.

"Oh, while I think of it," he said while putting down his tea cup on the trolley, and returning to his desk, "You must get some yellow fever and smallpox injections. You can get them from your own doctor, or any hospital specialising in tropical diseases.

"Okay, I'll get on to it right away," I said, in my best executive voice.

"And another very important thing,," he said as he sat down behind his desk. You must go today to the passport office and get yourself a passport, if you haven't already got one. Wendy will give you a letter to the Passport Office explaining the urgency of the situation, so I am sure that there will be no problem in that direction. After that, you will be required to come back here to sign your contract."

Then suddenly standing up whilst consulting his watch, he said, "Now Jake, you will have to excuse me. I have an important meeting to attend, and I'm late already. So, I'm afraid I must ask you to go and get on with your side of things, and let us meet again, the day after tomorrow to see how you are getting on and at the same time, you can sign your contract."

Again, I could not help noticing again his neurotic, sideways-on way of walking as he traversed the office to hold the door open for me.

"You forgot to tell me how and when I get paid," I said, as I too stood up to leave.

"Did I?." His raised eyebrows accentuated the nonplussed look on his face. "Oh, sorry. Well...very briefly..." he again looked at his watch, this time anxiously; "You collect your salary for the six weeks for the outward leg of the tour, plus another half week's pay to cover the week you have to spend in Jo'burg, at the airline's office there in Johannesburg. As to the return leg of the tour, you will come to our offices here to get that. You will be paid for both the outward and inward parts of the tour in pounds Stirling. Unless of course you request to be paid in a different currency."

"No, that sounds fine with me," I said, as we shook hands, prior to my leaving.

I was on cloud nine as I floated down the stairs of that grubby little building and out into the even grubbier little back street, called Windmill Lane.

Even though it was raining hard, I walked the three miles or so back to the apartment. The thick, heavy downpour was not bothering me in the least. My legs may have been walking, but my heart was dancing. Everything, the shops, the street traders, even the rubbish on the pavements looked fresh and new. I was buzzing with a crazy, thrilling kind of excitement. The mixture of flying for the first time, visiting so many foreign places for the first time, plus being in the dark, mysterious continent of Africa—all this overlaid by the knowledge that the pain of not knowing what I was going to do when my job ended was creating a glow of excitement that spread right down to my toes.

I went straight to the bedroom, took off my soaked-through clothes, put on one of the earl's silk dressing gowns and while still drying my hair with a hand towel made my way to the study. I grabbed a piece of the Earl's stationary and excitedly began to make a list of all the things I had to do in the ten days remaining before my African jaunt.

I started by writing down 'Pay the Rent'. Then I crossed it out. I was not going to give any more rent money to Jack. This was not because he had failed to pay back the money he owed me, nor was it out of any villainy on my part. It was simply out of necessity. The way I saw it, paying Meri, plus two additional weeks pay to tide her over until one of Jacks 'bastard partners' takes over the apartment, as well as money for her food, and a little bonus for all her kindness, was about all the exchequer could handle—especially bearing in mind that I would not be receiving any money for six weeks until I get to Jo'burg.

But I guess there was still another reason why I decided to do a 'runner'. I still had a smouldering rage rumbling away deep down inside me, at the injustice of getting the sack from the club, and it had been stoked up somewhat by the knowledge that one of those responsible for my being fired, was going to take over my flat and, worse still, be looked after by my Meri.

Even though I see now that this was an unfair résumé of the actual position, that was the way I felt at the time. And anything I could do to get my own back on these Liechtenstein motherfuckers, well that was just fine with me—although why I thought that by not paying my rent, I was somehow getting back at Jack's partners, eludes me.

Then I wrote down, 'Visit the family and tell them'.

Again, no sooner had I written it down that crossed it out. Ever the devout coward, I decided to take the peaceful route and visit them in the normal way but say nothing regarding what I was about to do. I convinced myself that it was far better to write and tell them, but not post the letter until the day I leave. Prompted by fear of the repercussions that would undoubtedly follow were I to tell them of my decision, I managed to convince myself that no matter how annoyed Aunt Sarah is going to be at my doing it this way, she will forgive me when I return and show her how much money I have made. According to my reckoning, the total amount of money I was due to earn from just twelve weeks playing was a few pence under one thousand, one hundred and thirteen pounds. Even including the costs of buying presents for the family and Meri (which I intended to buy during the return leg of my tour, after having been paid in Jo'burg), I was still going to end up my first tour of duty with at least a thousand pound in my pocket. And, on top of that, I would have a job in Mister Coverdale's office, earning the same huge salary.

'I will be such a big shot upon my return' I thought, ' that Aunt Sarah and Uncle Harry will certainly forgive me for running out on them in such an underhand way.

Then I moved to making a list of what to pack, and what to place in storage because when I return, even though I will be quite well off, I will have nowhere to stay.

Having completed that task, my thoughts as ever in those youthful days, turned to sex. In this I was lucky. On checking my diary, I saw that I had noted Evelyn's return to London was on the Thursday and Friday before I leave the country. So, being a person who likes to think that planning one's life is better than not doing so, I saw that my sex life over the last remaining ten days will consist of six nights of jerking off (I used to like to give myself a couple of days off every now and then), and two nights of fucking.

All that was left now was to get my passport, yellow fever and smallpox jabs, and I was ready to do my jungle thing.

Two days later, I was back in President William D. Coverdale's office to report that everything was fixed regarding my passport and that I was booked in to get my yellow fever and smallpox jabs the very next day.

"Well done my boy. Well done indeed." Then he picked up his phone to tell Wendy to bring in my contract. I noticed while he was speaking to her that on the desk in front of him was an open copy of 'Sporting Life'.

After he had put down the phone, he asked me if I had any other problems he could help me with. I told him about finding somewhere to store my records, my books of music and my few trinkets as well as some clothes I was not taking with me.

"No problem at all," he told me. "We have a spare office on this floor with plenty of space to keep your bits and pieces. Bring them over on the Friday before you leave. We'll look after them until you want them back again. Don't worry at all about that."

"I was now surer than ever that good ol' Pres. Coverdale was the nearest thing to Jesus I had ever met. Then the door was pushed open by Wendy, wheeling in the trolley bearing my contract plus a bottle of Champagne and two glasses.

"Oh good" He said as she came in. Then turning to me: "Jake, I thought that after you had signed we'd drink a toast to a long and successful association."

I was really hooked on this guy Coverdale. I like to think it was the reason why I did not bother to read the contract before I signed it. Coverdale had quickly pointed out that the sum of money I was to be paid and that the date for my departure was all correct and that the other parts of the contract were, "Just a load of the usual legal rubbish," that I need not bother my head about. So I signed. He gave me my copy. Then, from a desk drawer he retrieved an envelope in which was a gold coloured airline ticket. "This is your airline pass, which allows you to travel as crew. Don't lose it whatever you do, because without it, you will not be allowed back on the aircraft."

I swore on everything holy that it will never leave my personal possession. We drank our champagne toast, and after agreeing on what date he will be expecting me to show up at his office to commence training for my future life as an important executive, I left his office with my heart flying higher than any plane in the entire Hermes-Air fleet.

Of course I was not to be allowed to get out of the country without any aggravation. My evil, sadistic little sprite wouldn't give me that kind of unalloyed satisfaction. The very next night after I had signed my contract, I got a telephone call at the club from Herschel Weinstein, Lola's personal manager. He was phoning me from Rome to tell me that he has now got himself involved in another movie, nothing to do with that "Heap of shit Lola's in, but something really good Jake" Then he went on to tell me that he can get me a part in the movie. I would be the young English aristocrat who plays jazz piano in this Parisian night club which is central to the plot. "There is a good speaking part too for you Jake. I can get you ten thousand dollars for the five week shoot, which will all be in Paris. Plus, I think I've also got you a night time job playing in a new jazz place they're opening here. We're talkin' about a grand a week for you with bass and drums. So what do you say kiddo?"

I had of course to turn it down. But to put it politely, I was fucking annoyed and fucking frustrated by having to do so.

Then, I got a call two days before my departure, from Candy. She phoned me at about three o'clock in the morning, clearly pissed, to tell me that her proposed marriage was off and that she has had the abortion and now wanted to see me. I knew that I dare not tell her about my African trip, in case it got back to my Uncle and Aunt, and, as I had not yet worked out what lies and double talk I was going to put into my letter to them, I had to be very careful about what I said.

"Where are you phoning from?" I asked.

"Boston" she said. "But I am coming home just as soon as I can. The bastard I was supposed to marry first tells me that he doesn't want to be a father again. So I go through with the damned abortion, only to then be told that he wants to put the wedding off to give him time to come to terms with the fact that the woman he is marrying was not a virgin when he first had sex with me. I just told him to fuck off. So I'm coming home Jake and I need to see you sweetheart."

"When will you be back?"

"I'm not sure. Just as soon as I can get on a plane or boat or something."

"I think that the best thing then, is for you to phone the moment you return and I'll drop everything and we'll get together."

"Do you really mean that Jake darling?" I noticed that she was going into her kittenish routine.

"You know I do" I said, really hating to tell such a nasty lie, but I could not think of what to say that would make her feel good, and at the same time, not give the game away to my Uncle and Aunt.

"That is really great," she purred. "Let's try to pick up where we left off. What do you say?"

"Absolutely" I said.

After a long pause she said. "I'm drunk Jake."

"I know."

And after another long pause; "Tell me you love me."

I hated the way one lie led to another. But I said it: "I love you"

"Oh boy" she said happily. You won't regret this Jake darling. We are going to be great together. God, I can't wait to get my hands on you again. I don't care how many women you've be screwing while I've been away. Just make sure you've got rid of them by the time I get back."

"I promise. Goodbye baby, until then."

"'Bye my darling."

After I put the phone down, I lay back on my bed, feeling just plain lousy. I did have a lot of time for Candy and lying to her in this way was a shitty thing for me to have done. As it was, the whole idea of going to Africa had been severely soured by Herschel's fantastic offer. Now this Candy thing had made it seem even worse. As I turned over to try to get back to sleep, I was sickened, not only by my lost opportunity in film land, but also and equally at the realisation of how many people I was upsetting.

Coda

And so it was, on the thirtieth of March, in the year of nineteen hundred and fifty, that I, together with two medium size suitcases, plus one heart thumping with excitement, made my way across the tarmac with my fellow passengers towards the flight that was to take me to Brussels.

I did visit the family once more, and I also phoned them a couple of times, but made no mention either of getting fired from the club, nor of my new job. Earlier that morning I had posted off my letter to them, telling them about the trip, but enshrouding it in the most outrageous lies. I was already hip to the fact that my Aunt and Uncle set great store by the ridiculous concept that it was wonderful to mix with the super-rich. I also knew that the idea of going into business for oneself was for my Aunt, something to be desired over almost any other aspiration.

So I used both of these crazy notions in my letter. I told how I have been suddenly invited, all fares and expenses paid, to visit a South African college friend of mine, now back in Johannesburg, and whose father is a multi-millionaire. I said that better still; he is flying up to Tunis to meet me so that we can travel the largest part of the journey together. I added this additional frill because I knew that my Aunt would not worry so much if she felt that I was not travelling on my own. I promised faithfully that I would write regularly, and be back in London 'in a couple of weeks or so'. I also thought it a good idea to stretch the lie a bit further by adding, that when I return, I will probably be giving up playing the piano for a living, because my friend's vastly wealthy father wants me to go into business with his son in London. I knew the old motto; 'The bigger the lie, the more likely it is to be believed', and so I trusted that my whoppers would go down well.

Saying goodbye to Meri was hardest of all. If there is anything more upsetting to a normal male than the sight of a woman crying, it is the sight of a woman crying bravely. Assuring me through her tears that she will be alright, and that I must look after myself, she suddenly flung her arms around my shoulders (she was too short to reach my neck), and with her body racked with spasms from the sobbing, she managed to say, "I like master bery much. BERY much." I told her that I liked her more than any other girl in the world (which was in a way, true), and I promised to write and tell her all about my trip. I also promised to come and see her when I return.

I also left a note for Candy, telling her more or less the same load of nonsense that I had told my Aunt and Uncle. The main difference was that I told her exactly when I will be back in London and asked her to wait for me.

I also met up with Jack on the Friday before leaving. We met in a little bar off Curzon Street for a farewell drink. He gave me the Rhodesian address of his ex-wife and told me to look her up if I get the chance. He also told me that Eliot was now engaged to an American millionairess and that their marriage would be his first and her fifth. When I asked him if he could see a way out of his financial problems, which he had explained were very, very serious, he said he could not. Little did either of us know that within a short time all his problems would be a thing of the past. Three months later, Jack Montgomery died as a result of a cerebral haemorrhage (although I was not to learn of it for another year or so).

What I also could not have known as I fastened my seat belt was that I was flying into a new life; one that would bring me the great love of my life, but also one that would involve me in violence and even murder, including having a Mafia 'contract' out on my life, as well as having to live an enforced exile out here in Cuba.

If I live long enough, and if you have the stamina, I'll tell you about that later.

END OF PART ONE.